P9-CKD-137

"Love the BKI team…motorcycle, undercover alphas… an amazing premise for a series, and Julie Ann Walker continues to rock it with amazing story lines!"

—*Smitten with Reading*

"Full of hot alpha men, strong witty females, blazing passionate sex, and tons of humor. The balance between it all is spectacular. Black Knights Inc. is hands down my favorite romantic suspense series."

—*Guilty Pleasures Book Reviews*

"Hysterically funny amidst the action, danger, and sexy romance."

—*Drey's Library*

"A great love story, lots of action, and so much humor I was laughing out loud."

—*Love to Read for Fun*

"The humor, wit, and unique warmth…are [things] I associate with Ms. Walker as part of her trademark style."

—*The Romance Reviews*

DISCARDED

"One of the best romantic suspense novels I've read so far this year. Well written, full of drama, action, laughs, and love, you will enjoy every second."

—*Romance Witch's Reviews*

"Steam-worthy sexual attraction and pulse-pounding action only accentuate the fabulously executed plot."

—*Tome Tender*

Also by Julie Ann Walker

Black Knights Inc.

Hell on Wheels
In Rides Trouble
Rev It Up
Thrill Ride
Born Wild
Hell for Leather
Full Throttle

The Deep Six

Hell or High Water

TOO HARD
TO HANDLE

JULIE ANN WALKER

sourcebooks
casablanca

Copyright © 2015 by Julie Ann Walker
Cover and internal design © 2015 by Sourcebooks, Inc.
Cover art by Craig White

Sourcebooks and the colophon are registered trademarks of Sourcebooks, Inc.

All rights reserved. No part of this book may be reproduced in any form
or by any electronic or mechanical means including information storage
and retrieval systems—except in the case of brief quotations embodied
in critical articles or reviews—without permission in writing from its
publisher, Sourcebooks, Inc.

The characters and events portrayed in this book are fictitious or are
used fictitiously. Any similarity to real persons, living or dead, is
purely coincidental and not intended by the author.

Published by Sourcebooks Casablanca, an imprint of Sourcebooks, Inc.
P.O. Box 4410, Naperville, Illinois 60567-4410
(630) 961-3900
Fax: (630) 961-2168
www.sourcebooks.com

Printed and bound in Canada.
MBP 10 9 8 7 6 5 4 3 2 1

To the Writer Chicks who keep me company through daily emails, who keep me sane when my screws threaten to come loose, and who keep encouraging me to "write the next damn book, Jules!" Cheers!

The true soldier fights not because he hates what is in front of him, but because he loves what is behind him.

—G. K. Chesterton

Prologue

Goose Island, Chicago, Illinois
Thursday, 5:28 p.m.

"CALM DOWN, DUDE. IF YOU KEEP GOING ON LIKE THIS, YOUR brain will explode. And I really don't want to get any of it on me."

Penni DePaul recognized the voice of the man speaking as she followed the redheaded behemoth named Geralt through the narrow gate on the side of the big warehouse that housed Black Knights Inc.

"It's not my head I'm worried about," came a booming bass response. "It's yours. I mean, Ozzie, man, you know that woman is buckets o' crazy, right?"

"Maybe," Ozzie replied just as Penni rounded the corner, stopping when Geralt's gigantic biker boots took root atop the patio pavers. "But if she is, she really puts the *hot* in psychotic. Am I right?"

Peeking around Geralt's massive back, Penni's eyes landed on Ethan "Ozzie" Sykes. He was sitting in a bright red Adirondack chair with his back to her. And from what little she could make out, he was looking pretty good for a guy who'd nearly had his leg blown off. The leg in question was secured in a brace and propped on the stone lip of a big fire pit built into the center of the courtyard behind the warehouse. The courtyard itself was surrounded by outbuildings and a fifteen-foot-high brick wall topped by razor wire and a crap-ton of security cameras.

To the inexperienced, Black Knights Inc. looked as it was meant to look, like the work area and living space for a group of rough and rowdy guys who built fantastical custom motorcycles in a not-so-nice part of town. *The latter requiring all the high-tech security, don't you know?* But Penni wasn't inexperienced. She was well aware of the cold, hard facts behind BKI's chrome and leather facade. On her last assignment she'd worked with Ozzie and two more of the Black Knights, and she could say without a shadow of a doubt that they did a whole lot more than design shiny things that ate asphalt for dinner and roared like steel beasts.

The motorcycle shop was nothing but a front for the most secretive, most whispered-about government defense firm ever to be redacted from all of Uncle Sam's files. Granted, it was a really *excellent* front, considering that the three guys she'd worked with during The Assignment—that's how she'd come to think of the mission that had changed her life forever—had all been a little bit scruffy and a whole lot tattooed. *Handsome-as-sin Hells Angels look-alikes…*

"And if you must know," Ozzie went on, "I happen to *like* crazy. It makes for really interesting conversations. Besides"—he took a swig from a beer with a red label that read "Honker's Ale"—"she seems like she'd be a hellcat in the bedroom."

"Kee-rist, man!" The guy who belonged to the bass voice was sitting at a picnic table laden with what appeared to be huge vats of potato salad, coleslaw, and baked beans. He plunked his beer bottle atop the table's surface with enough force to send foam geysering from the longneck.

"I know that pretty face of yours means you're used to women throwing themselves at your feet," he added, "but the only reason she flirted with you at the bar last night is because she's a fuckin' reporter who's been nosing around this place for years looking for a fuckin' story. So even if a nutso in nylons *is* your screwed-up idea of a cup of tea, her fuckin' J.O.B. should make any appeal she has shrink up quicker than an Eskimo scrotum."

The man certainly had a mad penchant for colorful descriptions. And f-bombs. And *scars*. His craggy face was lined with more than its fair share.

Penni didn't know exactly what she'd expected to happen after the taxi dropped her in front of the mammoth gates of BKI and she told Geralt, who'd been manning the gatehouse, that she needed to talk to Dan "The Man" Currington. But it certainly wasn't to be led to a backyard barbecue complete with smoking grill and three guys lounging around on mismatched lawn furniture while arguing about the merits and drawbacks of getting jiggy with some nameless newspaperwoman. The third man was wearing a green John Deere baseball cap and strumming an old Martin six-string, looking for all the world like he was completely ignoring the other two.

The smell of cooking meat hung heavy in the cool breeze. It competed with the wet, fishy aroma of the nearby Chicago River and the hoppy deliciousness of the open beer bottles. In fact, if it weren't for that whole security-camera/razor-wire thing they had going, Penni would have said the air around Black Knights Inc. was less supersecret spy-guy lair and more laid-back, good-ol'-boy hangout.

"Yeah." Ozzie nodded vaguely, scratching his chin. "The reporter thing is a *bit* of a drawback."

"A *bit*?" Scarface sent Ozzie an incredulous look, prompting the man playing the guitar to finally jump into the fray.

"I don't know why you're surprised, *mon ami*," he said and Penni instantly identified his smooth-as-silk voice and sweet-as-molasses accent from a phone conversation she'd had with him during The Assignment. His name was Rock. But while the famous Rock was big and bulky, *this* Rock was lean and wiry…and sporting a pretty spiffy pair of scuffed-up alligator boots. "You know Ozzie can't see past the upside of a thing, especially when that thing has boobs, until ya point out the downside of a thing."

Ozzie turned to grin at Rock. And even though he was in profile, Penni noticed the expression looked a little…*different* from the one she'd seen on his face three months ago. It was duller. Sadder. *Harder* somehow.

Her mind returned to the hotel bombings in Kuala Lumpur—the ones that had left her colleagues, her *friends*, dead—and started picking at the memory like a scab. What lay beneath burned and ached, but she'd learned a thing or two over the past few months. One of which was how to take a deep breath and push aside the ugly thoughts so they didn't rise up and overwhelm her in grief. She wasn't entirely sure time healed all wounds as much as it simply taught a person ways to stanch the chronic bleeding.

Geralt, heretofore known in her mind as the Carrot-Topped Colossus, must have sensed a lull in the men's debate. He cleared his throat and said, "Speaking of skirts"—his accent was one hundred percent Windy City, his words running together like cars colliding on the Eisenhower Expressway—"we got one here who says she's looking for Dan Man."

Penni was trying to decide whether or not she should take offense at being labeled "a skirt" when Scarface and Rock jumped from their seats. Ozzie craned his head around the side of the Adirondack chair. And suddenly she was...

Not scared, exactly. In her thirty-three years she'd faced down a lot worse than three flag-waving, gun-toting, pretend motorcycle mechanics. But now that she was here at Black Knights Inc., on the brink of telling Dan that she hadn't been able to get him out of her head since The Assignment, and that she—

"Agent DePaul!" Ozzie crowed, pushing up from the chair and grabbing the crutches leaning against it. He hobbled over and threw an arm around her shoulders, squeezing her tight. The move was made awkward by the crutch shoved in his armpit. "Forget about my fantasy shag-o-rama with ace reporter Samantha Tate," he told Rock and Scarface. *Shag-o-rama? Christ almighty.* "Because my future wife has just arrived!"

Uh-huh. Sure. Because while they'd worked together in Kuala Lumpur, Ozzie had gaily—and quite insincerely—asked her to marry him at least a half-dozen times.

She turned to grin at him now, grateful for his exuberant welcome and the balm it was to her frayed nerves. But her smile faltered when she saw his eyes.

He *was* different.

Gone was the spark, the bright golden glow that

seemed to shine from within him. Now there were shadows lurking behind his sapphire irises. Deep shadows. Dark shadows. Shadows that told her all his good-natured joking was a studied act, a slick veneer to cover up what was hurting and broken inside him.

She wasn't sure if it made her feel better or worse, knowing she wasn't the only one irrevocably changed by The Assignment. On second thought, she *was* sure. Worse. It definitely made her feel worse.

But what are you going to do?

Keep on keeping on, that's what. A phrase her father had taught her to live by.

"Your future wife, huh?" she asked Ozzie, determined to play along. If he insisted on wearing a false happy face, far be it from her to pull off his mask. "What makes you think I'll take you up on your offer of marriage this time when I've turned you down every time before?"

"Well, why else would you be here?" He wiggled his blond eyebrows. "I mean, it's obvious you've come to your senses and decided to make me the happiest man on the pl—"

"Dim your love-lights, you oversexed jackass," Scarface said, crossing his arms over his chest when he came to a stop in front of them. He was a mountain of a man. Close to six-and-a-half feet of bulging, flexing muscles. "I'm blinded by the bullshit shining in them."

"Oversexed? *Me?*" Ozzie's tone and expression epitomized incredulity. "You're one to talk. I'm surprised every morning that Becky can walk out of your bedr—"

"Not in front of our guest," Scarface growled, leveling Ozzie with a look Penni was surprised didn't curdle the latter's balls. "Especially not before the introductions have been made."

"Typical." Ozzie shook his head. "You can dish it, but you can't take it."

When a vein the size of a garden hose appeared in the center of Scarface's forehead, Ozzie quickly relented and officially introduced Penni to Richard "Rock" Babineaux and Frank "Boss" Knight, a.k.a. Scarface. After shaking the men's hands, Penni turned to extend the gesture to Geralt and thank him for the escort.

The giant redhead ran a hand over his bristly crew cut and said with a dramatic leer, "Believe me, the pleasure was all mine. And if you decide not to take Ozzie up on his offer of ball-and-chaindom, how about you and me grab a cup of joe before you leave, yeah? Ya see"—he had the audacity to slow wink at her before turning a smug smile toward Ozzie—"I've always had a thing for NYC accents, especially when that accent comes with a broad whose legs go *all* the way up."

From "skirt" to "broad." She wasn't sure it was an improvement. And didn't everyone's legs go all the way up to…well…wherever all legs went? Hips, usually?

"Back off, you big ginger!" Ozzie bellowed, pushing Geralt's shoulder but failing to budge the Carrot-Topped Colossus an inch. "I saw her first!"

"Oh, sure." Geralt made a face. "'I saw her first.' The go-to gambit of small-minded men with even smaller d—"

"Gentlemen, please," Penni interrupted, her head spinning with the whirlwind that was her first five minutes at Black Knights Inc. And then there was her stomach… It was so jittery at the thought of what she was about to do that she marveled her lunch was staying down. She'd been so peaceful, so serene when she'd made the decision to come. But now that she was actually here, on the brink of confessing everything? *Yeah, no.* And Ozzie and Geralt? Well, they weren't helping a damned thing.

Her father's voice echoed inside her head. *When you find yourself in a gaffle, Penelope Ann DePaul, the only way out is straight ahead.*

Her dad had been chockablock full of little adages like that.

"It's not that I'm not *extremely* flattered at being reduced to the chew toy in a game of tug-of-war between two big, slobbery dogs…" She lifted a brow, letting both men know when she used the term "dog" she wasn't referring to the four-legged variety. She was fully aware this little tête-à-tête had nothing to do with her and everything to do with them having an excess of testosterone, which forced them to latch on to any excuse to growl and posture and insult one another. *Men.* She shook her head. "But I really *do* need to talk to Dan."

Geralt had the good sense to bite the inside of his cheek and turn the color of the cherries they put atop the charlotte russe pound cakes back in Brooklyn. But Ozzie? He just grinned wider. *The good-looking lout.*

"We'll let you talk to Dan," Boss said, narrowing his eyes, "if you can assure me this doesn't have anything to do with that bad business in Malaysia."

To her utter horror, when she opened her mouth, what initially came out was, "I-I-I—" *Hello?* What sorry sonofabitch had gone and tied her tongue in knots? Swallowing, she tried again. "I'd really rather discuss this with Dan, and I—"

Before she could finish, three women burst from the back door of the warehouse, laughing uproariously. There was a petite blond with a lollipop stick protruding from her mouth. She was carrying a huge casserole dish filled with…peach cobbler, by the smell of it. Beside her was a tall, curvy woman with an amazing mass of chestnut hair. She was holding a baby swaddled in a Chicago Cubs blanket—the little bundle cooed and burbled and waved a pudgy fist in the air. Bringing up the rear and rounding out the trio was a dusky-skinned, dark-eyed beauty who walked over and slapped Rock on the ass before she realized there was a stranger in their midst.

"And who do we have here?" the black-haired woman inquired, snaking an arm around Rock's waist. Rock brushed an inky lock away from her face and bent to press a tender kiss to her temple.

"Vanessa," he said in that sweet southern drawl that screamed Louisiana bayou, "this is Agent Penni DePaul."

Penni opened her mouth to remind him that she and Vanessa had spoken on the phone during The Assignment and to correct him on that whole "agent" business, but she closed it again when he quickly introduced Becky, the blond, and Michelle, of the chestnut hair. Penni also made the acquaintance of the cooing baby, one Jacob Michael Sommers, Jr. Or JJ for short.

These people are more than coworkers, she realized with a start after Becky set the casserole dish on the picnic table and walked back to the group, popping the sucker from her mouth so she could drag Boss down to steal a loud, smacking smooch. *They're family. A big, noisy, loving family.* Dan's *family. And I'm intruding on them. On* him.

Okay, sure. She'd known before she ever hopped on the plane headed west out of Reagan National Airport that just because Malaysia had been the catalyst for her making some huge decisions about the path of her life, it didn't mean Dan had done the same. And she'd been fully aware that just because what passed between them during those hellacious twenty-four hours had turned out to be momentous for her, it didn't mean it'd held the same importance for him. But now, after seeing the impressiveness of Black Knights Inc. in person, after meeting the host of people who filled Dan's life, she couldn't help but wonder if he'd given her as much as a passing thought.

She considered tucking tail and running. It would be so easy to turn around, walk out that gate, and forget she ever—

No. *No!* She wasn't a coward. She'd come here to say her piece. And you can bet your ass that's exactly what she was going to do. Squaring her shoulders, she glanced around at the faces staring at her expectantly and blurted out, "I sort of feel like a broken record here, but I really need to—"

"Talk to Dan," Boss finished for her. "Just as soon as you tell us what this is all about. Because if the Secret Service has a problem with the way he handled things in Kuala Lumpur, then it's me you need to be having a conversation with, not him. When it comes to BKI, the buck stops right here." He hooked a thumb toward his football-field-sized chest.

See? Family. Sticking up for each other and closing ranks when it looked like she was trying to insert herself into the middle of them. Once again, a sliver of doubt lodged in the back of her brain. All right already, who was she kidding? It was more than a sliver. It was a full-fledged *log* of doubt.

"It doesn't have anything to do with that, I swear to you," she assured him. "What I want to talk to Dan about is sort of…well…" *Geez, this is getting awkward.* "It's personal."

"Hmm," Boss hummed.

Hmm? That's all he had to say? Just…*hmm?*

Apparently so, because for a couple of eternal ticks of the clock, they all just stood there. Her looking at them. Them looking at her. The baby burbling and the meat sizzling on the grill. Somewhere on the river behind the outer wall a tour boat passed by, the guide regaling the passengers with stories of Baby Face Nelson and Al Capone.

Finally, Becky waved a hand through the air and laughed. "Whew! Is it just me? Or did this barbecue turn into a tension convention? Penni"—she crunched down on the sucker, chewing noisily—"you don't have to tell this big lug anything." She nudged Boss with her elbow, making him grunt. "Because the truth is, Dan's not here."

"He's not? Where is he?" Penni should have known better than to ask that question. All she received in answer were shuttered stares. "Uh-huh." She nodded. "Sure, I get it." When she caught herself rubbing a finger over the little bump on the bridge of her nose, she quickly dropped her hand and tightened her fingers into a fist. "Can you at least tell me when he'll be back?"

Becky looked up at Boss. She obviously saw acquiescence in his face—although Penni couldn't make out anything behind his intense scowl—because she admitted, "We don't know. Could be days. Could be months."

"*Months!*" Penni squawked, her heart plummeting so fast she was surprised she didn't see it lying on the pavers at her feet. And those shoulders she'd just squared? Despite her best efforts, they drooped dejectedly. She'd screwed up her courage and come all this way...

"I think we should tell her where he is," Michelle murmured, the first thing she'd said since the introductions.

Penni looked up to find the woman bouncing the baby and eyeing her intently. She blinked and considered digging a finger into her ear because she wasn't sure she'd heard correctly.

Obviously Boss was having the same problem. He shook his head. "Excuse me, Shell? What the hell did you just say?"

"Yes." Michelle nodded, still looking at Penni. "I definitely think we should tell her where to find him."

Chapter One

Cusco, Peru
Friday, 4:55 p.m.

"Yᴏᴜ ᴇᴀᴛ ᴀɴᴏᴛʜᴇʀ ʙɪᴛᴇ ᴏꜰ ᴛʜᴀᴛ ᴅᴀᴍɴᴇᴅ ɢᴜɪɴᴇᴀ ᴘɪɢ ᴀɴᴅ I swear the next thing you'll see is my Technicolor yawn."

Dan "The Man" Currington glanced over at his friend and teammate and lifted a brow. In the two days they'd been in the little city nestled in a high valley of the Andes Mountains, Dagan Zoelner had yet to sample the local delicacy. And since it was an unwritten rule among operators—and men in general, come to think of it—that outgrossing each other rated just under out-insulting, outshooting, and outfighting each other, he reached into the tinfoil-wrapped snack he'd purchased from a street vendor, pulled off a drumstick, and sucked the juicy grilled meat from the bone. The devil in him insisted he chew slowly and make *nom-nom* noises.

Zoelner's upper lip curled back. He shuddered and scooted to the opposite end of the bench, tucking his chin into his scarf.

Mark one for the Dan Man! Dan put a checkmark in the *W* column of his imaginary scoreboard of life.

"For the record," he said, licking his fingers and absently noting the way the cool, dry air whispered down from the mountaintops, interrupting the rhythmic burble of the fountain at their backs and teasing the ends of his hair, "I've eaten way worse. Undercooked, day-old goat meat in the Qandil Mountains of Iraq comes to mind. That shit'll grow some pretty radical hair on your chest. I guarantee."

Although they were lounging lazily on a park bench in the big square in the center of the city, Dan's eyes clocked the movements of every tourist that passed by him. Cusco was bustling with travelers hoping to make it down to Machu Picchu before the rainy season set in and the area around the ancient Incan ruins turned soupy. But it was one particular face he was looking to find, the same face he'd been looking to find for what was beginning to seem like an eternity. *Fuckin'-A*.

"*Also* for the record," he continued conversationally, keeping up the appearance that he and Zoelner were just part of the crowd, sightseers out enjoying the day, "they don't call it guinea pig. They call it *cuy*. And it's kinda g—"

"Since apparently we're putting things on the record today," Zoelner interrupted, "I'd like to add that, *for the record*, it's a rodent."

"So's a rabbit. A guy like you musta eaten a rabbit at some point, right?"

"*Wrong*." Zoelner shot him an emphatic look. "When it comes to meat, I'm a fan of the big three. Beef, chicken, and pork. The holy trifecta of barn-yard animals. And what the hell do you mean by *a guy like me*?"

Dan stuck his tongue in his cheek. Zoelner had been pricklier than a porcupine the last forty-eight hours. And Dan would have chalked up his bad mood to the fact that they'd yet to complete their assignment to capture and exfiltrate *hombre numero uno* on Uncle Sam's shit list, *except* that Chelsea Duvall had joined their little clandestine venture two days ago. And *that* had made their dynamic duo a tension-filled trio and—

"He means that besides being a grumpy Gus pain-in-the-butt, you're a guy with a job that requires you to go on missions to the ass-ends of the earth, where the holy trifecta of barnyard animals sometimes isn't on the menu." A rusty-sounding female voice echoed through their tiny earpieces.

And speak of the devil.

"Funny. I don't remember opening this conversation up to comments from the peanut gallery." Zoelner scowled. He *always* scowled when talking to Chelsea… or *about* Chelsea. The two had been coworkers back in the day. And Dan supposed they were sort of coworkers *again*, given that Chelsea had officially been named the CIA's liaison to Black Knights Inc.

"And *for the record*," Chelsea continued, as if Zoelner hadn't spoken, "rabbits were part of the scientific order Rodentia until sometime around the turn of the twentieth century. They've since been reclassified to something called Lagomorpha, which means they aren't technically rodents anymore, but—"

"I don't give a fiddler's fuck *what* they're classified as," Zoelner interrupted. "My point is, I haven't eaten one. And in case you were both unaware"—he slid Dan's half-consumed snack a wary glance—"there's always chicken available. *Always*. Or beans! Dear God, what's so wrong with getting your daily dose of protein from an innocuous little legume?"

"Nothing's wrong with it," Chelsea admitted. A subtle smacking noise sounded over the airwaves. "It's just that beans are bland, not nearly as tasty as other, say, *meatier* choices."

Zoelner blanched just as a bus made to look like a trolley car trundled by on the brick street in front of them, belching exhaust fumes into the crisp mountain air. "Are you eating something, Chels?" he inquired hesitantly.

"I skipped lunch," came Chelsea's reply. "And when I heard Dan chewing, I realized my belly button was rubbing a sore spot on my backbone. So I asked the baker's son to go out to get me a snack."

"What *kind* of snack?" Zoelner ventured to ask.

"*Cuy.*"

Zoelner made a retching sound and Chelsea's low, husky laugh resonated in their ears.

Dan shook his head. He, for one, was glad she'd joined them. She added some much-needed comic relief to two guys who, due to their natures and a few karmic punches in the gut from life, were typically sullen and withdrawn.

"I was thinking about our sleeping arrangements, Chels," Dan blurted. Number one, because it was sure to freak Zoelner out. And number two, because he was bored as shit. From the very beginning, this assignment had been nothing but schlepping ass from one South American city to the next, following leads that either turned out to be a whole lot of hooey, or else didn't pan out because the CIA kept fucking things up by being all bull-in-the-china-shoppy. *The overeager sonsofbitches.* And *for the record*, this current lead was looking to wind up at the same deader-than-dead end, so what was the harm in stirring the pot that held Dagan Zoelner and Chelsea Duvall and livening up his day?

Sure enough, Zoelner turned to him, eyes wide, expression plastered with *What the hell are you doing?* Dan let his eyelids hang at half-mast and paired them with a shit-eating grin.

"What do you mean?" Chelsea's tone was cautious.

Dan's grin widened. "I was just thinking it's sorta unfair for Zoelner and me to get the soft feather bed and leave you on that rickety ol' cot." The room they'd rented above the bakery a quarter mile from their current position had approximately the same square footage as a Triscuit, smelled strongly of powdered sugar and yeast, and came equipped with one full-sized bed and one pint-sized cot. Masquerading as a group of money-tight backpackers in order to keep a low profile came with certain disadvantages.

"Besides," he continued, "Zoelner doesn't like it when I'm the big spoon. And I refuse to be the little spoon. So I was thinking maybe if this lead doesn't pan out, you and I could switch places tonight, and—"

"*No!*" Chelsea and Zoelner barked in unison. Dan had to bite the inside of his cheek to keep from laughing out loud. Zoelner flipped him the bird by way of pretending to scratch his eyebrow with his middle finger.

"I'm perfectly fine with the cot," Chelsea insisted.

"And I don't let you be the big spoon because I'm afraid of what you'll do to me in your sleep," Zoelner added. "Every damn night you dream about that chick you worked with in Kuala Lumpur. And then you moan and whisper, 'Penni, oh, Penni!' It skeeves me out."

If Dan was the blushing type, he would have been red from the tops of his ears to the tips of his toes. As it was, he simply swallowed and hoped Zoelner couldn't see how just the mere mention of Penni's name made his blood run hot.

"Penni?" Chelsea asked, the timbre of her voice that of a woman who smelled gossip in the air. "Ooooh, do tell, Dan. And don't leave anything out. I could use a good romantic story. The tediousness of this assignment is getting to me."

The smirk Zoelner sent him was evil enough to scare the devil himself, and Dan could do nothing but tip his head, giving the guy points for summarily turning the tables. "You won that round, you big penis-wrinkle," he whispered from the corner of his mouth. Louder, he tried to sidestep the issue. "And tedious, Chels? Really? You've only been doing this two days. Try three months!"

"Yes, yes," she agreed. "You poor, abused clandestine government operators. I'm sure there's moss growing on your weapons as we speak. Now stop stalling and spill."

So much for sidestepping…

"Nothing to tell," he insisted, the *cuy* having lost its appeal. He folded the tinfoil around the little carcass and tossed the whole thing in the trash can a couple of feet from the end of the bench. Fishing in the hip pocket of his jeans, he snagged a pack of Chiclets—the only gum he'd been able to find in all of Peru—and popped a couple of the candy-coated squares in his mouth. The taste of spearmint exploded on his tongue.

"Nice try," Chelsea snorted.

"Fine." He sighed, sending Zoelner a look that promised slow, painful retribution for bringing up this particular topic. "Agent Penni DePaul was part of the Secret Service detail attached to the president's daughter when *el Jefe*" — that's how the boys and girls of BKI always referred to the commander in chief…when he wasn't in the room with them, of course — "saw fit to send me, Steady, and Ozzie in to provide backup support. Penni and I had to work together when everything went to hell in a handbasket because of Winterfield's black-hearted treachery."

Even had *el Jefe* not tasked BKI, and Dan specifically, with bringing in the asshole, he would have considered it his own personal mission. Not only did he have an inherent stake, given the hell he'd been through in Malaysia, but he'd also decided this job was the perfect opportunity for him to show all his friends and teammates that he was back to being an asset and not just a grief-stricken asshat. To thank them for putting up with his sorry self when he'd spent a year sitting at the bottom of a whiskey bottle, followed by another year doing his damnedest to crawl back out.

But fat lot of headway I've made on the mission so far. Winterfield was still in the wind. And Dan couldn't think of a more ridiculous way to try to catch the guy than sitting around and hoping to see him pass by. But their Intel had only specified that Winterfield might be meeting a buyer in Cusco so…yeah. *Whatcha see is whatcha get…*

"And after it was all over?" Chelsea prompted, dragging his mind back to Penni. Although, in truth, in three months it'd never strayed all that far from the woman. Which was a problem. "Then what happened?"

"What do you think happened? The only thing that *could* happen, given she's a Secret Service agent and I'm…" *A widower. A drunk. A—*

"A wannabe street punk from Detroit Rock City?" Zoelner supplied, pronouncing it *Dee-troit*.

"Hey, don't knock Motown, man," Dan harrumphed. "As Kid Rock once said, 'Cars and rock 'n' roll. It's a good combo.'"

"I think Dan meant that she's a Secret Service agent and he's a supersecret, legally suspect, blacker-than-black operator," Chelsea added not so helpfully.

"Legally suspect?" Now it was Zoelner's turn to harrumph. "How many times do we have to go over this? It's not that what we at BKI do for the president is *illegal* necessarily. It's just that we sort of skirt around the edges of international law…or find the loopholes. And *you're* one to talk. The evil shit The Company has been known to get up to makes all of us at Black Knights Inc. look like angels sent straight from heaven."

"That mighta been pushing it," Dan mumbled, hoping Zoelner had distracted Chelsea from the topic at hand.

He should have known better. "Zip it, Z," she said, "and let Dan finish."

Dan envisioned her pulling a bowl of popcorn into her lap and hunkering down for a long, sordid tale. So he was doomed to disappoint her when he finished succinctly with, "Long story short, we went our separate ways."

For a couple of seconds, silence reigned in his earpiece. Then she made a rude noise. "Why do men do that?"

"Do what?" Zoelner asked.

"Leave out all the good parts?" she grumbled.

"Because those good parts are filed under None

of Your Goddamn Business," Dan informed her as a vision of Penni as she'd been the last time he'd seen her, mourning and exhausted, flashed through his head.

Agent Penelope Ann DePaul had the understated, honest type of beauty most men didn't immediately pick up on. But the more you looked at her, the more breathtaking she became. Because not only did she have dark, shiny hair, deep brown eyes—*kind* eyes, that's the first thing he'd noticed about her—and a set of legs that should be illegal, but she was the sort of woman who displayed innate grace and tended toward straight talk. The kind who'd never faked a laugh or an orgasm or—

Oh, perfect.

The thought of Penni in the throes of rapture, what she would look like with her head thrown back, her long neck arched, was enough to have the moron behind his zipper twitching with interest. And just in case Zoelner hadn't yet noticed the untimely bulge behind his fly—the man had a mean eye when it came to details—Dan hooked an ankle over the opposite knee and surreptitiously stuffed his hands into the pockets of his jacket, pulling the material over his lap.

"Fine," Chelsea harrumphed. "Be that way. But at least tell me this." Dan groaned as if his nuts were caught in a vise. "You're dreaming about her every night, right?"

Roger that. Dreams so hot, so vivid, he was surprised none of them had been wet. And considering he was currently sharing a bed with Zoelner? Yeah, talk about having some explaining to do.

Then again, he supposed his current dreams were

better than the nightmares he'd been suffering for most of the past two-plus years. Nightmares of his wife covered in blood and dead in his arms, shot by a psycho right in the courtyard of BKI where she should have been safe, where he should have kept her safe...

He shuddered, hunching deeper into his jacket. He figured he was past the worst of his grief. He no longer spent his days wishing for death. But thinking back on that awful evening was still like scraping a fingernail over a raw nerve. He suspected it always would be.

Living in the past is victimization. *Living in the future is* manipulation. *Live in the* present...

One of the many mantras he'd picked up at AA whispered through his head, and he did his best to shake off the heavy weight of heartache that made him want to reach for a drink. Instead, he concentrated on the now. Easy enough when Chelsea got tired of waiting for him to respond and inquired, "So then why haven't you tried to contact her?"

"Well, 'cause she made it pretty clear she didn't want—" His words came to a halt so fast he thought maybe his larynx came equipped with air brakes.

"What?" Chelsea demanded impatiently. "What did she make clear?"

Dan ignored her, rubbing a hand over the back of his neck.

Zoelner immediately sensed the change in him. "What?" he asked, casually reaching inside his jacket pocket for his weapon. "You have that feeling again?"

He was referring to the creepy, crawly sensation Dan had suffered since they landed in Cusco. One minute he was fine. The next minute, it was like a whole colony of invisible ants skittered over the back of his neck and scalp. "You don't *feel* that?" he asked.

"Dude," Zoelner said, "look who you're talking to. I pretty much live in a constant state of paranoia. I think it's a factory setting Langley installed."

"That and the ability to blend into a crowd and go statue-still at the drop of a hat," Dan added, never before having seen anyone quite as chameleonlike as Zoelner.

"Eh." Zoelner shrugged. "That has less to do with Langley and more to do with my old man."

"Oh, do tell," Chelsea piped up. She was *determined* to get a story out of one of them.

"Some other time," Zoelner said. "Like, maybe next century."

Whatever Chelsea said in response was lost on Dan because he got another jolt of bad juju.

Damnit! What *was* that?

Ever so casually he allowed his gaze to swing around the square, wondering if the unending hunt for Winterfield and the accompanying boredom had finally gotten to him. If his subconscious had decided to stimulate things a bit by making him sense something that wasn't there.

No one by the fountains looked hinky or suspicious. Neither did anyone on the park bench across the way. As for the flagpoles…

His eyeballs came to a stop so quickly he assumed they left tread marks on the backs of their sockets. He rubbed a hand over his face, blinking. Okay, so his eyes were playing tricks on him. He shook his head. Hard. Hoping to untangle whichever wires had crossed on the pathway from his retinas to his brain.

"Whoa. Did a bug fly into your ear or something? What the hell is up with you?" Zoelner demanded.

Dan swallowed, his heart stuttering, tripping, galloping, then stuttering again. "D-do you see that woman over there?" He indicated the direction with his chin. "The one who looks like she could be Marisa Tomei's sister?"

"Where?"

"By the flagpole." He could hardly breathe.

"Which flagpole? There's more than one."

"The gay pride flagpole."

"What?"

"*The rainbow flag! Jesus!*" Dan barely refrained from pointing. A strange buzzing sounded in his ears. Maybe Zoelner was right about that bug.

"Now who's being the grumpy Gus? And just FYI, around here a rainbow flag doesn't have anything to do with gay pride. It's used to represent the Incan culture and—" Before Dan could tell him to shut the hell up, Zoelner stopped himself. "Christ in a cardigan sweater," he muttered. "I've obviously had way too much time on my hands. I'm pretty sure I read the entire Peruvian guidebook."

"Goddamnit!" Dan had reached his wit's end. "Do you see her or not? The one with the ice-cream cone!"

"Yeah, I see her," Zoelner finally said. "So what?"

"Do you need me to fly the drone around?" Chelsea's excited voice sounded in Dan's earpiece.

Part of the deal that'd been made a little over forty-eight hours ago with the CIA was that the spooks would agree to stop looking for Winterfield themselves and let Dan and Zoelner work the case alone *if* Chelsea Duvall was allowed to join the mission and report back to The

Company bigwigs on any progress. As an added bonus, the CIA had thrown in a drone. Nothing that could drop bombs, mind you. Just a little aircraft about the size of an extra-large pizza box, big enough to support a long-range camera lens and the gizmos necessary to uplink directly to military and government satellites. Sitting in their rented room with her laptop open, Chelsea had been piloting the craft high in the airspace above Cusco, taking photos of the folks in and around town, hoping for something to pop.

"No," he told her emphatically. "No need for the drone."

"How do you know?" she demanded.

"'Cause it's Penni DePaul."

Zoelner chuckled, actually *chuckled* beside him. Of all the times for the guy to grow a sense of humor. "Holy shit! Are you serious?" he said.

Dan glanced over at his teammate only to discover that the fuckhead was checking Penni out, letting his eyes drift down her lean, delicately curved frame. Even dressed in jeans, boots, and an open parka—the highs in Cusco hovered around seventy degrees Fahrenheit, but the lows in October dipped close to freezing—she was obviously a long, tall glass of water, just as Ozzie had once described her. It wasn't jealousy Dan felt as he watched Zoelner drink her in. Because jealousy would be ridiculous; he had no claim over her. But it sure as shit was *something*. A close cousin to jealousy maybe. One that prompted him to revert to his middle-school self and say, "Take a picture, asswipe. It'll last longer."

"And *that's* what I wanted to hear!" Chelsea crowed. "The drone is on its way!"

Chapter Two

"I GOTTA ADMIT, I IMAGINED I'D SEE SOME CRAZY SHIT IN Cusco." A deep voice with a familiar habit of smashing two words together sounded over Penni's shoulder. It vibrated through her, liquefying her bones from the marrow out. And her heart decided to go ahead and switch places with her stomach. "But the craziest thing I've seen so far is you."

Sonofa... Her bones might have turned to liquid, but her muscles hardened to stone, jerking her shoulders up around her ears. She hadn't been prepared to see him. Not yet. Not for a couple more hours, when she planned to knock on his door and invite him out to dinner so she could ply him with wine and food before she laid her heart open and—

"What the ever-lovin' fuck-all are you doing down here, Agent DePaul?"

Agent DePaul? Surely after everything they'd been through, they were, at the very least, on a first-name basis. Or maybe, just as she'd feared, she'd read more into their time together than she should have. And that did *not* bode well for the reason she'd come...

She swung around, preparing herself for the sudden impact of his eyes. Yep. Just as she remembered, they were the exact color of the climbing vines that grew up the back of her childhood home on Hancock

Street. She was also ready for the punch of his hand-some face—his square jaw seemed perpetually dusted by light-brown beard stubble, and his broad forehead tended to support a whorl or two of his wavy, sand-colored hair. What she *wasn't* prepared for was his expression. To put it mildly, it was about as welcoming as a roadkill dinner.

In response, her heart—indecisive organ that it was—decided to change places with her toes.

"Well, hello to you too, Dan," she said, congratulating herself for pulling off nonchalant, considering she was dealing with liquid bones, stonelike muscles, and organs that refused to stay in their proper places.

"Cut the bullshit, Agent DePaul," he growled. Coming out of any other man, that low, grumbling sound would've seemed ridiculous. Coming out of him? Well, it sort of fit. Because even back before she knew what he really was, she'd noticed the way danger seemed to drift around him like smoke above dry ice.

He looked around as if he expected someone to be with her. "I don't believe in coincidences," he said…er, growled. He really was very growly. "I'm here. You're here. And if the Secret Service thinks it has a dog in this pony show 'cause of what went down in Malaysia, then I've got news for you, honey."

Honey? *Honey? Oh, no he di-int!* "Skirt" she could handle. "Broad" was okay too. But "honey"? Well, not when it was said in *that* tone! She hoisted her purse higher on her shoulder and thought, for a whole two seconds, how satisfying it would be to smash her ice-cream cone over his head.

In the end, she couldn't make herself do it. *Damn my mad love for chocolate double scoops!*

"It took us turning some serious screws before the CIA dipshits would agree to pull back and let me and Zoelner handle this on our own. If you think I'm gonna let you guys come in here and pick up where they left off, loitering around every corner, making Winterfield afraid to poke his head out of his hole, you've got another think coming. And, just so you know, I'm not an idiot. For the last two days I've known someone was watching us and—"

"Dan?" she interrupted, making sure her voice was syrupy sweet despite the fact she was hard-pressed not to smack him upside his wonderful, ridiculously handsome head. This was not going at all according to plan.

"Hmm?"

"How's about you shut your piehole." When she got worked up, the Brooklynese really came out in her. "Because I don't know what the hell you're talking about. And I haven't been here two days. I just got in two hours ago." And then pieces of what he said sank in. "Wait…you're here to apprehend Winterfield? Winterfield's in Cusco?"

Just the mention of the man who was ultimately behind the deaths of her colleagues made her blood run with gunpowder and her heart beat to the rhythm of a death march.

"We think so," Dan said. "But we've thought he was a lotta places before, only to find out he wasn't, Agent DePaul."

Agent DePaul. Agent DePaul. If he Agent DePauled her one more time… "I'm *not* Agent DePaul anymore," she informed him. "So you can drop the formalities. I'm just plain Penni now."

"Huh?" His chin jerked back like she *had* smacked him upside the head. She supposed there was some satisfaction there.

"My name," she said. "It's just Penni. Penni DePaul."

He shook his head, blinking at her. "I know your name. *Jesus!* Did you think I could forget you after everything—"

"Hello there!" A man with a shock of thick brown hair and a pair of storm-cloud-gray eyes walked up to them. Now she wanted to smack *him* upside the head. Geez, she was feeling particularly smacky today. Dan was just about to say something good—the *first* good thing that'd come out of his mouth—and this asshole interrupted him. "You must be the inimitable Agent Penni DePaul. This big lug's told me all about you."

He slung an arm around Dan's shoulders and Penni lifted her eyebrows, turning to Dan. Now her silly heart decided to sprout wings and fly around outside her body. She really was going to have to have a conversation with the organ later. Right now she was too preoccupied with the idea that Dan had actually talked about her.

Did that mean there was hope? Was it possible there was a chance for—

Now, don't get ahead of yourself, Penni!

Right. Good advice.

"Oh, he has, has he?" she asked. Again with the nonchalance. *Damn, I'm good!*

"That's affirmative." The new arrival nodded, an odd sparkle in his eye. "He talks about you every night in his s—"

Dan elbowed Gray Eyes in the ribs hard enough to

have the wind rushing from his lungs. He doubled over, and when he stood up, the expression he pinned on Dan was incredulous. "Uh…*ow!*" he said, rubbing his side.

"You think that hurt?" Dan made a face. "Then the five-fingered sandwich I'll put in your crotch basket if you don't zip it is gonna be a bona fide killer."

"Oh yeah?" Gray Eyes stepped forward. "Try it. It's been a while since you and me have taken a trip to Fist City."

Penni rolled her eyes so hard it was a wonder they didn't get stuck backward. Apparently, it was her lot in life to be surrounded by men suffering from bad cases of too-much-testosterone-itis.

"If memory serves," Dan said, "you came out of the last tussle a little worse for wear while I didn't have as much as a scratch on—" He stopped so suddenly that Penni frowned. Her frown deepened when a brief look of horror skated across his features. And then, before she knew it, Gray Eyes was apologizing.

"Sorry, man," he said. "I didn't mean to bring up that day and—"

"No." Dan shook his head, causing a lock of blond hair to curl over his eyebrow. It was quite delightful, really. That lock of hair. *Grrrr. Stupid hormones!* And speaking of too-much-testosterone-itis, since the first moment she and Dan had locked gazes, she'd been afflicted with a chronic case of too-much-*estrogen*-itis. "That was my fault," Dan finished.

All right already. She was obviously missing something here. She glanced back and forth between the two men, trying to determine the truth in their faces. But each of their expressions were…well…

expressionless. She frowned some more, taking a lick of her ice-cream cone.

"Let's change the subject, shall we?" Gray Eyes finally said, extending his hand in Penni's direction. "Hi, I'm Dagan Zoelner."

"Shit. Sorry." Dan shook his head as if physically jostling away whatever had momentarily overshadowed him. "Dagan Zoelner, meet Agent Penni DePaul."

"Hiya." Penni shook Zoelner's hand. "And it's just plain Penni DePaul now," she corrected for what seemed like the bazillionth time in the last twenty-four hours.

"Huh?" Dan scowled at her. That seemed to be his favorite word today.

"It's just plain Penni DePaul now. There's no more 'Agent' in front of my name."

"What do you mean?" he demanded.

"I think she's trying to say she's no longer with the Secret Service," Zoelner supplied helpfully.

Thank goodness *someone's* synapses were firing. Three months ago, she would have said Dan was one of the most intelligent guys she'd ever had the pleasure of working with. Now? Well, for some reason he was intent on doing his best impression of the dullest knife in the drawer.

"Is that true?" Dan asked, placing a hand on her arm, concern knitting his brow. She did *not* notice the way the heat from his broad palm seeped through the fabric of her parka, or the way his touch reminded her of how it'd felt when he pushed her shirt aside so he could kiss the top of her shoulder.

Okay. Forget about it. Of course she noticed. *Of course* she remembered!

"Yep." She nodded, mesmerized by the gold flecks rimming the green around Dan's pupils, reminded that he smelled like the air after a thunderstorm...rich and clean and electric. "Civilian Penni DePaul." She snapped him a saucy salute with her ice-cream cone. "At your service."

And then he didn't just smell like a thunderstorm, he looked like one too. His expression turned so violent, she would not have been surprised if lightning bolts shot from his eyes. His jaw ground so hard she fancied she could hear the enamel on his teeth cracking like thunder. "If those fuck-sticks fired you 'cause you"—Fuck-sticks? That was a new one—"broke protocol that night and stayed out past that ridiculous curfew," he ground out, "then I—"

"No." She was quick to cut him off. "It wasn't that."

"What protocol?" Zoelner asked, looking back and forth between them. "What curfew? What are you guys talking about?"

"The midnight curfew the Secret Service enacted after that clusterfuck"—now *clusterfuck* she knew very well—"in Colombia, where a bunch of their agents got caught with ladies of the evening in their hotel rooms," Dan spat.

"Ladies of the evening?" Zoelner smirked. "Is that for the benefit of our mixed company, or have you been reading historical romances again?" The idea of big, bad Dan "The Man" Currington with a Georgette Heyer novel in his hand made the corner of Penni's mouth twitch.

"You're missing the goddamned point," Dan growled. And there he went again, Mr. Growly Growlerton.

"Which is?" Zoelner asked.

"That the Secret Service thought it could tell its own agents when it was bedtime."

Zoelner turned to her. "And I take it you broke your curfew?"

"I did," she admitted, still coming to terms with what breaking her curfew that night had meant. "And it saved me from the incendiary device the terrorists had planted under my hotel bed." But it'd left her the sole survivor among the Secret Service agents who'd been on The Assignment.

"Hot damn. That was a lucky break," Zoelner mused, eyeing her curiously. Then, "If you don't mind me asking, what caused you to go against protocol?"

She glanced over at Dan, remembering how they'd been seconds away from getting down and dirty in his hotel room. That night they'd finally given in to the chemistry that'd been bubbling between them. No, on second thought, it wasn't chemistry. It was astronomy. Because she'd been the moon to his earth, seduced into his orbit by the sheer force of his gravitational pull.

"Ah." Zoelner nodded sagely. "I get it." He rubbed a hand under his chin. "And that explains more than you know."

"What do you mean?" She stuck out her tongue to catch the stray drop of ice cream that threatened to roll over her fingers.

"Nothing," Dan cut Zoelner off, his eyes zeroing in on her tongue like a sniper taking aim at a target. Heat instantly washed down her body from the top of her head, making her toes curl inside her boots. They'd resumed their usual position now that her heart was no longer taking up the space. "And back to the point, which is…" He made a rolling motion with his hand. "You're no longer with the Secret Service?"

"I'm not." *Now* they were getting down to brass tacks.

"Why?" he demanded. "What happened?"

"Well, I—"

"Never mind," he quickly cut her off, causing her brow to furrow in frustration. "Why you're out of the Service is less important than why you're here now. 'Cause if you're not part of some attempt to apprehend Winterfield, then you're in Cusco to…" Again with the rolling hand.

"To talk to you." There. She admitted it.

"To *me*?"

"To you." Inexplicably, the song sung by the Mad Hatter and the March Hare in *Alice in Wonderland* skipped through her head. *A verrrry merry un-birthday… To me!… To who? Oh, you!* And like the Mad Hatter's conversation, this one seemed to be all over the place.

Finally, Dan asked, "Why?"

Okay, so she hadn't exactly planned to say this in the middle of a busy Peruvian square, much less in front of an audience, but the way things were going, if she didn't take the opportunity to tell him what was in her head, what was in her heart, and—

Penni-pie, just pull up your big-girl panties and do it! Her father's advice echoed through her head, ever the voice of wisdom and reason.

She screwed up her courage and blurted, "Because I—"

"Holy shit!" Zoelner spat, cutting Penni off. She blinked over at the man. *Damnit!* He had the worst timing. "You two look alive if you want to stay that way."

Now it was her turn to say, "Huh?"

"What is it?" Dan was suddenly on point. She could feel the tension radiating from him like he was a live wire. As she casually followed the direction of Zoelner's stare so as not to draw too much notice to herself, her instincts and training allowed her to immediately spy what had snagged his attention.

"We've got a skinhead packing heat at three o'clock," Zoelner said, and Penni noticed he'd gone eerily still. No part of him moving. Even the wind refused to tease the ends of his hair. Then he started cataloging the guy's features, and the quick, businesslike descriptions told her he wasn't talking to her or to Dan. "Looks Eastern European. No neck. Has one of those narrow skulls suggesting he won't be winning any Academic Decathlon championships."

A quick glance at his left ear revealed the tiny, flesh-toned earpiece. Part of her wondered who was listening in. The other part of her lightbulbed the fact that she'd landed herself in the middle of a live operation, despite having been assured by the folks back at Black Knights Inc. that Dan wasn't too busy to talk to her.

Great. Just...grrrreat! Never let it be said that life in Penni Land wasn't chock-a-block full of twisty, turny excitement.

"I see him," Dan muttered, shoving his hands in his pockets and glancing away so it didn't look like all three of them were staring at the guy crossing the square not twenty feet away. "A lot more brawn than brain."

"More like a blunt-force object," she added helpfully, "as opposed to a precision instrument."

"That's him in a nutshell," Dan said. "Chelsea? You got an angle on his face?"

So it was *Chelsea* listening in. Whoever the hell Chelsea was, she was obviously somewhere close with a camera in hand. Instinctively, Penni reached over to her left side where her service weapon was kept in a shoulder holster.

Only…it wasn't there.

And boy, oh boy, it was one heck of a momentary shock to feel nothing but ribs beneath her fingers. For the first time in a really long time, she felt completely, inexplicably vulnerable. No big surprise she didn't particularly care for the sensation.

She couldn't hear what Chelsea said to Dan, but she figured it was a negative on getting a bead on No Neck's face, because Dan cursed, grabbed what was left of her ice cream, and lobbed it into a nearby trash can.

"What the… *Hey!*" she complained, her heart breaking as she watched the top scoop smash against the metal side and slide over a huge glob of bubble gum. Before she could say more, he wrapped a hand around her arm and started pulling her after No Neck.

Okay, okay, she felt like griping, hoisting her purse back onto her shoulder when it slipped to dangle from her elbow. *I know how to play the game of cat and mouse. No need to manhandle.* But she'd always prided herself on being a smart woman, and Dan's patience seemed to be scraping the bottom of the barrel today. And since her arrival—*surprise!*—didn't appear to be helping matters, she simply asked, "So what's the plan?"

"We have a drone in the air," he said. So Chelsea wasn't close with a camera; she was sitting in a control center at a console or in a room somewhere with her laptop open. "But because of the direction he's facing and the surrounding mountains, we can't get a wide enough angle," he continued, lacing their fingers together so it looked less like he was frog-marching her across the square, and more like they were a happy couple out for a stroll.

A jolt of awareness shot up her arm when his wide, callused palm touched hers.

"We need to snap Skinhead's photo," he told her, increasing their pace, "so we can run his mug against the facial recognition software back at BKI and Langley."

It'll be fine if you fly to Peru, Becky had said when Penni balked at the thought of hopping on a plane and distracting Dan from whatever he was doing. *He's just twiddling his dick down there, anyway. Has been for nearly three months now.*

Twiddling his dick, huh? Well, Penni had five choice words for the woman: "drone," "facial recognition software," and "Langley."

As they hustled across the square, she was tempted to glance into the sky even though she knew the drone was probably flying so high there was no way for her naked eye to see it. Zoelner abandoned them, cutting to the left and picking up his pace in an attempt to outflank No Neck and get ahead of him. It was a classic tailing technique. Put one party in front. Another behind. And trade places if and when necessary.

She and Dan took up the "party behind" position and trailed No Neck onto one of the busy cobbled roads fanning out from the square. The street was lined on both sides by two-story buildings made of plaster and stone. In this part of Cusco, the first floors were occupied by trinket shops, convenience stores, and small eateries. The top floors, with their brightly painted balconies, were where the owners of the shops made their homes.

The air on the little avenue was redolent with the smell of exhaust, cooking meat, and frying pastries. A gang of gnarly-looking street dogs rooted in an overturned trash can. And a taxi screamed around the corner, rattling and beeping at the tourists who had the bad sense to tarry in the street.

No Neck glanced over his shoulder at the woman who squealed when the taxi's side mirror came within inches of her hip, and Penni sucked in a breath when she saw his eyes. They were ice-blue and completely devoid of emotion. Seriously, looking into those cool, empty pools, she would not have been surprised to learn he was blood brothers with a snake.

Dan squeezed her fingers.

She peeked over at him, and even though he winked, the expression on his face was clearly *keep your shit together*.

Right. Because even if her head was spinning—you know, having suddenly been sucked into the cyclonic craziness of an operation; she was really going to have to strangle Becky for that dick-twiddling comment— she was a trained agent. Except... Oh, *crap*. No Neck hooked a right onto an even *smaller* street.

To be clear, the size of the street wasn't the problem. The *problem* was the steep incline of the little thoroughfare and its accompanying sidewalk—which was nothing less than a long flight of stairs. Cusco was built in the valley, but it quickly climbed up the sides of the surrounding mountains. And like the Big Bad Wolf, Penni was instantly huffing and puffing. *Unlike* the Big Bad Wolf, she'd be hard pressed to blow out a candle, much less blow anyone's house down.

Dan turned to her. "Y'okay?" Two words smashed into one.

"We're doing a lot more legwork than I planned when I decided on these boots," she told him.

"Bullshit. You're not acclimated." Due to Cusco's elevation, the air was incredibly thin and she was having a hell of a time catching her breath. Scratch that. She *wasn't* catching her breath.

"S-stop giving me the"—*pant, pant*—"evil eye. You're only allowed to use it if you're"—*pant, pant*—"Italian. I think it's a law or something." What she wouldn't give for one of those little wheeled oxygen carts the concierge at her hotel had been passing out to the out-of-breath out-of-towners when she'd checked in.

"You're a lot sassier than I remember," he grumbled, slowing their climb when Zoelner popped out from around a corner up ahead, taking his position in front of No Neck.

Thank Christ for small miracles. She couldn't have kept up that pace for one second more.

"Oh, you mean I'm sassier than I was"—*pant, pant*—"after all my friends and coworkers were killed?" She sucked in a deep breath that didn't seem to contain one drop of oxygen. "Is that what you mean? Because I'm pretty sure"—Geez, her heart was pounding. Her ears buzzing. Little spots of light danced in front of her eyes—"that situation didn't really lend itself to sassiness. What? What's that look for?"

"I'm just trying to decide whether or not I like this new, mouthy Penni DePaul," he said, brow quirked.

"Oh, you like me." She winced at the stitch in her side. And even though she sounded confident, truth was, she waited, *literally* breathlessly, for his response.

She hadn't been herself in Malaysia. She'd been a mess both emotionally and professionally, and Dan's calm, his self-assurance, his all-around badassedness—*Is that even a word? Well, if it's not, it should be*—had been the only things that'd kept her from falling completely apart. But the fact of the matter was, he didn't really know her. Not the *real* her. The smart aleck. The tomboy. And maybe he *liked* his women vulnerable and fragile and—

"Roger that," he said. She didn't have long to wonder if he was talking to her or the woman in his ear when he added, "I've sorta had a thing for ball-busting broads since Susie Edwards threw a rock at my head during second-grade recess. Musta been born with a little bit of masochist in me."

Again with the "broad." Of course, the way Dan said the word made it sound good. She would've blown out a breath of relief if she had a breath to spare. And he must've sensed some of what she was feeling because the smile he gave her was as sweet and dry as the wind blowing down from the mountains. But the light shining in his eyes? Forget about it. It was anything but sweet and dry. Just the opposite. It was hot and liquid, churning and burning and making her wonder if it was possible for her underpants to combust.

Yep. He liked her. And more than that, he *wanted* her. It was there in his face. He was letting her see it.

No holds barred. And then she was dizzy for a reason that had nothing to do with the lack of O_2 in the air.

She opened her mouth to tell him…well…*everything* when Zoelner called, "Hey, you guys!" in his best Sloth from *The Goonies* voice. He was ten steps in front of No Neck, waving frantically, his iPhone held out in front of him like your average, overly exuberant tourist. "Fancy meeting you here! Now, smile for the camera!"

"Smart," she whispered when No Neck glanced up the steep steps at Zoelner. But before Zoelner could take the picture, No Neck ducked into the doorway of a convenience store. The move caused his jacket to fan out, and Penni got a good long look at the piece he was carrying in his shoulder holster. *Christ on the cross!*

"You think he looked up long enough for Chelsea to snap a photo?" she asked as they stopped in front of the souvenir shop located a handful of steps below the doorway of the convenience store.

Dan cocked his chin, listening to something she couldn't hear. "Roger that. Now do as Zoelner says and smile for the camera."

"Cheese," she said when Dan threw an arm around her shoulders. In contrast to the cool mountain air, he was hot as a furnace. Curling into him seemed like the most natural thing. And allowing him to hold her up since her under-oxygenated muscles were complaining about the task was an added benefit.

"Got it!" Zoelner crowed the second after the flash on his iPhone blazed. Then he was skipping down the steps toward them. Penni saw No Neck exit the convenience store and continue his way up the hill. "I suspect it's too soon to have his identity?" Zoelner murmured once he was in front of them, pantomiming showing them the photo while simultaneously listening to Chelsea's response.

"Chels says yes it's too soon," Dan said for Penni's benefit since she wasn't wearing her own earpiece. *Bless him.* "His mug shot is being run through the software now."

"Okay. So while Chelsea tries to determine just exactly who he is," Zoelner said, still smiling, still waving his hands around like they weren't having a really serious, supersecret conversation, "let's follow him. See where he goes with that big gun strapped to his side."

"That's not a gun," Penni grunted. "That's the *Mona Lisa* of death. Did you get a good look at it?"

"A T/C Contender," Dan said. "Rifle-like accuracy and power in a handgun. Whatever Skinhead is doing here, he wants to do it with precision and from a distance."

Zoelner twisted his mouth and bobbed his eyebrows. "Hot damn! Maybe we're *finally* on to something. You two want to keep pulling up the rear position and let me—"

"Forget about it." Penni shook her head. "I'm done for."

"Can't catch her breath," Dan explained.

"Ah." Zoelner's expression was concerned. But Penni didn't know if it was for her or because No Neck was getting away.

"You two go on," she said. "I'll head back to my hotel once I can—"

"Fuck that," Dan interrupted. "I'm not leaving you alone. Not when an Eastern European douche-canoe packing a T/C Contender is on the loose."

"Awwww. You're sweet." But the expression she shot him said he was anything but, succinctly conveying

Hey! Former Secret Service agent here! Still, a part of her *was* touched—in a girlie, gooey, totally undignified way. "But I can take care of myself."

Zoelner and Dan exchanged a look. It lasted only a second and they never said a word, but somehow they'd come to an agreement because Zoelner said, "Okay. I'll go it alone and check in should anything interesting happen."

Penni watched him take off up the stairs, hands shoved in the pockets of his jacket. He whistled a snappy tune and stopped occasionally to peer into a shop window. You know, like a tourist would do. But all the while he closed the distance to No Neck.

"Really, Dan"—she turned back to him once Zoelner was out of earshot—"you don't need to stay with me. I didn't come down here to interfere with—"

"Penni DePaul." The way he said her name made it seem like he was tasting it, rolling it around on his tongue. Since his arm was still around her—yeah, she'd noticed—it took very little effort for him to push her back until her shoulders hit the wall of the souvenir shop. Then he was bracing his hands on either side of her head, leaning in, his eyes the only spot of disparate color against the whitewashed plaster of the buildings across the street. They seemed to burn with intensity and suddenly she was hot. Suffocating. And not just because the air was thin. It felt like she was wrapped in ten layers of thick wool.

"In case I gave you the wrong impression earlier…" he growled. Mr. Growly Growlerton. "I want you to know how damn *good* it is to see you again."

Chapter Three

"IT'S GOOD TO SEE YOU TOO, DAN…"

His name, spoken so softly, caused Dan to suffer a momentary loss of the present. The street and buildings around him dissolved into the swanky Novotel hotel in Malaysia. Time reversed itself and suddenly it was three months ago, when she'd pushed him back against the door of his room and they were on each other like icing on cake…

"Dan…"

She was alive in his arms, a warm, writhing mass of sweet femininity. Her mouth hot and hungry. Her fingers and hands…everywhere. It was insane. Amazing. Fast. Too fast. He didn't have time to think. And maybe that was her whole plan, since not fifteen seconds ago he'd been about to put on the brakes and call the whole thing off.

She fumbled with his belt buckle and shoved his pants down his legs, pulling hers off a split second later. Then she was dragging him toward the bed and his eyes were superglued to her high, tight, panty-clad ass. Somewhere along the journey, his boxers went the way of his pants. And then she was crawling onto the bed, turning to beckon him with a sultry grin and bedroom eyes.

"Condom," she husked when he was about to launch himself on top of her.

He spun to snag his discarded pants so he could root around in the pocket for the rubber he knew was in there. When he swung back, she was on her knees on the bed, her lush bottom lip caught between her teeth. She looked so damned beguiling. So damned tempting. So damned…everything he'd been missing. He hesitated.

"Do we need to go through it again?" She lifted a brow, referring to the speech she'd just given him about not usually doing this kind of thing, but being willing to take a chance on him because she felt they had a strange, unexpected connection.

And that was the whole goddamned reason behind his continuing reticence, wasn't it? That strange, unexpected connection. Because even though he'd convinced himself that his wife would be the first person to cheer him on in finding life again, finding love or lust or even just companionship again, it still felt disloyal to her memory to have such an intense attraction to another woman.

And it was intense. Utterly carnal. Profoundly sexual. Stronger than anything he'd ever felt before. Which made the sense of disloyalty that much worse.

"If you've changed your mind, I understand," she said softly. "We can just forget about it." The way she smashed the words together in that quintessentially New York way made it sound more like fuhgeddaboudit.

Hell's bells, she was adorable. A tough, streetwise, long, tall, sexy-as-hell Secret Service agent who made all his internal gyroscopes go so crazy he didn't know which way was up.

"No." He adamantly shook his head, the phrase he'd

heard at his last AA meeting echoing inside his heated skull: Get up, suit up, show up, grow up, don't give up… no matter what. And to his eternal dismay, the truth was he had given up. For a really long time. And he hadn't shown up. For just as long. But he was done with all of that useless self-pity and narcissistic despair. He was taking his first step out of the darkness and into the light. And he was doing it with a wonderful, kind, intelligent woman. As for the growing up, if one particular part of him grew any more, it'd likely split its skin. And suiting up? Roger that.

"*I haven't changed my mind,*" he assured her, ripping open the foil packet with his teeth. "*Not on your life.*"

When he rolled on the condom, she licked her lips. Her dark eyes sparkled hungrily as she watched the thin rubber slide over his painfully sensitive, angrily engorged erection.

He went to her then, pressing her back on the mattress, loving the way her shiny brown hair fanned out against the pillow. His pillow. His bed. This wonderful woman. He bent to claim her mouth, whispering the pet name he'd given her only minutes before. "Brooklyn." And that's when…BOOOOMMM!…all hell broke loose…

He came back to himself when her breath fanned over his cheek. She smelled like chocolate and the promise of a warm woman in the middle of cool sheets. He wanted to eat her up and take her to bed. Wait… Reverse that. He wanted to take her to bed and *then* eat her up.

Which wasn't really anything new. He'd wanted to do that since day one.

And because she'd been the first person of the female

persuasion he'd had any interest in after his wife died, he'd convinced himself that was the reason he couldn't get her out of his head. Because she *was* the first. And like firsts, she'd taken on this massive, larger-than-life importance in his mind just as first kisses, first loves, and firstborns tended to do.

Of course, now that she was here, standing in front of him, he had to admit the reason he hadn't been able to forget her wasn't because she'd been the bright, shiny beacon of hope he'd used to guide himself out of those last few feet of the gutter, but because he was drawn to something about her. Inevitably. Inexplicably. Like a honeybee to nectar. Like the tide to the moon. Like a goddamned moth to the flame.

"Brooklyn," he whispered into the soft shell of her ear, feeling her shiver delicately against him, smelling the scent of rosewater that clung to her skin and hair. That smell had plagued him since the day they'd parted, lingering in his dreams at night.

"You remember." Her voice was husky, hoarse. It went to his head like top-shelf whiskey. Making him dizzy. Making him burn.

"I couldn't forget."

That was God's honest truth. He couldn't forget her. No matter how hard he'd tried. And now she'd flown to the other half of the world to talk to him. Which *had* to mean she couldn't forget him either, right? Did she think maybe there was something for them? Something between them? Something more than lust fueled by the madness and mayhem and adrenaline rush that had been Malaysia?

The idea filled him with dread and longing and hope—and more dread—as a million and one questions raced through his brain. But the one he asked when he pushed back to look into her warm, dark eyes was, "How in God's name did you find me?"

A delightful flush rode high on her cheeks. He recognized it for exactly what it was. Awareness. Arousal. Whatever had been between them, whatever connection they'd made, was still there. And more than that, it'd grown during their long—too damn long—separation.

The realization had his heart beating so hard he could feel it in the fingertips he pressed against the plaster wall on either side of her head. In his toes encased in hiking boots. And…uh…other places. Yeah, definitely other places. One look at her, one smell of her, and his idiotic libido was throwing a kegger and streaking around like Frank the Tank in *Old School*.

"Well…I made a trip to Chicago," she told him, licking her lips. The dart of her pink tongue nearly had him panting. He wanted so badly to kiss her, to suck that sweet tongue into his mouth until he was drunk on all things Penelope DePaul.

"And rolled up to the gates of Black Knights Inc., I presume?" he asked, brow raised.

She bobbed her chin. Her delightful chin. It needed nibbling on, didn't it?

"So *now* the question becomes…just how the hell did you convince my lovely friends and coworkers to send you to me in the middle of a mission?"

She winced, and he barely resisted the urge to kiss the tip of her adorable nose. "First of all, I didn't have to convince anyone of anything. I just asked. Nicely. You'd be amazed what asking nicely will get you."

"Really?" He conjured up all the things he might ask her to do to him later. *Nicely.*

He pushed away from the wall and shoved his hands deep in his jacket pockets. It was either that or he was going to start molesting her right there on the street.

"Second of all, I didn't *know* you were on a mission. And certainly not one as important as bringing in"— she lowered her voice to something barely above a whisper—"Winterfield."

She unconsciously ran a finger over the tiny bump on the bridge of her nose. He'd learned early on that she only did it when she was nervous or frightened. And sometimes when she was really, *really* turned on. Why he found the little quirk so damned charming was anyone's guess.

"And third of all, Becky said…" She trailed off. Blushed. And that had his eyebrow sliding up his forehead. Ass-kicking, gun-toting, former Secret Service Agent Penni DePaul blushing?

"What? What did Becky say?" He could only imagine. Rebecca "Rebel" Knight née Reichert was as brash and balls-out as the kick-ass motorcycles she designed from scratch.

Penni cleared her throat. He braced himself for the worst. "She said you were just down here twiddling your dick."

He coughed. "Roger that. That sounds like Becky."

And he supposed he shouldn't be all that surprised his friends and teammates had jumped at the chance to send Penni his way. Until ten minutes ago, he *hadn't* been up to much—to his everlasting dismay. And all those assholes back home had been pushing him to start living life again, to start seeing women again. They probably thought Penni's arrival on their doorstep was a gift sent straight from heaven. A sign that maybe all their good-natured ribbing and nudging and heart-to-hearts had finally paid off.

In his mind's eye, it all became clear. He saw them hustling her onto a jumbo jet headed to the Southern Hemisphere before she could pack an extra bag or think twice or—

"Dan," she whispered, laying a hand on his wrist. The muscles beneath her touch jumped, and it took everything he had not to press her back against the wall and claim her mouth in a kiss he knew would leave them both breathless. It seemed almost unnatural… this attraction he had for her. Or maybe it was the most natural thing in the world, because it was instinctive and intrinsic. "I…"

She hesitated. Was it because, despite his best efforts, a low growl sounded at the back of his throat? He played it off with a cough. Like he'd had a tickle on one of his tonsils.

"What is it, Penni?"

She opened her mouth. Then closed it again, frowning.

Her uncertainty had him relenting. "I think I know what it is," he told her.

She blinked up at him, her soft brown eyes huge and sparkling in the setting sun shining over the mountain peaks and between the buildings. "You do?"

"It wasn't just adrenaline and lust and…and *whatever* back in Kuala Lumpur, was it?"

Her mouth fell open, an invitation that was almost

impossible to resist. She shook her head slowly, searching his face.

"You told me then you'd decided you had to stop letting the job be your life. That you were looking to start making real, human connections," he continued, watching her watch him, trying to see if what he was saying was on target or if he'd missed the mark by a mile. "You and me"—he wagged a finger between them—"we made a connection, didn't we? A real one."

"Yes," she hissed, a whisper of sound that held so much meaning.

"And you came all this way to see…what? If I felt it too? If I thought so too?"

She snapped her mouth closed and nodded, so much hope shining in her eyes that he didn't dare tell her about all his doubts, all his misgivings. He was a bad bet when it came to relationships. For many, *many* reasons. But she'd find all that out for herself. Eventually. For now, he gave her the simple truth. "I felt it, Penni. I *still* feel it."

She bit her lip and took a step toward him, her gaze focused on his mouth. And like a caged beast that'd been starved for days, he leaped at her, taking her in his arms, intent on tasting her. Then a husky voice that was *not* hers sounded in his ear.

"Uh. Sorry to interrupt," Chelsea said.

A lightbulb blazed to life over Dan's head. A bright, shiny reminder that he and Penni weren't alone in this conversation.

Sonofabastard! How could he have forgotten about the tiny microphone hidden behind the top button on his jacket, or the earpiece lodged in his left ear? But he knew the answer to that. Two words: Penni DePaul. When she was near, nothing else seemed to matter.

With no small measure of regret *or* embarrassment, he stepped away from Penni, pointing at his ear and widening his eyes so she'd know Chelsea was talking to him. The delightful woman clued in to the same thing he'd just realized and turned cherry red. Her cheeks were the exact color of the 1978 Camaro he'd fixed up and cruised down Eight Mile Road when he'd been a seventeen-year-old punk who thought he was a cool mofo.

"What's up, Chels?" he asked.

"*You*, I suspect," Chelsea said, her voice full of innuendo.

"Can it," he told her, feeling his own cheeks heat.

"What? There's no shame. I mean, she's a hottie. Way to go, Dan Man. Get down with yo bad self."

Lord save me. "Get to the point, Chels," he demanded. "You know who or *what* Skinhead is?"

"Bad motherfriggin' news, that's what. Z," Chelsea said. "Where are you? I lost you when you turned down that alley between…" She rattled off a couple of streets whose names Dan recognized from the map of the city he'd studied.

"I followed Skinhead into what I suspect is his hotel," came Zoelner's response, clear as a bell. *Technology. You gotta love it.* Or hate it. For example, when you were trying to have a private conversation. *Cock and balls.* Zoelner was never going to let Dan live down the things he'd just said to Penni. "I'm sitting at a table at the downstairs restaurant waiting to see if he comes out or if Winterfield comes in," Zoelner finished.

And even though Dan couldn't see him, he knew Zoelner had his phone raised to his ear, pretending to talk into it. Dan couldn't imagine running ops before the cell phone had been invented, when a guy or gal had to deliberately drop something and duck under a table in order to respond to an order or a question.

"Which hotel is it?" Chelsea asked.

Zoelner named one of the ritziest boutique joints in town.

"Stay there," Chelsea commanded. "I'm going to land the drone and come to you. Dan, you and Penni meet us. Two couples sharing a meal will look less conspicuous than one guy loitering alone. I'll fill you all in on what I know then."

"If dinner includes *cuy*," Zoelner complained, "I'm out."

"Oh, sack up, you big weenie," Chelsea grumbled.

"Big weenie?" Zoelner mused. "Aw, Chels, I knew you snuck a peek when I was in the shower yesterday morning."

"Ugh," Chelsea grumped, and if it was possible for someone to roll their eyes with their voice, she'd just done it. "What is it with you men and your preoccupation with the size of your junk?"

Dan stopped listening as the two of them quickly devolved into an argument that included Chelsea suggesting Zoelner do something with his *junk* that Dan was pretty sure was anatomically impossible. Instead, he turned to Penni and was struck anew by how lovely she was, especially when she was wearing that expectant, almost eager expression. And even though a part of him was excited by what this new development with Skinhead might mean, a larger part of him couldn't help but think this was a fucker of a case of bad timing.

Three months on Winterfield's trail and nothing. Then today, just when Penny arrives on his doorstep, *bam!* Their first real lead.

"We, uh…" He ran a hand over the top of his head and shrugged. Seriously, what else could he do? "We think we mighta caught a lucky break and stumbled onto something. I know you didn't fly all the way down here for this, but right now I…*we* could use your help. You up for some drinks and dinner with a side of espionage?"

Something flickered across her face. Something he couldn't quite put his finger on. Something that caused the semaphore flags in his head to lift up and start waving around. Then she shrugged. "Sure. Why not?"

A breath of relief that seemed to come from nowhere rushed out of him. But that relief was short-lived. Because as he placed her hand in the crook of his arm, escorting her up the stairs toward the hotel, he suddenly felt like the sword of Damocles was hanging over his head, a portentous doom awaiting him if he made one move in the wrong direction with her.

Trouble was, he had no idea which direction was the *right* one…

Chapter Four

DAGAN ZOELNER WATCHED DAN AND PENNI APPROACH THE table he'd appropriated after following Skinhead into the small boutique hotel. The spot had a killer view of the lobby with the added perk of a straight-ass shot down the hall that led to the bathrooms and the back door. Only way their not-so-friendly friend with the T/C Contender was exiting the place without being seen was if he spidermanned his way out of his bedroom window and down the exterior wall. And given the size of the guy…

Yeah, right. Not happening.

"Hey, you guys!" Zoelner said, standing and folding Penni into a hug. "Fancy meeting you here!"

"You need to get some new material," Penni whispered, hugging him back to keep up the pretense of old friends. "My sense of déjà vu can only take so much."

He winked after he released her, lowering his voice to respond, "Duly noted." When he turned to shake Dan's hand, it was to find the guy trying to scowl him through the floor. Zoelner's chin jerked back. "What's *that* look for?" he demanded.

"It's okay to go ahead and turn off the charm now, asswipe," Dan grumbled.

"What charm?" Zoelner asked, although he knew

exactly what the problem was by the way Dan moved to stand proprietarily close to Penni. If they'd been dogs, this is the part where Dan Man would lift a leg to mark his territory.

"The hugging and the winking," Dan grumbled. "*That* charm. And while you're at it, bat those baby grays at somebody else too."

Zoelner shook his head. "Slow your roll, dude. I heard you stake your claim." With a subtle point to his earpiece, he added, "Loud and clear."

"I knew you weren't gonna let that slide."

"What was your first clue?"

"I don't know," Dan said drolly. "Maybe the fact that you are, indeed, an asswipe?"

"Can either of you explain to me why men do that?" Penni interrupted before he and Dan could devolve into a really fun round of name-calling.

"Do what?" Dan turned to lift a brow at Penni's pursed lips.

"Stomp around each other, growling and snarling, all big and bad like you have dicks the size of redwoods. Or maybe *not* having dicks the size of redwoods is the problem, huh?" Her eyes twinkled with mischief.

Dan choked and Zoelner crossed his arms, nodding. "I like her," he told Dan. "And I take back the part where I said I'd let you keep that claim you staked." He bounced his eyebrows at Penni because he knew it was guaranteed to tick Dan off. And right on schedule...

"What did I just tell you about turning off the charm?" Dan demanded.

Penni chuckled at the two of them. The sound was

low and sexy. It must've hit Dan Man's eardrum like a wet tongue, because Zoelner watched the guy gulp and immediately adjust his stance.

"In reality," Zoelner told her, reclaiming his seat, "men tend to feed each other regular helpings of shit because, simply put, it's fun. And it's the only way this asshole and I"—he hooked a thumb toward Dan—"have entertained ourselves these past few months."

And that was the straight-up truth. There were very few men Zoelner could spend ninety-three straight days with. Dan Currington was one of them. Probably because they shared the same warped, slightly dark sense of humor, were completely comfortable with hours, sometimes days, of silence, and knew each other well enough to agree that chitchat about the past was strictly off-limits.

Dan pulled out Penni's chair so she could sit. After settling himself, he threw an arm around the back of her shoulders. Zoelner cocked a brow when Dan's fingers started twitching like he was tempted to twirl them in the ends of the silky brown hair that trailed over his hand.

Dude has it so bad, he thought.

And then Penni adjusted her chair, causing her hair to tease Dan's wrist, and Zoelner saw the exact moment the poor guy couldn't stand it a second longer. A muscle jumped in Dan's jaw before he gently caught a lock of hair between his thumb and forefinger, rubbing the strands together.

Okay, so the dude didn't just have it bad, he was flat-out ass-over-teakettle. Maybe not in *love*, but at least in *lust*.

Zoelner couldn't be happier. He'd been there the

evening Dan's wife was murdered. It'd been heartbreaking, soul-shaking, one of the hardest things he
had ever witnessed. Harder still had been standing by
and watching Dan sink into a pit of self-destruction
and despair so deep that Zoelner thought there was no
way Dan would ever pull himself back out again. But
miraculously, he had.

By his motherfuckin' bootstraps.

And now here he was, back in fighting shape and on
an assignment some might consider the most important of his career. Add to that the fact that Dan seemed
willing to open himself to another woman—enter
Penelope DePaul—and it spoke of an inner toughness,
an intrinsic courage and strength, that Zoelner could
only marvel at.

In short, Dan "The Man" was one ballsy, brave, bru-
tally badass sonofabitch, able to take life's hard knocks
and not only keep standing, but also thrust out his chin,
ready to take another punch. Zoelner was proud to be
able to call him his friend.

He glanced across the table at Penni, noting how her
cheeks were flushed with heightened awareness, her
eyes sparkling with desire. The sexual tension between
her and Dan was so thick you could slice it with a butter
knife. The pheromones hanging in the air so heavy
Zoelner thought he could almost smell them.

Good for you, bro, he thought. *Fuckin' good for you.*

Then all thoughts of Dan and Penni disappeared when
Chelsea burst through the front door of the hotel like a
pint-sized wrecking ball. Carrying a backpack and her
ever-present monstrous satchel purse, she was dressed
in leggings, a long wool sweater that came to just above

her knees, and a pair of hiking boots with thick socks rolled down over the top.

On any other woman, the tree-hugging/granola/ backpacker getup would not have been flattering. But Chelsea was blessed with more curves than a barrel full of rope, so she could make a garbage bag look good.

Holy fuck. He silently whistled, watching her trudge toward their table. *That must be jelly because jam don't shake like that.*

He'd made the mistake of actually *saying* that to her once. He would *never* be that stupid again. His shoulder still hurt from where she'd drilled him with a tiny balled-up fist and accused him of calling her fat.

Fat? Oh, hell no. She was delightfully plump. In. All. The. Right. Spots.

"Hello everyone!" she said cheerily, taking the seat beside him. She leaned toward Penni, lowering her voice so only the three of them could hear. "Nice to meet you."

"You too." Penni nodded and smiled widely. Just a quartet of old chums on a holiday together.

Which was sort of funny when Zoelner thought about it. Considering Chelsea would probably say she'd been put on this planet not so much to be his chum but to torment his every waking hour. Case in point, how her subtle perfume reached out to him, tunneling up his nose and hitting whatever part of his brain controlled the thermostat on his blood. The stuff started to boil. And just like that, he went from coolheaded and composed to inexplicably hot and horny.

It was a problem.

One he'd yet to find a solution to, despite the fact she busted his balls every chance she got.

She turned to smile at him. *And the ball-busting will commence in 3...2...1...*

"Did you miss me?" she asked.

"Like I'd miss a toothache," he told her sweetly.

"Perfect. Just as I'd hoped. Now, straight to business." She set aside the backpack, and covertly pulled her earpiece from her ear now that they were all together and there was no need for alternative forms of communication. Then she waited until he and Dan followed suit. With a sleight of hand, the two of them tucked the little devices into their hip pockets. Chelsea deposited hers into a side pouch of her satchel and opened the menu the waiter had placed at her seat, saying conversationally, "I have Ozzie doing his magic with the hotel registry."

The "magic" she referred to was Ethan "Ozzie" Sykes's utter genius when it came to all things technological. If it was connected to the Internet, Ozzie could hack into it, fry it, or serve it up with a side salad. "He's trying to figure out which room our friend is in," she continued, her eyes skating down the menu. "Once he does, he's going to see if he can book us into a room adjacent and..."

She trailed off, then whistled and lowered the leather folio that listed the five-star hotel's culinary choices. Glancing at Zoelner, she pointed at the menu. "I hope you're paying. My expense account gets maxed out at Mickey D's."

"Oh, sure." He nodded, then shook his head. "You forget I used to *have* one of those expense accounts. And if I recall correctly, its upper spending limit was the equivalent of a small country's GDP." The Central Intelligence Agency was in the business of buying off warlords, cartels, and regimes. One meal wasn't going to bust its budget.

Dan leaned over to whisper in Penni's ear, and Zoelner suspected he was explaining Chelsea's situation and credentials to her. Of course, the way Penni flushed bright red at his nearness, the dude might as well have been whispering sweet nothings while nibbling on her earlobe.

And on the subject of nearness and sweetness... Chelsea's proximity and her damned perfume were driving Zoelner insane. He quietly, covertly scooted his chair away from her.

"Just the same," Chelsea said. "This is one meal where I won't insist we go dutch. What's that? What are you doing?" She frowned at him, glancing at the space separating their seats.

Busted. So much for covert. Maybe he should have his spy license taken away. Oh, right. Spies didn't have licenses.

"I...uh..." He looked at her like a kid who'd been caught with his hand in the cookie jar.

Her frown deepened although her golden eyes continued to sparkle with mischief and life. They were killer, those eyes of hers. An exotic contrast to her café au lait skin and pitch-black pixie-cut hair. Her mixed heritage meant that her coloring was both striking and unique. So much so that most people stopped in their tracks to stare when she walked by.

Oh, sure, she tried to hide it all behind a professional demeanor and black-framed glasses. But it was like trying to hide a sparkling crystal vase under a cocktail napkin.

She pushed her glasses up her cute nose and narrowed her eyes at him. "Well?" she demanded when he just continued to sit there, mouth slung open so wide he was surprised he wasn't attracting flies.

"Uh…" he said again, like the true genius he was.

She tsked and shook her head. "What's with you? Did you take an awkward pill this morning or what?"

And if Dan thought Penni was subject to bouts of sassiness, then Special Agent Chelsea Duvall was queen of the condition. The woman wore her attitude like a fashion statement. Luckily, Zoelner was saved from having to come up with a witty rejoinder to the awkward pill question—FYI, he didn't have one—when Chelsea looked at her watch and cursed.

"Sorry, guys. I need a second." She reached into her satchel and pulled out her phone. Glancing at the screen, she groaned.

Zoelner saw the missed call and couldn't resist taunting her with, "Oooh, you're in so much *trouble*."

"Shut it, Saturday Night Fever," she scolded him.

His chin jerked back. "Saturday Night Fever? What the hell are you talking about?"

She lifted a brow at the jacket he'd hung over the back of his chair. "If the lapels on that thing were any wider, you could fly away on them."

He glanced at his new leather coat and frowned. He'd bought it off a street vendor two weeks ago in La Paz. He'd thought it was pretty cool, kind of retro. But now every time he wore it, he was going to think of John Travolta.

He scowled over at Chelsea and realized from the devilish glint in her eye that had been her plan all along. Racking his brain, he tried to come up with a pithy reply. But he was saved from the effort when the sound of Dolly Parton singing "9 to 5" jangled from Chelsea's phone.

"Better not make her wait," he said, tucking his tongue into his cheek. "You might get a spanking when you get home."

As far as pithy replies went, it wasn't his best. But it seemed to work just fine because the look Chelsea shot him as she thumbed on her phone was so frosty he was surprised he didn't see snowflakes forming in the air.

"Ma!" she said. He loved it when she talked to her mother, because her southern accent peeked out. "Now's not a good time. I told you I might…" She quieted and then blew out a sigh that was a Broadway production worthy of a Tony Award. "Yes, Mother," she mumbled, her tone contrite. "I'm sorry. I didn't mean to shout. Yes, ma'am. Okay. I'll talk to you later. Promise." And then, to his delight, she looked around the table, color rising in her cheeks before she whispered as quietly and as quickly as she could, "Love you too."

After she hung up, he opened his mouth but she lifted a firm finger. "Not a word," she warned. He took a breath. "Ah!" She waggled her finger in front of his face, and he snapped his jaws shut.

For all the headache and heartache Chelsea gave him—and heartburn sometimes too—she made up for it by tickling his funny bone on a pretty regular occasion.

Unfortunately, I have another *bone I'd much prefer she tickle.*

Dear God! And it was thoughts like that that made their working together completely untenable…

—◦◦◦—

So…not the best *way to project an aura of professional-
ism and poise*, Chelsea thought as she shoved her phone
back into her purse. And cue the music…

"I'm sorry," Penni said. "Was that…really your
mother?" Chelsea looked up to find Penni's expression
was one of incredulity. And maybe…was that a hint of
suppressed humor?

She stifled a groan. "Indeed, it was," she admitted
lamentably. "See, before I was named the official liaison to these jokers… Dan, did you tell her?" When Dan
nodded, she continued. "Well, before that, I was nothing
more than a technician."

"Which we all know is code talk for the men and
women who scour the Internet and reams of Intelligence
documents for the telltale signs and signatures of plots
and threats," Dan said quietly. "Don't sell yourself short,
Chels. Folks like you, sitting at a desk somewhere, are
far more integral to the everyday safety of Americans
than people like me and this monkey." He hooked a
thumb toward Z.

"Aw, thanks, Dan," she said. She really liked Dan.
He was the definition of "a good guy."

"Who you calling a monkey?" Z lifted a brow. And
although she was sure he would argue the point, he was
a good guy too.

"If the fez hat and cymbals fit, my friend…" Dan winked.

Chelsea loved the byplay between the two of them.
Listening to them banter the last couple of days had been
like getting backstage tickets into the minds of men. "Aw,
look at you two," she said, "being all Rocket and Groot."

Z blinked at her, his eyes narrowed. She sighed at the familiar expression. Dagan Zoelner was far too serious. Oh, sure, he liked to mix it up with the insults and the wisecracking—if there was one truth, it was that Z possessed a razor-sharp wit. But even when he was joking around you'd be hard pressed to see a smile on his face.

Chelsea had decided to make it her life's goal to rectify that wrong And she managed it occasionally by busting the man's Bs—as he so often put it. With the right quip, the right insult, the right witty reply at the right moment, she could coax…not a smile, necessarily…but certainly a grin out of him. She lived for those instances. Because when Z smiled, it was like the sun coming out after a hurricane. Brilliant and blinding and so beautiful you almost couldn't stand it.

"Rocket and Groot? I don't know what that means," he said.

"You know, *Guardians of the Galaxy*?"

He just shook his head.

"The anthropomorphic raccoon and the tree thing?"

Now he simply lifted a brow.

"You really should get out more," she told him before turning back to Penni. "Anyway, back to the original topic. Until recently, I spent most of my days locked in an office. Which means this new position I've taken is not something my mother is accustomed to."

"I thought most family members didn't know about…" Penni let the sentence dangle, then finished with a carefully worded, "the specifics of what you do and who you do it for."

It was customary for family and friends of CIA agents

to be under the impression that their loved one worked for another, *safer* government agency. It protected everyone in the equation because a person couldn't be blackmailed or tortured for information they didn't have in the first place.

"Oh, my mom knows I work for the Bureau of Land Management." Chelsea leveled a meaningful look on Penni. "But she's also one smart cookie, and when the Bureau of Land Management sends me out of the country, she worries. A lot." She blew out blustery sigh. "The curse of being an only child. Now"—she picked up her menu— "enough about me, let's talk about our friend upstairs."

"Who is he?" Z asked eagerly.

After three months on assignment with nothing to show for his time, Chelsea knew he was more than ready to get this party started. And oh, how she loved seeing the light of anticipation glowing in his storm-cloud eyes. Z was one of those men who was classically handsome, with a broad forehead, high cheekbones, and a chiseled jaw—which made his ability to blend into his surroundings just that much more astonishing. But he was never more attractive than when he was neck deep in the middle of some crazy mission and his adrenaline was running.

"His name is…" She lowered her voice to something barely above a whisper even though it wasn't really necessary. They were far enough away from the next table that their conversation couldn't be easily overheard. In fact, thanks to the high, echoing ceilings and the tile floors, the noise inside the restaurant was something close to a dull roar. "Andrei Kozlov."

"Sounds Russian," Z said with a grunt.

"*Is* Russian," she replied. Then added, "Ultra Russian," for effect.

"For God's sake, what does that even mean? *Ultra* Russian?" Z turned to address Penni. "In case it wasn't obvious, Chels missed her calling. She was really meant for the stage."

"Don't act like you don't love it," Chelsea told him. "What's life without a little drama, huh?" He opened his mouth to argue—he enjoyed arguing with her almost as much as she enjoyed taunting him—but she went back to the topic before he could. "When I say he's ultra Russian, I mean he's..." Again she glanced around before whispering, "KGB."

For a couple of seconds, silence reigned around the table. Then, "I thought those guys went the way of the dinosaur when the Soviet Union collapsed," Penni said, continuing to peruse her menu, pretending they were having the usual small talk while deciding what to eat.

"Officially they did," Dan informed her. "But unofficially they formed the Federal Security Service, now known as the FSB."

"Pfft." Chelsea waved a hand of dismissal. "Words, shmerds. Once KGB, always KGB."

"And you all think he's here to...what?" Penni asked. "Buy Intel from—"

"Lord Voldemort," Chelsea interrupted. She wasn't superstitious by nature, but this mission made her twitchy. "Call me crazy, but if we are *finally* on the right track here, I don't want to jinx us by saying his name out loud."

"Who is Lord Voldemort?" Z asked, frowning.

Who is... "Didn't you read Harry Potter?" she demanded, glaring at him.

"Uh, no," he told her. "Because they're children's books and I'm a thirty-five-year-old man."

She blinked, giving him the same look she would have if he'd been growing a pair of feet out of his ears. "You say that like it's a valid excuse."

"She means He-Who-Must-Not-Be-Named," Penni supplied helpfully. Chelsea had already convinced herself that she liked former Secret Service Agent Penni DePaul. But finding out the woman was a fellow Potterhead sealed the deal.

"You-Know-Who," Chelsea added. And when Z just stared at her, she threw her hands in the air in disgust. "First no *Guardians of the Galaxy* and now no Harry Potter? Have you been living under a rock, or are you being willfully dense? Because I have to say, if it's the latter, it's not a good look on you."

One corner of his lips quirked. *Almost. That almost did it.*

"Oh, you're talking about Winter—" he started and she had to slap a hand over his mouth.

"Yessss," she hissed. When she removed her hand, she curled her fingers around the spot his breath had warmed. Although Z gave her no indication that he considered her anything more than a colleague, a coworker, a...*pest* most days, she couldn't stop herself from wondering how it would feel to kiss those finely formed lips, to press herself tight against that broad chest, to...

Ahem! Okay. Back to business. It was either that or her chair was going to melt out from under her.

"And yes to you too," she said, turning back to Penni.

"I think it's highly likely Comrade Kozlov is here for the same reason we're here—because He-Who-Must-Not-Be-Named is in town. And this is the *first* time our Intel has panned out."

Penni frowned before tucking her menu into her lap. "Which means you think He-Who-Must-Not-Be-Named"—Z sighed beside Chelsea, and she could tell he was annoyed at the overly long, overly complicated nickname—"is in possession of information the Russians might want."

"That and then some," Chelsea said, her stomach hollowing out at the thought of the havoc Winterfield had already wrought and the chaos he could still create. "The data he stole was immense. Worth a pretty penny to any foreign government, be it friend or foe."

"Christ almighty," Penni breathed.

"You said it," Chelsea agreed.

For a while no one uttered a word. Then Penni looked tentatively at each of them and finally ventured, "Uh, mind if I ask why your people"—she bobbed her chin toward Chelsea—"decided to pull back and let you three work the case alone? I mean, considering Wint…er, considering Lord Voldemort is one of your own, I'd think The Company would be sticklers about being the ones to bring him in." Her New York accent dropped the *r* sounds on the ends of her words, making "sticklers" sound more like "sticklahs."

"In a different situation," Dan said, tapping his menu against the table, "that'd be the case. But, until recently, the CIA had themselves a little rodent problem."

Ugh. Until about six months ago, Chelsea would've bet her best handbag it was impossible to have *one* traitor inside the CIA, much less *two* of them.

"Rodent problem?" Penni asked, eyebrow raised.

"A mole," Dan clarified.

"Oh," Penni said. Then, "*Oh!* You mean someone *besides* He-Who-Must-Not-Be-Named?"

"Just so you know," Dan said, "I'm on Zoelner's side when it comes to the nickname. The Harry Potter references go against my better judgment as a man of advancing years."

Chelsea snorted. "Advancing years my ass, Dan. You're a good decade or two away from needing Fixodent and fiber pills. And just so *you* know, I'm pretty sure a mole isn't actually a rodent either. I don't remember where in the hierarchy of biological classification they fall, but—"

"Jesus!" he swore. "Seriously? I guess I shoulda paid more attention during my middle-school science classes 'cause I'm zero for two today."

"Huh?" Penni blinked.

Chelsea waved a hand in dismissal. "It goes back to a conversation we were having earlier and… You know what? Doesn't matter. To answer your original question, The Company had a second mole who was disseminating classified information to our enemies. And given there was a fire-hose-sized leak inside our ranks, the president didn't trust us to find him on our own. So these two"—she shot a finger gun first at Z and then at Dan—"were tasked to run a simultaneous and clandestine snatch-and-grab mission. Sort of like, *May the best men win.*"

Unfortunately, *no* men had won. *Yet*. Chelsea hoped that wouldn't remain the case for very much longer. Her reputation within the CIA—and, you know, the fate of the world—hinged on them bringing Winterfield in sooner rather than later. *No biggie*.

"So you're telling me there are *two* traitors inside The Company?" Penni whispered. Her face was the picture of astonishment.

"*Were* two," Chelsea stressed, defending her organization. "The other has been found and is being interrogated."

"And the capture of the second mole meant we could come out of hiding and let the spooks know we were also searching for…*You-Know-Who*," Z said.

Chelsea beamed at him for playing along with the no-name game. He gave her a long-suffering look and shook his head.

"But having two teams in the field never works," Dan added. "Not only is there inevitable dick-measuring and stovepiping when it comes to Intel, but there's also competition to be the ones to actually get the job done. So we convinced 'em to let us take over."

Chelsea watched Penni give Dan the side-eye. "You're telling me you were able to simply *convince*"— Penni made the quote marks with her fingers—"the CIA to back off in their search for one of their own rogue agents?" She snorted. "Spectacular tale. Have you thought about adapting it for the stage?"

A Potterhead *and* spunky. Penni DePaul just climbed a notch higher on Chelsea's imaginary list of potential best gal pals.

"Well, we *may* have had some help," Dan admitted

with a lopsided grin. "Someone above our pay grade mighta been the one to *actually* call 'em off."

"Uh-huh." Penni nodded. "I would have liked to be a fly on the wall when they got *that* order."

"Considering that in their eagerness to bring in Wint…the sorry SOB, they've been about as covert as a car wreck, barging in like Keystone Cops and blowing whatever chance Zoelner and I had at snatching him," Dan said. Chelsea winced at the truth in his words. Her colleagues *had* screwed things up pretty spectacularly over the last few months. "I figure they shoulda been happy to be kept in the loop," he finished.

"Which, as you've already guessed," Chelsea said, "is where I come in. I'm the loop." And she was *determined* to do the CIA proud. *I mean, somebody has to, right?*

Their conversation came to a halt when the waiter arrived to take their drink orders. "Let's make this thing look legit, shall we?" she mumbled. Then, louder, "You like Malbec, Penni? They have a great one here from Argentina." She pointed at the menu.

"I, uh, I'm still trying to get used to the altitude," Penni said. "I'll stick with sparkling water."

"Same here," Dan piped up from beside her.

"I guess that leaves you and me." Chelsea turned to Z, one brow raised. "Care to have a glass?"

Before he could answer, Penni leaned over to Dan and whispered, "Just because I'm not having any wine doesn't mean you can't have any."

Chelsea felt Z immediately tense beside her. Together, they glanced across the table at Dan. She winced at the look of regret and humiliation that skittered across his face.

"It sorta does," Dan said, rubbing a hand over his jaw. "Since I'm an alcoholic."

The way he said the last word, so full of shame, it may as well have been "pedophile" or "murderer" or "tiny-baby-kitten-torturer." Chelsea's heart split down the middle in sympathy.

"Oh," Penni said, her dark eyes going wide, blinking. "Oh, well…"

The silence that followed those three words was so crushing Chelsea thought she could hear her bones creaking under the pressure of it.

"Hey, we all have our shit, right?" She kicked Dan's ankle under the table. Her expression the facial equivalent of *Hold your head up, Dan Man. You don't have anything to be ashamed of.*

"Yeah." Dan nodded, one corner of his mouth hitching down. "It's just some people's shit stinks worse than others'."

Chapter Five

GEORGE WODEHOUSE SAT AT THE BAR IN THE POSH HOTEL, nursing a pisco sour—a famous Peruvian cocktail—and wishing he could hear what the quartet at the table was saying. Unfortunately, he didn't dare move closer for fear he'd draw unwanted attention to himself. And even if he *did* dare, he wasn't certain it would do him any good. The acoustics inside the restaurant were terrible. He'd very likely need to be sitting on their laps to make out what they were discussing.

Bollocks!

He was conjuring up more creative curses when his mobile came to life inside the front pocket of his trousers. He thumbed on the device without looking at the screen. Spider had already phoned to demand an update on his progress, so there was only one person who would be ringing now.

"What have you learned about the woman?" George demanded of Benton, the computer whiz kid Spider had hired straight out of Oxford University.

George hoped the tall brunette who had joined Daniel Currington and Dagan Zoelner in the square earlier and who was now sitting and eating dinner with the two men and the woman, Chelsea Duvall, would yield more satisfactory answers than the others had. And hopefully let him know he was on the right track in ghosting those who were tracking down Winterfield. In the years he'd been under Spider's purview, George had learned numerous things. One was that it was easier to hunt the hunters than the prey because the hunters were so much easier to spot. Another was that jumping from the shadows to kill the prey once he or she was located was the work of an instant.

"Quite a lot actually," came Benton's reply.

"Truly?" George asked, surprised. He took another leisurely draw on his drink, listening to Benton relay what he'd discovered about the newcomer. After a bit, George interrupted, "What does that mean? She *was* Secret Service. Was she sacked?"

"No. According to her file she turned in her resignation two weeks ago and officially turned in her badge less than seventy-two hours ago."

George kept one eye on the group while using the other to peruse the menu the bartender plopped in front of him. "Considering the trouble you had finding out anything specific about the other three, it surprises me you know so much about this woman," he admitted, pointing to the menu and indicating he'd take an order of the bean salad with tomato and onions. Since he was here and it was the dinner hour, he may as well enjoy some of the local flavor. "I'll take the check too, please," he told the bartender, dropping the mobile away from his mouth. "I might need to duck out in a bit."

Another thing he'd learned since coming to work for Spider was *eat when you can*. He never knew when a mission might force him to go out on the hunt or else go into hiding. And neither occupation generally lent itself to readily available food.

"Sorry," he apologized to Benton after lifting the phone. "So…the information on the woman?"

"The Secret Service is more of a *policing* body than an Intelligence body. So their employees' records don't receive the same brand of whitewashing by the government," Benton said. George could hear the lad's fingers flying over a keyboard, and he wondered what Spider had over on Benton. It had to be something pretty good to keep the kid on his payroll instead of going to work for some high-paying high-tech firm.

"And you're *sure* about the other three?" he asked. The thought that he might have made the wrong decision in Lima had a cold sweat popping out on his forehead.

"Look," Benton insisted, "the only people who enjoy paperwork and documentation more than we Brits are the Yanks. The lack of readily available information on the other three when they were or *are* all supposed government employees? I don't buy it. If Daniel Currington was simply a Navy man before going on to build motorcycles in that shop in Chicago, I will eat my shorts. And that other bloke? Dagan Zoelner? Does he really look like the type of guy who would choose to be a bean counter for the Federal Reserve? And then if he *was* a bean counter for the Federal Reserve, why would he leave that cushy job to become a mechanic?

"And don't get me started on Chelsea Duvall. There is nothing other than her employment record to suggest she actually works for the Department of Land Management. The projects she's worked on have come to naught. There's no record of her being involved in any protests or government lobbying. Everything I find on her is superficial at best. So, yes. I'm sure the three of them are more than they seem. But I could hack into the Pentagon's main computers if you want proof of—"

"No, no." George was quick to cut him off. "No need to go skulking about and risk raising red flags."

From the corner of his eye, George studied Daniel's face. The man was handsome in a young Paul Newman kind of way. But where Newman had once had a soft, boyish charm, Daniel Currington looked hard, as if he'd seen and done too much in his life. And that…*hardness*, paired with Benton's certainty that Daniel was some sort of government agent, gave George hope that he was indeed tailing the correct men.

"So you think I wasn't wrong to follow them here from Lima?" And though he would not have wished it so, his voice betrayed his need for validation.

"I don't," Benton insisted. "In fact, I'd go so far as to lay down a bet that your instincts have proven correct once again, Georgie Boy."

George winced just as he did every time Benton used the ridiculous nickname. George was no boy. Quite the opposite. He was a man. A cold, hard man who'd carried out more than his fair share of cold, hard deeds. And when Spider had sent him to find and kill Winterfield before the United States had the opportunity to apprehend and interrogate the man, he had assumed the task would be easy enough. After all, he'd done similar things before. Stalked and killed those foolish enough to leave Spider's organization or, worse, *betray* Spider directly. But as the weeks turned into months, and the CIA agents he ghosted continued to come up empty-handed, he'd begun to worry he might fail at his task.

Spider did not abide defeat. Of any kind. And the man

was a mad genius when it came to meting out punishment for such. George had learned that the hard way…

An image of his beloved daughter, Bella, her arm in a cast because it had been broken in three places, flashed behind his lids when he squeezed his eyes shut. The story her boarding school teachers told was that she took a tumble off her mount when the horse startled at something. But George knew better. Whatever had surprised Bella's pony had Spider's fingerprints all over it. And Bella's pain and suffering had been George's penalty for not living up to Spider's standards.

So when one of the CIA agents he'd been trailing met with Daniel Currington—though George hadn't known Daniel's name at the time—at an outdoor cafe across from the Parque Central in the Miraflores neighborhood of Lima and an argument immediately broke out between the two men, George's interest had been piqued. He'd wondered just who and what this newcomer was, and had desperately hoped that whoever he was, he could help lead the CIA to Winterfield, thereby leading *George* to Winterfield.

When the newcomer pulled his mobile from his pocket, quickly dialing a number and briefly speaking to whoever was on the other end before handing the phone to the CIA agent, George had moved in. Pulling out the chair of a little bistro table a few feet from the men, he'd signaled the waiter, ordered a coffee, and shaken out the local newspaper just in time to hear the CIA agent say into the phone, "Yes, sir. But if we were just allowed a little more time to— No. No, sir. I understand, sir. Okay. I will."

While pretending to peruse the headlines, George

had watched the CIA agent hand the phone back to the newcomer. "It's all yours now," the agent had snarled. "Let's see if you guys can do any better than we've done. He said you're to head to the airport ASAP. Your plane is fueled and ready for the flight to Cusco."

Then the CIA agent had uttered a few choice words under his breath before pushing up from the table and stalking away, his back and shoulders stiff with barely repressed anger.

At that point, George had been faced with a dilemma. Follow the CIA agent and his group, just as he had been doing for nearly three months, or hastily have Benton book him travel to Cusco so he could keep an eye on this new fellow. And though his instincts had told him he'd just witnessed a "changing of the guard," so to speak, it'd still been a difficult decision to make. In the hours since he'd made it, he'd second-guessed himself no less than a thousand times.

"So what will you do now?" Benton asked.

George sucked in a deep breath that brought with it the smell of top-shelf liquor and rich spices. "What I've been doing for months," he admitted. "Watch and wait. Hope this bunch has better luck than the last. And hope no more mysterious players appear. I would prefer to keep the body count on this one to a minimum. It seems so useless to eliminate *all* of them."

"Can't leave any witnesses," Benton grunted. "You know Spider."

Yes indeed. George did know Spider. All too well. And George wouldn't fail the man again. For his daughter's sake…

———〜〜〜———

Well, this is awkward as hell…

Even though Dan knew the food he'd eaten during the most uncomfortable meal of his life was delicious—mostly because Chelsea had commented on it a half dozen times while making *nummy-nummy-nummy* sounds—he hadn't tasted a single bite. It might as well have been cardboard.

He wished he could claim that was because he was too busy paying attention to the lobby and the exits, keeping a weather eye out for Kozlov. But the truth was, he was completely and totally preoccupied by Penni. She'd closed up tighter than a clam after he told her he was an alcoholic.

Not that it'd been a *silent* meal by any means. Chelsea had made sure of that, peppering Penni with dozens of questions—literally dozens; he'd stopped counting at twenty—about her childhood, where she grew up, and what it'd been like to have a policeman for a father. Chelsea even went so far as to ask Penni her favorite music group. Penni admitted she usually said Led Zepplin to sound cool. "But," she went on, "The Band is really my all-time favorite because my dad loved them and would play 'Up on Cripple Creek' on the boom box while sitting out on the front stoop after his shift." Which Dan happened to think was *still* pretty damn cool.

And it hadn't stopped there. Dan now knew that Penni's favorite color was red. Her favorite dish was rigatoni with short-rib ragu served at Piccoli Trattoria on Sixth Street in Brooklyn. And she was a born and bred Mets fan. "The Yankees are just a bunch of overpriced jackwads." Her words. Not his. And Chelsea had managed to uncover all of this while still continuing to argue with Zoelner on a pretty regular basis.

So when Dan said Penni clammed up, it was more of a feeling than anything else. A subtle sense that she'd pulled away from him.

Not that he could blame her, of course. What sane woman *wouldn't* think twice—no, *ten* times—about starting something with a guy who had a vicious bastard of a monkey on his back? A monkey he couldn't promise wouldn't someday get the better of him and make life a living hell for all those around him.

He sighed and tried to tell himself it was better this way. Better for her to know now. But he couldn't quite make himself believe it. Because he *had* planned to tell her. He'd just planned to do it after they'd had their heart-to-heart. And maybe after he'd seduced her a time or two...or twenty. You know, when she'd be soft and sated and far more inclined to take a chance on him.

Is a chance really what you want?

The question buzzed through his brain like a chain saw, cutting into his consciousness and making him wince. The truth was, he wasn't sure. The concept was as frightening as it was fascinating. What he *was* sure of was that he would have liked the opportunity to mull it over.

So much for that...

Sighing, he wiped his lips with his napkin and tossed the cloth square atop his plate. When the waiter came to clear it away, Dan turned to Penni and opened his mouth to say... *Hell's bells!* He wasn't sure *what* to say to her. Thankfully, he was saved from having to say anything when Chelsea suddenly returned to the real reason for this ill-fated dinner.

"But here's something I don't get," she said. "If Kozlov is here to buy information from Lord Voldemort, what's with the T/C Contender? That's a weapon you choose when you want to take someone out. Not something you carry for personal protection." She scrunched up her nose. "Do you guys think it's possible we're on a bad chase? You know, one of the wild-goose variety? Is Kozlov in town for something entirely different and we're wasting time and energy trailing him?"

"Only two ways to find out," Zoelner said. "The first is we get ears inside his room and hope we hear something that'll give us the lowdown on his business here."

"And the second way?" Chelsea asked.

Zoelner shrugged. "We follow him and see what or who he has in mind for the dangerous end of that boom stick."

"Speaking of the first way…" Chelsea said, downing the last of her wine. There was a part of Dan, the *thirsty* part, that watched the final ruby-red drop disappear. She rummaged around in her giant purse until she located her phone. "Let's check with your favorite in-house computer geek and see what he's come up with."

They all waited expectantly while she made the call. There were a lot of "yeah, okays" happening on her end. At one point, she glanced up at Dan, making a slightly startled, slightly considering face—which was a concern. Then she signed off, laid her phone atop the table, and folded her hands in front of her.

"Well?" Zoelner asked impatiently when she didn't immediately begin filling them in.

"Yeah," Dan added, more than a little impatient himself. "What Zoelner said. *Well?*"

Although, in truth, impatience was a *secondary* emotion, considering Penni's warmth and rosewater smell reached out to taunt him, reminding him that even though *emotionally* she'd pulled away, she was still *physically* very, very close. Too damn close. Close enough to touch. Close enough to kiss if he leaned over just a scant few inches.

Chelsea cleared her throat and shoved her black Buddy Holly–style glasses up her nose before sliding her phone back into her ginormous purse. "Ozzie was able to find out which room Kozlov is staying in even though, apparently, he was using an alias." She lifted her eyebrows meaningfully. If they needed a second reason, besides the T/C Contender, to suspect Kozlov was in Cusco on nefarious business, registering under a false name was it. "As chance would have it," she continued, "the suite next door was vacant. Ozzie booked the room under Penni's name, using Penni's passport number."

Chelsea let her eyes swing back and forth between Dan and Penni. "He also, er…" She had the grace to scrunch up her nose. "Well, he checked Penni out of the other hotel. Her bag is waiting at the bellman's station for her to pick up."

"What?" Penni choked at the same time Dan muttered, "Sonofabitch."

Besides being their in-house computer geek, Ozzie was also their in-house matchmaker. And he'd been trying to get Dan together with Penni since Malaysia. In fact, it'd been Ozzie who'd insisted Dan go up to her in the bar that night before the bombings. It'd been Ozzie who'd shoved him out on the dance floor with her. And it'd been Ozzie who'd tucked the condom in

Dan's pocket—the one he never got the chance to use. Apparently, the asshole was still attempting to play the part of Cupid, even from nearly four thousand miles away. Determined to keep Penni in the middle of their operation whether she wanted to be there or not.

"Sorry." Chelsea winced. "But, you know, maybe this is for the best."

"How do you figure?" Dan demanded, sliding Penni a glance he hoped conveyed two things. One, *I'm sorry*. And two, *Ozzie is a no-good, interfering, grade-A douche nozzle*.

To his surprise, Penni reached over and squeezed his thigh. But just when he'd begun to think maybe he was imagining her emotional retreat, she hastily removed her hand, brushing a finger over the bridge of her nose.

Annnnd, so much for wishful thinking. Then, *sonofa-bastard! There it is again!*

The sensation of his skin trying to crawl off the back of his neck was becoming as familiar as it was annoying. He turned in his seat, scanning the restaurant and bar. Nothing but tourists and the locals who were serving them and—

Wait a minute… Did he recognize the guy in the brown flat cap over at the bar? The hat was the kind golfers and hipsters liked to wear, and surely was not all that common in Cusco. He narrowed his eyes, studying the man's profile, but save for a bit of beard stubble and a receding chin, there wasn't much to see. Then another man walked by wearing an almost identical cap, and Dan shook his head.

So much for "not all that common in Cusco." Man, he was losing it.

"It means she *has* to stay in the suite if she wants a

soft place to lay her head tonight," Chelsea said. Dan swung back around, rubbing a hand over his neck. "And since you're our resident jack-of-all-trades gear-wise"— she hauled the backpack out from under the table and handed it to him—"you need to be in the suite too. Which will be the perfect opportunity for you two to discuss…uh…whatever it is you two need to discuss. Just as long as you remember to turn off your mic this time." She glanced pointedly at the top button on the jacket he had draped over the back of his chair. "We'll stay in touch by cell."

Which sounded good in theory. In reality? He figured the only thing Penni probably wanted to talk about was how soon she could catch a flight back to the States.

"Jack-of-all-trades gear-wise?" Penni slid him an intrigued glance, and he realized that even though they'd gotten pretty chummy in Malaysia, truth was, she didn't know much about him.

"Yeah, I was a Navy mechanic before I…got into more specialized work," he told her, foregoing mention of the Navy SEALs and Black Knights Inc. out of habit. "Which means if it has moving parts or wiring, it's right in my wheelhouse." With a tilt of his head, he indicated the backpack he'd taken from Chelsea and tucked beside his chair. "And that thing's chock-full of all the goodies we need to get ears inside Kozlov's room."

"Pfft." Chelsea waved a hand through the air. "Don't let his humble act fool you. He's a real-life MacGyver. Give him a paper clip, a rubber band, and some C4, and he'll build you a rocket ship to the moon."

One corner of his mouth twitched. "That mighta been pushing it."

"Seriously." Chelsea nodded, looking at Penni while jerking her head in Dan's direction. "He's awesome. A good man to have around."

Okay. And now Chelsea was being *beyond* obvious, trying to convince Penni that even though he was a lowdown, no-account drunk, he still had some redeeming qualities. He closed his eyes and prayed for the floor to open up beneath him. Luckily, Zoelner came to the rescue.

"Not to interrupt this Dan's Great and You Should Give Him a Chance Fest"—*So much for the rescue. Jesus!*—"but if he and Penni are up in the room getting ears on while discussing personal issues, then what the hell are you and I supposed to be doing?" He wagged a finger between himself and Chelsea.

"Well, *I'm* headed back to the room above the bakery," Chelsea told him. "Ozzie is supposed to send me everything he can find on Kozlov."

Zoelner glanced pointedly at her purse and the phone that had disappeared somewhere inside it.

"Silly rabbit." Chelsea tsked. "He can't very well transmit the docs to my cell."

"Why the hell not?" Zoelner asked. "It's encrypted out the wazoo."

The look she gave him said she suspected his IQ fell far to the left of the curve. "True enough," she admitted. "But there's encrypted and then there's *encrypted*. My laptop has air-gap networking. My cell phone does not."

Zoelner raised a brow.

"One is completely secure," Chelsea explained. "One is not. Do I have to say it again?"

"What?"

"Silly rabbit."

Zoelner shook his head. "You and Ozzie." He snorted. "You two would make quite a pair."

"I know." Chelsea grinned. "And so does he. Which is why he keeps asking me to marry him."

Zoelner made a rude noise. "Like I've told you a million times, that guy is nothing but hot air and hormones." He turned to Penni. "How many times has Ozzie proposed to *you*, may I ask?"

"Including the even dozen times he managed it while booking my flight here?" A smile as bright as a Roman candle curved Penni's beautiful, kissable, irresistible mouth.

Of course, thinking about Ozzie flirting with her dulled the impact of the expression a bit. And something inside Dan, whatever that something was that wasn't jealousy but a close cousin of the emotion, once again reared its ugly head. Ozzie was too handsome for his own good, and too charming for the good or safety of all womankind.

Inexplicably, Dan imagined himself punching the bastard in the peanut pouch. The fact that he found the fantasy so satisfying probably called into question that whole "close cousin" of jealousy thing he was trying so hard to convince himself of.

"*See*, Chels." Zoelner jerked his head in Penni's direction, his tone smug. "Told you."

Chelsea rolled her eyes. Something she always seemed to do whenever Zoelner was winning one of their unending arguments.

"But back to the point," Zoelner said, his tone self-satisfied.

"Do you even remember what the point is?" Chelsea asked with false sweetness.

Ignoring her question, Zoelner reiterated, "So *they're* going to go upstairs to get ears on Kozlov." Dan opened his mouth to remind Zoelner that Penni had not agreed to any of this. There was probably still time for her to rebook the room in her original hotel. Come to think of it, he hoped she *would*. He didn't like the idea of her staying next door to a Russian packing a Thompson/Center Contender. But before he could say anything, Zoelner continued. "And you're going to go back to the bakery to geek out with Ozzie over your air-gap network. So what the hell am *I* supposed to do?"

"Well," Chelsea said, "first you can go take a flying leap. Second, you can pay the bill." She ticked the items off on her fingers. "And third, you can hang around here until Dan can wire Kozlov's room. Just in case Kozlov decides to leave the premises beforehand and you need to follow him. Sound like a plan?"

"Uh…*parts* of it," Zoelner said, rubbing a hand under his chin. Dan couldn't tell if Zoelner wanted to strangle her or strip her naked. It was definitely one or the other.

"Good." Chelsea batted her lashes. "So should we all put our hands in the middle of the table and yell *Break*?"

And Dan finally saw his chance. "Wait a goddamn minute here. Penni hasn't agreed to any of this."

He didn't want to look over at her. He didn't want to see pity or regret or…who knows what in her face. But he'd spent quite a long time hiding from the hard things, the things guaranteed to hurt him. And by God, he was hell and done with being a yellow-bellied coward. He turned to face her, girding himself for whatever awful expression she wore.

And there it was. That look. But inexplicably, and despite the fact he'd always prided himself on being able to read people, he hadn't the first clue how to decipher it. It certainly wasn't awful. It was…contemplative, maybe? Sort of…curious? He felt the movement of her eyes across his face like a physical touch, hesitant and warm. Goose bumps erupted up his arms and across his back.

What the hell, he figured. *Nothing ventured, nothing gained.*

"Do you still *want* to help us?" And even though he didn't say it, they all knew he was really asking if she still wanted to go upstairs and discuss the reasons why she'd come all the way to Cusco to talk to him.

She lifted that cute, kissable chin of hers, and with her dark eyes still searching his, she hesitantly asked, "Do you still *want* my help?"

Once again, and despite the fact that it made him sound a bit desperate, he gave her God's honest truth. "I do."

Chapter Six

Palacio Mario Hotel, Suite 402
Friday, 8:02 p.m.

SHE WAS A PRIZE ASS.

Like, seriously. Take her to the county fair, pin a blue ribbon on her, and name her Best in Show. Because she could *not* think of a worse way to respond to someone admitting they had a drinking problem than with a brilliant muttering of *Oh…oh well*.

I mean, who in God's name does *that?*

Penni answered her own question with, *Me, apparently. Prize Ass Penelope Ann DePaul.*

But she'd been so…*shocked*, she guessed was the word. The Dan Currington she knew was not only confident and sexy as hell, but also the most self-controlled, steadfast, and disciplined man she'd ever worked with. To find out he struggled with sobriety stunned her, quite frankly. Stunned her straight into idiocy apparently. Because if her brilliant muttering of *Oh…oh well* hadn't been bad enough, her extreme embarrassment over that far-less-than-stellar response had caused her to act all stilted and weird during dinner. So much so she wasn't entirely sure *she* wasn't the one who'd taken that awkward pill Chelsea spoke of.

And to make matters worse—oh yes, they got worse—the whole time she'd been checking into the room next to Kozlov's, the whole time she'd ridden the elevator up to the fourth floor, the whole time she'd fumbled with the key in the door, Dan had stood silently beside her.

Which wasn't the worse part.

The worse part was the *way* he'd stood silently beside her. Close but not too close. Maintaining his distance instead of crowding her like he usually did, like he was a magnet and she was metal and it took everything in him not to slam into her until there was nothing left between them but a paper-thin sliver of electrically charged air.

You bet your ass she'd felt that distance the way one might feel the loss of a limb. Like something she depended on had suddenly been stripped from her, leaving her raw, shocked, and completely off balance.

She was still feeling that distance as she sat on the bed in the lavishly appointed suite with its colorful Incan-inspired textiles, watching Dan pull out all manner of things from his backpack. But for the life of her, she didn't know how to bridge the gap.

How about you jump his bones? This time the voice in her head was definitely her own. Thank God! She couldn't imagine her father offering her *that* advice.

And sure, if she wrestled Dan onto the big four-poster bed and had her way with him, *that* might make up for her prized assedness. But she hadn't traveled all the way to the Southern Hemisphere to knock boots with him. Or at least she hadn't traveled all the way to the Southern Hemisphere *just* to knock boots with him. She'd come here to talk to him about…so many things. Some of which he'd already guessed, but some of which he hadn't.

Then Kozlov had happened. And dinner had happened. And the plan for her to check into the suite had happened. And now she found herself in the midst of a very important mission, which meant knocking boots or taking the time to sit down and have a good ol' fashioned heart-to-heart were both pretty much out of the question.

"Huh," she said, watching him pull a bug detector from his backpack. He set the instrument to vibrate instead of beep. *Can't have our neighbor overhearing our little search, now can we?* "We used that same model in…" She caught herself before she said *the Secret Service*. "…my job," she finished lamely.

And lame responses seem to be my stock in trade today, don't you know? Geez!

"That's because it's the best model out there," he said. His matter-of-fact tone seemed to echo across the gulf that had formed between them.

Checking a hotel room for listening devices was the first thing anyone working in the wide world of espionage did, be they Secret Service agents, tattooed motorcycle mechanics/clandestine operators, or others. Sort of like the first thing people in their line of work did upon clandestinely appropriating a vehicle was to disable the interior light that comes on when the door opens.

Tricks of the trade. Learned through trial and life-ending error. She shuddered.

Dan ran the bug detector all around the room, taking special care with the wall that connected their suite to Kozlov's. He paused here and there, flattening his hand against the plaster. And near the corner, he leaned in to put his ear to the wall.

Penni almost quipped, *When Chelsea and Zoelner talked about getting ears inside Kozlov's room, I think they meant something a little more high-tech. Har-har.* The joke fell so flat inside her own head that she didn't dare send it out into the world for fear of the resounding splat it would make.

Then Dan bent to press his hand to the floorboard and the move caused his sweater to pull up while his Levis pulled down. The gap created was enough to give her a peek at the tan muscles in his lower back. Enough for her to see the waistband on his black boxer briefs. Enough to have her remembering another hotel room in another foreign city and the way he'd held her, kissed her, *touched* her...

Her blood grew warm at the recollection of his lips, his big hands, his hard body against hers. Moving. Brushing. Rubbing. Liquid heat bloomed low in her belly and between her thighs. She crossed her legs and squeezed, chastising herself. *Really, Penni. You just convinced yourself that now is not the time.*

Right. She had done that, hadn't she?

"Looks like we're in luck. No electronic creepy crawlies to worry about," he said, pushing to a stand. *Whew!* Not seeing his broad back and underpants helped to return her focus. Sort of. *Okay, not really.* "He won't be able to say the same for too much longer." He hooked a thumb over his shoulder and crossed back to the bed.

The way he walked, all sinewy coordination and fluid movement, reminded her of a wild animal. Something big and sleek and powerful. The ache to touch him, to hold him, to harness all that power for herself was incredibly strong, tempered only by the silence in the

room as he selected a few things from the stuff on the
bed, reloaded his backpack with the rest, and sauntered
back to the adjoining wall.

For a few seconds she watched him run his hand
along the plaster again, the quiet growing, growing,
growing until it was almost deafening. Almost...*crushing*. Like a hundred pounds of pressure pushing against
her eardrums.

She couldn't stand it!

"I've noticed there's some...er...*tension* between
Chelsea and Zoelner," she finally finished. Okay, and
all things considered, that wasn't a bad start. Neutral
ground on which to begin a tentative conversation that
would hopefully help close the distance between them.

"Ha!" His bark of laughter echoed around the room
as he taped something to the wall that looked like the
round electrodes used in hospitals to hook up a patient
to the machines that charted their vitals. He stuck some
wires into the electrode and then twisted the opposite
end of the wires around themselves before threading
them into a metal tip. He then inserted that metal tip
into a handheld digital recorder.

Setting the recorder on top of the dresser, he moved
to the other end of the wall and said, "*Tension*. I guess
that's one way of putting it." He repeated the procedure
with the electrode and the wires and the recorder. This
time he set the device on the seat of the plush crimson
chair pushed into the corner. "But I'd say it's more a
case of mutual lust or mutual loathing. Hard to tell the
difference sometimes."

Indeed. Although that'd never been *their* problem.
Pretty much from the start it'd been mutual lust and

mutual *liking*. Then again, that was before she'd made such a fool of herself at dinner. Before the Grand Canyon had sprung up between them. She ventured, "And do you know *why* there's so much tension?"

He shrugged, and she totally did *not* notice the way the hem of his sweater rode up to reveal his belt buckle. All right already. So maybe she did notice that it was the same belt buckle she'd fumbled to unhook three months ago when—

Whew! Is it just me? Or is it getting hot in here?

The line from the song by Nelly ran through her head…*so take off all your clothes*. And, yeah. That's just what she wanted to do. Take off all her clothes. Then take off all *his* clothes. To her utter shame, she had to remind herself yet *again* that she wasn't there to jump his johnson, that he was on a mission and didn't have time for…well…*whatever*. While doing that, she shrugged out of her parka and tossed it on the bed.

"There's some history there," he said, shoving his thumbs through the front two belt loops on his jeans so that his long, tan fingers made a little frame of his man bits. She'd become enamored of that stance in Kuala Lumpur, thinking at the time that he did it intentionally to draw the eye down to his rather… er…*impressive* package. But now, knowing him, she realized it was inadvertent, although it was no less hot.

Holy shit! What was with her?

"What history?" she managed even though talking was becoming more and more difficult. Her tongue felt heavy, swollen…like *other* parts of her.

"Hell if I know."

"I just figured, given the last three months, that you and Zoelner had talked about—"

"Stop right there," he interrupted, frowning at her. "Men *don't* talk. At least not about feelings or relationships or anything that really matters."

He flipped on one of the devices. A low hiss issued from its speaker, followed by what sounded like scratchy music. When he clicked on the second device, the same low hiss and muted music emerged from it. Lifting a finger for quiet, he cocked his head and listened. Then he nodded as if satisfied and pulled his cell phone from the hip pocket of his jeans. Punching in a number, he held the phone to his ear. After a second, he said so softly she had to strain to hear him, "Chels. It's me. We're wired up here." Penni jumped when she heard his whispered voice coming from the speakers of the digital recorders. "Nope. But there's music playing. I'm pretty sure he's in there."

The music was coming from Kozlov's room? She stared at one of the devices in wide-eyed wonder.

"Roger that. Okay. Will do," he finished softly. Stuffing the phone back into his hip pocket, he turned to her. "Where were we?"

"Forget that for a second," she whispered and pointed to the electrodes and the wires and the recorders. "What *are* those?"

He glanced over his shoulder, then came to sit beside her on the bed. The mattress dipped under his weight, and she slid toward him. When her hip made contact with his, she caught herself before she let out a relieved sigh. Being next to him, *touching* him, felt right in way that nothing in her life ever had. Right and wonderful and...*exciting*. It's like he was both a comfort and the cause of her internal chaos at the same time.

He leaned in and his voice was a bare whisper. "The stickers that look like electrodes are actually high-powered contact microphones." His breath fanned her cheek. It smelled like spearmint gum, cool and fresh and completely delicious. "They detect vibrations through the walls. Attaching them to digital recorders allows us to record the sound next door. And because they don't have transmitters or send out signals, they can't be picked up by traditional bug-detection devices."

Both of her eyebrows were sitting near her hairline when she pulled back to search his face. In all her years as a Secret Service agent, she'd never heard of such a thing. "Handy," she mouthed.

He shrugged. But despite his nonchalance, she had to agree with Chelsea's insistence that he was a good man to have around.

"Now," he whispered, "I think we were talking about Chels and Zoelner."

"We were? I don't remember." In fact, she didn't remember much of anything except his nearness. Where was she again? What was her name? All she could focus on was stopping herself from running her finger over the little crescent-moon-shaped scar on the side of his jaw.

One sandy blond eyebrow inched its way up his forehead. His mouth twitched.

She leaned in, inhaling his electric scent. "And besides, I don't think we should be talking." She hooked a thumb toward the devices.

"It's fine." His voice was deliciously low and growly and just loud enough to be broadcast through the speakers. Then he lowered it further still, until only her ears picked up the sound. "They're not recording right now. Once *he* starts talking I'll hit the record button and we'll have to zip it. Until then, we just need to keep our voices down so they don't carry."

"You *are* MacGyver," she mouthed. Then she batted her lashes. "Build me a rocket ship to the moon. Pretty please?"

"And *there's* the new, sassy Penni DePaul I've been missing," he whispered.

She leaned in, shivering at his nearness, his heat, and said softly in his ear, "I already told you, *sassy* Penni DePaul is the *old* Penny DePaul. Not the new one."

"Whatever," he murmured, putting his mouth so near her ear she could feel his lips move. Then he inhaled. *Did he just smell me?* "I thought I'd lost her at dinner, so I'm happy to see she's making a return performance. Even if it means she's currently razzing my raisins."

If she wasn't mistaken, he'd just taken a step to close that uncomfortable, emotional Grand Canyon between them. The relief she felt had her leaning into him until they were shoulder to shoulder. His body was a fortress beside her, big and solid and imposing. She wanted to crawl inside him and let him protect her from all the things she was afraid of, from all the things she needed to tell him but couldn't. Which was silly and not at all like the bold, gutsy woman she'd always prided herself on being, but there you have it.

And speaking of the things she needed to tell him, speaking of being bold and gutsy, it was time to explain what had happened downstairs. She blew out a silent breath and turned to pull his ear down to her mouth. Since she was all legs, when they were sitting side by side, he was much taller than she was. "I want to talk about what happened at dinner and apologize for—"

He pulled back and put a finger over her lips. It was warm and calloused and had her heart fluttering against her rib cage. "Shh," he mouthed. His words were barely a whisper when he said, "If you're gonna say you're sorry for being appalled that I—"

She grabbed his wrist—*Christ*, his skin was hot—and removed his finger from her lips. "I wasn't appalled," she assured him, raising her voice, not caring that the devices picked up the sound, because this was something she needed him to understand. "Not at all. I don't judge you or think less of you because you fight the battle with booze. Hell, my favorite uncle is a recovering alcoholic. I *know* what it takes for a man to dance with the devil every day and still come out the victor."

He smiled then. It was a little sad. A little ashamed. She wanted to kiss it right off his lips. "Dance with the devil," he mused. "Never heard it put that way, but I guess that pretty much sums it up."

She searched his face, trying to think of what else she could say to convince him she wasn't put off by his alcoholism. But then he lifted his hand and ran a finger over her cheek. It was a delicate caress, not meant to be incendiary. Just the same, fire erupted across her skin. And whatever words she'd been forming slipped to the back of her throat when he whispered so quietly, "Brooklyn…"

Her breath caught at the sound of the nickname he'd given her. Her heart skipped one beat. Then another.

The whole world condensed down to this one room. This one man.

"Can I—" He hesitated and she wanted to cry out, *What? What? Can you what?* She'd grant him anything. Everything. Finally, he finished with, "Can I kiss you?"

She closed her eyes. She suddenly felt dizzy. Okay, so screw the mission. "I thought you'd never ask."

—∿∿∿—

Penni's words—those sweet, irresistible words—had Dan releasing all the pent-up air in his lungs in one long, silent sigh. And because the truth seemed to be working so well for him today, he decided to offer her one more unassailable fact. "I've missed you, Penni." Because he hadn't lowered his voice, his whispered words were picked up by the speakers, lending them even more meaning, more emphasis.

Her eyes rounded, seeming to take up her whole face. "I-I've missed you too, Dan," she murmured haltingly, her voice cracking on his name, like saying it aloud was both pleasure and pain.

And that was all he needed to hear. All he needed to *know*. Even though he still wasn't sure what was between them, whether it was nothing more than an intense physical attraction that would burn bright and extinguish itself quickly once they gave themselves over to it, or if it was something more, something precious and rare and *lasting*, he *was* sure that whatever it was, he wanted to see it through to the end.

The realization had a warm glow blooming in the center of his chest, in a place he hadn't realized had been a cold, black void. The glow grew, spreading outward until his whole body was diffused in delicious, wondrous heat. Looking into her pretty face, watching her wide, dark eyes search his uncertainly, he recognized that warm glow for what it was…

Hope.

Hope that perhaps there could still be more to his life than daring and duty and daily dances with the devil.

With tender fingers he traced her high cheekbones, the length of her nose, and finally, her perfectly formed lips. She was sweet as sin, her skin delicate as a daisy as she held still beneath his caresses. And when he whispered reverently, "You're so beautiful," she opened her mouth to protest. But he leaned forward and silenced her with a kiss.

It was supposed to be tender, sweet, subdued. And it started out that way. For one second. Two. Then it quickly changed. Because *holy hell*, her mouth was just as he remembered. Hot and delicious. *Eager*. She opened to him without any coaxing, giving herself willingly, wantonly. Her agile tongue sought his, swooping past his teeth to tangle, to tease, to plunder in that charming way he dreamed about every night.

Her flavor was a mix of the chocolate cake and decaffeinated coffee she'd ordered for dessert. It went to his head like a bottle of rye, making him dizzy, making him feel drunk. On her taste. On all things warm and womanly. On Penelope Ann DePaul.

"Dan…" She breathed his name against his lips, winding her lithe arms around his neck and pulling him forward until they were breast to chest. Heart to heart.

"Ah, hell," he hissed when she caught his lower lip between her teeth and bit gently. The little sting of pressure let him know she wasn't *all* gentleness and light.

And ain't that *the truth?*

Because he knew from experience that behind those large, luminous eyes lay the heart and soul of a passionate woman. She increased the pressure on his lip before sucking it strongly, easing the bite of her teeth with the bold, liquid swoop of her tongue.

His blood ran wild. Ran hot. His heart thundered as he fed her his breath and accepted hers in return. As they licked and sucked and ate at each other's mouths until it was hard to know where her lips and tongue began and his ended.

He had no idea how long they remained that way, kissing as if they'd never kissed before. As if they'd never get a chance to kiss again. Like all their longing and desire and passion had to be expressed right here. Right now. As quickly and urgently as possible. Until finally, with a throaty moan, she pushed at his shoulders.

He thought she was shoving him away, and his disappointment was so keen it hit him like a round fired from a rifle. But then she was climbing on top of him, straddling his lap and pulling at the hem of his sweater with frenzied fingers.

Sweet, sweet Jesus…

The backs of her hands were cool against his stomach. Goose bumps erupted across every inch of his skin, making the hairs on his body stand straight. Up, up, *up* she pulled his sweater, gathering the material along the way and exposing his belly and chest to the air inside the room and the heat radiating off her.

He was so relieved she wasn't putting a stop to things

that he would swear an invisible choir of angels was standing behind him singing, "Hallelujah! Hallelujah!" He would have warned them they needed to cover their eyes, because the things he had in mind for Penni's corporeal body weren't something celestial bodies should ever see. But he couldn't bear to break the suctioned seal of Penni's hot, hungry lips.

She rocked against him, against the painful erection straining his fly. He growled his encouragement, gripping her delicately curved hips to help her in the glorious bump-and-grind. It hurt so good. And she was so hot. Her woman's heat scorched him even through their clothing, singeing him, igniting his passion into a roaring conflagration.

"A little help," she groused, placing a string of biting kisses along his jaw while trying to wrestle the sweater over his head. Her voice echoed quietly through the speakers.

"My pleasure," he whispered softly, releasing the hard grip he had on her hips and lifting his arms.

Whipping off his sweater, she tossed it heedlessly behind her shoulder. And then she was drinking him in, her eyes skimming over the flesh of his shoulders and chest like a physical touch. He shivered in response. Then he was holding his breath, because she started to pet him, running her hands over his shoulders and chest reverently, lovingly. Like he was something precious. Like he was something rare, and worthy, and *wanted*.

He lost it.

Whatever hold he'd had over himself, over his lust for this amazing woman, was broken. With a low growl, he grabbed her waist and twisted until he pressed her back against the mattress, finding his place between her spread thighs and claiming her beautiful, bedeviling mouth in a kiss that burned them both down to ashes…

Chapter Seven

PENNI WAS LOST IN A WORLD OF SENSATION...

Smooth, tough skin marred by the occasional scar slid beneath her searching fingertips. Scratchy facial hair abraded her tender cheeks and chin. A hot, wet tongue dallied and danced and dove deep, driving her crazy.

Dan...

She was lost in a world of Dan and she never wanted to find her way out. Wanted, instead, to stay wrapped in his arms, inhaling his scent and feeling his knowledgeable kisses and caresses. Forever. Until she expired. Until time ended.

With a moan that was picked up by the speakers, he broke the suction of their lips, pushing to support himself with his arms. "Jesus, Penni," he whispered.

From the hair that dusted his chest and thinned to a single line running down the center of his corrugated stomach, to the expanse of his shoulders so broad and uncompromising they looked as if they could support the weight of the world, from the bulge of his pectoral muscles crowned by the flat, brown disks of his nipples, to the shaggy blond hair that fell forward over his forehead and temples, he was, in a word, *gorgeous*. Gorgeous in the way healthy, virile men were gorgeous. All heat and hardness and *h-h-holy shit!*

And then there were his eyes. They cut like lasers

through the air between them, singeing her with their molten warmth, drilling into her soul, seeing so much. *Too* much? More than she was ready for him to see? *Perhaps*…

"We need to stop," he said, his voice so soft and hoarse it sounded like it'd rolled over gravel on its way out of the back of his throat.

Right. Of course. Stop. "The mission," she mouthed, nodding jerkily, trying to catch her breath.

"No." He shook his head, then leaned close and whispered in her ear. "Not the mission. The *talk*. We still need to—"

"Later," she murmured. She didn't want to go there. Didn't want to be dragged back to the real world. Not yet. For now, for just a little while longer, she wanted to stay immersed in the world of Dan. In the universe of lust and longing he created.

And since plying him with food and wine before laying her heart open was no longer an option—well, at the least not the wine part—she figured succoring him with a bout of hot, sweaty sex would do the trick just as well. *Better* even. And bonus! *This* way, she'd get to roll around in the sheets with the most beautiful man on the planet!

At least that's how she rationalized it as she trailed a finger over the length of his neck, delighting in the hard, steady pulse at the base of his throat. Lower, the skin over his clavicle was smooth and hot. She marveled at the size and density of the bone beneath. Dan was a big man. And for the first time in her life, she felt small. Almost delicate by comparison.

"Penni," he breathed his protest.

She couldn't have that. "Shh," she whispered. "Not now."

Letting her fingers drift to his flat, brown nipple, she scraped the little nubbin with the edge of her thumbnail. It sprang to life and Dan hissed. The veins in the side of his throat stood out in harsh relief.

"Fuck me," he groaned, his words picked up by the speakers and momentarily drowning out the sound of the scratchy music. Somehow that just made what he'd said even more salacious, even more sexy. *Yes*, she thought. *Fucking you* is *the plan.*

His hips flexed forward, and then *she* was the one hissing. Because the hot column of his erection was a rod of temptation, a steely shaft of promised satisfaction against her swollen, heavy sex. *Aching* sex. And when he stroked forward again—rubbing, teasing—the friction was amazing. Hard. Rough. Almost enough.

He watched her with eyes like lava, glowing and hot. "You like that," he grumbled, stroking forward again.

"God, yes," she said breathlessly, giving him the truth, because he hadn't hesitated once all evening to do her the same honor. And that was just one more reason on a long list of reasons why she'd sought him out. His honesty, his integrity, his tenacity and toughness had been a boon to her in Malaysia—and had messed with her mind ever since. Every man she'd met in the past three months, every man she knew from before, fell short by comparison.

"Can you come this way?" he whispered in her ear, stroking forward again.

Her eyes nearly crossed. Her clitoris gloried at the decadent friction.

"Yes," she whispered back.

He smiled then, and it was hot and warm, like a

promise. Before she could tell him she didn't *want* to come that way, she wanted to come with him *in* her, he reclaimed her mouth in a kiss that had starbursts exploding behind her eyelids. Little flashes of incandescent light streaked and slashed, dazzling her, dazing her. His hand snuck beneath her sweater. His palm was hot, callused, lusciously abrasive—a working man's palm.

"So soft," he husked against her lips. "So soft you make me even harder."

As if to prove his point, he increased his thrusts, moving against her in a carnal, age-old rhythm. She wanted to cry out. To tell him to undress her and screw her and satisfy them both. But his tongue was back in her mouth, and little jolts of pleasure were beginning to thrum through the bundle of nerves at the top of her sex. She knew that making him stop would be the worst kind of torture…

—⁓—

Penni DePaul. Sexy, sultry, sinfully seductive Penni DePaul…

She was back in his arms. Back beneath him. Where he'd dreamed of having her for more than three months. And she was the sweetest thing. Lithe and lean and sinfully soft. Dan skated his hand up her smooth belly to gently cup her breast. The high, tight mound seemed to scream, "Touch me! Touch me!" and you can bet that's exactly what he did. Gently squeezing. Softly molding.

With a quiet moan she caught his tongue between her teeth. Sucking. He imagined how good it would feel to slide the swollen head of his cock between her lush lips, letting her suck on it with the same force. The thought alone was almost enough to have him spilling in his boxers. But he wasn't a fifteen-year-old copping his first feel. And besides, before he found his own release there was Penni. Penni, Penni, wonderful, wickedly wanton Penni to attend to.

He pulled back to glance into her luminous eyes because…well, just because he wanted to see her, to see that look on her face. And there it was. "When you look at me like that…" He didn't go on. He couldn't. He didn't have the words for the way she made him feel.

"What look?" she mouthed, rubbing herself against him.

His eyes crossed and the top of his scalp felt like it was trying to pull away from his skull—the pleasure was that good, that ferocious—but he still managed to whisper, "Like I'm your favorite toy."

She tugged his head down and said softly in his ear, You *are* my favorite toy."

"You're gonna kill me, woman," he husked, thrusting his hips and watching her eyes close. Her lips curved into a smile and she grabbed his ass, encouraging him on. Meeting him stroke for stroke.

She bedeviled him, beguiled him, teased and tormented him until he thought he'd go mad. He wanted her more than he wanted his next breath. More than he'd ever jonesed for a whiskey, neat, ice on the side. And that pretty much said it all. "And you're loving it, aren't you?" He bent to whisper against the delicate shell of her ear. "You're loving making me crazy."

She didn't answer. Just nodded. Her soft hair tickled the side of his face. Her breast was warm and firm beneath his palm.

"Hasn't anyone ever told you that paybacks are hell?" he asked softly, finding her beaded nipple through the lace of her bra and pinching delicately.

She drew in a sharp breath, then whispered huskily in his ear, "Well, shit. And here I was banking on them being heaven."

And that did it. He was done messing around. He'd had a fantasy since Malaysia. The fantasy of seeing her come apart in his arms, seeing her *come*. Every. Which. Way. And now he was determined to fulfill it. He told her as much. "I've dreamed of making you come this way, from the friction of our clothed bodies."

"Dan…" His name was a wisp of sound. An incantation that anchored him in the here, the now, the moment. This wonderful, pleasure-filled moment.

"I've dreamed of taking you with my fingers," he admitted, pulling back to see her lovely neck arched. Her pulse fluttered strongly at the base of her throat. He pressed his lips to it, feeling her heart racing, knowing he was the cause of its mad tempo. Being wanted, *feeling* wanted, went all through him. It was a thrill, a joy he hadn't experienced in a very long time.

"I've dreamed of rubbing that secret spot inside you and making you come so hard you squeeze my knuckles until the bones grind together," he whispered. He loved the harsh sound of her quickly indrawn breath and the little moan of longing and titillation that followed. Both were just loud enough to be caught by the speakers, mixing and mingling with the music still coming from the room next door.

Some women didn't like it when a man talked dirty. They were embarrassed by having their wants and needs and desires put into words—which Dan always thought was a crying shame considering that the mind was the biggest sex organ, and stimulating it in every way possible was never a bad thing. But to his utter satisfaction, Penni did not appear to be one of those women. With each brazen word out of his mouth, her hands grew more frenzied, her arching thrusts more desperate.

Emboldened, getting hotter, hornier—which he wouldn't have thought possible—he continued. "I've dreamed of putting my mouth on you."

"Sweet Christ."

"Of licking and laving you and tasting your release."

"Yes," she hissed in his ear before he claimed her lips in a kiss that was as carnal, as wanton, as his words. When she started to tremble, he broke the suction of their lips and spoke the coup de grâce. "And I've dreamed of putting my cock in you. Thrusting over and over until—"

"Dan, please," she begged.

Oh, but she needn't beg. He intended to see every one of his dreams made into reality. At least that was the plan...

His plan got blown to shit when the muted jangle of a ringing phone interrupted the sound of Penni's catching breaths and little cries of ecstasy on the brink. He tried to ignore the disturbance, pistoning his hips faster, harder, determined to—

Ring, ring! Ring, ring!

"*Privyet*," a deep voice said in Russian, followed by, "*Da. Da*, okay."

"Jesus H. Christ," Dan groaned as he vaulted off the bed and raced over to the far wall. "Today should be named a holiday for fuck-all bad timing," he whispered right before he switched the devices to record and thumbed down the volume so that Kozlov's voice was barely audible.

When he turned back to Penni… *Aw, hell*. The look on her pretty face rated about a nine…no, ten, that was definitely a ten…on the I'm Ready to Explode scale. *Join the club*—if his dick was any harder, he'd likely pass out. And when she bit her lip, grimacing, he shook his head and chuckled silently. It was either that or break down crying.

"Sorry," she mouthed, pushing to sit crisscross-applesauce style in the middle of the mattress. With hungry eyes, Dan watched her pull her sweater down over her stomach. Then she tried to smooth the hair his fingers had done a number on during their all-too-brief bout of…whatever it was. Heavy petting and dry humping, he supposed, although he couldn't remember the last time he'd indulged in either. Suzie Sheffield in the back of his Camaro after the state championships his senior year in high school came to mind.

Trying to shake off the lust that was riding him hard—*Ha! As if!*—he bent to grab his discarded sweater. *Ow! Sonofa*—If Penni was going to be around for a while, he should definitely invest in some jeans that were a bit looser in the crotchal region. Refusing to think about the look on her face after she'd taken the sweater off him, he tugged the garment over his head. Of course, not thinking about that look was hard to do while he threaded his arms into the sleeves and glanced at her only to discover it was plastered all over her face. *Again*.

He swallowed the groan perched at the back of his

throat and cursed Fate or Destiny or Father Time or whoever the hell else was responsible for fuck-all bad timing as he pulled the sweater's hem down over his chest and stomach.

———

Well now, that's *a crying shame*…

The thought drifted like fall leaves on a cool breeze through Penni's overheated brain as she watched Dan pull down his sweater. When he'd tugged it over his head, it'd caused his sandy hair to riot boyishly. And then it had slid over his shoulders, covering the traditional heart-and-arrow tattoo that was inked over his bulging right deltoid muscle. But neither of those things were as heartbreaking as watching the wool cover six-pack abs and the intricately scrolled letters of the tattoo just below his belly button. *No Guts, No Glory* the bold, black design read.

And that's the flat-out truth.

If there was one thing Dan "The Man" Currington had in spades, it was guts. Though, as far as she could tell, he didn't do the things he did—putting himself in danger, taking on the treacherous jobs—because he was chasing glory. Quite the contrary. During The Assignment, she'd overheard a phone conversation he'd had with someone. "When Uncle Sam comes calling, it's our job to answer. And when the work is done, we don't take a bow."

Those words, *his* words, had struck her, reminding her of the time she asked her father why anyone would decide to become a police officer, decide to walk that thin blue line day after day for crappy hours and even crappier pay. Her dad had explained it simply—as had been his way. "Some men crave the adrenaline. Others get off on the power." And then he'd said, "But sometimes, Penni-pie, once in a blue moon, a man is simply born a gladiator. A *defender*. It's in his blood. Stamped on his DNA. And when you find yourself in the presence of a man like that, you know it. You can feel it."

Her father had been one of those men. And for a long time, she wasn't sure she'd ever meet another. But then she'd met Dan. When she'd heard him say those words, she'd known that besides being big and beautiful, he was also a battle-hardened gladiator, a defender, a *hero* in every sense of the word. And she'd been trying to have her way with that big, beautiful, battle-hardened hero ever since.

"Winterfield…"

Penni's heart jumped like a startled rabbit as that one word stood out among all the Russian quietly rolling through the speakers. The familiar *zing* of adrenaline spiked through her system and was the equivalent of a bucket of ice over the inferno of her libido. All the lingering ache, all the liquid longing was gone. Just like that.

Her wide eyes swung to Dan. She saw his jaw harden. *Nope. Scratch that.* His entire *body* hardened. He marched stiffly over to the dresser to stare so forcefully at the digital recorder that she was surprised he didn't melt it with his gaze alone. After Kozlov signed off with a gravelly-sounding *do svidan'ya*, the tinny music clicked back on, followed by the quiet but unmistakable *crack-snick* of a break-action weapon being loaded.

The hairs on Penni's arms started crawling around like they were alive, and she sat in stunned silence as Dan quickly switched off the digital recorders before reaching into his hip pocket to extract his phone. As he punched in a number, a muscle twitched in his cheek.

"He was just on the phone," Dan growled softly after his call was connected. He unhooked the recorder that was on the dresser and started for the bathroom, motioning for her to follow at the same time he snagged his jacket from the end of the bed. "I'm gonna put in a call to Vanessa back at BKI and have her translate his conversation." Penni knew from her time in Malaysia that Vanessa was BKI's onsite language expert.

"I'll get her on speakerphone," he continued. "You and Zoelner mic up so you can listen in. Call and tell him the plan. Oh, also...I've turned off the digital recorders so we no longer have ears inside Kozlov's room. Make sure Zoelner keeps his eyeballs peeled in case the Russian jets."

Penni grabbed a seat on the toilet lid and watched Dan lay the phone on the white marble bathroom vanity before reaching into his hip pocket and extracting the tiny flesh-colored earpiece. After inserting it, he shrugged back into his jacket and, with the edge of his thumb, flipped a switch no bigger than the head of a ballpoint pen behind the microphone made to look like the top button on his coat. Checking the time on his big, black diver's watch, he closed the bathroom door to ensure as much privacy as possible and said, "Check, check. Either of you copy me yet?"

Dagan Zoelner must have already mic-ed up and copied him because Dan made a face and answered with, "That wasn't an invitation for ass-hattery, Zoelner. And for your information, no." He flicked her a glance that had her raising an eyebrow. "That's a...negative. We didn't have time to talk because we got…uh…distracted by other things."

Distracted. That was *one* way of putting it. Another way would be to say that, just like anytime the two of them found themselves alone in a confined space, they were all over each other like cold on ice cream.

She was glad she didn't hear what Zoelner said in response to Dan's admission, because whatever it was, it caused the tips of Dan's ears to turn red. She gave him the evil eye. She *was* Italian—well…*part* Italian anyway, on her mother's side—so it was her right. And just in case her expression didn't clearly convey her desire for him to *ix-nay* all talk of their, ahem, *distractions*, she sliced a finger across her throat.

He rolled in his lips, stifling a grin. But all the humor disappeared from his face when he said, "I copy you, Chels. I'm getting Vanessa on the horn." Snatching his phone from the countertop, he dialed and held it to his ear. "Yo, Ozzie," he said once the connection was made. He flicked her another look and added after a beat, "You know goddamn well she made it here safe and sound. You used her passport to reserve the very room I'm standing in. Now, stop dicking around and making stupid innuendos. Put Vanessa on the phone. We finally have a lead."

When Dan lowered the cell, switching it to speaker, the sound of Meat Loaf wailing and Ozzie humming the chorus to "Paradise by the Dashboard Light" issued through the little speaker and bounced around the white subway tiles that lined the walls of the bathroom.

A couple of seconds later, Vanessa's deep, throaty voice thrummed through the phone. "Turn that racket off, Ozzie. I can't hear myself think."

"First of all," Ozzie said, "Mr. Loaf does not produce racket. He is one of the preeminent tenors of the past century. Second of all, with a body and a face like yours, Van"—his voice was suggestive even through the cellular connection, but Penni would swear on a stack of Bibles that there was a slight edge to his tone—"you don't need to strain yourself thinking."

"What have I told you about flirtin' with my woman, cocksucker?" Rock's drawl issued from somewhere off in the distance.

"All of you shut up," Dan barked. "Chels and Zoelner, you two picking everything up on my end?" He waited a tick, then said, "Good, so now everyone listen to this."

He clicked on the digital recording at the same time Meat Loaf began "praying for the end of time." The instant Kozlov's voice sounded, however, the music back in Chi-Town was muted. And then for a couple of minutes, there was nothing but the rolling echo of Kozlov's fluid Russian filling the bathroom. Again, when the man's recorded voice distinctly said "Winterfield," Penni's skin started crawling.

"Well?" Dan asked, thumbing off the digital recorder. "What was that all about? What did he say?"

"He asked whoever he was talking to if they thought their Intel was reliable," Vanessa said. "They must have convinced him it was, because he's going to be in the Plaza San Francisco ninety minutes from now where he will, and I quote, 'Get Winterfield and finally, after so many years, bring justice to Mother Russia.'" She managed a fairly spot-on Arnold Schwarzenegger impersonation on that last part.

"Pretty sure the Governator is Austrian, not Russian," Ozzie added quite unhelpfully.

Dan ignored Ozzie and thanked Vanessa for her translation before turning off his cell phone and shoving it back into his hip pocket. "Okay," he said. "So it sounds like Kozlov and his trusty T/C Contender are in town to ensure Winterfield takes a dirt nap." Penni knew by the way Dan cocked his head that he wasn't talking to her, instead lending an ear to Zoelner and Chelsea's responses.

"Nope. I'm done with code names. You're just gonna hafta get over the superstitious mumbo jumbo," Dan said, no doubt responding to something Chelsea said. "Winterfield, Winterfield, *Winterfield*. There. It's done. We're moving on."

Penni rolled in her lips. Even in the middle of a heart-pounding mission, they were an entertaining trio. And given a different set of circumstances, she would have liked to simply sit and watch them all spar and bicker.

A few more moments passed while Dan listened to his partners. Then he blurted, "How the hell would I know why? Maybe in all that shit Winterfield stole there was something on the Russians. Maybe the Russians got wind he planned to sell that something, and they wanna make sure he finds out what's behind Door Number One"—Door Number One being the coffin lid—"before he can do the deal. Whatever the reason, it sounds like the Russians think Winterfield is gonna be in or around Plaza San Francisco in the next ninety minutes. So what's the plan?"

Then the three of them ran through some options. Since Penni was only hearing a third of the conversation, she was hopelessly lost. She clued in to at least *some* of their thinking when Dan said, "If that happens, it'll be our lucky day. We can be in the air headed for the States in thirty minutes. Now, where should we meet?" A beat of silence, then, "Roger. That's a good idea. I remember the place. See you both in a bit." The way he smashed his words together made it sound more like *see y'both inna bit.*

Before she could ask what exactly they had come up with—not that it was any of her business, but her curiosity was absolutely *killing* her—he propped his foot on the edge of the claw-foot tub and pulled up the hem of his Levis to reveal his ankle holster. Inside was a Bersa Thunder CC handgun. It was small, meant for concealed carry. But with an eight-round magazine that held .38-caliber bullets, it was still mean enough and deadly enough to persuade most guys to rethink any less-than-gentlemanly impulses.

"If I was going with my big, bad, protect-the-woman instincts," he said, pulling the weapon from its holster and seeming to weigh it in his hand at the same time he weighed his thoughts, "I'd ask you to stay here where you'd be safe." He passed her the gun. She hesitated to take it, but when she finally did, she noticed the metal was warm from his body. "But after what happened in Kuala Lumpur, you have as much right as anyone to be there when we capture Winterfield."

Her mouth dropped open. Her eyes flew wide. Everything inside her came to a screeching halt except for her stomach. It turned upside down and spewed hot, stinging bile up the back of her throat.

Sweet Christ.

Dan cocked his head, his eyes narrowing into considering slits. "That is," he said, "if you *wanna* be there."

The image of her partner Julia's charred corpse flashed before her eyes, causing a lump the size of the Rock of Gibraltar to form in her chest. The memory of that night, of seeing her friends reduced to ash and gore, cut into her like it always did. Like shrapnel. Leaving her bleeding and disoriented.

She was supposed to be *done* with this kind of work. Done taking chances. Done putting herself in harm's way. But…all her teammates, all her *friends*, deserved justice. They *deserved* to have Winterfield spend the rest of his life rotting in a dingy, cold eight-by-ten. And, as Dan said, it was her right, her *duty*, not only to her lost friends but to the country she'd served for over a decade, to help put him there.

She paused a second longer, her inner war waging one final battle.

"Penni." Dan placed a hand on her shoulder. The pressure and heat of his palm had her eyes jumping to his concerned face. "I didn't mean to put you on the spot. I just thought—"

"No," she interrupted him. "You didn't." Then she slid out the clip, checked to see that it was full, and glanced back up at him. Now that her decision was made, determination burned like a hot coal behind her breastbone. "Let's bring that sorry sonofabitch in once and for all."

Chapter Eight

HELLUVA PLACE FOR A HOMICIDE...

The thought ran through Dan's head as, arm in arm with Penni, he passed by Chelsea, who was pretending to be a distracted tourist studying a map of Cusco while loitering on a park bench in the corner of the little square. Save for Chels, the place was deserted, thanks to the near-freezing temperatures that had descended the instant the sun sank behind the mountain peaks. The sightseers were back at their hotels, fighting the chill with a late dinner and drinks...or with each other. And the locals, having no one around to sell to, had closed up shop for the day and gone home to seek their own reprieve from the night's frosty breath.

Cusco was one of those cities that rolled up the streets after dark. The only nightlife to be had was tightly contained around the city center, and the rest of the place pretty much turned into a ghost town.

"Ghost" being the operative word. Dan wasn't given to melodrama—he left that to Chelsea—but the little square was spooky. The kind of setting that belonged in a Stephen King novel.

A few decorative streetlights lit the perimeter around the grassy area, leaving big puddles of inky black shadows everywhere, especially beneath the trees. The only sounds to breach the silence were the burble of the fountain and the shushing sound of his and Penni's footsteps. And the air was redolent with the earthy smell of damp cobblestones and the sharp bite of an electrically charged atmosphere.

A storm brewed somewhere close by. And it was as if the sky overhead was holding its breath…waiting for something portentous to happen. *A lightning strike and a low mist creeping across the ground would make the scene complete.*

Dan shivered inside the warmth of his jacket and led Penni toward their rendezvous point. It was an old building around the corner and a block down from the square. Besides being in a great location, it was undergoing renovation so it was guaranteed to be empty. And batting three for three, it also sported a conveniently large portico that cast a massive black shadow they could easily dissolve into. Which is exactly what he and Penni did.

Shrugging out of his backpack, he set it on the sidewalk beside the double doors to the main entrance of the structure. Five seconds later, his lock-pick set was in his hands. Ten seconds after that, the door to the building was open. After replacing his lock picks in his backpack, he shoved the bag just inside the entry and turned to find Penni's arms crossed, her mouth pursed.

"What?" he asked innocently. She glanced pointedly at the open door, and he quietly cleared his throat. "Let's just say that growing up on the mean streets of Motor City taught me a thing or two."

"Uh-huh." She nodded, then shook her head when he

couldn't stop the smirk pulling at his lips. He sobered and pointed to her purse. "Keep it or store it?" he inquired quietly.

"Store it," she said, pulling the strap over her head and handing it to him. He tucked it beside his backpack inside the building and then joined her in leaning against the outer wall. Silently, they waited for Chelsea to arrive and for Zoelner to check in and give them Kozlov's location.

Dan and Penni had followed the Russian from the hotel when he'd left it a mere ten minutes after they'd finished the call to BKI—obviously the Russian liked to arrive early to these types of things. But they'd been forced to hand off tailing duty to Zoelner when Kozlov made one turn too many on his way to the square, and they feared their continued presence on his six would draw the Russian's attention.

Kozlov was good. Cautious. Taking a circuitous route to his destination. But they were better.

I hope it stays that way.

Dan rubbed his hands together to calm his nerves at the same time Chelsea—having skirted around the block—approached from the opposite direction he and Penni had chosen to take. Penni shivered beside him. And without thinking, he threw an arm around her shoulders, hugging her close and offering her his body heat. She glanced up at him, the tip of her nose rosy with cold, and gifted him with a soft smile. It struck him as a sweet invitation to bend down and take a taste of her lips.

Some of what he was thinking must have been wallpapered across his face, because when Chelsea stopped beside them and shoved her glasses up her nose, she whispered, "Ugh. You two need to get a room."

Dan offered her a withering glance he wasn't sure translated in the darkness. "If you recall," he said softly, "we *had* a room."

A feisty smile split Chelsea's face. "Oh, that's right. So, besides the interruption of Kozlov's call, how did *that* go?"

"Not as far as I'd have liked it to go. If we'd had ten or fifteen more minutes…*then* maybe," Penni said.

Dan choked and glanced down to find her grinning up at him unabashedly. "You're not making this easy on me," he warned her.

"Good." She winked. "Means I'm doing something right."

And then they just stood there, staring at each other, grinning at each other, *wanting* each other.

"Holy crap," Chelsea said. "I don't know whether to be jealous or sick."

"Be jealous," Penni informed her, her tone heavy with innuendo. "Be very, very jealous."

"Oh really?" Chelsea tilted her head toward him. "That good, is he?"

"Better," Penni assured.

Both women turned to look at him appraisingly. And when he scowled, they dissolved into giggles. It had been his experience that when women got together, they just naturally joined forces and started making easy targets of the men around them. In an effort to divert their attention away from the invisible bull's-eye on his chest, he released Penni to activate the button on the side of his diver's watch. When the little light came on, he pointedly checked the hour. "Almost go-time," he said, pulling his Ruger from his jacket pocket and gently thumbing off the safety.

His ploy worked. Instead of continuing to poke fun, Penni reached into her coat and transferred his little Bersa Thunder into the front waistband of her jeans.

Convenient, he thought, eyeing the placement and thinking of the ease with which the weapon would be available for a quick draw. *If you're a woman. If you're a guy, you risk shooting your balls off.*

Figuring a bullet in the butt was better than one through the dick, he placed his handgun in its normal position...tucked into the waistband at the small of his back. Maybe not as quick a draw, but he liked his pecker with just the one hole, thanks.

"Are you sure it was a good idea to give her a weapon?" Chelsea whispered, eyeing the Bersa and Penni with equal distrust, the feminine camaraderie having vanished so quickly Dan was surprised he didn't see a puff of smoke.

He started to jump to Penni's defense. But Penni grabbed his hand, squeezing his fingers and telling him without words to keep his mouth shut. Like a smart man, that's exactly what he did.

"I've been trained to handle every kind of firearm, from a six-shooter to a sniper rifle," Penni said quietly, her adorable chin jutting out just a touch.

Ho-kay. So she can definitely fight her own battles. Two things occurred to him then. One, the hotheaded New Yorker in Penni lurked just beneath the surface—he'd probably do well to remember that. And two, the woman had a set of balls on her to shame an elephant. *Damnit!* Both made him like her more.

"That's not what concerns me," Chelsea whispered. "What concerns me is that after what happened in Malaysia, you might be tempted to blur the line between justice and revenge. We need Winterfield alive. We have no idea what he's sold or to whom. There could be a ticking time bomb out there somewhere. We have to bring him in for interrogation or we could find ourselves in the midst of another 9/11." Chelsea's golden eyes seemed to be on high beam when she pinned a look on Penni.

"Look," Dan insisted quietly. Truth was, he enjoyed a good catfight as much as the next guy. But not when the cats in question were women he both liked and respected. "We're all professionals here. Penni knows what's at stake."

Chelsea studied Penni's face a second more, and Dan was about to remind her that regardless of what she thought, she wasn't calling the shots. But before he could open his mouth, Chelsea must've seen something in Penni's expression that eased her misgivings, because she nodded. "Okay, good. So then let's do this the right way."

She reached into her satchel and pulled out an earpiece and clip-on microphone. She handed both to Penni. "Mic up and do a quick sound check," Chelsea instructed, tossing her satchel to Dan and motioning with her chin toward the door at his back.

Penni inserted the earpiece and clipped the microphone to the collar of her parka while he turned to place Chelsea's satchel beside Penni's purse inside the building.

Quietly shutting the door behind him, he almost jumped when Penni's hushed tone slid through his earpiece. "Check, check. You guys copy me?" And either it was the intimacy of having her East Coast accent swirling around in his ear—*you guys* sounded more like *yous guys*—or it was the cold of the night, but something made goose bumps erupt up his spine.

"Copy that," Chelsea said.

"Roger," he managed through a clenched jaw.

"I'm picking you up too," Zoelner's whispered voice suddenly sounded in their ears. "Welcome to the show, Penni," he said. "And taking a page from Chelsea's book, let's get straight to business. Kozlov is set up on the northwest corner of the square. He's sticking to a dark spot between a building and an alley. And going by his body language and the fact his head is on a swivel, I'd definitely say he's waiting for someone. I'm hanging back a couple of blocks. I suggest you guys take up positions near the other three corners so we can cover all the angles should Winterfield make an appearance or Kozlov make a move."

"I'll take the southeast corner," Penni said, a consummate professional even if she no longer carried the Secret Service five-point star to prove it.

Before she could turn away, Dan laid a hand on her arm. When she looked up at him, there was a question glowing in her big, dark eyes. "Penni, don't..." he began.

What? Don't what? Holy shit, there were so many things he didn't want her to do that he didn't know where to begin. *If this breaks bad, don't try to be a hero. Don't put yourself in danger; catching Winterfield isn't worth losing your life. No matter what Chelsea said, don't hesitate to take a shot if you have to.*

"Don't take any chances, okay?" was what he ended up going with. "You and I have unfinished business to take care of when this is all over."

"That 'hell to pay' you spoke of?" she asked, one corner of her mouth twitching, one dark brow arched flirtatiously.

"Heaven," he promised her. "I thought we agreed it'll be heaven."

Chelsea shook her head and Zoelner's soft groan of disgust sounded through Dan's earpiece. Right now he didn't give a good goddamn that they had an audience. Neither did Penni, apparently, because with a wink and a quick squeeze of his fingers, she went up on tiptoe and kissed the side of his mouth.

"Don't worry about me," she breathed against his lips. "I'll keep chicky," she added.

Dan remembered the saying from Malaysia. It was her unique way of letting him know she was not only exercising her Second Amendment rights, but that she was zoned in and staying frosty. It should have calmed him, given him a sense of relief.

It didn't.

And when she turned and strode purposefully down the sidewalk, sticking to the shadows, her footsteps barely audible, he was surprised to discover that letting her disappear around the corner was one of the hardest things he'd ever had to do…

―◦◦◦―

Deep into the darkness peering, long I stood there wondering, fearing…

Penni shivered and cursed her English teacher to

a life plagued with flimsy toilet paper and stray Lego pieces for introducing her to Edgar Allan Poe's "The Raven." Poe possessed a mad penchant for creating a sense of creepy foreboding with words alone, and why that particular stanza from his famous poem should come back to her now was a mystery.

Although, on second thought, maybe it wasn't so mysterious after all. Because as she stood hidden on the dark stoop of a closed coffee shop, eyeballing the eerily quiet square, she could quite easily imagine a raven alighting atop one of the park benches, its shiny black head cocking, its beady eye glinting in the low light given off by the nearby street lamp, its cawing voice calling hauntingly, *"Nevermore!"*

Goose bumps peppered every inch of her skin. The hairs on her head stood stick straight. Her panting breaths crystallized in the night air, swirling and coalescing like specters in front of her before disappearing.

She zipped her parka up as far as it would go before shoving her frozen fingers back into her pockets. The place was atmospheric. She'd give it that. And maybe it was the lower oxygen level, but the air around the square seemed abnormally still. Almost breathless.

Or maybe that's just me.

No joke, she was having a hard time making her lungs work properly. They kept wanting to seize up on her. Which could have something to do with the fact that her nerves were stretched piano-wire tight, the muscles in her entire body burning because she'd kept them tensed for so long. That inner war she'd thought was over and won continued to see the occasional skirmish, and she asked herself for the hundredth time since she left the hotel if she'd made a mistake in agreeing to help.

You already said you would, her old man's voice whispered through her head. Some folks had little angels or devils sitting on their shoulders and giving advice. *She* had Sergeant Gerard DePaul. *And you're not a woman to go back on her word*.

Flippin-A. In death as in life, her dad was right as rain. Which meant…

Relax. Breathe. Hold steady.

She was in the process of forcing her shoulders down from where they'd crawled up around her ears, twisting her head back and forth to relieve some of the tension, when Chelsea's rusty-sounding voice whispered through her earpiece. "Penni, I don't know what you just did, but there's a faint silver sheen coming from your location."

Penni glanced down and saw a strip of reflective fabric on the underside of her parka's collar. When she'd raised her zipper, it'd revealed the strip. *What the—?* How could she not have noticed that when she bought it?

"Son of a suck-ass bitch," she hissed, ripping her zipper down to once more conceal the offensive material. As if to add insult to injury, the teeth on the zipper made an overly loud *scriiiiitching* sound. She winced. Then she held her breath and waited.

They all did.

Utter silence reigned as one second stretched into two. Two stretched into ten. The pounding of her heart was like the ticking of a frantic clock. *Lub-dub…tick-tock*. And just when she was about to blow out a relieved sigh, Zoelner said, "Kozlov's moving, ducking into the alleyway." Her internal alert system flashed from yellow to red. "I'm following," Zoelner added unnecessarily.

Pressing back into the doorway, Penni strained her eyes toward the northwest corner of the square. She could see nothing beyond the gentle glimmer of the water spurting from the fountain and the subtle ripple of shadows across the ground when a cold breeze rustled the leaves on the trees.

It went without saying that losing track of the modern-day equivalent of a Russian KGB officer in a back alley in Cusco was way down on her list of Safe Things to Do on a Friday Night. Unfortunately, that's apparently what had happened when Zoelner cursed and said, "I'm at the mouth of the alley. He's not here. Everyone maintain their positions until I can pick up his tail."

Unease coursed through Penni's veins. *Come on, come on, Zoelner. Get eyes on.*

"Okay, I'm at the other end of the alley," Zoelner finally said. "Kozlov has ghosted. Fuck. *Fuck.* I'm heading south around the square toward Penni's position in case Kozlov saw what Chelsea saw and he's coming to investigate."

"I'll hold my location," Chelsea whispered.

"I'll make my way to Penni from the opposite direction," Dan told Zoelner. "Penni, babe, you needa get the hell outta there."

"One step ahead of you," she said, looking both ways and sliding from the shadows to hastily descend the stoop's two narrow steps. She'd gone no more than twenty paces when a massive baseball mitt of a hand emerged from nowhere and nearly yanked her out of her boots.

She screamed—or squealed, really—as she was jerked around the corner and shoved up against the cold back wall of the coffee shop. A half second later, a heavy forearm slammed across her throat, cutting off her air and her squeal.

"Penni! *Penni!*" Dan's dismayed voice blasted through her earpiece.

"Who are you?" Kozlov's face was an inch from hers. His narrowed blue eyes were ice picks stabbing at her. His facial features were as blunt as a closed fist. And considering the unnatural flatness of his nose and cheekbones, it was a fairly good bet that many closed fists had made them that way. Fear blazed through her like napalm, burning across her nerve endings.

"Why are you here?" he demanded, easing up just enough so she could croak out an answer—not that she was going to answer him.

Oh God. Oh hell. Oh shit.

"Oh *fuck!*" she heard Dan hiss. *Okay, and that works too.* "Hang on, Penni! I'm coming!"

Hang on? Forget about it. In what world was she the damsel in distress who waited to be rescued by the white knight…er…in this case, the Black Knight?

Channeling all her fear and adrenaline, and ignoring the way her brain buzzed from lack of oxygen—blue really wasn't her color—she dug her nails into Kozlov's forearm and tried to yank it down at the same time she brought her knee up. Hard. Aiming for his wedding tackle with enough force to ensure he wouldn't be procreating anytime soon.

Unfortunately, he was prepared for the move. He

swiveled his hips at the last second and her knee missed its intended target, slamming ineffectually into his muscled thigh. "Mmph," he grunted on impact as— "Uhhhh!"—she struggled to breathe.

This can't be happening! Oh sweet Christ, I have to—

Desperate, she dropped a hand from his forearm to instinctively reach for her service weapon. She hesitated only a fraction of a second when she remembered she wasn't wearing her shoulder holster. But that fraction was enough. She was able to get a grip on the butt of Dan's little Bersa Thunder, but Kozlov was right there with her, wrapping his thick fingers around her wrist and slamming her hand against the wall the instant she pulled the weapon free. Pain exploded up her forearm as white lights burst in front of her eyes. The Bersa fell to the cobblestones with an echoing *clink* and a clatter.

"*Suka!*" Kozlov hissed. His hot breath washed over her face, thick with the smell of high-dollar whiskey and cigarettes. When his lips curled back in a snarl, they revealed tobacco-stained teeth.

Penni didn't speak Russian, but judging from his tone and expression, she was pretty sure he'd just called her something that would translate into "bitch."

Must breathe. Must breathe. Must… Oh, thank God!

"Let the woman go," Dan commanded, having materialized out of the darkness like an avenging angel. He pressed the lethal end of his Ruger tight against Kozlov's temple and snaked an arm around the Russian's throat. She squeezed her eyes shut as relief rushed through her so quickly she felt dizzy. Or maybe that was the lack of O_2.

And, yes. Okay. So turns out she *was* the damsel in distress who needed a Black Knight to rescue her.

Maybe she'd feel bad about that later. For now, all she felt was gratitude.

"I *said* let the woman go, asshole," Dan demanded. "Or instead of putting a bullet in your brain, I'll be tempted to reach down your throat to pull your backbone out through your mouth."

Whoa. And she thought Kozlov was scary? Penni opened her eyes to find Dan's concerned gaze searching her face. She nodded jerkily, letting him know she was okay. You know, if she could…Just. *Breathe*.

"No problem." Kozlov lifted his hands in the air, his Russian accent rolling the *R*.

The instant his forearm disappeared from her neck, Penni filled her hungry lungs with bright, glorious air. She didn't even care that its biting cold flayed her tender throat on the way down. *Okay. Okay. It's okay*. The mantra circled around in her head a couple of times, and she pressed a shaking, reassuring hand to her stomach.

"Now, nice and easy," Dan growled—normally she found that animal-like snarl sexy as hell, but she had to admit, it could be damned unnerving too—"I want you to ease that big piece out from under your coat. And before you think of trying anything, you should know I'm a total cliché. I got a hair trigger and twitchy finger."

"No problem," Kozlov said again.

When the big Russian reached inside his jacket, Penni bent to retrieve the Bersa. Her wobbly knees betrayed her at the last second and she muttered a foul word, catching herself with a hand pressed against the coffee shop's back wall.

"Penni?" Dan asked urgently.

"I'm fine," she assured him again.

She'd just wrapped her fingers around the Bersa's polymer grip when Kozlov took advantage of Dan's momentary distraction to slam an elbow into his face. *Thunk!* The obscene sound of bone hitting bone echoed dully down the dark street.

Penni was on her feet in an instant, taking aim and curling her trembling finger tight against the .38's trigger. But it was too late. Dan's head whipped back, blood gushing from the wound over his left eye where the skin had split open on impact with Kozlov's elbow.

For a big man, the Russian was extremely fast. He twirled like a top in Dan's arms, managing to get a hand on Dan's wrist and angling the Ruger away from his head. And then the fight was on! The two men became a blurry tangle of arms and legs as they spun toward the opposite side of the street. Each used his free hand to pummel the other. Each grunted with the exchanged jabs, twisting and turning and struggling for dominance over the weapon.

Dan! No!

Fear left a sour taste in Penni's mouth. These things could turn bad at the drop of the hat. One false move, one missed opportunity, and it could all be over. If Dan ended up on the wrong end of that gun because of her, because her mutinous knees had failed her, she'd never forgive herself.

"I can't get a clean shot!" she hissed, her blood roaring through her veins so quickly it burned. "Dan! I can't get a—"

She didn't finish because Kozlov slammed Dan's hand into a street sign and the Ruger dropped into the road.

Christ! *Christ!*

Penni closed one eye and sighted down the Bersa's short barrel. Her hands were shaking so badly she was ashamed of herself. But even if they hadn't been, she wouldn't have dared take the shot. Not when one inch in the wrong direction could mean the difference between hitting the Russian and hitting Dan by mistake.

Punches. Kicks. Body blows. Face strikes. It was terrifying to watch them dance and dodge. And strangely quiet. Neither man uttered a word. Just the occasional grunt when a brutal blow landed with particular force.

Penni recognized some of Dan's moves as Krav Maga. The CQB—close quarters combat—technique combined boxing and wrestling with various forms of martial arts. It was invented by the Israelis and taught to America's Navy SEALs. And it was as effective as it was impressive. Despite Kozlov's greater bulk, Dan was gaining the upper hand.

Now, if only he'd get out of the damned way so I can get a clean—

Bongggg! Dan slammed Kozlov's head into the metal side of a pay phone bolted to the curb. *Huh. Do those still exist?* Apparently. And Dan put the apparatus to good use. Grabbing the receiver off the hook, he used the cord as a garrote and started strangling Kozlov, the big veins in the Russian's neck stood out like snakes with the strain of it. Kozlov frantically gripped the cord, trying to get his fingers between the garrote and his throat. But it was no use. Dan was way too strong. And *way* too determined.

When Kozlov's eyes bulged from his crimson face and his booted feet scrabbled against the cobblestones,

Penni saw her opportunity. Racing across the street, she bent and retrieved Dan's dropped Ruger. Luckily, this time she managed to keep from almost ass-planting. And then, with a weapon in each hand, she slowly made her way around to the front of the men, aiming both the Ruger and the Bersa straight at Kozlov's midsection.

"Stop fighting him or I'll fill your belly with lead," she warned, amazed her voice sounded so incredibly steady when her insides were jiggling around like a Jell-O mold...

Chapter Nine

"YOU HEARD THE LADY," DAN HISSED THROUGH gritted teeth as he yanked the pay phone's cord tighter. "Stop fucking fighting and you might just live."

Kozlov must have realized he was overpowered and outgunned. And proving he was smarter than he looked, he went slack in Dan's arms. Without taking the pressure off the improvised garrote, Dan reached inside Kozlov's coat and carefully removed the T/C Contender from the Russian's shoulder holster.

Once the weapon was secure, he unwound the pay phone cord, slammed the receiver back onto the hook, and shoved away from Kozlov before the big Russian could gather his wits and make any sort of counter move. Placing himself at a ninety-degree angle from Penni, Dan joined her in drawing down on the motherfucker, enjoying the Contender's solid weight at the end of his arm. He knew if he fired, the roar of the handgun would be loud enough to shake the ground. And the thought of its lethality almost gave him a government operator stiffy.

Or maybe that's just the adrenaline…

Blowing hard and wiping the blood from his eye with his free hand, he spared Penni a quick glance. He wanted to go to her and take her in his arms, to assure himself that she was safe and whole and unharmed. But he didn't dare allow Kozlov an opening. And besides, the expression on her face when she shot him a look said it all. Coolheaded and clear-eyed, Penni had everything under control.

Balls to shame an elephant…

If he ever again found himself trying to take down a trained Russian spy, he could do a lot worse than having former Secret Service Agent Penni DePaul by his side. But he probably couldn't do much better.

Swiping more blood from his forehead and flinging it onto the cobblestones—head wounds always gushed like a damned geyser; it was annoying—he saw Zoelner race around the corner and skid to a stop. Once Zoelner verified with his eyes what he'd been hearing through his earpiece, that they had everything under control, he planted his hands on his knees, let his head hang between his shoulders, and started panting.

"Nice of you to show up," Dan said drolly. Despite the brutality of the fight—he was going to have bruises galore up and down his left side thanks to Kozlov's thunderous right hook—it had lasted no more than a few dozen seconds. No doubt Zoelner had been busting ass in their direction every single one of them.

"Shit," Zoelner wheezed. "Holy shit."

One would think the guy didn't have an ounce of energy left in him. But that was proved dead wrong when Chelsea started around the opposite corner. Her toe had barely cleared the lip of the curb before Zoelner did a one-eighty so fast he was nothing but a blur. When he stopped, his Beretta 92 was aimed right between Chelsea's wide eyes.

Her squeal of surprise damn near deafened Dan.

And his peripheral vision told him Penni winced. The weapons she had trained on Kozlov didn't move an inch, however, remaining locked, loaded, and rock-fucking-steady.

Alice Cooper once said that "the minute you step on stage, you get eight feet taller." Well, this must be Penni's stage. Because she was proving to be a veritable Amazon.

A warm glow of admiration filled him and pushed out against the chill of the night. He couldn't wait to finish this goddamned mission and get her alone for two, maybe three days, and *show* her just how much he admired her.

Zoelner obviously wasn't having any similar feelings toward Chelsea. "Damnit!" he hissed at her. "You don't sneak up on a guy like that! I almost dropped the hammer on your ass!"

"Please," Chelsea scoffed, straightening her collar and recovering quickly. "This was not made"—with a Vanna White–style flourish of her hand, she indicated her rather curvaceous physique—"to sneak." As if to prove her point, she pressed her palm against her side and winced like she had a stitch. "But since the gang's all here, let's not waste any time." She took a second more to catch her breath, using the brief lull to quickly catalog Kozlov's features. Then she said, "It sure is fancy meeting you here, Andrei."

Huh, Dan thought, frowning. *So I guess we're just gonna throw all our cards on the table.*

Kozlov was down on one knee in the street, rubbing his abused throat. But he went completely still at the sound of his name. "You know who I am," he snarled.

Now, Dan was no expert when it came to male beauty, but he knew enough to lay down pretty steep odds that Kozlov wouldn't win any awards for looks, even on his best day. Given the Russian's right eye was already swelling, as were his lips, Dan would go so far as to say that if you looked up the term "fugly" on Urban Dictionary, you'd see a photo of the Russian FSB officer.

"We *do* know who you are." Chelsea advanced another step, careful not to obscure Penni's aim. "We know you are Russian Federal Security Service. We know you checked into your hotel under the alias Peter Sayankin even though your real name is Andrei Kozlov. We know you came to Cusco via Buenos Aires." That last bit she must've discovered while she and Ozzie were chatting over their air gap network. "And we know you're hoping to meet up with Winterfield in about"—she checked her watch— "forty-five minutes."

Aha. And now Dan got her game. Make Kozlov think they already knew all the important things in the hopes of conning him into telling them the not-so-important things. Basically, bluff. *Smart cookie, that one*.

"Who are you?" Kozlov narrowed his one remaining good eye, turning to spit on the ground as if in punctuation.

"Whoa," Zoelner said, tucking his Beretta into his waistband and crossing his arms. It made the lapels on his leather jacket flare wide. "Looks like you dropped something there, Andrei."

Chelsea shot Zoelner a look that clearly conveyed, *You're not helping*. Zoelner answered with a laconic shrug.

"If you don't mind," Chelsea said, "I'm going to refrain from answering that, Andrei." With a subtle jerk of her chin toward Penni and Dan—both of them continued to keep Kozlov in their sights—she indicated without words that *he who has the weapons gets to ask the questions*.

Kozlov glanced over at Dan, his eye swelling more and more each second. Dan had a pretty mean right hook too. "Could you point that some place other than my head, cowboy?" the Russian asked. "Like you, I prefer a hair trigger."

"Oh, sure thing." Dan nodded, dropping his aim from Kozlov's head down to his crotch. "Better?"

Kozlov scowled.

"So now that we all know where we stand, and now that your mission is officially in the garbage, how about you help us out, Andrei?" Chelsea asked, her voice ringing with false sweetness. Zoelner had once said she was a lion when it came to hunting for information, fierce and indefatigable. Obviously her ferocity didn't just apply to scanning reams of Intelligence documents.

A light in the second-story window of the building across the street clicked on, proving the block wasn't *entirely* deserted. Kozlov glanced up at the glow, then leveled a look on Chelsea. "You really wish to do this here, *golubushka*?"

Chelsea tilted her head like she was trying to decide if that was an endearment or an insult.

"The alley." Zoelner jerked his chin toward the narrow cobblestoned path cutting behind the coffee shop. "There are no windows back there."

"A dark alleyway?" Chelsea made a face. "Yeah, that seems appropriate."

"Move," Dan ordered Kozlov, motioning with the T/C Contender. "And keep your hands where I can see 'em, or you and me are gonna have ourselves a problem not easily fixed with anything other than a bullet."

"Okay, cowboy," Kozlov said, raising his hands above his head. "You are the boss." Slowly crossing the road, Kozlov started whistling a tune Dan recognized as the Russian national anthem.

Cheeky bastard, he thought with a hint of admiration. It was just a *hint*, mind you. Because following close behind Kozlov, the Contender at the ready, Dan wouldn't hesitate to shoot the sonofabitch should he so much as look at him sideways. He knew Penni was at his back, even though he didn't dare take his eyes off his target to verify it. Truth was, he didn't need to. That weird, wonderful connection they shared meant he could sense when she was near him. And by the sound of a hissed argument, Zoelner and Chelsea were bringing up the rear.

As a group they shuffled past a pair of rusting blue dumpsters that reeked of molding coffee grounds. Something small and furry darted out from under one of the bins, running on fast feet toward the opposite end of the alley. The temperature inside the narrow expanse was markedly warmer, and when Dan spared a quick glance to his left, he realized why. There was a small vent spewing steam from the boiler in the basement of the coffee shop.

"That's far enough," he told Kozlov once they were half a dozen paces past the dumpsters.

When the Russian stopped and turned, Chelsea murmured, "Excuse me," as she squeezed by Penni and Zoelner to come stand beside Dan. A look down into her eager face had him fighting a grin and saying, "Okay, tiger. He's all yours."

She nodded her thanks. But before she could say anything, Kozlov preempted her with, "I will not say a word until you tell me who you people are." The second-to-last word sounded more like *pipple*. He seemed to be amazingly unconcerned that three weapons were currently aimed at the softer parts of his body. Then again, the FSB wasn't known to employ wilting lilies.

"I thought I made it clear that *we're* the ones asking the questions," Chelsea spat.

Kozlov shook his head, his busted lips curling back to reveal discolored teeth. "Like you said, my mission is ruined. So why should I answer your questions? Why should I give you anything?"

Chelsea considered him for a second, and Dan took the opportunity to appreciate the Dance of the Spies she and Kozlov were performing. When he worked with the SEALs, information sharing between foreign Intelligence agents wasn't a big part of his job description. His had been more of the get in, blow some shit up, and get the hell out kind of gig. And the work he did for BKI was so black it gave credence to the phrase *If I told you, I'd have to kill you*. So watching two spies squaring off, trying to feel each other out, was surprisingly entertaining.

"Fine," Chelsea allowed. "A little tit for tat isn't too much to ask. The answer to your question is we're the ones who've been sent in to do what those before us haven't managed."

Kozlov lifted a brow and glanced around at the four of them. Dan had to admit they looked like quite the motley crew. Probably *especially* him. He took another swipe at the wound on his forehead and noticed the blood was congealing in his eyebrow. The cut was finally clotting. So...silver linings and whatnot.

"And what is that?" the Russian asked.

"Bring Winterfield down," Chelsea finished with dramatic flair.

As if the whole of Cusco conspired to join her in her theatrics, a puff of steam belched from the vent near the trash bins, swirling into the cool air. Somewhere off in the distance a dog snarled and barked before falling silent. A dark cloud moved over the silver crescent moon, casting the alleyway into even deeper, more malevolent shadows. And *damnit!* There it was again! That creepy, crawly sensation.

Dan rubbed a hand over the back of his neck and thought, *Seriously?* A cold, dark night in a foreign country, a dimly lit alley, and an American agent going head-to-head with a Russian agent while a muddy sense of gloom and doom hung in the air? If Dan was writing a bad spy novel, this is the exact scenario he'd describe. In fact, it was so clichéd it was almost trite. And he suddenly understood why Chelsea had said their new location was appropriate.

"Please," Kozlov scoffed, the word sounding more like *pliz*. "That is nothing. The information I have is worth far more than your cryptic answers."

"Well"—Chelsea shrugged—"the way I see it, you can either tell me what you know, or I'll have Winterfield do it as soon as we apprehend him. If I have to go with option number two, I can assure you I'll have my tech guys post your photo, name, and occupation on every social media site from Facebook to Twitter to Tumblr. It's so hard to do this kind of work when the whole world knows about you, isn't it?" she asked with feigned sympathy.

Dan shuddered at the mere idea and Kozlov regarded her for what seemed like an eternity, a muscle twitching fitfully in his bruised jaw.

"And if *that* doesn't convince you," Chelsea continued, "how about this? You either cooperate with me, or I'll make it known to anyone who will listen—the president, the world press, whoever—that Russia was actively seeking to procure stolen information about foreign governments from a rogue U.S. spy. Given the trouble you guys are already in with the international community regarding that bad business in Ukraine and Crimea, I'd think you'd want to avoid another black eye on Mother Russia's pretty face. You and I both know your country can't survive another round of sanctions."

Wow. As Aretha Franklin would say, "R.E.S.P.E.C.T." Special Agent Chelsea Duvall had some serious props. Dan tipped an imaginary hat to her.

"Fine," Kozlov hissed. "Ask your questions."

Chelsea grinned. "See? It's an easy decision when you think about it, isn't it? So first things first. What's your beef with Winterfield?"

Kozlov cocked his head, his one good eye narrowing. "I do not understand this expression."

"Oh, sorry." Chelsea shook her head. "Let me rephrase. We intercepted a phone conversation you had that led us to believe you're here to kill Winterfield."

Something strange passed over Kozlov's features, but it was so fleeting Dan wondered if it was anything or just the play of shadows. "Why the hell would you do that?"

"Ha!" Kozlov's bark of laughter echoed down the alley. "So contrary to what you would have the world believe, you Americans are not gods. You do not see all and know all."

If only he knew just how true that was, he'd be dancing in the street…uh…alleyway.

"Feel free to gloat with your cronies over vodka shots when you're back at the Kremlin," Chelsea growled impatiently. "For now, answer the damn question. Why are you here for Winterfield? What has he ever done to you?"

Kozlov reveled in his own self-importance for a second or two more. If Dan thought it would help move things along, and if his hands weren't currently occupied with the Contender, he would have slow-clapped for the jerkwad.

Finally, Kozlov shrugged. "It is not what Winterfield has done. It is what he has."

"And what's that?" Chelsea asked.

"We have reason to believe Winterfield knows the location of Stanislav Rubashkin." By the way he said the name, it was obvious he expected them to recognize it.

Dan glanced at Zoelner. *Nope*. The former CIA agent shrugged with his eyebrows. One quick look at Penni's *ya-got-me* expression had his gaze landing on Chelsea. *Bingo*. She was blinking rabidly behind the lenses of her glasses.

"Is that why he's here in Cusco? To sell you Rubashkin's information?" The color was running high in her café au lait cheeks.

"No." Kozlov shook his head. "Our sources say

Winterfield is here to meet a man who goes by the name of Khalid al-Rahma."

"Which sources would those be?"

"Those ones we have inside the AQAP," Kozlov admitted. All Dan's mental bells and whistles started clamoring at mention of Al-Qaeda in the Arabian Peninsula. *Not good. This is so not good. Fuckin' Winterfield!* "Al-Rahma is one of theirs. He has a reputation for procuring the unprocurable."

"And what unprocurable thing is al-Rahma supposed to get from Winterfield?" Chelsea demanded.

Kozlov shrugged. "That we do not know. And we do not care."

Dan blinked. Was it just him? Or was this thing getting ridiculously convoluted. *Damn spies and their pretzel machinations and twisty, turny logic.* He much preferred the kind of work that had clear parameters and precise objectives.

Chelsea started pacing back and forth, her brow furrowed in concentration. "So let me see if I have this right. You think that among the reams of Intelligence Winterfield stole from the CIA is the current location and alias of Rubashkin. You heard from your sources inside the AQAP that Winterfield would be meeting this al-Rahma character here in Cusco to do some kind of deal. So then you're here to what?" She suddenly stopped pacing and turned to pin her golden gaze on Kozlov. "Wait a minute. You're not here to *kill* Winterfield." She blinked at Kozlov. "You're here hoping to approach him to make a deal about Rubashkin."

And *that* had been the shadow Dan saw pass over

Kozlov's face when Chelsea made that comment about him being here to take out Winterfield. She'd made a wrong assumption based on his side of the phone call. They *all* had.

"It is past time Stanislav Rubashkin pay for what he has done." Kozlov spat on the ground like saying the man's name left a bad taste in his mouth. *Justice for Mother Russia…* It suddenly made sense. Even though nothing else did yet. *Who* was Rubashkin?

"There you go dropping things again, Andrei," Zoelner muttered.

Chelsea shot him an emphatic look that said, *Cut it out*. Again, Zoelner answered with a laconic shrug.

Kozlov's expression turned sour. "And just so we understand each other, Russia does not pay good rubles for something she can get for free."

"Meaning what?" Chelsea asked. "You just planned to catch Winterfield and beat the information out of him. And so the T/C Contender is for?" Kozlov opened his mouth, but she held up a hand. "Let me guess. Al-Rahma."

"One less radical on the face of the earth."

Chelsea glanced up and down the alley. "So where are your friends, huh? Where's your backup?"

"Please," Kozlov scoffed. "Your government may have forgotten how to handle these matters, but Russia has not. When you want to catch a rat, you do not send in a whole regiment."

And that had been Dan's *exact* point to the CIA barely two days ago. Although he would not like to think he had anything in common with Kozlov, he had to admit they were of like mind in this one particular regard.

"You send in one very mean rat terrier," Kozlov finished proudly, the *V* in the word "very" sounded like a *W*.

Chelsea checked her watch. "And the terrier was planning to capture the rat in Plaza San Francisco thirty minutes from now."

Looking at Kozlov, Dan realized once again that the fate of the nation had come down to good ol' DFL. *Dumb fuckin' luck.* Which Zoelner's happenstance spotting of the Russian in the square definitely qualified as. More often than anyone would probably like to concede, that's how it happened, and he thanked his lucky stars every time it did.

"Is there anything more you can tell us about Winterfield's meeting?" Chelsea asked.

Kozlov shrugged indifferently. "Nothing. You know it all. Now I would like my weapon back, please." With a jerk of his chin he indicated the Contender still aimed at him.

Dan scoffed. "Not on your life, comrade." *Is this guy for real?*

"A pity," Kozlov sighed. "It was one of my favorites. But, then again, I have many favorites." The warning in his tone was clear as he straightened his jacket, touched a finger to his busted lip, and smiled at Dan. The look on his face said, *Until we meet again…*

Dan made sure his own expression responded with *Looking forward to it, fuckhead.* And, *ooooh!* Wasn't supersecret spy-guy stuff fun?

"Now"—Chelsea cocked her head at Kozlov, tapping a finger against her chin—"what to do with you?"

"What? This is a question?" The Russian glanced back and forth among the four of them. "I have given you what you want. I have no weapon. My mission is, as you say, in the garbage. So you will let me go, yes?"

Penni caught Dan's eye and mouthed, *Is this guy for real?*

Under different circumstances he would have laughed out loud that she'd just put his thoughts into words.

Chelsea chuckled. "You're funny, Andrei. I think I like you."

Zoelner snarled something under his breath. But when Chelsea turned to him, he straightened and blinked innocently, like he hadn't just threatened to have the Russian strung up by his balls. "Suggestions, Z?" she asked. "This is more your area of expertise than mine."

"Take him to the rendezvous point, gag him, and hog-tie him until we see if his information pans out," Zoelner said, as if the answer was obvious.

"Yeah," Dan wholeheartedly agreed. "What he said…"

Chapter Ten

"I KNOW I STUMBLED INTO THIS MISSION AND IT'S PROBABLY none of my business," Penni said when Chelsea clicked off the phone with her supervisor after telling the man to alert the marshals about the mysterious threat to some guy Zoelner had never heard of, "but care to fill me in on what the heck all that business concerning Rubashkin was about?"

"Yeah." Dan shook his head so fast Zoelner was surprised the move wasn't accompanied by the cartoonish *aye-eee-aye-eee-aye* sound effect. "I hate to sound like a broken record, but what *she* said…"

Zoelner glanced over at Chelsea. Normally the woman had a face that promised heaven, but in the dim light of the street lamp shining in through the window, her current expression looked like hell. She might have put on a brave front while interrogating Kozlov, but it'd taken its toll on her. She was used to sitting safe and sound in a cubicle, not demanding answers from a Russian thug who would have happily killed her, given a chance.

The air inside the deserted building was as heavily scented as a South Side hooker. But instead of dime-store perfume, the smell was sawdust and plaster. It filled Zoelner's nose and mouth when he sucked in a breath, preparing himself for whatever bombshell Chelsea was poised to drop.

"Stanislav Rubashkin is the former military intel-ligence colonel for the KGB," she whispered. "He defected to the U.S. after the Soviet Union fell in '91."

Boom!

And there it was.

Zoelner glanced into the far corner where he'd left Kozlov after he duct-taped the Russian's wrists and ankles—double duct-taped them actually; Kozlov was a big boy. "Cocksucking sonofabitch," he hissed. "That jackass is real? I thought he was just a crazy rumor."

"Nope." Chelsea shook her head, glancing furtively in Kozlov's direction. The Russian was nothing but a big, shadowy blob against the still darkness of the corner. "No rumor. Rubashkin is as real as it gets."

"How come I never heard anything about that?" Penni asked. "I mean, I know it was way before my time, but it had to have been huge news and I—"

"You don't know anything about it because it was never reported," Chelsea said. "Rubashkin was a course unto himself in CIA Hush-That-Fuss 101."

"Huh?" Dan's intense scowl was visible even in the near-dark room.

"The CIA took him, held him, debriefed him for almost two full years, and then they handed him over to the U.S. Marshals Service, who have been hiding him ever since," Chelsea explained.

Zoelner watched as Dan and Penni exchanged a look.

"You see, Rubashkin cut a deal," Chelsea went on. "He gave us an unfettered peek into the lives, finances, and ties of the movers and the shakers behind the Iron Curtain, told us everything we wanted to know about how the Soviet Union operated and who was likely to rise to power after its fall. And in exchange, we agreed to give him full immunity, a new identity, and protection from the long arms of his former friends in the KGB." She pushed her glasses up her nose. The glasses thing— half sexy, half nerdy—was too charming for words... usually. But not when the hand she used to do it with was shaking like an addict's in the middle of detox.

Zoelner didn't realize his feet were moving until he'd already closed the distance to her. "Hey." He lifted a hand, then faltered. Touching Chelsea was never a good idea. She was so soft, so immensely touchable. And putting his hands on her, even in the most innocent ways, always reminded him that what he really wanted to do was put his hands on her in very *un-innocent* ways.

Which was a *problem*. Only partly because Chelsea had never given him any indication she'd welcome his touch, innocent or otherwise.

Or maybe you're just a big ol' pussy.

Allowing for that possibility, he forced himself to grab her shoulder. "You okay?" He gave her a little squeeze.

Soft. So unbearably soft...

"Yeah." She nodded, standing a little straighter and lifting her piquant chin.

And tough too. A dichotomy that worked on him like pasties and thongs worked on other men.

"Sounds like Rubashkin was a real winner," Penni muttered, disgust lacing her tone. "And by *winner*, I mean a rat scurrying from a sinking ship." She took Dan's hand, threading her fingers through his. And when Dan dragged her close to his side, Zoelner wondered if the two of them realized they were already acting like a couple. He envied their ease with one another. How they just seemed to naturally fit together. Two pieces of a puzzle clicking. No pretense. No bullshit.

Which reminded him…*What the hell am I supposed to do with my hand now? Do I drop it? Do I leave it on Chelsea's shoulder?* "Easy" and "comfortable" certainly were *not* words he would ever use to describe his relationship with her. Choosing the first of his two options, he hoped to cover up any awkwardness by rubbing his hands together like he needed to warm them.

It seemed to work. Chelsea didn't appear to notice anything amiss as she agreed. "You said it. But we gave our word to protect him in exchange for the information, so that's what we've done. What we'll continue to do. I'm sure the marshals are moving Rubashkin as we speak. Just as a precaution."

"What a phenomenal waste of taxpayer money," Dan grumbled, shaking his head.

"Can't argue with you there," Chelsea agreed. "But hey, let's look on the bright side here. If it weren't for Rubashkin, we never would have stumbled across Kozlov." She hooked her thumb toward the corner. "And without Kozlov, we never would have known about al-Rahma. And without al-Rahma, we never would have known when and where to expect Winterfield."

Her face brightened, a grin suddenly stretching her lips. Chelsea had the best smile. Her teeth flashed white, her cheeks plumped, and her happiness shined in her eyes, making them glint like polished gold. "Hey, guys, you do realize we're *finally* about to bring Luke Winterfield down, right?"

Zoelner took a page from Kozlov's manual and spit on the ground in punctuation. "It's way past time."

"Right." Dan bobbed his chin, releasing Penni's hand to wrap an arm around her shoulders. Penni's arm went around his waist just as naturally as you please. "So, then, what's the plan?"

"If Kozlov's Intel proves correct"—Zoelner glanced at his watch—"we could have our hands on Winterfield in fifteen minutes."

"Which means we need to call the ground crew at the airport and tell 'em we need the plane gassed and ready to go on the tarmac," Dan said, already digging in his hip pocket for his phone.

"And we need a way to *get* to the airport," Zoelner added, exchanging a look with Dan. After three months together, they no longer needed to say anything to come to an understanding. Dan nodded, just a quick jerk of his chin that said, *Roger that*.

Zoelner turned to Chelsea.

"Uh-oh." She frowned. He wondered if she realized it made the freckles across her nose stand out. "I know that face. I'm not going to like what comes next, am I?"

No, she probably wasn't. But of the four of them, she was the least qualified for what might happen next. Which meant they needed to put her to work on something she *was* qualified to do. And *then* there was the added perk that he would able to concentrate a lot better knowing she wasn't in the shit. Chelsea might be the bane of his existence most days, but he also happened to care for her. "How are you at hot-wiring a car?"

George remained one with the shadows of the news-paper stand as the foursome exited the building. He watched them head quietly toward the square, and Spider's orders rang viciously clear inside his head. *No witnesses! No loose ends!*

He hadn't been able to hear everything discussed in the alley—when the steam from the coffee shop's basement boiler hissed into the space, it had drowned out their voices—but he'd heard enough to know the Russian now fell into both of those categories, a witness *and* a loose end. George had also caught the bit about Winterfield's expected arrival in the plaza at ten o'clock, which meant he had time to dispatch the Russian and get back to the square to see if, indeed, Winterfield showed.

If he did, George would kill the bastard and the hodgepodge quartet that had apparently been tasked with bringing him in. If Winterfield *didn't* show, well…then George would simply continue to watch and wait and hunt the hunters until they finally led him to the prey.

He took a moment to congratulate himself for making the call to follow Daniel Currington from Lima to Cusco. Then he stepped from the gloom, shoving his hands deep in his pockets and keeping his head down so the brim of his ivy cap obscured his face. There was no real concern about street cameras in Cusco—probably one of the main reasons Winterfield had chosen the city as a rendezvous point—but old habits were hard for George to break.

Waiting until he could no longer hear the foursome's footsteps, he slowly crossed the street, sliding easily through the shadows cast by the surrounding structures. Peering through the window of the building the others had exited, he patiently let his eyes adjust to the darkness inside. One more little lesson he'd learned since coming to work for Spider: *It never pays to rush.*

One second became two. Two soon became ten. With each of his quiet breaths fogging against the windowpane, George fancied he could hear the cold night whispering to him of secrets locked in the dark, of ancient civilizations reaching an invisible hand forward through space and time to keep a bony finger on the pulse of the present.

The Incans had been a brutal culture by modern standards. Sacrificing their own children to the gods in times of famine and illness. But they had also created great civilizations and beautiful art that transcended the passing of centuries. That dichotomy intrigued George. Perhaps because he saw a bit of it in himself. There was the half of him made up of love and life. The half he showed his daughter. And then there was the half of him made up of darkness and death. The half that did Spider's bidding no matter the consequences.

George's whimsical musing came to an abrupt halt when he saw what he was looking for. Over in the far corner a bulky shadow moved. The Russian. Trussed and helpless. An easy target.

Sliding silently toward the building's entrance, George tried the knob and smiled when it turned. Slipping inside, he closed the heavy wood panel and leaned against the door, feeling the weight of certainty settle atop his shoulders. In approximately ten seconds, the Russian would be dead by his hand.

With a sigh, he let go of the half of himself that was love and life and let the half that was darkness and death reign supreme. Pulling the handcrafted Perkin

440C stainless-steel hunting knife from the sheath at his back, he took a step toward the Russian. Nine seconds… Closing his eyes, he pictured his daughter. *I do this for her.* Seven seconds… He squeezed the burl wood handle tightly and started jogging toward his prey. Five seconds… The Russian spotted him and started grunting and struggling against his restraints. Three seconds… Clearing his mind of everything but the task, George skidded to a stop beside the Russian who was now on his side on the floor, floundering like a fish. One second…

George bent down, fancying himself the specter of death poised to strike the fatal blow. And that's exactly what he did. With one hand on the man's shoulder for leverage, he shoved his hunting knife into the base of the Russian's skull, past the rows of fat wrinkles that stretched all the way up into his narrow, bald head.

George's aim and his blade both proved true, the latter slipping over the uppermost vertebra and severing the Russian's spine in an instant. The man didn't even have time to squeal his surprise.

A good kill. A clean kill. George could take comfort in that.

Wiping his blade on the Russian's coat, he ignored the tangy scent of blood and spinal fluid that drifted up his nose. After sheathing the knife, he straightened, turned, and walked purposefully for the door. *One down. Five more to go…*

Oh, sure. You can all run and shoot and simultaneously protect the wee folks of the world. But can you see patterns in online search algorithms? Can you locate terrorist cells based on their digital footprints alone? Can you tie a cherry stem in a knot with only your tongue. Huh? Can you?

To say Chelsea was butthurt and embarrassed by her assigned role was like saying Antarctica was cold. A bona fide case of *well, duh*. First there was Penni with that whole "trained to handle every kind of firearm from a six-shooter to a sniper rifle"—which, okay, truth be told, just made Chelsea like the woman more; *chick is badass, fo sho*—and now *this*. Reduced to playing the part of the valet and the bellboy. It was shameful. Humiliating.

Everything is coming up Chels! Not.

"For crying out loud, I passed all my marksmanship tests," she harrumphed, looking up and down the street before jimmying the lock on the back door of the old Volkswagen cargo van circa 1990-something.

Z had given her specific directions to the vehicle. "It's perfect," he'd said, pointing her down the street. "Old enough to easily hot-wire, big enough to hold all of us should we need it, and while I was trailing Kozlov, I saw its owner hop on the back of some girl's scooter and take off for what looked like a hot date. You shouldn't have to worry about getting caught in the middle of snatching it. You can't miss it. It's the one with the big yellow sun on the side."

Right. Perfect. The one with the big yellow sun on the side. *Appropriate, considering this whole day has been nothing but blue skies, sunshine, and glittery unicorn farts*, she thought sarcastically. "Passed with flying colors I might add," she went on.

"Stay off the goddamn line unless you have something to report, Chels," Z commanded. "When things start happening here, they're going to happen fast. I don't want to miss something Dan or Penni says because you can't let it go that you're underqualified for this job."

And *that* was the true crux of her problem, wasn't it? Not that she'd been relegated to a supporting role—*when Penni, who is now officially a* civilian, *is still invited to the show. Grrr!*—so much as that Z thought playing a supporting role was exactly where she belonged.

It stung. More than Z probably realized and *far* more than Chelsea would ever admit to anyone but herself.

Silently fuming, she sprung the lock on the bus—See? She had crazy awesome skills!—and tossed Dan's backpack, Penni's purse, and her satchel inside. Sparing one final glance around, assuring herself she remained unobserved, she jumped in after their gear. Climbing over the two rows of rear bucket seats, she slid behind the wheel. And there she sat for a couple of seconds, wondering exactly where things with her and Z had gone off the rails.

They'd always verbally sparred with each other. In fact, the first conversation they'd had, way back when he was still with the CIA and she was a wet-behind-the-ears analyst, had been an opening salvo. A shot heard around *her* world.

It had happened during a meeting when she'd been trying to explain a particularly difficult theory about online surveillance to a group of uninterested operators. Z, a hotshot field agent at the time, had leaned over to one of his colleagues and whispered, "The minute she started throwing around words like 'skeuomorphism' and 'site aggregators' it was my cue to go."

"You mean it was your cue to go look them up?"

she'd asked, trying to portray bluster and bravado even though she was a hot mess of anxiety inside. It had been her first time leading a meeting and she wasn't doing a bang-up job of it.

Of course, any facade she'd managed to maintain was obliterated when Z lifted a surprised brow at her, a challenging light shining in his eyes. She'd blushed from the roots of her hair to the tips of her toes. And from that day on, they'd taken great delight in one-upping and insulting each other. But it had always been in fun, in jest, a battle of the wills that left her titillated and excited and looking forward to the next clash.

Then something changed. Something that had added a sharp edge to all their encounters. Something that made them skittish and unsure of each other. Something that—

Oh, who are you trying to fool, sister? You know what happened.

Yes, she did. And to this day, she regretted it with her whole heart.

Shaking her head and lamenting all the things she couldn't undo, she reached up to disable the interior light that would come on when the doors were opened. That was pretty much lesson one in stealing a car. A blinking interior light could draw unwanted attention on a cold, dark night such as this one.

Lesson two was to check the sun visor, the glove box, and beneath the floor mats. No use going to the trouble of hot-wiring a vehicle if the owner had been kind enough to leave behind a spare set of keys. Going through the motions, she tried to breathe through her mouth. The van smelled strongly of BO and barbecue sauce, evidence that the owner liked his slow-roasted meats more than his showers. She did *not* envy his date. And unfortunately, no keys.

So we do it the old-fashioned way.

Pulling the little tool kit she'd scrounged from Dan's backpack out of her pocket, she found the Phillips head screwdriver and went to work on the two screws holding the plastic steering column cover in place. After a bit of elbow grease that had her panting—*Holy crap, I need to hit the gym more*—it came free. She set it between the seats.

Pulling a little Maglite flashlight from her pocket, another tool she'd pilfered from Dan's backpack—the man had everything but the kitchen sink in that thing—she stuck it between her teeth and ducked down to study the wiring.

Okay, Chels. She gave herself a pep talk. *If they're going to consign you to being a lowly hot-wirer, then you'll be the best damn hot-wirer out there!*

Shining the light on the innards of the steering column, she saw the standard trio of bundles. It took her a second to identify the wires that led to the signal indicators and the cruise control on one side, the lights and wipers on the other, and those that attached to the battery, ignition, and starter.

She didn't realize she was muttering to herself around the flashlight until she heard Dan whisper in her ear, "Problem?"

Damn. So much for being the best hot-wirer out there. "No," she assured him after pulling the flashlight from between her teeth. *Come on. You have* one *job to do.* "It's just been a while."

"The battery wires are almost always red," Dan advised. "Make sure you don't—"

"I know," she hissed. "You're not the only one with a little MacGyver in you."

"Keep the line clear," Z growled again. "It's almost Miller time."

Keep the line clear, Chelsea pantomimed the words. *It's almost Miller time.* She wished she was standing in front of Z so she could roll her eyes and tell him, "Oh, please to the power of ten. Your big, bad alpha male operator material is so cheesy Velveeta wouldn't touch it."

Maybe after this was all over, she'd let him know how little she thought of—*Aha!* She finally located the battery wires among all the other wires. And they were *not* red, *thank you very much.* They were maroon. And she'd still pinpointed them. Like. A. Boss!

She shot an imaginary fist in the air, replaced the flashlight between her lips, and moved on to the next step. Which was the easy part. She stripped the insulation off the battery wires and twisted them together, careful not to let them touch any metal parts of the van. If they did, they could short out and then she'd be dunzo, having proved to Z that even playing a secondary role, she wouldn't be up for any Oscars.

And now for the finale. She took a moment to shake out her hands. They were aching from the exertion and from the cold. She blew into them for a couple of seconds. Once the sensation was back in the tips of her fingers, she carefully stripped the insulation away from the starter wire. Holding her breath, hoping she didn't electrocute herself, she sparked the starter wire against the battery lines.

Hheee-hubba-hheee.

The engine tried to sputter to life, but it sounded like an old man after climbing three flights of stairs. *Come on, baby. Show Mama what you got.* She sparked the wires again.

Hubba-hubba-hu-vroom!

"Yes!" She slapped the van's console and sat up in the driver's seat. Stepping on the gas, she revved the engine to keep it from dying. Then she yanked the wheel hard left and right to break the steering lock. Once it was free, she put the van in gear and slowly pulled from the curb. "I've secured the vehicle," she said. "I'll park around the block and wait for your signal."

"Nice work, Chels," Dan's voice sounded in her ear.

"Yeah," Z said. "Good job. Now shut up and keep the line clear."

Damned by faint praise…

Chapter Eleven

BUT THE SILENCE WAS UNBROKEN, AND THE STILLNESS GAVE no token...

Again with the Edgar Allan Poe. Penni was going to have to send a strongly worded letter...er...email—*who writes letters anymore?*—to that teacher when she got home. Young, impressionable minds should not be exposed to such nightmarish prose, the kind that stuck with a person even years later. Because who knew when it would pop up to haunt them? You know, like on a dark Peruvian night in the middle of a stakeout to catch one of the world's most fiendish men.

Okay, in Mrs. Pogue's defense, when she'd been teaching "The Raven," she probably hadn't envisioned any of her students finding themselves in this *precise* scenario. *So maybe the old gal deserves a pass.*

"We got company coming in from the east." Dan's voice sounded low and deliciously gravelly in Penni's earpiece. "Could be Winterfield. Right build. Right height. Everyone hold their positions until I verify his identity."

Edgar Allan Poe and his eerie poem were instantly forgotten. *Because who has time for rhythm and rhyme when it's officially go-time?* Even though no one could see her or hear her thoughts, she made a face when she realized what she'd just done.

"He's wearing a hoodie," Dan continued. "I can't get

a clear view of his face. Gimme a coupla seconds. I'm moving closer."

Penni lifted her wrist, squinting down through the darkness. Twenty-two hundred on the dot read the hands on her watch. *This is it*, the soft breeze that ruffled the leaves on the trees seemed to whisper. *This* has *to be it!*

Her idiotic heart, which hadn't really settled after that encounter with Kozlov—and talk about the stuff of nightmares—became a fist hammering against her breastbone. Worry and dread took up all the remaining dead space inside her. And for a moment, just a blip of time, she struggled against the instinctive desire to turn tail and beat feet for the nearest room with thick walls and a locked door.

She had so much to lose. And Dan…

Yeah, Dan. The warp and weft of her entire reason for being here. He had faith in her ability to watch his back. Trusted her to do what needed to be done if things with Winterfield and his AQAP contact looked like they might be headed toward a very *un*-Disney-like ending. Which meant that backing out now was not so much a case of that ship having sailed, but more like a case of that ship having *sunk*.

She couldn't let him down. She *wouldn't* let him down. Not when the thought of anything happening to him hurt like heartbreak. And for the millionth time since Malaysia, she wondered how it was possible to come to care so much for someone so quickly.

"I have another player approaching from the west." Zoelner's whispered tone held equal parts anticipation and excitement. "Blue coat. Black beard. Twitchy as fuck. He could be al-Rahma."

Penni slipped deeper into the shadows under the awning of the souvenir shop Dan and Zoelner had designated her OP—observation position. They'd chosen the spot for two reasons. It had an unencumbered view of the square. And if need be, she could aim and fire from behind the cover of the big masonry posts that flanked both sides of the front door.

"I don't want you to put yourself in any danger," Dan had said. "If it comes down to a choice between our hides or yours, I—"

"Forget about it," she'd told him, pressing a finger to his lips. When his hot breath tickled her skin, she threw caution to the wind and went up on tiptoe to kiss him. Just a quick peck. Just a sweet promise. His mouth was so warm, wonderfully firm yet incredibly soft in the way of men.

"Brooklyn," he'd whispered against her lips, his strong arms coming around her to hold her tight when she would have stepped away. She closed her eyes and took a moment to exult in his embrace. The roadway beneath them dissolved into a blur. The cold became something more understood than actually felt. The beep of a car horn off in the distance sounded like it was a million miles away.

Basically the whole world turned into a hazy, lazy kaleidoscope of nothingness. And in the center of that nothingness was Dan. Big, bold, brave Dan. "Brooklyn…" He whispered the pet name again, thrilling her with the intimacy of it. "You have no idea how much I—"

"Save it for later, Romeo," Zoelner had interrupted, and Penni wondered if the man practiced bad timing or if it just came naturally to him. Either way, it had her feeling smacky again. "We need to get set up…"

"Suspect moving toward the fountain," Dan said now, and Penni saw the hooded man emerge from a side street. He walked quickly toward the center of the square, hands shoved deep in his pockets, not looking this way or that, his strides short yet unhesitating.

"Potential al-Rahma is looking to intercept," Zoelner quickly replied. "I think this is it."

"Move in," Dan hissed and Penni's heart was no longer a fist banging against her ribs. It was a giant ham hock of a hand squeezing her throat. Curling her fingers around Dan's Ruger—he'd taken the Bersa, leaving her with the Ruger's better aim, longer firing range, and bigger clip—she sighted down the weapon's barrel, bracing it against one of the posts to combat the shaking of her hands. Blowing out a breath, she slipped her finger off the trigger guard and onto the trigger, noticing the latter was worn smooth from years of use.

Maybe they should *have chosen Chelsea for this and left me to hot-wire the van…*

The thought barely had time to finish swirling through her head before the world dissolved again. Only this time it wasn't Dan's handsome face that filled her vision. It was Mr. Hoodie. She kept his head lined up dead center in the three-dot sight. From one breath to the next, and with a few pounds of pressure, she could turn his skull into a big bowl of chunky salsa. And even though she'd never killed anyone, never *had* to kill anyone in all her years with the Secret Service, she knew she wouldn't hesitate to one-eighty that status quo if it looked, for even a split second, like Dan might be in trouble.

And speaking of Dan…

From the corner of her eye she saw a shadow move from the street into the square. If she hadn't been expecting it, she wouldn't have noticed it. Noticed *him*. Dan "The Man" Currington. Dan "Her Man" Currington…maybe…hopefully? Honestly, she wasn't sure. It all hinged on what happened once she told him—

Not now.

Right. *Right*. Now was not the time. Quickly filing away her thoughts under Shit to Be Dealt with Later, she searched the darkness beneath one of the trees surrounding the fountain. There. She spotted him again. Just a slightly deeper shadow in and among all the other shadows. He was as quiet as death. As still as a coffin. And now he was standing no more than ten yards from the potential bad guys.

Be careful, she begged him silently. She could smell the fear on her skin, taste its bitter flavor on her tongue.

"It's him!" Zoelner hissed. "It's Winterfield! Move, move, move!"

She watched mesmerized, terrified, locked-and-loaded and ready to fire should one of the men happen to see Dan and Zoelner materializing out of the night's inky blackness and turn to take a shot at them. But she needn't have worried. Winterfield and al-Rahma were completely clueless, caught totally off guard when Zoelner popped up behind al-Rahma at the precise second Dan materialized behind Winterfield, their guns held tight to each man's head as if the whole thing had been choreographed and practiced for months. Al-Rahma instinctively turned to fight and Penni's finger tightened on the trigger. But Zoelner clocked him in the temple with the butt of his weapon and the blow dropped the man to his knees.

"The next time won't be a warning, motherfucker," Zoelner growled. "It'll be a bullet in your brainpan." Al-Rahma held his wounded head and whispered something foul-sounding in Arabic. Zoelner must have understood it because he barked out a laugh. "Not even on your best day, you piece of shit," he said.

As for Luke Winterfield? He proved something Penni already knew. That he was a filthy, stinking, no-good coward. Because he didn't even attempt to put up a fight or run away. He simply raised his hands over his head and hissed a nasty word that translated through the mics Dan and Zoelner were wearing. Not that she would have *wanted* him to put up a fight, of course. Not with Dan on the receiving end of any resistance. But still…it was all a little anticlimactic.

"Luke Winterfield," Dan growled. "Under the authority granted to me by the government of the United States of America, I hereby inform you that you're totally fucked. You made a choice to sell out your country and now you're gonna face the consequences. Reap the whirlwind, asshole."

"Nice," Zoelner said. "Have you been holding on to that one for a while?"

"Came up with it in Bogotá," Dan admitted, a definite grin in his tone.

"I like it."

"Thought you might."

"Really though," Zoelner went on, "I was expecting some quote from Ted Nugent or Eminem."

"I *can* come up with my own material, you know," Dan insisted. "It's just I like to give credit to my hometown whenever I can. To make up for the place getting such a bad rap."

"Maybe it's because so much bad rap has come out of there," Zoelner mused. "Insane Clown Posse comes to mind."

"Hey," Dan whispered urgently, "don't say that too loud. You'll have groups of juggalos beating down your door."

Zoelner snorted.

"And just so you know," Dan went on, "what I've learned out of this lifetime is you should be proud of where you come from."

"I'm waiting…"

"Kid Rock said that. Via his Twitter account."

"And *there* it is."

Penni wanted to scream. Were they really standing there shooting the shit after finally catching Winterfield? Acting like it was no biggie that they'd just interrupted a deal with a member of the AQAP? Pretending like there was nothing at all urgent about the situation? *I mean, really?*

Chelsea must have been having similar difficulties because she piped up with, "Are we doing this or what? I'm still waiting for the signal to come get you guys."

"Roger that, Chels," Dan said. "We're r—"

Boom!

A shot rang out over the square, making Penni jump at the same time al-Rahma's head erupted like a melon loaded with firecrackers. Blood sprayed in a terrible arc, shining black in the dim light cast by the nearby street lamps.

What the hell? Where did that—

Boom!

Another shot blasted through the cold air, the round ranging wide, hitting the middle tier on the fountain and shattering the ceramic. Penni heard the crash of the broken pieces into the water in the base of the fountain at the same time Dan yelled, "Down! Down! Get down!"

Boom!

A third shot grazed Winterfield's arm before Dan jerked him to the ground. Winterfield's scream of agony echoed around the plaza. That, combined with the unmistakable sound of gunfire, had lights flashing on in two of the second-story apartments up the street to Penni's right. Every dog within ten blocks started barking and howling and setting up a terrible ruckus.

She noticed all this as an aside since every part of her was focused on the spot where she'd seen a muzzle flash. She ran through the four rules of marksmanship. Rule one: steady position. *Check*. Her right forearm was still braced solidly against the post. Rule two: aim. *Check. Check*. She lined up the Ruger's three-dot sight until the spot she thought she saw the muzzle flash was dead center. Rule three: control breath. *Triple check*. She punched all the air from her lungs. Rule four: *Squeeze trigger…*

Bam! Bam! Bam! The Ruger kicked like a mule in her hand as she lit up the dark spot catty-corner to her across the square. She could hear Winterfield bellowing like a wounded bull and Dan and Zoelner yelling orders to each other, to Chelsea, and to her. But she'd stopped comprehending English, concentrating entirely on laying down cover fire.

Time slowed to a crawl. Her heart was a steady, deliberate *lub-dub*. Her breathing was a calculated inhale and exhale between rounds. She counted off her shots to keep track of how many bullets remained in her clip. *Four, five…*

The column she was braced against took a round. Then another. The noise of the lead projectiles burying themselves in the thick post seemed oddly muted. And then she realized that was because her heart wasn't a steady *lub-dub*; it was a dull roar between her ears. Her breathing wasn't a calculated inhale and exhale; she was panting so loudly she sounded like she was auditioning for the role of Darth Vader. A chunk of concrete flew off, grazing her face, and she was slingshotted out of the momentary time warp.

Sonofa—

Now nothing was happening in slow motion. The whole world seemed to be spinning out of control, thrust into a chaotic twirl as she adjusted her position, aimed for the muzzle flashes, and let loose with another round of return fire. The Ruger belched .45-caliber bullets at a pulse-pounding rate, perfuming the air with the scent of cordite, slinging spent shell casings off to Penni's right, and making the muscles in her wrist and hand burn from exertion.

From the corner of her eye, she saw the van Chelsea had hot-wired come screaming around the corner. Its tires gripped the damp cobblestones in an effort to remain upright as the whole vehicle tipped ominously.

"Goddamnit, Penni! Get down! Protect yourself!"

Dan's terrified yell blared not only through her earpiece, but also through the air itself. *Oh goodie!* Apparently she was understanding English again.

And boy, oh boy, how she would have loved to obey his order. But he and Zoelner would be sitting ducks if she did. Not to mention Winterfield. Really, she didn't mention Winterfield because *who gives a flying frick about that traitor's sorry ass?* But since she *did* give many flying fricks about Dan, and Zoelner by association, she ignored his command and continued to lay on her trigger—*eight...nine...* A mutinous terror had entered her bloodstream, making her veins burn.

So much to lose. So much to lose. So much to... The mantra spun around and around inside her head, dazing her, dizzying her.

Zzzzip! Crack! Another bullet slammed into the post, sending bits of concrete flying. She closed her eyes and ducked behind the pillar. The sound of sirens blared somewhere off in the distance. The clamor of the dogs seemed to have grown to a crescendo. And someone a couple of blocks away was yelling something in Quechua, the native language spoken by so many in the Andes.

When she opened her eyes again and stepped back into firing position, it was in time to see the van jump the curb and fly onto the grassy area of the square. Chelsea was headed straight for the fountain without a thought to applying the brakes, plowing over a trash can and grazing a streetlight. The latter ripped the mirror off the driver's side door.

Penni squeezed her trigger, attempting to keep the shooter occupied so Chelsea could make a kamikaze-style rescue. *Thirteen...fourteen*, she counted, her hand and finger now numb with the repeated shock of the Ruger's recoil. One more round and her clip would be dry.

"Reloading!" she yelled. Just the one word to alert Dan and Zoelner that they needed to keep their heads down while—

"Penni!" Dan begged. "Please just—"

Bam! The last .45 exploded out of the Ruger's mouth, flashing in the darkness. She ducked behind the post and ejected the used magazine before slamming in a new one. It took only two seconds but it felt like an eternity as the sound of the van coming to a jolting stop, its front bumper hitting the fountain with a *crash*, was followed by the echoing barrage of traded gunfire.

"*Go, go, go!*" Zoelner's bellowed command blared through Penni's earpiece as she jumped to her feet. She could see Dan and Zoelner pushing Winterfield toward the open cargo door on the passenger side of the van. Chelsea was leaning across the front seats, exchanging fire with the shooter through the open passenger window.

"Holy shit!" the little CIA agent screamed when a bullet hit the front windshield, shattering the glass around a golf-ball-sized hole and causing a series of cracks to snake across the entire expanse. "Hurry up! We're taking heat here!"

Dan turned and put the little Bersa to good use, firing into the darkness as Zoelner tossed Winterfield inside the van and jumped in after him. Penni joined in the fray, pressing the button on the side of the Ruger that slammed the slide forward and chambered the first round. When she squeezed the trigger, the deafening roar of the weapon drowned out all the voices shouting in her earpiece.

With one eye on Dan and the other on the sight, she started counting again. *Two…three…four…*

Once she had the shooter pinned down, Dan jumped into the van and pulled the door shut. Chelsea laid on the gas. The vehicle's tires spun uselessly in the wet grass before the treads finally found traction in the soil beneath. The van shot across the square in Penni's direction, careening around trees and taking rounds in its metal skin. Penni didn't allow herself to think about what would happen if the bullets managed to penetrate the vehicle's body and come to rest inside Chelsea or Zoelner or…Dan! *Sweet Christ!*

Hot tears streamed down her face, dripping from her chin. She paid them no mind as she continued to fire, hoping to draw the shooter's aim away from the van and back to her. *Seven…eight…*

It worked. The pillar in front of her sustained a volley of rounds that had her ducking to avoid the spray of concrete shards. Well, at least it worked for a couple of seconds. She barely had time to steady her shaky nerves when *ping-ping-ping!* The unmistakable ring of hot lead slamming into sheet metal recommenced.

She spun around, careful to keep her body behind the now chewed-up post. Aiming down the barrel, she counted off *nine…ten… Son of a suck-ass bitch!* She was almost out of ammo and desperately low on options. Those two things had spelled doom for many a well-trained agent.

"Penni…" Dan's voice sounded in her ear, and she

choked on the wave of relief that rushed over her like a tsunami. He was okay. He hadn't been hit. "Hang steady for a couple more seconds, babe." He wasn't shouting. He was speaking slowly, steadily. Which was probably why she could hear him over the cacophony of her barking weapon. "We're almost to you."

"I'm almost out of…" *Fourteen…Fifteen. Click! Click! Click!* "I'm dry, Dan! I'm out!" She ducked behind the pillar. And to say she'd been scared from the get-go was an understatement. She'd been pee-her-pants terrified. But now she was panicked too. She could feel the emotion's subversive effects twanging over her nerves, obliterating her thought processes, burning away her ability to reason.

She realized she was hyperventilating when bright spots danced in front of her eyes. But she couldn't make herself calm down and breathe. *So much to lose. So much to lose.* There was no oxygen in the air. There was no—

Eeeeerrrrtttt! The van's tires squealed like a dying animal as the vehicle rocked to a stop in front of the souvenir shop. Penni peeked around the pillar in time to see the cargo door slide open and Dan—beautiful, wonderful, *alive* Dan—beckon to her with an extended hand. "Now, Penni!" he commanded.

She hesitated as Chelsea reached through the driver's side window to lay down covering fire. *One bullet. That's all it will take to—*

"You can do it, babe." Dan's steady voice and glowing green eyes cut through the darkness. The combination was just the impetus she needed to stop crouching like a coward and get her ass moving. With a little cry that was an unintelligible prayer for mercy, she flung herself from behind the safety of the post and stumbled down the stairs straight into Dan's waiting arms.

He caught her up against his chest, holding her tight even as he slammed the door shut and bellowed, "Step on it, Chels!"

Chelsea stomped on the gas and the van fishtailed out of the square to the squeal of approaching sirens, bullets slamming into the bumper, and Dan whispering into her ear, "Jesus Christ, Penni. You almost got yourself killed."

Chapter Twelve

DAN KNEW CHELSEA WAS DRIVING LIKE A BAT OUT OF HELL down the streets of Cusco. He knew Winterfield was wailing and Zoelner was yelling at him to *shut up or I'll give you something to scream about!* He knew Penni's arms were around his neck as he braced them on the floor between the driver's seat and the first row of rear bucket seats where Winterfield and Zoelner were sitting.

But it all felt very surreal, like it wasn't happening in real time and he was stuck in a parallel universe. Some place that existed between the past and the present. When Penni had peeked around that post, ruby-red blood running down her face, his mind had been flash-fried back to another time, another place, and another woman he'd loved who'd been covered in blood and dead in his arms. He'd nearly lost it. His sanity, that is. He'd almost gone stark raving mad in an instant at the thought that he'd come so very close to losing another one.

"Dan?" Penni squeaked. "Ease up!"

And suddenly he was catapulted out of that weird in-between microcosm and back into the world of chaos and sound. Chelsea powered through gears like a bona fide NASCAR driver. The rubber on the van's tires squealed against the cobblestone streets. Zoelner slapped a hand over Winterfield's mouth, digging his weapon into the guy's ribs. And Penni was a warm, living, breathing presence—*thank you, sweet Jesus!*—in his arms.

He realized two things when his gray matter stopped trying on a straitjacket. The first was that Penni was wiggling to escape his embrace because he was squeezing her to him with every ounce of his strength, and was probably close to crushing her spine to dust. The second was that, during his moment of insanity, he'd compared her to his wife, to a woman he'd loved more than life, to a woman he'd given his body, heart, and soul to.

"Dan!" she squealed again, squirming with growing fervor.

"Shit!" he said. "Sorry."

Forcing himself to relax, he released her just as Chelsea took a corner on two wheels. Penni tumbled back into his embrace—which was fine by him; that's where he wanted her anyway—just as an emergency vehicle buzzed by them. The kooky, foreign-sounding *bee-doo-bee-doo-bee-doo* of the siren pierced their eardrums at the same time red and blue lights flashed inside the van.

Dan held still, waiting to see if the authorities were after them or if the Cusco five-oh were simply on their way to the square where all hell had broken loose. When the sirens quickly echoed into the distance, he blew out a blustery sigh. They did *not* have time to mess around with the local *policia*, waiting for the U.S. government to intervene on their behalf before they would be allowed to spirit Winterfield back to the States. It would be far better, and so much less hassle, if they could simply blow this joint before anyone was the wiser.

So far, so good…

Cradling Penni in his lap, he lifted her chin and used the soft cotton cuff of his jacket to wipe some of the blood from her face. "Shit, Penni…" He choked on his heart because it seemed to have taken up permanent residence in his throat. "What happened? Did one graze you?"

"What?" She blinked up at him, her eyes big and luminous in the lights of the street lamps strobing by the windows at a dizzying rate.

Chelsea laid on the horn and yelled out the open window, calling some poor pedestrian a jackass. Then she turned and quickly looked at Penni. "She's hit?" They were still wearing their mics, so every word was public fodder. "How bad is it?"

Dan ignored Chelsea and wiped more blood from Penni's face, gritting his teeth. This beautiful, courageous woman had taken a bullet to… Wait. No. There was only a small cut under her right eye. Relief hit him so fast he felt dizzy. Or maybe that was because Chelsea squealed around another corner.

Once Penni didn't have to hold on to him, the back of the driver's seat, and anything else to keep from sliding around on the floor of the vehicle, she glanced down at his sleeve. Seeing the stain, she reached trembling fingers up to her cheek to investigate. To his complete surprise, she chuckled—*chuckled*—and shook her head.

"I thought I was *crying*," she said, wonder and something that sounded strangely like satisfaction lacing her voice.

"Huh?" That seemed to be his word of the day.

"During the gunfight," she explained. "I felt this hot wetness running down my face and I thought it was tears. Thought I was being a total skootch." *Skootch?*

Oh, he did so love her Brooklynisms. "But I must've been cut by one of the flying chunks of concrete when the post was taking a beating."

Taking a beating. From goddamned bullets*!*

"Damn, Penni," he cursed, pulling her back to him and breathing in her delicate scent. Needing to assure himself once more that she was safe and solid and alive. "Seeing you there, spraying rounds like you were Rambo—"

"Rambina," she interrupted, her lips moving against his ear and her arms winding around his neck. "Let's hear it for the girls."

"Hear! Hear!" Chelsea concurred.

"Nearly gave me a heart attack," he finished because he had to get this next part out. "Don't *ever* do that again."

"Oh?" she whispered as another police cruiser zoomed by them, its siren bleating off into the night. "You mean don't ever save your ass again?"

And although he would not have thought it was possible at a time like this, he found himself chuckling. "You're a grade-A smart-ass, Penelope Ann DePaul. Anyone ever tell you that?"

"As a matter of fact, they have. And thank you for reiterating. Because I take being labeled a grade-A smart-ass as a compliment."

He snorted and squeezed her tighter because…well, just because he could.

"And don't act like you don't like it." Her breath feathered against his cheek and ear. She wanted this part to stay just between them.

So did he when he whispered, "I more than like it, woman."

And then as if his words thrilled her—or either she

just couldn't help herself—she gently kissed his ear-lobe. It was sweet, tender, in stark contrast to their hell-bent-for-leather race down the streets of Cusco. And it had that warm glow he'd felt earlier, that flicker of hope, replacing the icy cold fist of fear that had kept him in a choke hold ever since he'd been lying on the ground beside the fountain, watching her rain hot lead into the dark corner where the mysterious shooter had been doing his or her damnedest to fill them all full of extra holes.

As if Zoelner was reading his mind, he asked, "Who was that fuckass taking potshots at us? Kozlov? Did he get out of his restraints?"

When Chelsea skidded off the city streets and onto the road that would take them to the airport, Dan and Penni slammed into the back of the driver's seat. Automatically, Dan's hand went up to protect her head, which meant his shoulder took the brunt of the blow. The socket ached. His skin would most certainly be bruised. But he barely noticed either. All he cared about was that Penni didn't sustain one more injury.

Another image of her face, stark white except where the blood stained it red, superimposed itself over the memory of his wife in the first seconds after her death. But he was able to push the soul-shredding vision away before it got the better of him, before his stomach turned upside down and he lost his dinner, and before he was sucked back into that surreal in-between world where the past meshed with the present, and remorse sunk its teeth into him until all he wanted was a bottle—or two—of whiskey.

"Well?" Zoelner asked again. "Did anyone get a look at the shooter?"

"I didn't see who it was," Dan said. "But I doubt it was Kozlov. Unless—"

"Three minutes to ETA," Chelsea interrupted, her usually husky tone now sharp with surging adrenaline.

Penni shifted against him, turning her head toward Zoelner. "But who else would it be if it wasn't Kozlov?"

"You're all idiots!" Winterfield snarled, holding his wounded arm and rocking slightly in the bucket seat like a guy in some serious pain…or one who was out of his ever-lovin' mind. It was hard to tell the difference.

And for a man who'd sent the entire world into a tizzy, Luke Winterfield was remarkably…well, unremarkable. With mousy brown hair, a scraggly goatee, and wire-framed glasses, he certainly didn't look like the kind of guy who would be the target of an international manhunt. Quite the contrary. He looked like he should be wearing a pocket protector and working for Google.

"You have no idea who you're dealing with!" he finished, his voice cracking like a pubescent teenager's.

"We know *exactly* who we're dealing with!" Zoelner thundered. "A traitor. A jackass Judas. A motherfucking *scumbag*."

"Not me." Winterfield's eyes were huge and wild behind the lenses of his glasses. "Him! You led him right to me and now…" He started panting, rocking faster. "He's going to kill us all! He's going to put a bullet in each of our brains and—" He grabbed Zoelner's wide lapels and yanked until the two men were nose to nose. "We're dead!" Winterfield screeched. "We're all dead! You just don't know it yet!"

Dan exchanged a quick look with Penni at the same time Zoelner said, "Dude, you are completely corked."

"I'm not crazy," Winterfield said, releasing Zoelner and going back to his rocking. "I'm not crazy. I'm not crazy."

His repetition pretty much proved that the guy was, in fact, nuttier that a shithouse rat.

"What the hell?" Chelsea said. "The gate's locked!"

Dan craned his head around the seat and over the console. Sure enough. Not just locked. *Chained* and locked. *Goddamnit!*

"I told my contacts to make sure they opened it," he growled, annoyed, digging in his hip pocket for his phone. *What the hell am I paying them for?*

"Wouldn't it be quicker just to pick the lock?" Penni asked.

"Forget it," Chelsea said, throwing the van in reverse. After she'd gone some distance, she slammed the van into gear and revved the engine. "Okay, kiddies. Hold on to your hats. This next part will be a doozy!"

As if the entire ride hadn't already been a doozy? Dan shoved one boot against the metal leg of the passenger chair bolted into the van's frame and braced the other on the leg of the bucket seat. Tightening his hold on Penni, he palmed the back of her head and turned her face into his neck. He could feel her holding her breath. He did the same, closing his eyes and gritting his jaw as Chelsea stood on the gas. The wheels of the van spun, squealing and burning rubber. Then the whole vehicle shot forward. *Wait for it. Wait for it…*

Crash!

Chelsea plowed into the gate. When the metal of the van's front grill hit the metal of the gate's center posts, it sounded like the world was ending. Then with a mighty *bang*, the gate ripped away from its hinges and somersaulted over the roof of the van. Suddenly they were freewheeling across the grassy expanse that lined the closed airport's single runway, bouncing over uneven earth, being shaken around so much Dan felt like that Polaroid picture Outkast sang about.

Winterfield screamed like a... Well, Dan was about to say "girl," but that would be an insult to the two fierce, fearless woman in the vehicle with him. Zoelner cursed, trying to keep his seat and his weapon steady on Winterfield. And Penni tightened her hold around Dan's waist.

"Y'okay?" he grunted, trying to make sure he provided as much of a buffer between her and the hard seats and floor as possible.

"Yee-haw," she whispered against his throat, and *damnit*, he was smiling again. Fierce, fearless, sassy, with a monster set of balls. The more he was around Penni, the more he wanted to *stay* around her.

Chelsea never hesitated, pedal to the metal until finally the wheels found the edge of the tarmac and the ride evened out. Before Dan could catch his breath, the little CIA agent stood on the brakes and the van slipped into a sideways skid that seemed to last an eternity. The squeal of the tires sent tremors up his spine. The smell of burning rubber filled the interior of the vehicle until he almost choked on it. He didn't know how the hell Chelsea was able to keep the van from tipping over onto its side, but the vehicle finally came to a rocking stop, fully upright. She switched off the engine, and for a couple of heartbeats, the only sound was the *tick, tick, tick* of the cooling engine.

"Nice driving, Danica Patrick." He puffed out a breath.

Through the cargo window he could see the tail numbers on the Beechcraft King Air twin-turboprop plane *el Jefe* had secured for them when he initially tasked them with bringing in Winterfield. Dan and Zoelner had needed the aircraft to quickly hop around South America without having to wait on military transports or civilian flights. *Pays to have friend in high places.* And though the little King Air wouldn't get them all the way home—it didn't have the fuel capacity to make the entire trip—it could still get them headed in the right direction.

And if the airport crew had come through, which they *should* have, considering the mammoth retainer Dan had slid them under the table in the case of just such an event, then the little plane should be fueled, fired, and ready to rock.

As in most parts of the world, money was a universal language when you wanted a few laws or rules broken. Then again, maybe he was putting too much stock in the ground crewmen. After all, they'd failed to open the gate and—

His thoughts were cut off when Chelsea slammed out of the van at the same time Zoelner slid open the cargo door. Dan found himself staring into the wide-eyed faces of the crewmen. He didn't know if they were more taken aback that he hadn't simply called them to open the gate, that the van they were in was riddled with bullet holes, or that three out of the five passengers inside were bloody and bruised while one of the passengers—Zoelner—was making no bones about the weapon in his hand.

Chelsea ripped open the van's rear doors, shouldering his backpack, her satchel, and Penni's purse and trotting toward the steps of the King Air. Dan urged Penni from the van and hopped out after her. The first thing he noticed was the wind. It was absolutely *howling*. And the lights of the airport showed ominous black clouds roiling overhead, obscuring the tops of the surrounding mountains. *Great. Perfect. Another case of fuck-all bad timing.*

Hunching deeper into his jacket, he turned to Penni. "Get on the plane," he yelled above the turboprop's rumbling engines. The ground crew *had* come through with that part of the deal, at least. So he hadn't thrown *all* his good money after bad. *Another silver lining.* He was two-for-two in that department this evening.

"I'll stay—"

"I'll be right behind you!" he promised.

She searched his face and he could tell she wanted to stick by his side.

"Go on." He grabbed her shoulder, turning her and swatting her ass toward the plane.

She yelped and rubbed her delightful derriere while scowling over her shoulder. "It's a good thing I like you, you big Neanderthal!"

He winked and watched her trot toward the King Air, the wind blowing her silky hair every which way. Chelsea met her at the top of the plane's stairs, ushering her inside. Once he was satisfied she was safe and sound, he turned to see Zoelner shove at Winterfield.

"Move it!" Zoelner yelled.

Winterfield adamantly shook his head, remaining glued to the bench seat. Zoelner shoved his pistol into the traitor's face and thundered, "Out of the vehicle, asshole!"

"Fuck you!" Winterfield screeched. "If I get out of this van, I'm a dead man!" And like a toddler refusing bath time, Winterfield curled his fingers around the lip of the bucket bench and braced his sneakers against the seats in front of him.

Despite the wind whipping Dan's shaggy hair around his face, he saw the look Zoelner shot him. It said, *Can you believe this guy?*

"Time for a few come-along techniques," Dan advised, ducking his chin close to the mic on his jacket so he wouldn't have to yell. "A little well-placed pain always goes a long way."

Zoelner bobbed his chin and dug a thumb in the wound on Winterfield's arm. Winterfield screamed like the spineless sissy he was, but refused to release his hold on the seat. And it was like the world was conspiring against them, because right at that moment, the sky opened up. Frigid rain sheeted from the dark heavens and cut like sharp icicles into the exposed skin on Dan's face and neck.

Okay. Enough is enough!

"Jack Bauer his ass!" he hollered at Zoelner. "We don't have time for this shit!"

Zoelner gritted his jaw and twisted his thumb in Winterfield's injury. When that didn't work, he clocked Winterfield in the jaw. That did it. Winterfield howled, releasing his hold on the seat, and Zoelner shoved him out the door. But before he could hustle the traitor toward the waiting plane, the strangest thing happened. A black truck Dan was pretty sure he'd seen parked on a side street near the square—it was memorable because its bed was stacked with all manner of garden equipment, rakes, and hoes, and whatnot—came screaming toward them down the tarmac.

But that wasn't the strange part.

Or…at least it wasn't the *strangest* part.

The strangest part was the guy hanging out the driver's side window. His face was obscured by the buckets of rain pelting him unmercifully, but what *wasn't* obscured was the weapon he was aiming right at them…

Chapter Thirteen

THE LIZARD PART OF DAN'S BRAIN REGISTERED THE DANGER ahead of his rational mind. His Bersa was out and in his hand before he had time to think about making the move. He had already pulled his trigger when their mysterious assailant's first round slammed into the side of the van not six inches from Winterfield's head.

Winterfield screamed. Zoelner cursed. And the sound of gunfire had the three crewmen diving beneath the van.

"Get to the plane!" Dan yelled to Zoelner and it occurred to him that, in keeping with the night's theme, he'd channeled a little Arnold Schwarzenegger à la the classic film *Predator*. He very clearly remembered the scene where the Governator yelled, *Get to the choppa!* It played through his head as he squeezed his trigger again, satisfied when this round slammed into the truck's front windshield.

It was hard as hell to hit a moving target in perfect conditions. And these were *not* perfect conditions. His face and hands were already numb from the stinging cold. Icy rain slipped beneath his collar to slide down his back, making it feel like he'd received an electrical jolt.

"Move it!" Zoelner shoved at Winterfield with one hand, the other occupied by his Beretta as it barked out round after round in the direction of the advancing truck. They hustled across the tarmac in a classic scoot-and-shoot maneuver. But they still needed cover. Clearly the driver's target was Winterfield because another bullet dug into the runway not a foot away from the traitor's feet.

Employing the slow breathing technique he'd perfected as a SEAL, Dan was able to control his heart rate and stress hormone levels as he dropped down to one knee. He only had three slugs left in his clip. Which meant every single one needed to count. Closing one eye, blinking away the frigid water that clung to his lashes, he took a quick aim and fired. The little Bersa jerked in his hand, the .38 bullet flying true.

Bull's-eye! The truck's left front tire blew, the rubber shredding apart, rolling under the rear wheel, and leaving nothing but the bare rim to spark against the blacktop of the tarmac. It forced the driver to duck inside to steady the vehicle as it lurched violently, spilling half of the gardening equipment onto the edge of the runway with a mighty clatter.

Chelsea materialized in the open doorway of the plane, lifted her little Springfield XD-S 9 mm, and started wildly peppering the tarmac, the grass at the edge of the tarmac, and the truck's front bumper with lead. *What the…?* A quick glance showed her glasses were beaded with raindrops. The woman couldn't see a damn thing, but that wasn't stopping her from letting the bullets fly. Orange flashes blinked from the end of her muzzle, and between the *boom-boom* of Zoelner's Beretta, the *pop-pop* of her Springfield, and the loud roar of the rain falling from the low-hanging clouds, the air around Dan was a wall of sound.

It occurred to him then that a firefight was a bizarre thing…

For the untrained or unprepared, it was like hell on earth, so chaotic and quick it precluded the ability to make rational, reasonable decisions. So loud, so disorienting, that a person was reduced to their animal self, relying purely on instinct: fight, flight, or freeze. Take the ground crew, for example, cowering under the van instead of doing the smart thing, which would be to beat feet until they were hell and gone from the range of the weapons.

But for those few folks who'd survived the crucible of war, who were battle-hardened and used to the exchange of deadly gunfire, it was just the opposite. Whizzing bullets put everything in perspective. And the thing Dan realized as the world slowed to a series of halcyon images like a movie reel that was skipping frames—Chelsea grimacing as the weapon barked in her hand. Next frame, Zoelner slamming in a new clip and chambering the first round. Next frame, the driver of the vehicle fishtailing this way and that, still headed straight for them—was that for the first time in years he cared whether he lived or died.

After his wife's death, he'd tried his damnedest to join her by drinking himself into an early grave. Then, when his liver refused to give out on him, he'd sobered up. But even though he'd stopped actively seeking a way to punch his last ticket, it's not like he'd clung to life either.

The truth was, when he laid his head on his pillow at night, he didn't much care one way or the other if he woke up the next day. Life was just something to get through. And he whiled away the hours, the days by making sure he had a job to do. A duty to perform. A task to complete. It was nothing more and nothing less than that.

But now? Oh, *now* he had something to *live* for. Some*one* to live for. Penni and her big, dark eyes. Penni and her smart, sexy mouth. Penni and her hot woman's needs. She made him excited for the future. And, by God, if he'd gotten to this point only to kick it on a Peruvian runway in the middle of a rainstorm, he was going to be beyond pissed.

Eeeerrrrrtttt! He didn't have time for any more grand epiphanies because the driver of the truck screamed to a stop not forty yards away.

Who the hell is *this guy?* Dan wondered as he ducked to yell, "Make a run for it when you can!" to the three terrified men facedown and lying side by side like sardines under the van. Jumping to his feet, he raced after Zoelner and Winterfield, taking advantage of the cover fire Chelsea was providing and happy as could be that Penni—otherwise known as Señorita Weaponless—was having to sit this one out. His didn't think his heart could take watching another episode of her going all Rambo… uh…*Rambina* tonight.

Zip! A bullet whizzed by his ear when he jumped onto the plane's first step. His heart skipped a beat at the feel of the displaced air, but he barely had time for a silent *That was a close one* because Chelsea yelled, "Reloading!" and he glanced up to see her reach back for the clip in Penni's hands.

So much for sitting this one out, goddamnit! Penni was on her knees on the floor directly behind Chelsea, Chelsea's satchel open wide in front of her, another clip up and at the ready should the little CIA agent ask for it.

He should have known she couldn't stay out of it. The brave, beautiful, *beyond* consternating woman!

Winterfield dove past Chelsea and into the interior of the plane at the same time Dan and Zoelner spun to take up the slack left by Chelsea's reloading.

The driver's side door of the truck was open and the man, whoever he was—not Kozlov, Dan could make out that much through the gray haze of the rain—was using it as cover, turkey peeking around the side to take pot-shots at them. Dan sighted down the Bersa's little barrel, aiming for Mystery Man's ankles, knowing it was a long shot, but still…he had to try. His last two rounds needed to count for something more than simply forcing the guy to keep his head down.

Blowing out a steadying breath, Dan lined up his shot and… *Bam! Bam! Click! Click!* The little .38 was officially dry and he'd missed the shooter's ankles by a mere inch.

Hell's bells! "I'm out!" he yelled.

"I'll cover you!" Zoelner bellowed as one of his rounds hit the windshield on the driver's side door and shattered the glass. Dan saw his chance while the shooter was ducking. Careful to stay below Zoelner's and Chelsea's lines of sight, he half ran, half crawled up the remaining three steps.

Inside the plane was warm, dry, and strangely quiet compared to the chaos outside. He swiped a hand over his face and hair, squeegeeing away the freezing water. He saw Winterfield curled on the floor by one of the seats like the coward he was and Penni scrounging around in Chelsea's satchel, no doubt searching for another clip like the courageous warrior woman *she* was.

It took every bit of willpower he possessed not to yank her with him as he scrambled toward the cockpit.

But Chelsea and Zoelner needed her, and he couldn't sacrifice them just because he was terrified of history repeating itself and losing the woman that he… well, *whatever* it was that he felt for her. And since he *couldn't* drag her with him, the next best thing he could do was get the plane moving out of range of Mr. Mystery's bullets.

He slid into the pilot's seat just as Chelsea yelled, "I *told* you guys we shouldn't have used Voldemort's real name. I knew it would be bad luck!"

Bad timing and *bad luck. It's like Learn Your Fuckin' Lesson Day around here,* he thought, eyes zooming over the console, checking the gauges even as he was strapping in and slipping on his headset. Flight controls were free and correct. Altimeter was set. Flaps? *Check.* Tanks? *Full.* Parking brake? He flipped down the toggle switch. And when he saw that his mixture was a full-rich, just as it should be, he blew into his wet, frozen hands and reached for the controls.

"Let's blow this Popsicle stand!" he yelled into his mic so the others would know they were about to start taxiing.

Fear and purpose fueled his movements as he powered up. The plane responded like a dream, engines providing thrust as he used his feet to steer them down the tarmac and away from the man in the truck. The rain sheeted off the front windshield as the wipers worked like crazy to combat it. The runway lights were a dim blur. The radio squawked with air traffic controller jabber, but it wasn't coming from the local tower, as it was closed for the night.

Cusco airport was remote enough that it only saw a handful of flights each day, and those stopped long before sundown. So the good news? He didn't have to worry about air traffic on takeoff. The bad news? It was going to be a hell of a ride. The wind had to be blowing damn near 20 mph.

The *boom* and the *pop* of Zoelner and Chelsea's weapons came to an abrupt halt once he'd gone thirty yards down the runway. And when he heard the stairs fold in, the door close with a *thunk,* and the light on his console told him the door's lock was engaged, he wiped a hand over his wet brow, wincing when he inadvertently touched his wound. A second later, Zoelner, drenched and shivering, slid into the copilot's chair.

"We good?" Dan asked him. Just two words that conveyed about ten separate questions.

Zoelner knew what he was after. "The ladies are fine. I'm fine. Winterfield is still alive and still a fucking traitor. Let's get the hell out of here."

"I couldn't agree more," Dan said, turning the plane around when he reached the end of the runway. A quick look to his left told him the wind sock was standing straight and pointing fifteen degrees off center. The rain was still coming down by the bucketful. And the mountain peaks were completely obscured by clouds. He and Zoelner were going to have to rely on their gauges instead of their eyes.

"This is going to be one suck-ass takeoff," Zoelner said after checking the conditions outside and sneaking a peek at the wind sock.

Dan smiled. Getting his pilot's license had been part of his recovery. Initially he'd done it because it accomplished a few important things. One, it had filled a hole that had been left in the Black Knights' personnel. They'd *needed* another fixed-wing pilot besides Zoelner. There had been too many times in the last few years when the Knights had had to rely on contracted pilots to get them to and from where they were going. And in their line of work, where *mum's the word*, that was a problem.

Two, it had given Dan a goal to shoot for. Which, let's face it, he'd desperately needed. *You know, that whole not-caring-if-I-wake-up thing.*

Three, it kept him away from the bottle since flying drunk or hungover was out of the question. He was an asshole but he'd never be *that* much of an asshole.

And four, when he had the yoke in hand and he was up in the clear blue, the world seemed to come into focus, and all his problems, all his hurts and regrets seemed… less somehow. Smaller somehow. Maybe because at twenty thousand feet, the *world* was smaller.

But regardless of why he'd originally decided to get his license, the truth was he loved flying. And in the last dozen months he'd logged over a thousand hours through rain, sleet, snow, and gale-force winds. He was like the motherfucking U.S. Postal Service—nothing kept him from his rounds. And not to toot his own horn or anything, but he was a damn good pilot. *A natural*, according to his instructors.

So even though Zoelner was right that this takeoff was going to suck something fierce, Dan had no doubt that between the two of them, they could pull it off without a hitch. Chelsea wasn't as convinced.

"I don't like the sound of a suck-ass takeoff," she piped up from the back, their mics still keeping them all connected.

"I second that opinion," Penni's dear, sweet voice thrummed through Dan's ears.

He could have told Penni any number of truths right then, starting with *We don't have a lotta options* to *I'd sooner die than put you in any more danger*, but what he ended up going with was, "Don't worry, ladies. We got this." He winked over at Zoelner and saw one corner of the former CIA agent's mouth twitch. Though neither one of them liked to admit it, they absolutely *lived* for this shit.

He heard the ladies grumbling through his earpiece, their voices competing with the squawk and the chatter of the radio. And even though he would have loved to continue to listen to Penni, to have her voice in his head, he and Zoelner couldn't afford any distractions. Dan flipped off the power on his mic and saw Zoelner do the same. Then he reached under his headset, pulled out his earpiece, and stuffed it in the hip pocket of his sopping wet jeans before grabbing the throttle and shoving it forward. He got a little giddy when the thrum of the twin-turbo engines shoved them back in their seats.

The King Air ate up the runway like the aerial beast she was, gaining momentum by the second, the front edges of her wings gripping the air, impatient for lift. They'd just about reached takeoff speed when Mr. Mystery came barreling down the runway toward them. The truck's bare rim sparked against the tarmac and flashed yellow through the driving rain.

"Motherfucker!" Zoelner yelled, his knuckles white around the copilot's yoke. Water dripped from his hair and his ears as the Beechcraft shimmied and shook in anticipation of jumping into the air. "Whoever this guy is, he's a damned lunatic!"

Dan did not disagree, and he could not wait to leave the bastard behind. "Hold on!" he yelled, knowing his voice carried through the open cockpit door. And to borrow a line from Chelsea, "This one's gonna be a doozy!"

George slammed on the brakes, roaring his rage and frustration through the truck's broken window as the plane zoomed over his head. He laid on his trigger, aiming for the engines, but his clip was dry and he was forced to duck back inside to escape the nauseating scent of aviation fuel and the hot wash of air that buffeted the truck from side to side. He watched helplessly, impotently, as the plane climbed higher and higher into the night sky. Its red taillight blinking, taunting him when it disappeared into the rain and clouds overhead.

"Fuck!" he screamed, slapping the steering wheel over and over until his palm ached and his bones creaked warningly. "Bloody fucking hell!"

An image of his daughter flashed in front of his eyes. *Bella. Beautiful, sweet Bella.* She would pay for this mistake. He didn't know how, he didn't know when, but he knew it would involve pain. Spider would make sure of that. He he almost vomited up the bean salad he'd eaten at the bar.

He had not banked on the foursome splitting up back at the square. He had imagined they would all be on site to apprehend Winterfield, and his plan had been to catch them by surprise and take out the lot in one go. When only the men arrived on scene, he'd had to make a split-second decision. Wait and follow, and hope the quartet met up again so he could kill them together with Winterfield as he'd intended. Or take his shots when he had them and count on locating and dispatching the women afterward.

He'd gone with the second option. Unfortunately, it had turned out to be the wrong choice. Because *he'd* been the one taken by surprise by the former Secret Service agent who'd hammered his location with gunfire, forcing him to duck and cover. So now not only were Winterfield and the two blokes still alive, but both women as well. Bringing the total up to *five* witnesses and *five* loose ends.

Bella…my sweet, innocent Bella…

A lump grew in his throat like a metastasizing cancer, threatening to strangle him. He wondered when exactly his life had turned to shit. Was it the moment he received a surprise leave from Her Majesty's Royal Air Force and came home to find Bella's duplicitous whore of a mother in bed with his squadron leader? Or was it the instant he killed them in a red-eyed rage?

No. In reality, it was neither of those.

His life had turned to shit the second he tossed his revolver in the Thames.

Because some of Spider's "employees" had been in the shadows—doing *what* exactly George had never discovered, probably disposing of a body or something equally sinister—and they'd fished the gun from the murky water the minute George walked away.

Yes, that was it. That was the moment. Because even though George escaped being convicted of the crime— without the murder weapon, there was no solid proof he'd been the one to pull the trigger—he hadn't escaped Spider's web. He'd been caught up, trapped, and forced to quit the RAF and join Spider's minions, or else Spider would hand over the weapon to the police, sealing George's fate and leaving Bella all alone in the world.

But perhaps being alone is better than living with the shadow of Spider's wrath hanging over her head. If he could go back, he'd do it all differently.

"Fuck!" he screamed again, resuming his abuse of the steering wheel, trying to see a way out, and finding none. But just as he was about to give in to the fear and regret, the sorrow and shame, an idea occurred and his heart thundered with renewed vigor.

Snatching his mobile from the pocket of his overcoat, he shoved the stolen truck into gear. He'd managed to hot-wire the rusting old banger not thirty seconds after the group had careened out of the square with Winterfield in tow—another handy skill he'd picked up since coming to work for Spider. Pressing on the gas, he gritted his teeth when the bare rim screeched against the tarmac. He headed straight for the van and the ground crewmen who scrambled from beneath it. At the same time, he dialed Benton.

"Is it finished?" Benton asked once the call was connected.

"No!" was all George allowed on the subject, trying to see through the shattered windshield and the frigid rain blowing in through the broken window. "I need you to monitor air-traffic control for a flight with tail number…" He rattled off the twin-turboprop's designation, raising his voice above the sound of the wind and the truck's engine. The little plane didn't have the fuel capacity to get Winterfield and his captors all the way back to the United States.

If George was lucky, he could follow them to whichever Central or South American airport they were forced to land in and kill them while they were refueling or waiting to catch another flight. It was a long shot, but it was a shot. And he had to take it. "I'm going to steal a plane and go after them! But I'll need you to find out where they're headed!"

"This does not sound at all reassuring," Benton said, censure in his voice. "What happened, Georgie Boy?"

"Later!" George growled. "Just do your Boy with the Dragon Tattoo routine and track that flight!"

He hung up before Benton could say anything more. Standing on the brakes, he slid to a jolting stop, the truck's bumper barely an inch from the van's. In the next instant, he was slapping on his cap and slamming in a new clip.

"Get that Pilatus PC-12 gassed, greased, and ready to fly," he barked at the trio, gesturing with his weapon toward the plane parked in front of the nearest hangar. It was smaller than the Beechcraft twin-turbo. But it was just as fast and could cover the same number of miles before needing to stop to refuel.

"No hablo inglés!" one of them yelled.

Through the rain dripping from the brim of his hat, George aimed and put a bullet right between the tosser's eyes. The man's lifeless body crumpled onto the tarmac, blood mixing with the freezing rain to form an inky puddle behind his decimated skull.

The two remaining crewmen blinked down at the

corpse before turning dark, terrified eyes on George. "Either of you two claim not to *hablo* English?" he asked.

"I speak English, sir," one of the men said, the shorter, fatter one.

"Good." George nodded, shivering as a drop of icy rain snuck down the front of his coat and shirt. "Then do as I say or join your friend there." Of course, even if the fat man *did* do what George said, he'd still end up like his friend. But George would save that little surprise for later.

Chapter Fourteen

2,600 feet over Colombia
Saturday, 12:10 a.m.

"YOU STUPID BITCHES! YOU'RE BOTH DEAD, DO YOU KNOW that? Ow! Watch it, you ham-handed cunt!"

For a while there when Dan and Zoelner struggled to control the little plane against the turbulence kicked up by the storm and the wind sheers around the mountains, Penni had been absolutely green, we're talking so green Kermit the Frog would have been envious of her hue. And she was pretty sure her fingerprints were permanently embedded in the armrests of her seat. But eventually, what seemed like eons later and after she'd made about a dozen grabs for the barf bag but never actually barfed, they'd gained altitude and the ride evened out.

A couple of quick breaths of relief, and she and Chelsea had unbuckled so they could tend to Winterfield's wound. *Can't have the traitor dying of blood loss before he's interrogated and made to stand trial, don't you know?* But he'd started to fight them and then he'd started doing that rocking thing, and Penni had whispered to Chelsea, "I think this guy is about to go forty on us all."

"What does that mean?" Chelsea asked from the corner of her mouth, giving Winterfield the stink-eye.

"It's what we in the boroughs say when someone

looks like they're thinking about climbing into a clock tower with a rifle."

"Ah." Chelsea nodded her agreement. "Well, since there aren't any clock towers around, I'm afraid he might try to go forty on the door and attempt his hand at flying without a parachute."

"So let's secure him to his seat and *then* we can check his bullet wound," Penni had suggested.

Which is exactly what they'd done. While Chelsea held her Springfield between the traitor's eyes, Penni did the honors of duct-taping his arms to the armrests and his legs to the metal braces of his seat. Of course the minute they used the scissors Chelsea had scrounged from Dan's backpack to cut away the sleeve of his jacket and his hooded sweatshirt so they could get a look at his arm, he'd started with the insults.

Penni had a pretty tough skin. Most New Yorkers did. But the c-word was the last straw as far as she was concerned. "I think we should tape his mouth too," she muttered, her lip curled back.

"Oh good," Chelsea said, taking the tape from her and using her teeth to rip off a six-inch strip. "I was going to suggest it myself, but thought you might consider it cruel and unusual punishment."

"Are you kidding me?" Penni's chin jerked back. "Riding a packed, un-air-conditioned train out to Coney Island in August is cruel and unusual punishment. Taping this bastard's filthy mouth shut is a gift to mankind. We should be canonized for the effort."

Winterfield started howling and throwing his head around, resuming his litany of name-calling. Really, it was enough to blister a sailor's ears. But with the two of them working together, they were able to wrestle the tape over his dirty, *dirty* mouth. He glared at them, his glasses knocked askew, his nostrils flaring.

"Anyone ever tell you it's not nice to call people names, you traitorous piece of scum-sucking shit?" Chelsea asked.

Penni snorted at the contradiction in Chelsea's question. She liked the little CIA agent. The woman was funny and smart and had proved she could straight-up Chuck Norris an eight-foot fence.

"Okay," Penni said, willing her stomach to gird itself. "Let's see what we're dealing with." With Winterfield subdued in every way except a good, solid whack upside the head—*a girl can dream*—Penni pulled the material away from the blood drying on his arm. She hesitated when she saw the wound for what it was. A scratch. Like, seriously. The bullet had *barely* grazed him.

"You've got to be kidding me." Chelsea's jaw slung open, disgust lacing her tone. "All that hullabaloo over this? I've cut myself worse shaving my armpits."

"I guess we should…clean it?" Penni suggested. *Or maybe put a Mickey Mouse Band-Aid over it and kiss it better?* Although someone would have to be holding a gun to *her* head to make her put her lips anywhere near Winterfield. The man made her want to hurl.

"Why don't you grab the first-aid kit out of my satchel, leave me some antiseptic wipes, and take the rest with you into the lavatory?" Chelsea proposed. "Your cheek could probably use more attention than this little…*nick*." She flicked a finger at Winterfield's wound.

"Mmm, *mmmmmph*, bwphhhh," Winterfield grunted, still trying to insult them from behind the tape.

More anxious to get away from Winterfield's zealous, duplicitous eyes than anything else, Penni quickly agreed to Chelsea's suggestion. Five minutes later she'd washed all the blood from her face. Using a couple of butterfly bandages, she closed the little cut and stood back to study her handiwork. She might have a small scar, but whatever. Scars added character, right?

Like my face needs any more character. She rubbed a finger over the bump on her nose. It was courtesy of her father's genetics. She'd hated it growing up. But ever since she lost him, she'd grown exceptionally partial to that bump. Every time she looked in the mirror, she saw a little of her father. A little of his French ancestry amid all the dark-eyed, dark-haired Italian blood she'd received from her mother.

Brushing a lock of hair behind her ear, she noticed her hands were shaking. Come to think of it, so were her knees. *In fact*, so were her *insides*. She plopped down on the lid of the toilet and used one hand to support her head while pressing the other to her quaking stomach.

Christ almighty! It suddenly hit her how close she'd come to losing…everything. Dan. Her future. Her *life*. The life she was—

"Penni?" Dan's voice sounded through the bifolding door, muffled by the loud hum of the twin-turbo engines. "Y'okay in there? Chelsea said you came in to clean your—"

Hopping to her feet, she pushed open the door and managed a wavering smile when she saw him standing outside. He was hunched down, too tall to stretch to his full height inside the plane's fuselage. His eyes were rimmed with red, no doubt from the stinging rain. The stubble on his chin was quickly maturing toward a manly, full-grown beard. And thick, brown blood crusted over the wound on his forehead and caked in his eyebrow.

Despite all that, or maybe because of it, it occurred to her she'd never seen a more gorgeous man. He looked exactly like what he was, a staunch defender, a fearless gladiator, a guy who'd taken on the world and come out the victor. A hero. *Her* hero.

And, *oh*, how she wanted to kiss his handsome face. Run her hands all over his warrior's body. Throw her arms around his neck, hug him close, and never let him go. Tell him all the things that she was scared to tell him. All the things she wanted because she wanted…so much. Too much?

Probably, her father's voice cautioned.

She recognized the truth in that one word. The last few hours had been crazy, intense, but nothing had changed since that moment yesterday evening when she stepped inside the big gates at Black Knights Inc. *Really? Was that just yesterday?* Nothing was any clearer, any more settled, any more *certain*.

So make things more certain. Tell him…

No. *No*. Now was not the time. When his mission was over, when Winterfield was delivered, *then* she'd tell him.

"Jesus, Penni," he said, rubbing a hand down his face. The calluses on his palm made a scratchy sound against the bristles of his beard. He reached and tenderly brushed his finger down her cheek, below her butterfly bandages. "I'm so sorry."

"F-for what?" she asked, her voice more breathless than she'd like. Her knees definitely more rubbery than she'd like. She was still experiencing the effects of her delayed shock. And that, combined with Dan's bone-melting touch, had her bracing herself with a hand on the little vanity.

"For dragging you into this mess," he told her. "For putting you in danger. For making you do something you were hoping you'd never hafta do again."

Her quivering stomach stood stock-still. Her trembling knees became steady as rocks. *How can he possibly know that? How can he...* "What do you mean?" she blurted.

"That's why you quit the Secret Service, right?" His eyes searched hers, and maybe it was the way the light was shining from the vanity, but she noticed for the first time how his lashes were nearly black near the lids and graduated to platinum blond at the tips. "Because the horror of...of..."

"The Assignment," she finished for him.

"Huh?" He cocked his head and she nearly smiled. She'd known even before she finished speaking that would be his response.

"That's what I've started calling Kuala Lumpur," she admitted, knowing her expression was a little sad. She couldn't help it. Thinking about Malaysia would always be bittersweet. She'd lost so much—her friends and colleagues and the future she'd always thought she wanted. But she'd gained so much too. A chance to know Dan and to forge a life she'd thought was fading beyond her reach. "The Assignment," she clarified. "Both words are capitalized."

"Ah." He nodded. "'Cause of its significance. I get it. I've lived through some shit that qualifies for all caps too."

Had he? She wanted to ask him to tell her about it. She wanted to ask him…so *many* things. She wanted to *know* so many things, to hear his lifetime's worth of stories and dreams and hopes and disappointments. She opened her mouth, but he shook his head as if jostling his mind back on topic.

"Anyway," he said, "I figured after that, you lost your…uh…I guess you'd say *stomach* for this kind of work." He ducked his chin, staring up at her from beneath his sandy eyebrows. "And then you come to me and *boom!* You're right back in the thick of it. Am I right?"

"Something like that," she admitted.

"I'm so sorry." He shook his head sorrowfully.

"Stop saying that," she warned him. "Or I'll have to smack you upside the head."

A smile flirted with his wonderful, delicious lips. Then he sobered. "So what'll you do now? For work, I mean."

Now! Tell him now!

She jumped when the command echoed through her head. The move caused Dan's brow to furrow. "Penni?" He put a hand on her arm. His palm was wonderfully warm. "What is it?"

What is it? Oh, let's see… Delayed shock. Two cross-hemisphere plane rides in less than twenty-four hours. A queasy stomach. A voice that kept popping up to give advice when she least wanted it. A beautiful, dear man who hadn't the first clue that she—

"Hey." He moved his hand from her forearm back to her face, gently rubbing his thumb along her cheek. "Tell me what's going on."

Nope. She wasn't going to do that until *after* he'd delivered Winterfield. That's what she'd decided and she was sticking to it, damnit!

Coward...

Yeah. Probably. But until then, until there was no excuse not to lay her heart open and suffer the consequences, she was determined to distract herself. To give her mind and heart and hands to tasks she could accomplish, to things that didn't scare the bejeezus out of her. Grabbing the front of his wet wool sweater, she pulled him into the cramped space.

"Ow," he said when he bumped his head on the top of the door.

"Mother-flippin' hell!" she cursed when he accidentally stomped on her toe.

"Oof!" he grunted when she instinctively jerked her foot out from under his boot and her knee came precariously close to his family jewels.

"Ouch!" she squawked when he went to protectively cup himself and accidentally elbowed her in the sternum.

"Shit! Sorry," he grumbled, trying to back up and wincing when the paper towel dispenser dug into his back. He bent forward to avoid it and head-butted her.

"Sonofa—" She went to grab her throbbing forehead and stabbed him under the chin with her fingernails.

He jerked away and banged the top of his head on the ceiling. "Ow!"

"Damnit, Dan. Stop moving," she told him. And fifteen seconds ago, she wouldn't have thought it was possible, but she was giggling like a schoolgirl, snorting and snickering and grinning up at his consternated face.

God, it felt good to laugh. Since losing her friends and colleagues, since waving good-bye to Dan, and since trying to come to terms with the new direction she was taking in life, she hadn't had much occasion to do it. *What's that saying? Oh yeah.* More's the pity. Because laughing at Dan, laughing *with* Dan felt... freeing, *healing*.

"I feel like we should be auditioning for the Three Stooges," he grumped, a lopsided grin pulling at his lips.

"*Two* Stooges," she corrected and dissolved into another round of giggles.

"You wouldn't think it was so funny if it was *your* back that was trying to become one with a towel dispenser," he growled. Mr. Growly Growlerton. He was leaning forward to avoid the dispenser in question, and his warm breath tickled her lips. Her laughter disappeared when her blood ignited and started burning through her veins.

"Carefully..." she told him, still smiling, biting her own lip to keep from biting his. That bottom pad was just so plump and delicious and tempting as it shined pink amid all his sandy brown beard stubble. "I want you to shuffle around and sit on the toilet lid."

"What?" He lifted the brow that wasn't caked with blood. "Why?" He looked at her askance. The twinkle in his green eyes said he thought maybe she was up for joining the Mile High Club.

Which, okay, she *totally* was. When it came to Dan, she was up for just about anything. But no matter how she racked her brain, calculating angles and gymnast-worthy positions, she just couldn't see how they could make it work in the confines of the tiny lavatory.

Another instance of "more's the pity."

"I need to clean up that wound." She motioned toward his forehead.

"It's nothing," he assured her in that *guy* way that said, *I'm a badass and wouldn't complain even if I were missing a limb.*

She tried not to roll her eyes. "Even so, it'll make *me* feel better if we get it bandaged."

"Sure, okay." He shrugged his shoulders. "But don't think I don't know what just happened." He shuffled a couple of inches toward the toilet. When the heavy muscles of his thighs and chest brushed along the front of her, her nipples tightened into painful buds.

It's because his clothes are wet and cold.

At least that's what she told herself for all of a half second. In all honesty, touching Dan always felt incredibly carnal. Sexy and intimate in a way she couldn't quite explain.

It's because we have a connection…

Now *that* was the truth. *Had* been the truth since the first moment they laid eyes on each other, and *definitely* since the first moment he touched her. She could still recall the jolt she got when he shook her hand and his long fingers closed around hers. It'd been like a lightning strike to her core. A warm, delicious bolt of electricity that woke up a part of her she hadn't realized was asleep.

But the question was, were they connected on something more than the physical level? *She* certainly felt like they were. In fact, she *knew* they were. But that didn't mean Dan would agree with—

"I am well-trained in the ways of you women," he continued, pulling her from her introspection.

"Ways of women?" She lifted a brow. "I haven't the faintest idea what you mean."

He'd finally managed to get around her to sit on the toilet lid. To combat the aching loss of not having him pressed against her length, she busied herself pulling the door closed. Then she dug some antiseptic wipes from the first-aid kit and stepped toward her patient.

"That whole *It will make me feel better* shtick is the oldest trick in the *Women's Guidebook to Men*," he explained. "Get us to do whatever is it you want by appealing to our chivalrous natures."

"What two-bit, traitorous hussy gave you a copy of the guidebook?" she demanded. When she planted her hands on her hips, her left elbow slammed into the wall and her right elbow smacked the tissue dispenser bolted above the sink. "Ouch!" She rubbed at her funny bones, feeling laughter welling inside her again.

The whole situation was veering toward the ridiculous. The ridiculous and the strangely…*comfortable*. She'd never been as natural, as much *herself* around any man as she was around Dan. It was like they had been old friends, maybe old *lovers* in another lifetime. Which brought her to the last thing this situation was, which was *hot*. Being in a confined space with Dan was always sensual and provocative and filled with a sort of suffocating sultriness. Like he was taking up all the air as well as all the space. Like the heat from his body was turning the wetness clinging to his clothes to steam.

She imagined herself ripping off his sweater and jeans so she could run her tongue over every stray drop of water that clung to his firm, tanned skin.

Mercy.

She refrained from fanning herself by bending forward. "This may sting a little," she warned, not surprised to hear her voice was not her own. It was much lower, huskier…dare she say *sexier*? Carefully, her hands still shaking—now with unrequited lust instead of shock— she swiped the antiseptic towelette over the blood near his cut.

"You never did answer my question," he said.

"Which question was that?"

"The one about what you're gonna do now that you've quit the Service."

"Oh." She tossed the soiled wipe into the little trash bin and grabbed a new one. "As soon as I sell my condo in DC, I'm moving back to Brooklyn." *Unless you think there's a reason I shouldn't?* The question was right there. On the tip of her tongue. But she bit it back because she didn't want to scare the crap out of him. "My uncle, the one I told you about, the recovering alcoholic, runs a security firm. He's already said I could work for him. It'll be nice. A regular ol' nine-to-five."

"Is he your dad's brother?" he asked as she used the new wipe to wash away some of the blood that had crusted near his hairline.

"Yeah." She frowned down at him. "Why?"

"Just wondered if it ran in the blood," he said.

"What?"

"The need to protect people."

"Oh." She furrowed her brow, considering. Her uncle ran a security firm. Her dad had been a cop. And she had been with the Secret Service. "Huh. I've never really thought about it that way. Yeah. I guess you're right. Must be in the blood. And speaking of blood… I've cleaned up all the dried blood *around* your wound. Now I need to clean the wound itself. Brace yourself."

Dan didn't utter a word, didn't suck in his breath, didn't hiss when the big, crusty scab came away to reveal the angry, slowly seeping laceration beneath. His stoic silence was the very opposite of Winterfield's overblown theatrics.

When Penni ducked her chin, she discovered the reason for his reticence. The front of her V-neck sweater was gaping open, and he was staring at her boobs with a hungry intensity that stole her breath. She played it off with a teasing snort, shaking her head even as her nipples twanged with sensation. It was like his heated gaze was a physical caress, the movement of his eyes over the lace-covered peaks the equivalent of a warm, wet tongue.

"See something you like, sailor?"

"Roger that." He licked his lips, not even pretending to repent for having been caught ogling her goodies. "Helps keep my mind off the…oh…ow…owy…pain." He added a blatant whine to his tone in an effort to gain her sympathy.

"Oh, and *now* who's using the oldest trick in the

Men's Guidebook to Women? Appealing to the Florence Nightingale in *my* nature?"

His eyes flashed up to her, sparkling devilishly, his hands sneaking up to grip her hips. *God, he's hot.* Both metaphorically and literally. "And here I was hoping I was being subtle," he said.

"If there's a subtle bone in your body," she told him—was it her imagination, or had the temperature inside the little room jumped ten degrees in the last ten seconds?—"I'll eat that tissue dispenser." She gestured over her shoulder.

"Is that a bad thing?" he asked, his thumbs rubbing circles on her hip bones. She imagined those thumbs rubbing in the same circular motion on a totally *different* part of her body. Heat bloomed over her skin, under her skin, coalescing low in her belly. She turned to grab another wipe. It was either that or she was going to find a way to join that Mile High Club, and damn the pulled muscles and sprained joints that would inevitably follow!

"Eating the tissue dispenser?" she asked, one brow raised. "Well, I imagine it'll cause some mad indigestion and probably won't—"

"That I'm not subtle about what I want," he interrupted, his voice wonderfully low. It made the tiny room seem even more intimate.

"D-did I say it was a bad thing?" she asked, putting the towelette to good use on his clean, slowly seeping wound while simultaneously searching through the first-aid kit for more butterfly bandages. You know, just to give her hands something to do other than sneak up under the hem of his sweater and run all over his corrugated belly and mile-wide chest. The iron-y smell of blood reached her nose, competing with Dan's clean scent and the harsh, medicinal aroma of the antiseptic.

"Some women like a little mystery in their men." He shrugged one big shoulder. "They like the *not knowing*. They think it's exciting."

"Pfft," she snorted, tossing the last wipe away and then carefully pulling the two halves of his wound together with one of the bandages. The cut could probably use a stitch or two, but she hadn't the skill or the stomach for *that* task. *Needles?* She shivered. *No, thank you.* "You mean some *girls* like it," she corrected. Her proximity to him made her head spin and her knees tremble with the desire to straddle him and rock herself to completion against the huge erection straining the front of his jeans.

He didn't even pretend to hide it from her when he shifted atop the toilet and her eyes automatically pinged down to his fly. "I-I…" She had to stop and lick her lips. Her throat had gone completely dry. "I stopped playing games, including hard to get, when I was in my twenties."

"Mmm," he grumbled.

Now he was Mr. Grumbly Grumbleton. She couldn't decide who she liked better. Growlerton or Grumbleton. They were both sexy as hell. Applying two more butterfly bandages, she used a tissue to wipe away the few drops of blood that had welled out of the wound. She was in the process of backing away to study her handiwork when Dan tightened his hands on her hips.

"You have no idea how glad I am to hear you say

that," he rumbled. Mr. Rumbly Rumbleton? "'Cause I don't believe in playing games either."

"So what *do* you believe in?" Her voice was now so hoarse it sounded like she'd been eating glass. Some people didn't have a poker face. *She* didn't have a poker voice.

"Oh, I believe in a lot of things," he whispered, a muscle ticking in his jaw beneath his beard stubble. It made the crescent-moon scar twitch.

"Like what?"

"Like buying American-made cars. Like fireworks on the Fourth of July. Like moms and dads who dance in the kitchen after the kids have gone to bed. Like the magic of moonlight. Like babies. Like love."

And now not only was her heart pounding and her blood running hot, but there was also a lump sitting in the middle of her throat. The things he believed in were so pure. So simple. And to hear them come out of the mouth of such a complex, mysterious man who operated every day in a complex and mysterious world just made them all the more poignant.

"I also believe in asking for what I want," he went on, a dark, carnal gleam in his eyes. He pulled a wad of gum from his mouth and tossed it in the little trash receptacle. *Uh-oh. That's telling.* A thrill skittered through her. "I'll even ask for it nicely," he continued, "just like you said."

She cocked her head.

"When we were standing on the street in Cusco and you told me I'd be amazed what asking nicely would get me," he clarified.

She swallowed. Or *gulped*, really. And even though

her lungs were working overtime, she couldn't catch her breath. It was like all the air had suddenly been sucked out of the room. *Where's the mask that falls from the ceiling when a girl needs it?*

"Wh-wh-wh—" Seriously? She gulped again and managed, "What *do* you want, Dan?"

He licked his lips, those wonderfully male lips, and caught the bottom one between his teeth. "Can't you guess?"

"Tell me." She wanted to hear it. *Needed* to hear it. It thrilled her when he said he wanted her, when he explained exactly *how* he planned to assuage that want.

"You, Brooklyn," he murmured, palming the back of her neck and pulling her down until their lips were a hairsbreadth apart. As always, her heart tripped over itself at the nickname. "All I want is you."

"Tell me more," she whispered against his mouth.

"I want to kiss you on your soft lips and suck on your wet tongue until you beg me to do the same to the tips of your breasts."

"Yessss," she hissed the word, closing the distance between them until... Oh! Warmth. Liquid, bold, unhesitating warmth. That was his tongue plunging into her mouth to claim and conquer, to pillage and plunder.

Dan was not a man who hesitated. About anything. And he didn't hesitate now, kissing her like he always kissed her, kissing her like she'd never been kissed before. With an intensity that spoke of his unwavering self-assurance. He knew what she wanted, what she needed. And he knew he could give it to her. Period. End of story.

She realized then, standing there while he made love

to her with his mouth so expertly that her sex grew heavy and swollen with desire, that Dan's nickname "The Man" didn't have anything to do with him being loyal and upstanding and filled with the kind of macho knowledge that allowed him to build a rocket ship to the moon with a paper clip, a rubber band, and some C4. Or, at least, it didn't *just* have to do with those things.

He was "The Man" because, quite simply, he was *a* man. In every sense of the word. Domineering. Potent. Virile. Lionhearted. Powerful. And above all else, completely unafraid to be exactly who he was. To *show* her, no holds barred, exactly what he wanted from her, what he needed from her, what he *demanded* from her.

"Dan," she murmured against his firm yet deliciously smooth lips. His breath tasted minty and fresh. "Please."

"Please what?" he whispered back, taking a nip at her bottom lip. The sting was a challenge, as were his next words. "I told you what I want. Now *you* tell me what *you* want."

Wetness coalesced between her thighs at the thought of what she wanted. "What you said," she allowed.

"Tell me," he demanded again. "Give me the words."

The tips of her breasts stung, ached as they brushed against the lace of her bra with each breath she took. There was no room. No room to do all the things she wanted to do. But she needed something. Something he was forcing her to put into words. And it terrified as much as it titillated.

She was not as bold as Dan. Not as sure of herself. To speak her desires, her wants aloud, was admitting more than her simple physical urges. He would know how much she needed him. How much she wanted him. How much she *adored* him. In each and every way.

"Tell me, Brooklyn," he husked, his eyes a hot challenge. His fingers on the back of her neck rubbing and massaging, succoring her even as the hand on her hip inched back until his fingers curved around the globe of her ass in a blatant demand. He had her exactly where he wanted her, and he wasn't letting her go until she did as he commanded.

Well, okay then...

"I want you to take off my sweater and my bra." Heat climbed up her neck and cheeks.

"Yes?" He dropped his hand from her neck to grab the hem of her sweater. But he didn't remove it. Just allowed the backs of his fingers to brush against the quivering flesh of her stomach. "And then what?"

"I-I want you to kiss my breasts and suck on my nipples," she managed.

"Mmm," he growled. "That sounds right. Like we agreed."

"Hmm?" It was hard to pay attention to his words when he was standing and crowding her back against the little vanity. He was so hot. And huge! This bathroom was not intended for a man of his size.

"It sounds like heaven," he clarified, pulling her sweater over her head and carefully hanging it on the latch of the door.

She was panting, impatient. But she didn't have long to wait. He reached behind her back and, one-handed, flicked open the catch on her bra. Slowly, deliberately, he peeled it from her shoulders. Hooking one strap over the corner of the mirror, he turned back to her. They were thigh to thigh, squeezed into the tiny space. And the air was hot as a furnace.

Or maybe that's just me…

When he moved to resume his seat on the toilet lid, she felt the desertion of his big body like a physical blow. But he held her hand and pulled her toward him, her legs between his spread thighs, her breasts bobbing just above his head.

"You're beautiful," he said, eyeing her reverently.

She bit her lip and shook her head. "I've never had much up top, but I—"

"Shhh." He stopped her, gently cupping one tender mound in his hot, calloused palm. When he rubbed his thumb over the tip, she thought she might die. Sensation zipped from her nipple straight to the bundle of nerves at the top of her sex. Her knees shook. "You're perfect. High and tight, with these amazingly responsive nipples."

That last part, the amazingly responsive nipples part, was a recent occurrence. He lifted his other hand, cupping her opposite breast and giving it the same loving attention until both her nipples poked out like pencil erasers. "Given your coloring, I expected 'em to be darker. But they're the exact shade of cotton candy. So delicate and pink."

"Dan—"

"Bend down just a little," he instructed. "Let me taste 'em and make both our fantasies come true."

"Holy shit," she hissed, pressing her palm to the bulkhead behind him so she could bend forward enough to have the tips of her breasts level with his mouth. When his hot breath brushed over one super-sensitized point, a rush of wetness flooded from her core. And when he looked up at her, hunger and desire and…something she couldn't name sparkling in his eyes, she couldn't stand it a second longer. "Please," she begged, cupping the back of his head and pulling him forward that last inch. "I need to feel your lips on me."

And then he obliged her, opening his hot mouth around her nipple. He laved it with the flat rasp of his tongue, then he closed his lips around it and sucked. Strongly. Because somehow he knew that's what she needed.

She cried out. The pleasure was so good. Too good. And with each hard pull at her breast, she felt an answering tug between her legs. She slapped a hand over her mouth. With the engines humming, it wasn't likely those in the cabin could hear what they were doing, but—

"You taste amazing," he said. "Are you this sweet all over?" She knew it was a rhetorical question because he continued before she could answer. "I can't wait to find out…"

Chapter Fifteen

JUST AS PENNI HAD PROMISED, DAN WAS IN HEAVEN. Despite the tight spot, despite the fact there was a traitor sitting not fifteen feet from them, despite the lingering smell of blood mixed with antiseptic, he was in paradise.

Because he had Penni in his hands. In his mouth. Sweet, wonderful Penni and her little catching breaths and deep, throaty moans. She was so responsive. Made for love. Her nipples pebbled against his tongue, *begging* to be sucked. To be licked. To be laved.

He did exactly that. And with every pull of his lips, her hips arched forward just the tiniest bit. He imagined the move rubbed her sex along the seam of her jeans. Imagined she was hot and wet and wonderfully swollen. For him. For the pleasure he was giving her. For the pleasure yet to come.

"God, Dan," she said huskily, her fingers tousling his hair as she held him to her. "I need…"

She trailed off. And he knew by the hot blush that had stolen into her cheeks when he'd demanded she tell him what she wanted that dirty talk didn't come easily to her. But that just made it hotter. Made *her* hotter. That she was pushing her boundaries with him. For him. He didn't give her a reprieve.

"What?" he breathed around her nipple, playing with

the tip. Flicking his tongue against it just as he would against her hot little clitoris once he got her jeans off. "What do you need, Brooklyn? Tell me."

"I need you to make me... *Oh Christ*. That feels good," she moaned.

He didn't allow her to distract him. Moving to her neglected breast, he gave her nipple the same attention. And once it was standing hard and proud, he leaned back to look at his handiwork. Her breasts were so lovely. Small and firm and utterly feminine. They seemed a little rounder, a little fuller than they'd been in Kuala Lumpur. The same could be said for her hips. Quitting the Secret Service looked good on her.

"You need me to make you *what*?" he demanded, looking up to see her eyes on him. The brown pools were shiny and bright, her lids lowered with passion.

When Penni looked at him like that, like he was the only man in the world, he felt about ten feet tall and bulletproof. He had the sudden urge to pound his chest and roar.

"I need you to make me come," she said, biting her lip, running a finger over the little bump on the bridge of her nose. It was as much a sign of her uncertainty as it was of her need. The move was so totally, uniquely Penni. And so totally, unquestionably sexy.

"How do you want me to make you come?" he asked, one brow raised, loving the red flush that bloomed over her chest and stole up the length of her throat, obliterating the ring of darkening bruises there.

One look at them and he wanted to beat the shit out of Kozlov. *Again*. Because no one should ever mar the beauty of her ivory skin, the perfection of her long, lovely neck. Of course he forgot all about Kozlov when she opened her luscious mouth. "With…" She hesitated. He could see her screwing up her courage. It was as adorable as it was hot. "With your fingers," she finally whispered, her breaths coming fast, causing her beautiful breasts to bob in front of his face. "Just like you promised."

"Good." He nodded, a muscle ticking in his jaw in rhythm to the erection pulsing behind his fly. The thought of putting his fingers inside her, inside all that silken, wet heat, made him so painfully erect he thought it a wonder the button on his jeans didn't explode off and go pinging around the lavatory. "That's good, Brooklyn," he praised. "Now lift your foot and put it between my legs."

"Wha—?"

"I'm gonna take off your boot so I can peel one leg of your jeans off," he explained. "I want you to be able to spread your legs for me. I wanna do this right since you asked me so nicely."

Her nostrils flared. And even though she hesitated one second, then another, she did as he asked. Tackling her laces, he quickly removed her boot, surprised to find his fingers were shaking with want, with need, with a desire so hot he imagined he saw steam rising from his wet clothes. Then he went to work on the button of her jeans. She remained stock-still. Standing in front of him like a sweet, feminine sacrifice. So trusting. So certain that he would take what she offered and give her what she needed.

Her panting breaths were amplified in the small space, and he loved it. It made everything hotter, more urgent. Made *him* hotter and more urgent. Which was why it was such a test to make himself slowly, ever so slowly peel her jeans down over her hips, her thighs, her impossibly long legs. But he did it, to draw out his pleasure and his pain at seeing her long, lithe, womanly body revealed. She was wearing black lace panties. Just a wisp of material that teased and tempted him with the delights it covered.

He leaned forward because…well, just because he *had* to, and pressed his mouth over the lace between her legs. He breathed out, warming her already molten sex. Then he breathed in, and drank in the smell of her desire. It shot straight to his head like top-shelf bourbon. *Better* than top-shelf bourbon, because he knew that after he was finished here, he wasn't going to hate himself. This—being with her, touching her, giving her pleasure and letting her please him—was good. It was healthy. It was—

Out of nowhere he experienced that familiar sense of hesitation. That sense that he shouldn't want another woman so completely. But before it could take over, something strange and wonderful happened. A simple phrase drifted through his mind…*Stop holding on to what hurts and start making room for what feels good.*

And even though he knew he'd heard it at an AA meeting, he would swear it was his beloved wife's voice that whispered it inside his head. Dan wasn't sure he really believed in a higher power, in the promise of life after death, but he would swear that he could feel his wife telling him it was time. Time to let her go. Time to soldier on. Get busy living or get busy dying. And then he knew…

It was going to be okay.

He was going to be okay.

And just like that, she was gone. Leaving nothing behind but a warm sense of blessing, of permission, of encouragement.

A lump formed in his throat and he gripped Penni's hips, turning to lay his face against her warm stomach. He wrapped his arms around her bottom and hugged her to him as his heart, which he'd thought would remain a closed first for the rest of his life, slowly unfurled.

"Dan?" she whispered. "What…? Is something wrong?"

"No," he managed, shaking his head. His heart wide open. "No, Penni," he said, pressing a kiss to her stomach, loving how the muscles quivered against his lips. "Everything is really, *really* right."

Her fingers tangled in his hair, smoothing it back from his face. "Dan, I—"

"Shhh," he told her, hooking his thumbs in the waistband of her panties and sliding them down her legs. "Step out of 'em," he instructed. "And then lift your leg and rest your foot beside my hip."

"Dan…" His name was a plea for mercy. A plea for more. Which was exactly what he planned to give her. So, *so* much more. Along with the burning desire that arced through his veins like electrical jolts, he now possessed a sense of *rightness*. This was right. *They* were right. And he was determined to prove that to Penni. With every touch. With every word. With every kiss.

"It's okay, babe," he soothed. "I'm gonna give you everything you want."

A breath shuddered from her as she did what he asked. When she stepped out of one side of her jeans and panties and planted her foot beside his hip, he ran a hand up her long, slender thigh. The skin was creamy and smooth, the muscles beneath shaking delicately. He watched as goose bumps followed the path of his palm, waiting, teasing himself until finally, he allowed his eyes to drink in the whole of her. Save for the jeans and panties still pooled around her right leg, Penni was standing before him completely naked.

And she was glorious.

All sweet, delicate curves and inch after inch of smooth, tantalizing skin. He marveled at her beauty, everything that was hard and male in him responding to everything that was soft and female in her. And then, after a few moments, he glanced at the part of her that made her woman. At the part of her that held the secret of life, the core of mystery that men had been seeking to unravel since the beginning of time.

She was…*shaved. Holy fuckin' shit!*

Except for a very small patch of hair at the top of her slick channel, she was completely bare. Which highlighted just how ready, how needy she really was. All swollen and pink. Her lips dewy and plump.

If he thought he'd been hard before, he was wrong. Looking at her now had fresh blood filling him, stretching him until he hurt. Until every breath was agony because it caused his turgid cock to brush against the fabric of his boxer briefs. *Who the hell makes underwear out of burlap?* He'd never really noticed the problem before, but it was beyond evident now.

And, oh! How he wanted to taste her. Put his mouth on her and suck until she cried out and unraveled against his tongue. But that wasn't what she'd asked for. Those weren't the words that'd tumbled from her succulent lips. And so, with a reverence born of eons of women letting men put their hands on them, of delicateness allowing toughness a chance at touching something sinfully soft, he flattened his hand against the gentle curve of her lower belly and let his thumb rest at the top of her channel.

She sucked in a breath, the leg supporting her trembling. "Easy," he murmured his voice sounding like boulders rumbling from the back of his throat.

He was dizzy with want. Faint with desire. But he still managed to steady her by placing his free hand on her hip. Then, looking up at her, watching her intently, he slipped the callused pad of his thumb inside her slick folds. Finding the hard, swollen bud of her clitoris, he pressed. Just once. Just to test her.

Her eyelids fluttered. The muscles of her stomach quivered under his hand. And her head tipped back, exposing the length of her kissable throat.

He flicked his thumb, back and forth, back and forth, and gloried when her hips swung forward. She moaned. It was throaty and raw. He answered in kind. Only the sound that issued from the back of his throat was more growl than moan. The noise animalistic and hungry. Which pretty well summed up in two words the way she made him feel.

As for the way *she* felt? That would take a million words. But he'd start with scorching hot, decadently soft, wildly wet.

Roger that, that definitely described her. And all he could think was how good it would feel to release the button on his jeans, pull down his zipper, and impale himself into her wonderful, silky heat. But besides that not being what she asked for, he didn't have a condom. At least he didn't have one handy. There was a box in his backpack, but—

Why the hell didn't you bring it with you, numb nuts?

Oh, right. Because when he'd come to check on Penni, the last thing he'd expected was to be pulled inside the tiny lavatory to have his wound cleaned one minute, and have her naked and panting and begging him to make her come the next. Although, come to think of it, he should have known better. They'd proved over and over that whenever they were alone together, they couldn't keep their hands to themselves. The lust they felt—that intrinsic, elemental connection— always took over. And they *always* ended up here. Seeking pleasure from each other. Giving pleasure to each other.

"Open a little wider," he instructed. His nostrils flared as the scent of female need, of *sex* filled the small space when she let her bent knee fall wide until it was resting against the bulkhead. Her sweet, pink center and the swollen bundle of nerves beneath his thumb were revealed.

Is there anything in the world more beautiful than a woman's body? If so, he'd yet to discover it.

Continuing to gently ply her, he moved the hand holding her hip until he was cupping her sex. The heel of his palm added pressure to the work his opposite thumb was doing, and his fingers were poised at her entrance.

"Yessss," she hissed, her pulse beating heavily in her throat. It seemed to be racing in rhythm to his pounding blood. And when he pressed his middle finger into her, just the tiniest bit, just to the first knuckle, he thought he might explode in his jeans.

"More," she demanded, her hips swinging forward to try to accomplish the feat themselves.

"How much more?" he asked, loving to hear the words on her lips, loving to push her to the brink of her comfort zone.

"All the way more," she husked. "Until you're inside me to the last knuckle."

"Jesus," he swore, even as he accommodated her, sinking his finger inside her, pumping gently.

She moaned, flinging her arms out to flatten a hand against each side of the lavatory's bulkheads.

Soft. So unbelievably soft. Like satin. Like silk. *Hot*. Her inner walls were made of molten fire, burning the skin on his finger. *Wet*. She bathed his hand in her desire, making the gentle pumping motion slippery and wonderful.

And when he slipped a second finger alongside the first, all the while continuing to rub the little nub of swollen nerves, she hissed and encouraged him by groaning his name. He pumped two more times, stretching her, loosening her, and then he curled his fingers forward, searching, palpating, until…

There.

He found what he was looking for. That secret patch of swollen, slightly rougher skin. When he rubbed his fingers over it, she cried out and surprised him by immediately unraveling, her hips thrusting, her head back, her inner walls squeezing his fingers until his knuckles rubbed together.

"That's it," he encouraged her, continuing to use both hands on her. He was determined to make it last.

Seeing her come, *feeling* her come, was more erotic, more sensual than he could ever have imagined and he wanted it to go on forever. His dick pulsed so hard that for a moment, he thought he'd come too. But then he continued to ache, to throb, to *hurt*, and he knew he hadn't. Which was good. Because when he *did* come, he wanted to be inside her. He wanted to feel her walls closing, grasping, sucking along his shaft the way they were closing, grasping, sucking along his fingers.

God, she's gorgeous. Completely abandoned. Completely wanton. Completely woman. And that she would give herself to him so freely, so totally, made every cell in his body swell up like a peacock strutting for its mate. He felt...*possessive.* Greedy. Totally gluttonous. And then it occurred to him...he'd given her what she asked for. Now it was his turn.

His turn to taste her.

So when the last tremors of orgasm shuddered through her and she lowered her head, her eyes hazy with spent lust, he carefully removed his fingers and lifted them to his lips. He sucked her passion from his skin, and her taste... *Hot damn!* Her taste was both wild and sweet. It exploded on his tongue and set off a chain reaction that went to his head, his heart, and most definitely his dick. Just *pow!* Sex. The decadent flavor of it. The musky smell of it. The soft, slippery feel of it. The total, incomprehensible *want* of it. It was on him, around him, inside him. And while he sucked his fingers, he watched her watching him...

———

"I called Morales on the sat phone," Chelsea told Z, sliding into the empty pilot's seat. There was something decidedly unnerving about being in the cockpit of a plane when it was thousands of feet above the ground. With all the knobs and switches and levers, she felt like any false move, any inadvertent slip, could flip something and they'd immediately plummet out of the sky. Not wanting *that*, she crossed her arms around her middle and tried to stay as still as possible.

"Morales?" Z asked, fidgeting with a knob. "I thought I heard you talking to your mom."

"Well, I called my mom first and *then* I called Morales," she said, narrowing her eyes when he slid her a knowing smirk. "Not a word," she warned him.

"Okay," he relented. "So then what did the mighty director of the CIA have to say?" He pulled off his headset and turned to give her his full attention. She didn't like it. Partly because his piercing gray eyes were…well…*piercing*. And partly because, as Tattoo used to say on all the reruns she'd watched of *Fantasy Island*, *De plane! De plane!*

"Shouldn't you be paying attention to the controls?" she demanded, trying to become even smaller. She didn't like the looks of a blinking red light on the console. *At all!* "Like that one in particular." She motioned with her chin toward the distracting, angry-looking flicker.

"The plane is on autopilot," Z said, one corner of his mouth quirking. "And all that light tells me is that the door to the lavatory is locked."

"Oh." She nodded, sighing and allowing herself to settle a little more fully into the seat. "Dan and Penni are in there, uh, well…"

"I figured," Z said.

"Yeah," she agreed, then sighed again. The way Dan and Penni were together, hot to trot for each other while still completely at ease, made her wish for...so many things she didn't have. So many things she might *never* have.

"What?" Z cocked his head. In the dim light of the instruments, she saw how the move caused a mink-colored curl to hook around the top of his left ear. Which was a weird thing to notice but was par for the course, really, considering that everything about this day had been a little twilight zone-y. "Why are you wearing such a hangdog expression? I'd think you would be jumping for joy. You helped catch the CIA's most wanted man, something your colleagues couldn't do after months of trying. You'll probably get a commendation or a pro-motion for this."

"Bah." She waved a hand through the air, wincing when it came within inches of the yoke. She tucked her arm back around her waist. "I don't care about any of that." She realized how that sounded and was quick to clarify. "I mean, I care that we caught Winterfield, but I don't care about the other stuff. Besides, I didn't do much. *You* guys were the ones who managed all the heavy lifting."

"Oh, come on, Chels." He turned to face her more fully. His shoulders seemed too wide for the small space. She eyed the distance between his calf and that panel of knobs. "You did great back there and you know it. From interrogating Kozlov to hot-wiring the van to laying down cover fire...we couldn't have done any of it without you. And in case everyone else forgets to say it, *thank you*."

Thump! That was the sound of her jaw falling into her lap.

"What?" He lifted a brow.

She was able to reel up her bottom teeth. Barely. Shaking her head, she said, "It's just that you're not usually one for doling out praise."

He made a face. "I dole it out when it's warranted and deserved."

"Maybe so," she allowed. "Um…thanks then. I guess."

"You're welcome." He winked.

And there went her jaw again, falling into her lap. Dagan Zoelner never winked. And especially not at her. *Does he have something in his eye?*

Well, regardless of whether it was an intentional or unintentional wink, there was no denying his *praise* had been real. And she hadn't felt such a sense of accomplishment, such a sense of joy, since she won her eighth-grade spelling bee. A warmth spread from her stomach into her chest and further, into her cheeks.

"Well"—she played it off so he wouldn't know how much his words meant to her, how much *he* meant to her—"truth is, I think I prefer my tidy little cubicle and my endless lines of Intelligence to actual fieldwork."

"Not as fun as you thought it would be?"

"Ha," was all she said, which expressed what she was feeling precisely. "You know, I once heard a field agent tell another field agent that there's nothing more exhilarating than being shot at and missed."

"You think he was wrong?" Z asked, his eyes blazing through the low light in the cockpit to burn across her face. She always felt his stare like a physical touch. A *hot* physical touch.

"It was a *she*," she corrected, pushing her glasses up her nose. "And I don't think she was wrong. I think she was *cah-razy*."

He smiled. An actual, factual smile. The sight of his white teeth in the middle of his tan face was so sudden and blinding she almost lifted a hand to shade her eyes. She hadn't even been *trying* to make him grin, which was probably why his smile had caught her so off guard. And then it was gone. As quickly as it had appeared. And he was back to being Sourpuss Face Dagan Zoelner.

Damn. She blew out a disappointed sigh. "On the subject of being shot at and missed, who do you suppose that guy was at the airport? One of Kozlov's cronies, maybe?" she asked. "Kozlov could have been yanking my chain when he told me he was working alone."

"Fuck if I know." Z shrugged. "I didn't get a good look at him through the pouring rain."

"Neither did I," she agreed.

Then, for a few seconds they sat in silence, Z flicking his gaze over the control panel, her flicking her gaze over his handsome profile. She didn't like the idea of having to shrug and say *whatever* when it came to the guy at the airport, but there was nothing to go on and no way to investigate while she was twenty-something-thousand feet in the air. So she shoved it all aside and tried to clear her head. When she did, her mind wandered back to Dan and Penni, to the affection the two seemed to share, and before she even knew she was going to ask the question, she blurted, "Did you know Dan's wife?"

Z turned to her. Slowly. Then he sat perfectly still.

Eerily still. Which is how she knew she'd touched on a subject he in no way wanted to discuss. His words confirmed it. "One sentence in and I'm already hating the new direction of this conversation."

Still, she'd already broached the topic. *In for a penny, in for a pound.* "Did you?"

"No," he admitted after another long pause. "She died before I joined BKI."

"Oh." She nodded, then ventured, "Do you supposed Penni knows about her?"

"I have no idea."

"I don't think she does," she said contemplatively.

"What makes you say that? Do you read minds? Is there a crystal ball hidden somewhere in your giant purse?"

"She didn't know he was an alcoholic," she said, ignoring the jab at her satchel. "So I suspect she doesn't know he's a widower."

"Why would one have anything to do with the other?" he asked, frowning. "Dan's ashamed of being an alcoholic. So maybe *that's* why he kept it from her. There's nothing shameful about being a widower."

"Not shameful," she said, her brow wrinkled in thought. "But…I don't know. I think Penni would act differently if she knew."

"How so?"

"I don't know. I just think loving a widower would be hard to handle. Not knowing if you were second best. Not knowing if—"

"You think she loves him?" he cut her off.

"Yeah, maybe," she allowed. "Did he…love her, do you think?" she asked. "His wife, I mean."

Zoelner blew out an exasperated sigh. "Where are

you going with this? And how can I make sure to go the opposite way?"

"It's not like I'm sticking my nose is someone else's rose here, but—"

"Could've fooled me," he said.

"I keep thinking about her," she continued as if he hadn't interrupted. "I keep thinking about her and about Dan and about Penni." She turned to blink at him.

"Your words form a statement, but your face forms a question," he grumbled. His usually stoic expression was anything but. He actually appeared discombobulated. *Imagine that. Dagan Zoelner feeling awkward.* It was such a novelty she knew she just *had* to keep pressing.

"My question is, do you think Dan loved his wife?"

"Yes," he ground out. "I think he loved her. And I *know* her death nearly killed him."

"Mmm. The drinking?"

"Yes, the drinking," Z confirmed.

"I figured as much," she said a little sadly. That a man such as Dan, a loyal man, a courageous man, a *good* man could be brought so low…it didn't bear dwelling on. Yet, dwell she did until the silence in the cockpit grew, until the hum of the engines seemed to fill the space inside the plane and all emptiness inside her chest. "You have to be really brave," she finally said, almost to herself.

"What do you mean?"

"To be in love. Knowing that something terrible can happen and your heart can get smashed into a million tiny pieces. Knowing that you're giving someone that kind of power over you. Knowing that you have that kind of power over another."

For a few seconds, Z said nothing. Then he admitted, "I...think you're right." He waited a beat before adding, "You do have to be brave. Braver than I've ever been."

She searched his face and wondered why she should feel both thrilled and saddened by the knowledge that he'd never been in love.

"Me too," she murmured, swallowing and glancing out the window. A million stars dotted the black fabric of the sky overhead. A soft bed of clouds spread out like a quilt below them. "And to experience that kind of heartbreak and then have the courage and fearlessness to open yourself up to it again..." She trailed off. She wasn't sure exactly what it was she wanted to say. Whatever it was, it felt big. Too big to put into words. So she ended with, "I really admire Dan. I think he might be the bravest man I've ever met."

When she turned, she saw that for the first time ever Z's eyes weren't piercing. They were soft. Liquid. Like mercury, only warmer. "I *know* you're right about that," he said.

And then they simply stared at one another. Their eyes searching. Their hearts beating. Their breaths mingling in the small space. Chelsea wondered what was going on inside his head, wondered if he could guess what was going on inside hers. And for a while she thought perhaps it was possible for them to—

"So what did Morales have to say when you talked to him?" He turned away to fiddle with one of the digital displays, and whatever magic there had been in the moment was obliterated. Just...*gone*.

She mourned its loss. And for a couple of seconds she could form no words around the sudden lump in her throat. *It was only an apparition anyway, right? That brief second of communion, of shared understanding was only real in my head, right?* Running fingers through her hair—*Ow!* It was a mess. The rain had really done a number on it—she was happy her voice was steady when she finally said, "Not a lot. I asked him if he could pull some strings to compensate the owner of that van we demolished. I have no idea if there's such a thing as theft insurance in Cusco."

He snorted.

"What?" she asked.

"Only you would worry about the smelly van guy when you're in the middle of bringing in the most traitorous agent the CIA has ever trained."

She twisted her lips. "I'll take that as a compliment."

"You should."

Wha—? She reached over and put her hand against his forehead. He went completely still beneath her touch. She noticed how warm and smooth his skin was in contrast to the few strands of cool hair that had fallen over his brow.

"Chels," he said, his voice low and strangely husky. "What…uh…" When he swallowed, the sound seemed particularly loud inside the little cockpit. "What're you doing?"

"Checking you for fever," she told him, removing her hand and curling her fingers around her palm, trying to hold in the feel of his skin. "You're not yourself tonight."

He fixed on her a dark glance. "Am I usually that much of an asshole?"

She lifted a brow, sticking her tongue in her cheek.

"Not an *asshole* per se, so much as buttmunch and pain in the ass. Subtle but very important distinctions."

One corner of his mouth twitched. *Come on. Come on. Show me that smile.* But he simply shook his head and said, "So what did Morales have to say about you wanting to make sure smelly van guy was reimbursed?"

"He said he'd take care of it," she told him. "That along with sending someone to pick up the drone, the rest of our gear, and the bags Penni left behind. Oh"— she snapped her fingers—"and Kozlov. Morales said he'd have someone go release the poor guy before tomorrow's construction crew arrives to work on the building and finds a cantankerous, hog-tied Russian in the midst of the rubble."

"Poor guy?" Z shot her an incredulous look. "You know it might have been him trying to give us all a few fatal doses of lead poisoning back at the square, right?"

"Maybe," she allowed, her brow furrowed. "But I don't think so. I think it was that Mystery Man in the truck."

"Yeah," Z admitted. "You're probably right." Then he added, "Sounds like you've got it all worked—"

He was cut off when turbulence grabbed hold of the plane and shook it like a child brandishing a toy rattle. Chelsea's hands became claws digging into the edge of the seat as Z quickly slipped on his headset, grabbed the yoke, and checked the instruments. He started jabbering to someone on the radio, requesting they be allowed to descend into more stable air.

She thought about snatching the headset hooked over the bracket on the side of her chair so she could listen in to what air traffic control was saying, but she didn't dare release her hold on the seat.

"Roger that," Z said, drawing out the *R* sound. "We will maintain our current speed and position until the airspace clears up. But let us know when it does. It's getting pretty choppy up here. Over."

As if to prove his point, the plane rattled and shook and plunged a short distance before the wings gripped the air and stabilized. *I hate flying. I hate flying. Oh, how I hate flying.*

"Go tell Dan to get his ass up here," Z said. "And then you buckle up. It'll be bumpy for a while." It took Herculean effort to peel her fingers away from the edge of the seat. "And, Chels?" Z said after she'd stood to brace herself in the open door of the cockpit.

"Yeah?"

"Don't worry. Between Dan and me, we could pilot this sucker through a hurricane."

She swallowed, but her spit got stuck around her lungs and heart, which had migrated up into her throat. "Great," she said. "But let's not try that, okay?"

"If you insist." He grinned. And *winked*. This time there was no mistaking it for something in his eye.

Holy crap! I really have *entered the twilight zone…*

Chapter Sixteen

El Dorado International Airport, Bogotá, Colombia
Saturday, 3:45 a.m.

THE NIGHT WAS AS DARK AND WARM AS THE DESIRE STILL rushing through Dan's veins. He stood on the dimly lit tarmac, waiting to board the small private jet *el Jefe* had chartered to take them back stateside—they could have made it in the Beechcraft, but it would have required two more stops for fuel and taken a hell of a long time compared to the jet—and he couldn't stop thinking about what happened in that tiny lavatory...

"Your turn," she said, licking her lips and grinning down at him as he sat on the toilet lid. The taste of her was still on his tongue, his fingers still damp from her passion. "Stand up."

"Penni, I—"

She pressed a finger to his mouth, then softened the rebuke by rubbing along his bottom lip as if testing its texture, feeling the plumpness caused by her kisses.

"So soft," she whispered. "I think this is the softest part on your whole body."

"Currently?" He grinned. "I'd hafta agree with you."

She glanced down at the bulge straining his zipper and stuck her tongue in her cheek. "My point exactly. Now stand up."

He could see the spark of renewed desire ignite in her lovely brown eyes. It was thrilling to know he'd quenched her lust, her longing, but that the thought of returning the favor set her blood boiling again. "I'm not sure you—"

"I'm sure," she interrupted. "You asked me to tell you what I want. And I'm telling you, I want you to stand up."

Okay, then. *He swallowed. He was so hot, so horny, so completely* ready *he'd probably go off the minute she got her hands on him. But who was he to question the demands of a lady? Especially a lady such as her. One who was wickedly beautiful. One who was wonderfully* nude. *One whose current expression was that of the devil himself bent on a sinning spree.*

Hot damn...

Pushing to a stand, he gritted his teeth when his boxers and zipper rubbed against his painful erection. Then she went down on her knees in front of him. And just as it had done to men since the beginning of time, that submissive pose made everything that was male and dominant inside him growl with approval. In fact, he was pretty sure he was actually growling.

"Now Mr. Growly Growlerton," she said—Roger that, he was definitely growling— "let's get these jeans off, yeah?"

"God yeah," he agreed, hastily fumbling with his belt buckle.

She tsked and pushed his hands away. "No. Let me do the honors."

He bit his tongue to keep from begging her to hurry. Especially when she slowly, methodically undid his belt, carefully, teasingly unsnapped the button on his jeans, and deliberately, coquettishly unzipped his fly. She was probably one of those people who unwrapped her Christmas presents slowly too. Savoring the moment before the surprise. Saving the bows and being careful not to tear the paper.

"You're killing me, woman," he gritted, unable to resist tangling his fingers in her soft, charmingly messy hair. His heart was thundering out of control, no doubt trying to supply his brain and organs with what little blood wasn't pooled inside his raging hard-on.

Glancing up at him, she feigned a sympathetic pout. Then she cupped him through the denim of his jeans and squeezed. "Poor baby. We can't have that, can we?"

He had to shake his head because he couldn't speak. He couldn't breathe. *He could barely think, and even then, every single thought was focused on his need to feel her hands on him, skin to skin, her lips on him, her teeth and tongue and—*

Hell…

"Please," he managed, his voice so low he wasn't sure she heard him.

But obviously she had because she whispered, "Please what, Dan? Tell me what you want."

To hear his earlier words parroted back to him was both a tease and a challenge. And guess what? He was up to the task. Fuckin'-A he was! "I want you to pull down my pants. I want you take my dick in your hands. I want you to angle it toward your mouth. And then I want you to wrap those sweet lips around me and suck."

She'd asked for it. He'd given it to her. And he watched, a smile pulling at the corner of his mouth, as a deep red blush bloomed on her cheeks and across her chest. A sure sign of her excitement mixed with her self-consciousness. It was so damn sweet. So damn hot. So damn everything he'd ever wanted in a partner.

"Yes," she said. "I think I'll like that very much."

"I know I will." He braced himself when her long fingers hooked in the waistbands of his jeans and boxer briefs, pulling both garments down over his hips and beneath his ass. His dick sprang forward with such ferocity it was a wonder she didn't lose an eye. And the relief of being released from the confines of his pants was so acute it nearly dropped him to his knees.

"Wow," she whispered, her hot breath swirling around him. Even that small caress, that intangible touch was enough to make his shaft jerk and throb. He was so hard he was standing nearly vertical, so swollen with blood he was almost purple. "I knew you were a…a big man, but…" She hesitated. "You're… um…"—she bit her lip, blinking up at him—"going to be quite a mouthful."

It occurred to him then that maybe she wasn't up for this. Some women didn't like doing it, especially when it involved a piece of equipment that was…well… Okay, so he wasn't bragging here, but when the good Lord saw fit to add the twig to his berries, the big guy in the sky had looked around and upgraded to a stick. Dan had been in enough locker rooms to know that not only did he pack more than his fair share, but he also wasn't as…um… pretty as some. He shaft was thick, roped with veins, curved slightly upward, and his glans flared proud and plump at the end. For the unaccustomed, he probably looked a bit…aggressive.

"Penni," he husked, having to dig down deep in order to utter the next words, especially when all he wanted to do was grab the back of her head and press her face and mouth against him, "you don't have to—"

"Shut up," she told him, and he grinned. There's that adorably blunt New Yorker I know. *Then she wrapped a hand around the base of his shaft and angled him toward her mouth like he'd told her to do. When she licked her lips, his smile disappeared and he held his breath. But just as she leaned forward, just as her mouth opened, the plane hit turbulence…*

"There's been a change in plans," Chelsea said, dragging Dan from his delightful, *painful* reverie. He turned to see her drop her cell phone into her satchel, and covertly adjusted his stance since he was hard. Again. *Or maybe I should say still.* As far as he knew, he'd maintained his boner even while he and Zoelner had fought the turbulence of a passing thunderstorm, even when they had been forced to coast into the airport on fumes, and even though the digital display on his diver's watch told him over three hours had passed since he'd been in that bathroom.

He was the equivalent of a walking, talking side effect in one of those Viagra commercials. *For an erection lasting longer than four hours…*get laid as quickly as possible. At least that was the medical advice he was going to go with, whether it was sound or not.

"What kind of change?" Zoelner asked, hopping down the jet's four steps after having secured Winterfield inside the aircraft.

"The kind where we're headed to Chicago instead of Washington," Chelsea said.

Dan exchanged a look with Penni. She reached to take his hand and he didn't hesitate to pull her close to his side, taking comfort in her sweet touch, her solid presence next to him. They were supposed to drop Winterfield off at some interrogation site outside DC, and any deviation from that course could only mean one thing: bad news.

"What now?" Zoelner sighed, glancing over his shoulder to make sure the two pilots were nowhere around. Neither Dan nor Zoelner were licensed to fly jets, so a couple of Air Force flyboys who'd been stationed nearby had been brought in to get them all home, no questions asked. That went for the airport crew that had been scrambled into action in the middle of the night too. Once again, Dan thanked his lucky stars for friends in high places. Although, come to think of it, *el Jefe* and the Joint Chiefs probably qualified as friends in the *highest* of places.

"Morales said the Cusco assets he sent in to gather up our stuff and go release Kozlov discovered the Russian dead," Chelsea told them, her mouth twisting, her face filling with remorse and self-reproach. And, yeah, okay, Kozlov was probably a fucker of a guy who'd undoubtedly done some terrible shit in his life, but they'd left him there, taped, vulnerable, *defenseless*.

"Jesus." Dan ran a hand over his hair, his head spinning. *Why?* Why would anyone want to eighty-six Kozlov?

"It gets worse," Chelsea said.

Dan knew he was going to regret asking, but... "How so?"

"The ground crew at the airport is dead too. Morales's

assets say *policia* are surrounding the place and all flights into and out of Cusco have been canceled for the day."

"That dickhole in the truck," Dan growled, wishing he'd had the opportunity to put a bullet right between the bastard's eyes. He didn't know who the guy was or what the hell he was about, but by the sound of it, he'd murdered three innocent men. And, yeah, okay, so the ground crew weren't *completely* innocent. After all, they had taken a bribe to let Dan and company into the airport after closing, bypassing security and immigration and customs. But that didn't mean they deserved to be slaughtered for it. *Damnit!*

The night air around them was heavy with the smells of aviation fuel and wet concrete—the storm they'd flown through had hit Bogotá first. Penni squeezed his fingers and he glanced down to find her pretty face turned to him, judging his reaction to Chelsea's news. There was sympathy in her eyes—those kind eyes that had done a number on him since day one. The ground crew had been his contacts, his assets. And now they were dead because of the affiliation.

One more regret…one more black mark to add to my life's list.

Remorse hit him hard in the gut, and the impulse to drown his sorrows in a tall glass of Jack Daniel's was so tangible he could almost feel the tumbler in his hand, almost smell the hints of spice and nuts and smoke that whispered through the harsher notes of the alcohol. His mouth watered.

Penni gave his fingers another squeeze, as if she somehow knew where his mind had gone. It was enough to drag him back from the edge. Ground him in the here and now. He was able—with another look at her sweet face and a reminder that *you won't slip if you stay away from slippery places*—to push the craving away.

"You suspect he was the one who took out Kozlov too?" Zoelner ventured. "Maybe whoever he is, he was watching us, following us, and getting rid of anyone who seemed like they might know too much about what we were doing there. Maybe *that's* why you kept feeling like we were being watched, Dan Man. Because we *were*."

"But *why*?" Dan asked, his mind racing through possibilities and discarding them one after the other. Nothing about the Mystery Man made a lick of sense.

"No clue," Chelsea said. "And we're not likely to grab a clue anytime soon."

"Meaning?" Dan asked.

"Meaning our mysterious airport shooter has ghosted. He's nowhere to be found. But Morales is trying to track his movements."

"Which brings us back to the change in plans," Penni said. "Why does the killing of Kozlov and the ground crew mean we're taking Winterfield to Chicago instead of DC?"

Dan caught Zoelner's eye and knew the former spook was thinking the same thing he was. "Babineaux," they said simultaneously.

"What?" Penni glanced between them. "You mean Rock Babineaux? What does he have to do with it?"

"He's a highly trained interrogator," Dan explained. "Some might say he's the best in the biz. And I suspect, given the giant question mark that is our Mystery Man in Cusco, our commander in chief is insisting one of his own get first crack at Winterfield before he's handed over to the CIA."

"Oh-kay," Penni said slowly. "Um…*why*? I feel like I'm missing something here."

"Given the recent spate of traitors coming out of the CIA's woodwork, *el Jefe* doesn't trust that it's not another government spook who's gone AWOL, running around killing people," he explained. "And he doesn't want us to hand Winterfield over to the CIA before he has a chance to have someone he trusts interrogate the fucker."

Chelsea frowned and shook her head sorrowfully. "We haven't inspired much confidence lately, have we? Two rogue agents in the span of a few months." She hoisted her satchel higher on her shoulder and looked off into the distance where the air traffic control tower was lit up like a lighthouse against the blackened windows of the closed airport.

"So, we're headed back to the Windy City," Zoelner said, his eyes lingering on Chelsea's profile for just a *little* too long before swinging toward Dan.

"Roger that," Dan said. And despite everything, he smiled at the thought of taking Penni up to his room on the third floor of BKI's main warehouse. He'd shut the metal door, throw her on his bed, and do…*everything* to her. It was a good thing she was still holding his hand or else he might have unconsciously rubbed his palms together in lurid anticipation, like a cartoon villain.

And, oh great. His hard-on had softened at some point during their conversation, but now it was standing at full attention again. *Wonderful. Perfect.* He only had an eight-hour flight ahead of him.

"Ladies and gentlemen," one of the pilots called. The flyboy was standing in the open doorway of the jet wearing jeans and a T-shirt and a serious expression that looked sort of foreign on his youthful face. If the kid was more than twenty-five years old, Dan would eat his Ruger for dessert. "We are fully fueled. As soon as this emergency flight lands"—the pilot motioned toward the little red Pilatus PC-12 that was touching down on the runway—"we're green-lighted to go. If you all would, please." He motioned for them to board.

Chelsea was the first to climb the stairs, followed by Zoelner and Penni. Dan brought up the rear. And speaking of rears...he watched Penni's swing in front of him. *This is gonna be the longest eight hours of my life.*

"Emergency flight?" he asked the young airman once he'd made it to the top step.

"Yes, sir," the youth said. Dan could almost hear the salute in his tone. "Apparently the plane got caught in the storm that passed earlier and she's low on fuel."

Dan harrumphed. "Weren't we all. That squall was a bitch and a half."

"Yes, sir."

"I'll grab the door," Dan told him. "You get us ready to taxi."

"Yes, sir." The pilot turned and headed toward the cockpit. If Dan hadn't heard the kid speak earlier, he would have thought the lieutenant only had two words in his entire vocabulary. *Good ol' fashioned American military training right there, folks.*

When he swung back, he saw the Pilatus PC-12 taxiing toward the airport's main building. The hairs on the back of his neck suddenly stood up. He got that queasy feeling in the pit of his stomach. Narrowing his eyes, rubbing a hand over the back of his neck, he tried to see the pilot inside. But the distance was too great and the night was too dark.

Is it possible?

Nah, he quickly convinced himself. *There's no way.* Pulling up the stairs, he shut and sealed the door and convinced himself that he was just bone-tired, crazy horny, and jumping at shadows. The first two he was pretty sure he could take care of in due course. *Hopefully*, once he did that, the last one would go away on its own.

He turned into the cabin, noting Zoelner had cuffed Winterfield's wrists and ankles with zip ties and left the duct tape over his mouth. *Good. Nice and tight and ready for a* quiet *flight.* The traitorous CIA agent was proving to have quite the mouth on him. Dan just hoped that translated over to him spilling his guts to Rock. Because Rock might be the best interrogator in Uncle Sam's arsenal, but the guy hated doing it. Hated having to climb inside someone else's mind and go rooting around in the filth to find what he was looking for.

Behind the traitor, Chelsea and Zoelner were buckled in and in the middle of a heated argument about something that had Zoelner asking, "Do you think I'm an idiot?"

"Well, yeah," Chelsea said. "Sometimes. But that's beside the point."

Those two either need to duke it out or screw it out, Dan concluded, shaking his head.

Of course, thoughts of anything or anyone else vanished when he turned to find Penni waiting across the aisle, a warm glow in her dark eyes, a small smile playing at her lips as she beckoned him toward the seat beside her. *Naturally*. Like he would have chosen to sit anywhere else?

His mind flashed back to her on her knees, and of their own accord, his eyes darted toward the door of the lavatory. Would she be up for round two? When he plopped down next to her and pulled his seat belt tight, her hand landed on his thigh, precariously close to the bulge straining his zipper. *Roger that*. He figured he had the answer he was hoping for.

The pilots throttled up, taxiing toward the runway, and he knew he was grinning like an idiot. Again. If the woman hung around for too much longer, he supposed he'd have to get used to wearing the expression. And considering that for more than two years he hadn't had much to smile about, he fully expected to suffer from sore facial muscles. Not that he was complaining. Far from it. Being next to her, being *with* her reminded him what it was to feel good. To feel… Dare he say it? Happy?

He placed his hand atop hers, squeezed her fingers, and covertly slid her hand up his thigh until her palm was centered atop his hard-on. His shaft flexed at her touch and a *zing* of lust traveled up the length of his spine to explode at the base of his skull. His chest felt full, tight. Just like his jeans.

She turned to him, her expression slightly scandalized. Then she craned her head around to glance at the lavatory. With the jet engines revving and his heart beating wildly in anticipation, she grinned at him, wiggling her eyebrows and running a quick finger over the bridge of her nose.

So maybe it won't be such a long flight after all…

Chapter Seventeen

3,600 feet over Atlanta, Georgia
Saturday, 11:13 a.m.

GEORGE REACHED INTO HIS HIP POCKET, EXTRACTED HIS credit card, and swiped it through the slot on the satellite phone attached to the seat in front of him. After agreeing to the charges, he punched in the number and skimmed a glance over the blue-haired granny sitting on his left. The massive hearing aids in the woman's ears and the shouted conversation they'd had during the boarding process when she was confused as to which seat was hers assured him the dotty old pensioner couldn't hear a bloody thing. *Good. I don't want eavesdroppers.*

And that had his gaze sliding over to the keen-eyed Colombian woman across the aisle. *She* was another story. She'd been giving him the evil eye since he boarded. Which was why he kept his voice down when Benton picked up the phone after the third ring. "Whoever this is," Benton said without preamble, "you've got the wrong number."

"It's me," George hissed.

"What the bloody hell are you doing ringing me up on an…" After a pause Benton said, "On *this* line." George knew Benton had been about say *unsecured line*.

"I didn't really have a choice, now did I?" he demanded, smiling and shaking his head at the granny who offered him a slice of the apple she'd pulled from her purse. The core was brown and mushy, the smell of its overripe meat sickeningly sweet. George bet it'd been at the bottom of her bag for at least a week.

"Well, you know I'll have to chuck this phone as soon as we're finished," Benton said, irritation heavy in his tone. George wanted to reach through the connection and strangle the sod where he sat. Benton having to trash one of his myriad burner phones was the least of George's worries, but he couldn't let on how he felt. He would need Benton's help if he had any hope of salvaging his mission. Which meant he needed to keep the arrogant wanker happy.

"Sorry," he said quickly. "But look, I need to know what's ahead of me."

After tailing Winterfield and his captors through the air for hours, George had been forced to fly around a spot of bad weather before landing in Bogotá. It had only been a minor delay, but it had been enough. He'd barely finished taxiing the Pilatus PC-12 off the runway when he saw the private jet take off. And he'd known, with a sinking feeling in his stomach, with a heart as heavy as a block of lead, that his plan hadn't worked.

For many long minutes he'd sat inside the plane, cold fear making him shake, remorse and regret making tears stand in his eyes. *It's done*, he'd thought. *I'm finished*. But after a bit, he'd managed to shake it off. He couldn't quit. He couldn't give up. Not with beautiful Bella depending on him to do whatever was necessary, whatever it took to make sure he finished the task Spider had set before him.

Running a hand under his running nose, he'd quickly

called Benton, demanding the lad find him a way to trail the group flying north. Benton had been skeptical, of course. And he'd tried to talk George out of following Winterfield and his captors. In fact, Benton's exact words were: *You're completely crackers. You'll get yourself killed keeping on like this. It's over*.

Benton didn't know what was at stake for George though. He didn't know what was on the line. He must have sensed it, or else he heard the desperation in George's tone when George insisted again that Benton find him a way. Because after a bit of online wizardry with the international aviation sites, the computer whiz kid had been able to determine the private jet's flight plan terminated in Chicago.

Following that, Benton had booked George on the first civilian flight out of Bogotá. A private plane would have been better, but Benton hadn't been able to find one, and the Pilatus was out of the question because it was too slow and didn't have the fuel capacity to make the trip in one go. Luckily a civilian flight had been scheduled to leave for Chicago's O'Hare airport at 6 a.m., so the wait had been minimal and it had given George time to clean himself up before boarding.

But in the hours since, as George sat on the plane with nothing to do but think over all the things he'd done wrong, over all the things that could still *go* wrong, he'd started to go a bit crackers. Just as Benton had said. He needed something to occupy his mind. Something to keep him from envisioning all the ways Spider could make him suffer, make *Bella* suffer. He *needed* to start working on his strategy.

"You need to know what's ahead of you?" Benton

asked incredulously. "You mean if you make it out of the airport without the..." Again, he came to an abrupt halt. "If you make it out without being picked up," Benton finally finished.

"Picked up?" George demanded, lowering his voice when the black-haired cow across the way shot him a sharp look. He'd very much like to use the plastic fork the steward had left with the cold eggs and sausages to stab the woman in her beady left eye. "What do you mean?"

"I mean that mess you left in C—" Benton was becoming more and more agitated. He wasn't used to speaking on an unsecured line and therefore wasn't accustomed to choosing his words carefully. "That mess you left behind you," the kid finally said. "From what I'm seeing online, they're throwing over every rock."

And by "they," George knew Benton meant the Americans. And by "throwing over every rock," George knew he meant they were looking for him. A hard, sinking feeling took hold of his stomach. "Why?" he wheezed, absently squeezing the brim of his cap. It was his habit to pull the thing lower over his face when he was feeling vulnerable. A tell he'd tried to quell, but just couldn't seem to manage. "How? I mean, they can't possibly know—"

"They'll eventually connect the dots," Benton assured him. The dots meaning the shoot-out in the square, the filched truck, the dead crewmen, the stolen Pilatus, and then the civilian flight out of Bogotá where he'd had to use his assumed name, passport, and credit card. "You better just hope they don't connect them before you land," Benton finished.

Shit, George thought. Then aloud, "Shit!"

"Eh?" the granny beside him asked, cupping a gnarled hand around her ear. "You need to speak up."

"Sorry!" George nearly had to scream for her to hear him. "I'm not talking to you, love!"

"Oh!" She looked flustered, cute in that old granny sort of way. George tried to picture Bella growing old, tried to see her years from now as a sweet, deaf, wrinkled woman who'd lived a life of happiness and love.

If I have any say in it, he promised himself.

"No worries, love!" he told her, squeezing her hand. The bones felt as delicate as a bird's, her skin as thin as parchment paper.

"Love? You know I don't go in for that business," Benton said. "I like the ladies and ladies like m—"

"Not you, you daft bugger," George said. Then he got back to the point of their conversation. "Assuming they don't connect the dots before then"—*please, God, don't let them*—"I need to know what's ahead of me. I need you to find blueprints of the shop that isn't really a shop." They both knew he was referring to the custom motorcycle business. "Assuming that's where they're taking the bastard."

"*Señor*," the woman across the aisle said in heavily accented English. The way she was pursing her lips, one would think she'd been sucking on a lemon. "Do you mind? There are children three rows back."

George could see it all very clearly. He'd grip the fork, reach across the aisle, palm the back of the bitch's head, and jab the prongs straight into her eye. Blood would squirt. She would scream. And he would feel a momentary sense of satisfaction. But then he'd be wrestled to the ground, handcuffed, and arrested upon landing. And he couldn't have that.

"Sorry," he told her, smiling through his gritted teeth. Turning back to his conversation, he added, "I'll also need tools." And by "tools" he meant weapons. He'd had to toss his gun and knife before hopping on the civilian flight. "And something that makes a rather big, we're talking *huge* noise." And by "noise" he meant explosion. "And on the off chance I succeed and make it out, I'll need all new papers." And by "papers" he meant identification and credit cards. The ones he was using now under the name of Rupert Buttershaw—Spider's counterfeit paper maker liked his unique monikers— were going to be too hot. Because Benton was right: eventually the Americans *would* connect the dots.

"Understood," Benton said, reading between the lines. The kid was a right bright little shit, George would give him that. "You'll also need to ring Sp—" Benton quickly cut himself off. "You'll need to ring him up when you land. He wants to talk to you." The bottom fell out of George's stomach. "He's not happy."

"So what else is new?" George said tartly, disconnecting the call before Benton could respond.

Goose Island, Chicago, Illinois
Saturday 11:52 a.m.

"Who *are* you people?" Penni demanded from the backseat of the big, black Hummer when the vehicle's headlights lit up the massive metal door at the end of the underground tunnel. With a *pop* and a *hiss*, the aperture slid open, revealing the first floor shop of Black Knights Inc. and a row of gleaming, whimsically designed motorcycles. The screech of grinding metal and the booming bass of high-volume rock 'n' roll drifted inside the SUV. And Penni could just make out Becky Knight, blond ponytail swinging wildly as the woman used elbow grease—and a monster tool that looked far too big for her to handle—to whip a piece of sheet metal into shape.

"We're Batman." Dan chuckled, his voice all low and growly and Batman-y. "Er…Batman*s*."

"Geez, I guess so," Penni said a little breathlessly.

Boss had been waiting on the tarmac in the Hummer before their wheels ever touched down at O'Hare International Airport. After loading them up, he took a circuitous route through the city and into some random parking garage where they went around and around, down and down, until they hit the bottom level. It'd been eerily quiet and completely empty of vehicles. The light in the garage was strangely dim too. Sort of slasher-movie-esque.

Penni had been a split second from climbing into Dan's lap and demanding to know what the hell they were doing there—she'd never liked scary movies—when Boss headed toward the very back corner. The very *dark* back corner. With a furrowed brow and a pounding heart, she watched the colossus of a man reach up to press a button on a device attached to the driver's side visor. Then, it was a case of *What to my wondering eyes should appear*, because one whole section of the garage's cinder-block wall started moving.

What was revealed once it came to a stop was a dark tunnel just wide enough to fit the SUV. Penni felt a bit Aladdin-ish faced with the sudden emergence of the Cave of Wonders, and she knew her jaw was hanging open, her eyes wide and blinking. *What's next? Magic carpets? A genie?* The voice of the late, great Robin Williams echoed inside her head…*Yo! Rugman! Haven't seen you in a few millennia. Give me some tassel!*

She didn't know if she was relieved or disappointed that neither a magic carpet *nor* a genie appeared when Boss entered the tunnel and pressed the garage-door opener thingy again, and she watched as the cinder-block wall closed behind them. At which point, she had the genius thought of *h-h-holy shit!*

They were instantly plunged into darkness except for the lights on the console and the headlights shining into the tunnel. Wetness dripped from the ceiling, splashing on the windshield. Boss flipped on the wipers and began carefully driving down the narrow, dark, *spooky* shaft. And all the while Penni sat there, squeezing Dan's hand, blinking in astonishment, and wrinkling her nose at the damp, fishy aroma that invaded the vehicle. Then they'd reached the end of the tunnel and the huge metal door.

"We call it the bat cave," Dan said now as Boss pressed on the gas and drove through the open door and straight into Black Knights Inc. *Presto change-o, home sweet home.* "It's our bolt-hole dug under the Chicago River. Puts us directly on the mainland via that old parking garage."

"And our way in and out when we don't want to draw attention to ourselves," Boss added at the same time Penni turned to see a section of the brick wall of BKI's shop sliding shut behind them. It made a soft rumbling sound that competed with the roar of the Hummer's engine and the *bump, bump, bump* of the music's bass drum. Then, with a *snap* and a *thunk*, the seams in the bricks' mortar knit together perfectly. And just like that, you couldn't tell anything about the warehouse's wall was amiss.

Again, she had the brilliant thought of *h-h-holy shit*.

"And why aren't we drawing attention to ourselves today?" Zoelner asked from the seat behind them. He had volunteered to sit beside Winterfield in the third row of bucket seats, allowing Chelsea to ride shotgun.

"Because that fuckin' reporter has been nosing around again." Boss put the vehicle in park and switched off the engine at the same time Becky stopped grinding sheet metal and flicked off the boom box. It was strangely quiet all of a sudden, except for the whistling sound of Winterfield breathing through his nose. "No way was I taking the chance she might get a gander at dickhead."

"That's you," Zoelner said to Winterfield, his expression bland. "Just in case you were wondering."

Since Winterfield was still wearing duct tape, all he could do was glare.

The door beside Penni burst open to reveal Ozzie, leaning heavily on his crutches. His blond hair was mad-scientist wild and his face looked like a storm cloud. He was wearing a black T-shirt with white block lettering that simply read *Beam Me Up, Scotty*. The tongue-in-cheek sentiment was incongruent with his serious, slightly harried expression. "Hurry up and get out," he said, glancing furtively over his shoulder.

Well, that's a fine hi, how are ya. "What?" Penni frowned at him even as she ducked out the door. "Why?"

"Because she arrived early," he said, noting the bandages on her cheek and the bruises ringing her throat. He frowned, tsked like an old maiden aunt, and gave her a quick, absentminded hug. "Glad to see you made it back safe and sound," he whispered in her ear, his aftershave tickling her nose. "I swear I didn't think you'd run into any trouble down there. None of us did. If we had, we never would've agreed to send you."

"All's well that ends well," she assured him.

He pushed back to study her face. "And *is* all well?"

She glanced over her shoulder to see Dan unfurling his tall frame from the Hummer. The vehicle was big, but Dan was bigger. He looked all shoulders and legs trying to exit through the door. "I'm not…" She shook her head. "I don't know, exactly."

Ozzie flicked a glance at Dan, his expression turning contemplative before he pulled her into another hug. "There's still my offer," he whispered in her ear.

Penni's heart melted for the guy. Just a little. He was a womanizer, a playboy, and never seemed to take anything seriously. But under all that swagger and mockery beat a true heart. "You know," she speculated, "if you're not careful, some woman is going to take you up on that offer someday."

"Hey, dickhead," Dan grumped, dragging her out of Ozzie's embrace. "Keep your dirty mitts to yourself."

"I'll flip you for her," Ozzie said, pretending to dig in his hip pocket for a coin.

"Wow." Penni frowned at him. "Just when I think there might be hope for you."

He winked and leered.

She sighed and shook her head.

"Keep your eyeballs to yourself too," Dan warned, "or I'll be tempted to plant one on your kisser. See how it affects that silver tongue of yours."

"You wouldn't hit a wounded man, would you?" Ozzie leaned more heavily on his crutches, wincing and rubbing his leg like it pained him terribly. Then a grin split his handsome face and he reached forward, dragging Dan in for a bear hug. He slapped Dan on the back so hard Penni was surprised Dan didn't hork up a lung.

"Missed you like crazy, you sorry sonofabitch," Ozzie said. Dan couldn't see it, and Penni figured she wasn't supposed to see it either, but for just a second Ozzie's expression was heartbreakingly sad, almost...*anguished*.

"Whoa," Zoelner said after he pushed Winterfield out of the vehicle. "Should we give you two a couple of minutes alone?"

"Don't be jealous," Ozzie teased, shoving Dan away and dragging Zoelner in to wrap his arms around him. "There's enough of Ozzie to go around."

Chelsea hopped out of the Hummer at the same time Boss rounded the front bumper. "What do you mean she arrived early?" Boss asked, going back to Ozzie's original statement. "I thought she was scheduled to show in thirty minutes." He checked his watch. And then his questioning expression turned fierce when Becky—who'd finished putting away the giant grinding tool and setting aside the sheet metal—squealed and hopped into Dan's arms. She squeezed Dan's neck and peppered his cheek with kisses while telling him how happy she was to have him home. Boss waited barely a beat before grumbling, "Okay, *Mrs*. Knight. That's enough of that."

Becky pushed out of Dan's arms, rolling her eyes at her husband. "Don't tell me you're jealous."

"Well…*yeah*," Boss harrumphed, crossing his arms and scowling dangerously.

Apparently the men of Black Knights Inc. were terribly proprietary when it came to other men putting their hands on their women. That Penni should feel a little *zing* of pleasure that Dan had treated her like she was *his* made her want to kick her own ass. She wasn't some fawning heroine in a romance novel who needed to be the center of some chest-thumping man's desire to feel complete. She was a modern woman who'd proved herself capable of anything and everything— *without* a man by her side, thank you. But still…there it was. That *zing*.

Someone should take away my Girl Power Club card…

"Well, you'll just have to keep that green-eyed monster in check for, like, two more seconds," Becky said, wrapping her arms around Zoelner's waist and giving him a squeeze. Zoelner stiffened and patted her on the head like an older brother might do to a kid sister. But Boss didn't seem to notice the platonic nature of the embrace.

"One Mississippi, two Mississippi," he counted quickly, grabbing Becky's arm and pulling her next to his side. "And where's *my* warm welcome?" he demanded.

"You've been gone…what? An hour?" Becky reached into the hip pocket of her snug jeans to extract a Dum Dum lollipop. She used it as a pointer to indicate Dan and Zoelner. "They've been gone three whole *months*."

"Still…" Boss shrugged. And if Penni hadn't seen it with her own eyes, she wouldn't have believed the huge, hulking beast of a man could pout. But he did.

Becky chuckled and wrapped her arms around

her husband, laying her face against his broad chest. "There," she said. "Is that better?"

"Yes." A grin twitched at Boss's lips, highlighting the scar that snaked up from the corner of his mouth.

It hit Penni again. *Family*. This was Dan's family. And what would they think of her when they knew, what would *he* think of her when she told him that she—

"Good, great." Ozzie interrupted her thoughts. "The welcome homes are complete. Now everybody scram, because Geralt is stalling her, but he can't do it for too much longer. She's already suspicious, and if we keep her standing around out by the front gate, it'll make her even more so. Which is *exactly* the opposite of what this little show-and-tell is all about. We're trying to assuage her suspicions."

Penni was hopelessly lost. Who was *she*? And, totally off subject, but who actually used the word "assuage"?

Obviously she wasn't the only one suffering from *what-the-huh?* Dan was scowling so hard she was surprised his eyebrows didn't slide right down the center of his nose. "What the hell is going on here?" he demanded.

"Ozzie has agreed to give Samantha Tate a fuckin' tour of the warehouse," Boss grumbled.

Dan turned to Ozzie, blinking. The sunlight streaming in through the huge leaded-glass windows caught the blond steaks in his sandy hair and made them shine like spun gold. "That took some balls," he said.

"Actually"—Ozzie scratched his head—"it was Becky's idea."

"So it took some ovaries." Becky grinned. "A far more hardy reproductive organ."

"And you chose Ozzie to do the honors because…?" Dan let the sentence dangle.

"Isn't it obvious?" Becky gestured toward Ozzie's ridiculously handsome face.

"I feel so objectified," Ozzie mumbled.

"Just use all your charm and bullshit to distract her from asking any really probing questions," Boss said.

"You say that like it's *so* easy," Ozzie huffed. "I'll have you know, I've spent years honing my charm and bullshit to—"

"Who's Samantha Tate?" Penni asked Dan from the corner of her mouth.

"That nosy reporter Boss mentioned," he told her. "She's been on our ass like a bad rash since the day we opened our doors, always hanging around trying to get something on us."

"Like what?" she asked.

"You got me." He shrugged. "Proof that we're more than we seem? Something that'll get her name above the fold in the *Chicago Tribune*?"

"Yikes." Penni shuddered, knowing the reason Dan and the Black Knights were so effective was because they were such a clandestine group. Catching the eye of a reporter was seriously bad news.

"You said it," he agreed.

Boss, who'd stopped listening to Ozzie, added, "So Becky suggested we bring her in and show her around the place. Show her we *are* building bikes. Show her the CAD software Ozzie and Becky use to do the designs. Show her the painting process and the parts storeroom. And hopefully, once we've done all that, we'll have satisfied her curiosity." After a breath, he said, "And maybe then she'll leave us the fuck alone."

"But on the day we're housing and interrogating the world's most notorious traitor?" Zoelner asked incredulously.

"Mmmph," Winterfield said from behind the duct tape, still glaring in that menacing, slightly insane way that made the hairs all over Penni's body stand up. To coin a phrase the boys in her old neighborhood had liked to use, *I don't know nothin' from nothin'*. She was no psychologist after all. But she'd bet dollars to donuts that Winterfield had lost every single one of his marbles. Besides the whole World's Worst Traitor thing, there was just something *off* about him.

"We didn't *know* we'd be doing that until a few hours ago." Boss said, shaking his head and cursing.

"Fuck-all bad timing," Dan snorted.

"And then some," Boss agreed.

"So what else is new?" Dan asked.

"Nothing as far as I can tell," Boss said. Then his scare-away-small-children expression morphed into another grin. "It's damn good to have you back."

Whatever Dan opened his mouth to say was interrupted when Vanessa called down from the second-floor landing, "Geralt is bringing her in! Everybody look alive! Oh, hey!" A wide smile split her face when she saw Dan and Zoelner. "I was in Rock's office and didn't hear you guys arrive. Welcome home!"

"No time for that," Boss groused. "Zoelner, take Winterfield and lock him in the interrogation room."

"You have an interrogation room?" Penni asked Dan, looking at him askance. She's been impressed with what

little of Black Knights Inc. she'd seen while Becky and
Ozzie booked her flight to Cusco. But never in a million years would she have thought the warehouse came
equipped with an interrogation room. BKI headquarters
were like a CIA black site on crack and raised to the
power of ten.

"It's really just an old storage building that we've
turned into a gym. But it has soundproofing and heavy
things that we can tie our guest to," Dan said.

*Okay, so maybe not on crack. But still raised to the
power of ten.*

"Chelsea, head on up to the offices," Boss continued as if
neither of them had spoken. "I don't want Miss Tate to get a
look at you and start asking questions about who you are."

"Done." Chelsea pushed her glasses up her nose,
hoisted her satchel higher on her shoulder, and turned
for the stairs. "I need to check in with Morales anyway.
See if he's learned anything new on our mysterious airport shooter." Dolly Parton's "9 to 5" started wailing
from the bottom of her purse. "After I let my mom know
we made it home safe and sound." She made a face. "I
forgot to call her when we landed."

An amused noise sounded from the back of Zoelner's
throat, and Penni turned to see him fighting a grin.

"And you two." Boss leveled his gaze on Dan and Penni.

Dan instinctively reached for her hand. It was sweet
and charming that he always sought to touch her. And
when her palm was kissing his, when her fingers were
curled around his, she felt safe and wanted in a way she
never had before.

You keep this up and you really are *going to have
your Girl Power Club card revoked.*

"What about us?" Dan lifted a brow.

"Go hide yourselves upstairs in your room," Boss said. "I don't want Samantha Tate getting a gander at Penni either. Especially since she looks like she went ten rounds with a heavyweight."

Penni reached up to touch the bandages on her cheek.

Becky rolled her eyes and elbowed Boss in the stomach. It didn't budge the giant, but it did cause him to frown and blink down at his wife. "Good God, Frank," Becky harrumphed. "What have I told you about *thinking* before you open your mouth."

"What?" Boss asked, his tone completely baffled.

Becky turned to Penni. "It's not that bad," she assured her. "You still look beautiful." Before Penni could thank her—or call bullshit, more like—Becky winked at Dan and said, "When I heard you guys were coming, I put in an order at Downtown Dogs. Picked them up right about the time you were landing, so they should still be hot. Grab a few on your way up."

Zoelner, who was already marching Winterfield toward the back of the shop, turned and shouted, "I love you, woman!"

Dan pressed a hand over his heart, grabbed Becky's fingers, and kissed them. "I'm gonna name my firstborn after you. I swear it."

Penni felt a little stab somewhere in the center of her chest. Dan's firstborn. Dan's family. And where did she fit in? Did she fit in at all?

"Yeah, okay, good." Boss pulled Becky's hand out of Dan's. "I'm getting sick and tired of all you fuckheads pawing at my wife."

Dan chuckled, and Penni ached at the affection and

peace she saw glowing in his face. He was home, surrounded by the things and the people he loved, and he'd never looked better or more handsome. It was as if being back here brought out the sparkle in him. The shine. And she was as blinded by his brilliant smile as she was dazed by it.

He turned and extended a hand. "Shall we?"

Penni looked down at his broad palm and long fingers. Both were callused; both were hard. Both had given her pleasure like she'd never experienced before. Of course pleasure was the last thing on her mind when she suddenly realized the importance of what Dan being home really meant. There was no more putting off the inevitable.

Time to face the music, Penni-pie. Her father's voice sounded through her head.

I know, Dad. Give me the strength...

Swallowing, she placed her hand in Dan's, and walked toward the metal stairway that led to the second-floor landing. With every step she took, she was reminded again that what happened in the next few hours was going to shape the rest of her life.

Chapter Eighteen

"I'M ASSUMING BY 'DOGS,' BECKY MEANT HOT DOGS," PENNI said, her delicate hand held tight within Dan's. He just couldn't help himself. He felt better when he touched her. Whole somehow. Complete.

Well, that's scary as hell, isn't it?

He tried to shake off his sudden unease but didn't quite manage it. These feelings he had for Penni were equal parts wonderful and frightening. Wonderful because caring for a woman, *wanting* a woman was a heady, exhilarating experience. And there was the added bonus that when he was with her, he didn't think about taking a drink. Didn't *need* to take a drink.

Frightening because he didn't know where all this was leading. To bed, for sure. But then what? She hadn't flown all the way to Cusco just to engage in some bow-chicka-wow-wow. She wanted *more* from him. He figured she was going to *ask* for more from him in pretty short order, now that the craziness of the past twenty-four hours was behind them. And the question that kept nagging him was, *how would he answer her*? He didn't know if he could give her more. Didn't know if he *wanted* to give her more. Because giving her more was…well…*frightening*. And wonderful.

Fuckin'-A! It was circular logic, and he couldn't seem to break free of it. *Your mind is a dangerous place;*

don't go in there alone! The little slogans he'd picked up in AA worked for more than just giving him the occasional boosts he needed to avoid the booze.

"Dan?" Penni asked, pulling him to a stop once they reached the second-floor landing. "Are you okay?"

"Uh, sorry." He shook his head, realizing he'd been a world away. "What were you asking?"

"I asked if you're okay?" Her big, brown eyes were filled with sweet concern. *Kind eyes. Sweet eyes. Wonderful eyes that I could drown in, wallow in forever. Jesus!*

"No. Before that," he said, avoiding the question. The truth was, he wasn't sure he was okay, but he sure as shit didn't want to tell her as much and then have to explain why that should be. Since he'd never lied to Penni, not once, and since he didn't plan to start now, he figured escape and evasion were the best options.

"Oh, I asked if Becky was talking about hot dogs."

Okay. Good. A banal topic. He could work with that one.

"Roger that," he told her, leading her past the long row of closed doors that led to the Knights' offices on their left. To their right was the huge, open space that housed the big conference table and Ozzie's myriad computers. The place usually looked like NORAD. Satellite feeds, speakers squawking with positions and updates since inevitably one of the Knights was checking in from some mission or other. And '80s hair bands booming in the background because Ozzie had wretched taste in music.

Today, however, it looked like little more than what Ozzie and Becky and Boss were hoping to portray:

a high-tech custom motorcycle company. Designs for various bikes showed on every computer screen. Schematics for upgraded engines and wiring systems littered the long computer desk. A rebuilt V-twin engine sat on newspaper in the middle of the conference table. Lying beside it were hand tools and a pile of greasy rags.

"Wow," Penni said, looking around. "This place looks…"

"Different," Dan finished for her, tugging her toward the conference table where Peanut, BKI's notch-eared, overweight, sorry-excuse-for-a-mouser sat, crooked tail twitching as he eyed the white cardboard box with the slogan *Good Eats, Chicago-Style Treats!*

"Hello," Penni said, scratching Peanut's ears. At first contact, the cat started his engine, rumbling louder than Heartbreaker, Dan's custom-made Harley chopper. Peanut closed his yellow eyes in pure feline pleasure. The old tom was like Ozzie in that he adored all women equally and without prejudice. "And who are you, big boy? We didn't meet when I was here last."

"That's Peanut," Dan told her. "And he's as useless as he is fat."

Penni frowned and tsked at him. Turning to Peanut, she used that voice all women whipped out when they were talking to babies or animals. "He didn't mean it," she assured the cat. "You're not fat. You're just fluffy."

Dan scoffed before grabbing the box. He looked expectantly at Penni. "Are you ready to experience *real* heaven?" he asked, making sure his expression was serious enough for the solemn occasion. Three months was a hell of a long time to go without a Downtown Dog.

She blinked at him, her lashes ridiculously long and sooty. He couldn't wait to see them fanned out against her cheek when she threw her head back and closed her eyes in ecstasy. But first...sustenance. He was going to need his strength in the next few hours. And he did mean *hours*. Because that's how long it would take to do all the things to her that he'd been dreaming about. His stomach growled in hungry anticipation of the hot dogs at the same time the moron behind his zipper throbbed in hungry anticipation of finally, *finally* getting Penni exactly where he wanted her. Beneath him. Beside him. On top of him. Every which way...

"We are still talking about hot dogs, right?" She eyed him askance, her expression teasing.

"Yes and no," he admitted. "Because these are not just *any* dogs. These are hot dogs with a capital *H*. The preeminent hot dogs. The king daddies of hot dogs. The one, the only, Chicago-style hot dogs."

"Which means...what exactly?" Penni said, still scratching Peanut's head.

"It means that after you've had one of these babies"—he opened the box with a flourish and Penni had to wrap an arm around Peanut's substantial girth to stop the cat from leaping at the hot dogs—"your sickly little New York dogs will never taste the same."

Penni peeked into the box, her chin jerking back. "Those aren't hot dogs. Those are..." She shook her head. "I don't know what, but they're not hot dogs."

"Au contraire," Rock said, emerging from one of the offices and closing the door behind him. "They are the *best* hot dogs on the planet. An all-beef frankfurter on a sesame seed bun with a dill pickle spear, a slice of tomato, a squirt of yellow mustard, onions, and relish with just a *dash* of celery salt." He brought his fingers to his mouth, kissing them. "*C'est magnifique*."

"Or as we say 'round Detroit," Dan added, chuckling, "they're damn good eatin'."

Rock came over to wrap an arm around Dan's neck and pull him in for a sideways hug. "It's good to have you home, *mon frere*," Rock said. "And with a *W* under your belt to boot."

There was a time, not too long ago, when Dan wanted everyone to just back the fuck off and leave him the hell alone. Every single one of the Knights—and their wives or girlfriends—had coddled him, indulged him, and nagged him. All with equal frequency and equal fervor. But after he'd emerged from the fog of liquor, remorse, and self-pity, he realized it was probably by the grace of God and their constant nagging, coddling, and indulging that he'd survived the years following his wife's death. His friends, his teammates, his...*family* had closed ranks around him, letting him mourn. And then they'd kicked his ass in gear when his mourning looked like it might kill him.

With Rock's arm slung around his shoulders and the familiar smells of motor oil, bad coffee, and metal shavings filling his nose, two things occurred to Dan. One, he was happy to be home. BKI was no longer a reminder of what he'd lost. It was a memorial to all he'd had then, and what he had still. And two, he was a damned lucky man to have so many good and loving people in his life.

"When you say *W,* are you talking about Winterfield or Penni?" he asked Rock from the side of his mouth, shooting a glance at the latter. She was scolding Peanut to *stay put this time*. She'd had to pull the rotund tomcat off the table and set him on the floor twice already. In typical feline fashion, Peanut ignored her and hopped onto the seat of one of the conference table chairs before jumping onto the table itself.

"Both," Rock said, slapping him on the back and wiggling his eyebrows. "It's good to see you smilin' again, *mon ami*. Really, really good."

For the record—*Are we back to that?*—it *felt* good to be smiling again.

"So where's everyone else?" Dan asked Rock. The place was usually buzzing with more Knights than you could shake a stick at.

"Out in the field," Rock said, his mouth twisting. "We've been busy since you've been gone. I think *el Jefe* is trying to tie up loose ends before he leaves office." And that was a giant question mark none of them wanted to think about. What happened when President Thompson was no longer making his home at 1600 Pennsylvania Avenue? Thompson and his Joint Chiefs had been the ones to commission the opening of Black Knights Inc. And they'd been running the shop autonomously ever since.

Before Dan could comment, the sound of the huge front door to the warehouse clanging open had Rock adding, "Better get your food and get goin'. We're about to welcome a reporter into BKI, *oui*? Never thought I'd see the day."

"You and me both." Dan shook his head and grabbed a napkin from the pile stacked beside the box. Loading it up with two—*better make it three*—hot dogs, he told Penni, "Grab a couple and let's beat feet upstairs."

"You better save me some, you rat bastard!" Zoelner called from somewhere below, making Dan grin.

Rock chuckled and headed downstairs, presumably to start interrogating Winterfield. The heels of Rock's alligator-skin cowboy boots made clanking sounds on the metal treads of the stairs as he descended.

Setting Peanut on the ground for the third time— Dan's eyes automatically roved over the curve of Penni's ass as she was bent over—she straightened and caught him staring. He donned his most innocent expression, but he didn't fool her for an instant. She stuck her tongue in her cheek, lifting a brow. "See something you like, sailor?" she asked.

Sassy. God, he loved it. Loved…

Whoa. Stop right there.

"I thought we already went through this in the airplane bathroom." He fought a grin. "And the answer is the same. I *definitely* see something I like."

A flush stole up her throat to brighten her cheeks. She tried to hide it—the adorable creature—by turning, palming a napkin, and reaching into the box to grab a hot dog. With a twist of her mouth she ventured slowly, "And speaking of what happened in the prop plane's bathroom and what *didn't* end up happening in the jet plane's bathroom…uh…sorry about that. I know I gave you the impression we'd finish what we started, but I sort of…fell asleep. Which was a total weasel deal on my part, but—"

"Fell asleep?" he scoffed, watching her hesitate and then decide on a second hot dog. It had been a long time since last night's dinner. "More like you sawed logs like a lumberjack from before we gained altitude over Bogotá to when the wheels touched down in Chicago."

"I do *not* snore," she protested. Her rosy lips—those lips he was going to kiss for a thousand years once he got her up to his room—quirked in the most delightful way.

"Okay," he relented, motioning for her to follow him to the stairs that lead to the third floor. When he'd been married, he'd lived out in the little one-bedroom caretaker's cottage that was on the property—a remnant of when Black Knights Inc. was an old menthol cigarette factory. But since he'd become a widower, he'd moved into one of the rooms upstairs. It was cozy. Comfy. And, more importantly, it was *new*.

Not that he was trying to escape the memories of his wife. Quite the contrary, he cherished each and every one of them. But neither did he like being haunted by them when he looked at every wall, into every corner, at every piece of furniture. Moving out of the caretaker's cottage had been his first step in letting go of his past. The second had been rehab. "So maybe you don't snore. But you *definitely* slobber."

"I do not," she insisted. Their footsteps made *thumping* noises on the stairs.

"Do too."

"How would you know?"

"Because you used me for a pillow the entire way." And, oh, how he'd loved holding her in his arms. He'd forgotten how good it could feel, just…*being* with a woman. No fuss. No fight. Only a mutual trust and affection that allowed them to sleep side by side, heart to heart. It wasn't epic or filled with angst. It was simply *right*. And he'd slept better, *harder* during those eight hours than he had in years. "When you woke up, there was a huge wet spot on my sweater."

"Well, I blame you for that," she said, fighting a smile. She blinked rapidly when Peanut raced ahead of them. Considering the cat was a furry tub of lard, he was amazingly spry.

"How do you figure?" he asked her, pushing open the door to his bedroom and nudging Peanut aside when the mangy feline tried to slink inside. Like most men, Dan was into a bit of kink, but he could do without an audience. Especially one with whiskers and judging yellow eyes.

"Because you make such a *good* pillow," she said, smiling. Her cheek was bruised around the butterfly bandages, and the blotches marring the beauty of her throat had turned from red to purple. His heart tripped over itself when he thought of the danger she'd been in, of how he could have lost her and—

No. He cut off his thoughts. *She's here. She's safe. And by God I'm gonna make sure she stays that way.*

"I woulda thought I was rather hard for a pillow," he said, his blood warming, his breath catching when she stepped over the threshold into his room. *There. Now I've got her exactly where I want her.* The relief of it hit him. Hard. And he realized that all the months he'd been dreaming of her, all the months he'd been missing her, had led up to this moment, when she walked into his world, into his room, and, very soon, into his bed.

"Hard can be good," she whispered, her voice having gone charmingly husky. His dick twitched at the promise in her tone, the teasing invitation in her words. Then she turned beet red and burst into a peal of laughter as she backed into the room. "I can't believe I just said that. Look what you've done to me. You've made me into a woman who spouts corny one-liners."

"I happen to *like* corny one-liners," he assured her, wondering if he'd ever heard anything sweeter or more beautiful than her unreserved laughter. "As for what I've done to you…" He caught his bottom lip between his teeth, made sure the stare he gave her through the fan of his lashes was hot and predatory, and booted the door shut. "You ain't seen nothing yet."

"So…" Dan said, licking the last of the celery salt from his fingers. Penni watched the dart of his tongue and barely refrained from groaning. She knew just how talented that tongue was. "Was I right or was I right?"

She was sitting cross-legged in the center of his bed—yep, she was officially in Dan's bed and she had the butterflies to prove it—wiping a drop of yellow mustard from the corner of her mouth with a napkin. "Forget about it," she said around the last bite of hot dog. "Best hot dogs ever. I'm straight-up ruined for anything else." And *happy* to finally be able to keep all her food down. For a couple of months after The Assignment, it had been touch and go.

"Warned you." He smiled and hooked his hands behind his head, leaning back against the headboard and stretching out his long legs. He let out a contented sigh that was far from sexual, but it still hit Penni's ear like a hot kiss. "Man, it's good to be home," he said, sliding a satisfied look around the room.

The space was pretty much how Penni had imagined it. Polished wood floors, brick walls, and exposed piping and ductwork running along the ceiling gave the space a loft feel. And with a big wooden bed covered in a navy-and-green-striped comforter, a couple of metal bedside tables that supported mismatched lamps, and a big chest of drawers, the room was simple and masculine. Just like the man himself.

And *also* like the man himself, the space held a little mystery. There was a lacquered jewelry box atop the dresser. All pearly and white, it looked starkly feminine compared to the Ruger he'd placed beside it after he kicked the door closed, effectively sealing them inside his room. All alone. No likely interruptions.

There go the damned butterflies again. Geez.

And then there was the picture in the silver frame next to the old-fashioned alarm clock on the bedside table. It showed Dan with his arm around the shoulders of a cute redheaded woman. It was obviously old. Dan looked at least ten years younger in Navy dress whites, not to mention…happy, almost innocent. Penni couldn't help but wonder who the woman was. She opened her mouth to ask, but before she could, he pushed up from the bed and extended his hand. "Come with me," he said.

"What? Where?" She looked around like maybe she'd missed something. "I thought Boss said we were supposed to stay put until the reporter leaves."

"Bathroom." He hooked a thumb over his shoulder. And the butterflies that'd been flitting around in her stomach got together and made a bunch of babies, multiplying exponentially.

And even though she knew he wasn't inviting her for another assignation in a latrine—he didn't have that naughty gleam in his eye that said he was propositioning her—she still said, "You sure have a thing for bathrooms."

She was trying to cover up her nervousness by reminding him not only about the airplane lavatory but the hotel bathroom in Kuala Lumpur. Unfortunately, thoughts of that bathroom in Malaysia, about what had happened there and what it'd meant to her *and* to him, only *increased* her anxiety.

You're stalling.

Damnit! I know!

She just didn't want it to end. This feeling of being wanted, of belonging, of happiness and hope and promise. She didn't want the real world to intrude, to have to face his possible scorn or rejection. She wanted—

"When it comes to you"—he interrupted her tumultuous thoughts. And *there* was that gleam!—"I have a thing for *all* rooms." *See? Why can't it just stay this way?* "But in this case, I mean let's brush our teeth."

"Oh," she said, blinking. Then, "Oh!" Because she realized he wanted to brush his teeth so that when he kissed her it wouldn't taste like hot dog, onions, and relish. And he *did* want to kiss her. It was kind of obvious since every time she'd opened her mouth to wrap her lips around the hot dog, his eyes had zeroed in, burning with interest as he watched the frankfurter slip between her teeth.

Then again, maybe *kissing* her wasn't what he'd been envisioning.

Her blood grew warm. A soft flame flared to life between her legs. Her heart picked up its pace—which only aggravated the butterflies in her belly. They went wild. The time had come. There was no more putting it off. *Damnit.*

Courage, Penni. Have courage.

Yeah, right. Easier said than done.

"Do you…um…" She hesitated, swallowing. "Do you want to…talk first?"

A strange emotion flickered across Dan's face. It was gone before she could figure out what it was. "Do you?" he asked, giving her the perfect out.

"Not really," she admitted, seizing the opportunity with both hands because, you know, she was a total fraidy-cat, pansy-ass wuss. She just couldn't help herself. She wanted, just once, to know what it was like to lie in his arms, to love him and let him love her without bombs going off around them or Russian spies lurking in the next room. That wasn't too much to ask, was it?

Dan preempted whatever answer the voice in her head might have given when he grinned and said, "Neither do I."

Grabbing her hand, he dragged her off the bed. Two minutes later—after he'd pulled a brand-new toothbrush from the drawer of his vanity, cracked open the case, and handed it to her—she was standing next to him, her mouth full of minty suds, a goofy grin plastered across her face.

"What're you smiling about?" he asked, spitting toothpaste into the sink and filling a glass with water to rinse his mouth.

"Just that…" She had to stop and get rid of her own toothpaste before she could finish. "Who would have ever thought when we met three months ago that we'd be here now? Brushing our teeth together? Life's weird, isn't it?"

"Mmm," he murmured noncommittally. "I guess.

Although..." He grabbed her toothbrush, ran it under the faucet, and tossed it on the counter. "I hafta say that since the first moment I laid eyes on you, I *wanted* to be here, brushing our teeth together and—"

He pulled the collar of her sweater down, revealing her bra strap and shoulder. He bent to kiss her shoulder and his shaggy blond hair fell over his forehead. His eyes were lasers reflecting back at her from the mirror. His breath was warm, his lips cool from the water, and his tongue a bold sweep of liquid desire. When he kissed her there, she was helpless to resist him. Totally enslaved to his every want, his every need, his every demand.

"And *what*?" she breathed, her head falling back against his broad shoulder as sensation shot from the spot he was kissing, diffused through her entire body, and coalesced in her core. She was instantly achy, instantly needy. It was crazy how that happened. One minute they were sharing a companionable moment, completely benign, totally platonic. The next minute, all she wanted to do was to rip his clothes off and impale herself on the hard, male flesh he pressed against her bottom as he crowded her close to the vanity.

"And *everything*," he finally finished, his voice deliciously low. It rumbled from his chest into her back. "From the moment I laid eyes on you I wanted *everything*."

Before she knew what he was about, he released the collar of her sweater so he could grab the hem and whip the garment over her head. With an expertise that was both amazing and a little annoying— *just how many bras has he taken off in his life?*—he flicked open the clasp of her bra and dragged it from her shoulders, tossing it next to the sweater on the tile floor.

And then there she was. Naked. *Again*. Well, *mostly* naked anyway. There were still her pesky jeans and panties and socks to worry about—they'd both kicked off their boots before climbing onto his bed to eat the hot dogs.

Her reflection in the mirror revealed the rise and fall of her breasts as her breaths came short and fast. She'd never really thought of her boobs as anything to write home about. Sure, they were round and firm. But they were also a little on the small side. And her nipples were tiny. The areolas almost nonexistent around the buds of the nipples themselves, especially when they were puckered with desire, like they were now.

But when Dan looked at her, when he reverently cupped her from behind, his thumbs seeking the extended tips, she saw herself through his eyes. And she felt... beautiful. Soft and feminine. Flawlessly creamy and sensuously erotic. She shivered within the circle of his embrace, under the expertise of his hands and fingers.

"God, Penni," he murmured, his face next to hers, his eyes watching what his hands were doing. "You're so fuckin' gorgeous you make me harder than I've ever been before."

As if to prove his point, he flexed his hips forward, driving her thighs into edge of the counter and rubbing the length of himself against her ass. It was incredibly sexy, carnal even, watching what he was doing to her at the same time she was feeling it. He must have thought so too. Because he never took his eyes off her, off the reflected images of her breasts in his hands.

Her skin looked milky white compared to his long,

tan fingers. And the contrast between the rough calluses and scars on the backs of his hands, and the flawless flesh of her breasts was stark. He was man. Battle-scarred and tough. And she was woman. Soft and pliant.

He caught her sensitive nipples between his thumb and forefingers and gently plucked. She would swear she felt the sensation directly between her thighs. A rush of blood swelled her sex. A surge of wetness slicked her core, readying her for what was to come when finally, *finally*, the two of them would be together. Taking their time. Enjoying the pleasure and desire that had raged between them from the beginning.

She moaned her encouragement, rubbing her bottom against the steely shaft that throbbed so insistently.

"You want more?" he asked, watching her reactions.

"God, yes," she hissed. When it came to him, when it came to this, she had no pride. Only need. Only want.

He released one of her breasts so he could turn her chin. And then…oh, and then he kissed her. In that Dan way. Like a conqueror. Like a gladiator. All pillage and plunder and no waiting for permission.

The slick glide of his tongue into her mouth mimicked the motion of his hand at her breast. Every time he pushed past her teeth, he plucked her nipple. And eventually, she couldn't distinguish one form of pleasure from the other. It was all tangled up, tied up together. Her heart beat wildly against her rib cage. Her stomach quivered with want. Goose bumps peppered her skin, making the nerve endings beneath hyperaware so that every brush of his fingers, every hot rush of his breath was both agony and ecstasy.

"Dan…" His name was sigh, prayer, and entreaty.

"Tell me what you want," he whispered against her ear after he'd released her chin. His eyes pinned hers in the mirror, refusing to let her look away, refusing to let her hide.

"It's your turn to tell me what *you* want," she reminded him, her voice soft and low and full. "We were interrupted the last time, remember?"

He squeezed his eyes closed and moaned, rubbing himself against her. She knew the friction had to be building the ache as much as relieving it. "Yes, I remember." His voice was barely above a growl. "I remember you down on your knees in front of me. I remember the feel of your soft hands wrapped around my cock. I remember your succulent mouth opening."

"Is that what you want again?" she asked, watching his eyes flutter open. His lids hung at half-mast, a strong muscle twitched in his beard-stubbled jaw.

"What I want would shock you," he said. It felt a little like a challenge.

"Tell me," she whispered, arching back into him, increasing the friction of their bodies.

For a while he simply held her gaze in the mirror. She could tell he was debating, wondering if she could handle the bald truth of his wants. She held her breath, waiting, hoping he would tell her. She loved the thought of him trusting her enough to show her his most lustful, lascivious side.

She got her wish when he finally admitted, "I want to fuck you from behind and watch your face in the mirror while you come."

Sweet heavenly father! Just the sound of it, just the *thought* of it, had her womanhood contracting, pulsing,

aching. "Then do it," she told him, unconsciously reaching up to rub the bump on the bridge of her nose. "Do
exactly that."

*Who are you? And what have you done with Penni
DePaul?* It was a valid question considering she wasn't
an adventurous lover. Or, at least…she'd never been one
before. But maybe that's because she'd never been with
a man who made her feel safe enough to *be* adventurous.

Dan made her feel safe. He made her feel adventurous.
He made her feel…so many things. *All* the things.

His throat made a sticky sound when he swallowed,
his eyes searching hers in the mirror. "But don't you
want me to—"

"Do it," she interrupted him, her breaths coming fast
and hard, her nipples standing high and tight. "Just like
you said. *That's* what I want."

"Fuck me," he groaned, grabbing her hips and thrusting
against her ass like he couldn't help himself. Like he had
to rub himself against her or he would die.

She caught her lip between her teeth and grinned—
even *she* would say her reflection looked sexy,
coquettish; and she'd never claimed to be either in her
entire life. "I thought the plan was for *you* to fuck *me,*"
she said.

Chapter Nineteen

D<small>AN COULD NOT BELIEVE HIS GOOD LUCK</small>…

Penni was everything he'd dreamed about and more. He'd known she was sensual and passionate from their time in Kuala Lumpur. But he'd never guessed she was a sex kitten on steroids. Just when he thought he'd pushed her past the point of comfort, she surprised him by meeting him there and then taking it a step further. She was the perfect foil for him sexually.

And she was waiting.

Tomorrow he would probably scold himself for not taking his time when he undressed her. He pulled her jeans, panties, and socks off in one go and shoved them all aside with a careless foot. And he would *definitely* want to kick his own ass for not trying to be sexier when he disrobed for her. Instead of slowly undoing the button on his pants, teasingly drawing down the zipper to increase the anticipation, he shucked his drawers in record time and whipped off his sweater like it was on fire.

The bad thing about all that was he didn't savor the removal of each piece of clothing, glorying in each new inch of skin that was revealed. The good thing about all that was now they were both buck naked. And it was about damn time. He'd been waiting, *fantasizing* about the moment when there would be nothing between them. No barrier of clothing. No impediment for his seeking hands and mouth to overcome. Just flaming hot skin to flaming hot skin.

His reflection in the mirror looked huge compared to hers. Where her shoulders were narrow, his were broad. Where her arms were lithe and lovely, his were bulging and roped with sinew and veins. Where she was soft and delicate and smooth, he was hard and heavy and rough. Put together the disparity between them was…beautiful, sexy, highlighting the differences between male and female, man and woman.

"Do it." She braced her hands on the counter and shoved her sweet, round ass back at him. "Just like you said." Anticipation and desire made her voice breathy and rough.

When she bent over, her delicate breasts swung forward like ripe fruit. He wanted to pluck them, taste them, tease them. And he would. He *so* would. But first…

"Spread your legs," he commanded, his dick bobbing in time to his heartbeat. When she obeyed without hesitation, he growled his approval, smoothing his hand over her ass, noting the satiny texture of her skin, its warmth, and the subtle flush that pinkened it. She shivered, her eyes reflecting back at him when he glanced into the mirror. The chocolaty brown pools were liquid with need, hot with desire.

"Are you ready for me, Brooklyn?" he rumbled. Yes, rumbled. That was the only way to describe what had happened to his voice. It seemed to be coming up from the very depths of him, where he was full and heavy with a dark craving.

"Yes," she swore, shoving back into his caressing hand, wiggling slightly in invitation.

He could see that she was telling the truth. The folds of her bare sex were swollen and pink. An enchanting solicitation that eons of civilization had yet to conquer. When a man saw that, all his faculties scrambled. He became no better than an ape in the forest, one and only one thing on his mind. *Mate. Now.*

But Dan was able to avert the urge to spread her ass cheeks and womanhood and plunge inside because he knew he'd get there. And soon too. But first he wanted to test her, to feel how hot she was for him, how wet.

"Let's check to make sure," he said huskily, turning his hand so he could slide two fingers over her, into her.

"Dan!" She moaned his name and it was a siren's call.

The tips of his two middle fingers were poised just inside her entrance, and she was so hot she singed his skin. So wet she made his dick pulse and ache. A drop of passion gathered at his swollen tip, rolling over his head and down the length of his shaft. It was a tease and a caress. He shuddered at how painfully sensitive his skin was.

"More," she demanded, pushing back against his hand. "Give me more."

God. He loved it when she started spouting orders.

"Like this?" he asked, sliding his fingers inside her to his middle knuckles. She was so unbelievably soft, so satisfyingly responsive. At the intrusion of his fingers, her walls closed around him, pulsing, grasping as if she was welcoming him in, pulling him deeper, squeezing him tight.

"More." She wiggled her ass. Seeing the move, *feeling* the move made his cock throb so hard he was afraid for a moment there that the tip of his head had blown off. Once he assured himself that wasn't the case, he gave her what she was asking for, seating himself to the last knuckle.

"Christ, *yessss*," she hissed, closing her eyes and letting her head fall back.

She was ready. *More* than ready. So he began to pump. Slowly and softly at first. And then harder. Faster. She rode his hand unabashedly, meeting him stroke for stroke, her small breasts swaying, her soft pink nipples having darkened to a tantalizing rose. A deep flush bloomed over her collarbones and snaked up her throat into her face. Her mouth was open. Her breaths coming shallow and harsh. She no longer cared how she looked; she was concentrating everything she had on the pleasure he was giving her. But for the record? She looked amazing. So fucking sexy and erotic as she worked with him toward her own release.

"That's it," he crooned, the muscles and tendons in his forearm standing out as he pumped faster. He felt her walls contract around him once. A second time. He reached forward and caught her pebbled nipple, giving the tender bud a squeeze. She cried out and started unraveling. He felt her body clamping down on his fingers as she bathed his hand in her desire.

"Jesus," he breathed, his heart roaring, his breaths labored, his head spinning. "Jesus, Brooklyn. You're so damned sexy."

She didn't respond. She couldn't. She was in that wonderful orgasmic twilight when the body only functioned to shimmer with undulating waves of ebbing pleasure.

It's time. Time to make her all mine, just like I've dreamed. Finally. Finally.

Keeping his fingers inside her, softly moving them in and out to draw out the very last vestiges of ecstasy, he used his other hand to pull open the drawer on the vanity and extract a condom from inside. Tearing off the foil packaging with his teeth, he hissed when he placed the rubber ring around the throbbing head of his cock. He was so hard he hurt, his skin stretched so tight it was shiny. Then he fisted the condom down his length, pleasure bubbling at the base of his spine from the friction of his own palm.

When he looked up, he saw her eyes were open—well half-open, anyway—and sparkling back at him in the mirror. "That was…" she breathed, an enchanting grin pulling at the corners of her gorgeous mouth, "lovely."

He realized he was grinning back at her and quirked a brow. "You wanna make it even lovelier?" he challenged.

"Oh, *yes*." She nodded, catching her bottom lip between her teeth.

"Good." He slowly removed his hand, watching the retreat with hungry, avid eyes, watching as his fingers came away wet with her climax. Fisting himself, he gritted his jaw against the pleasure as he used her wetness to moisten his latex-covered shaft. Then he placed one hand on the small of her back and used the other to grab his thick base and bend himself forward.

When the plump head of his cock kissed her entrance, he saw her body open and flower around him, as if eager to draw him in. Her next words proved her need. "Please, Dan. I want you inside me. I *need* you inside me."

That's what he wanted too. What he *needed* too. But he also wanted to draw it out, this wonderful, carnal moment of joining. So he gripped her hip to keep her from thrusting back at him, and slowly, ever-so-slowly, inched forward, watching her body swallow him, seeing her part and stretch around his girth. It was agony. It was ecstasy. It was elemental and ethereal. Both corporeal and spiritual.

It's so right…

And there was that word again. He couldn't escape it. Didn't want to escape it, he realized with a start.

"Jesus, you're tight," he swore, her body squeezing him like a hot, satin-gloved fist.

"You're big," was her retort and he caught the devilish gleam of her eyes in the mirror's reflection.

"That too," he agreed. And he was doing it again. Grinning like an idiot.

Of course his grin melted away when he grabbed her shoulder for leverage, pulling her back at the same time he thrust forward. Her quickly indrawn breath mingled with the sound of his low groan. He was seated to the hilt. Totally surrounded by her. Totally immersed in her. Totally enslaved by her. And it was heaven.

"Wait," she said breathlessly, reaching back to grab his hip. The bite of her little nails into his flesh—a warning—was just as much pleasure as it was pain. "Just let me…" She swallowed, holding his eyes in the mirror. "Give me a second to get used to it, okay?"

"S-sure," he was able to grit out, remaining stock-still even though every instinct he had told him to thrust. Hard. Fast. Over and over until the orgasm building inside him exploded. Until the world around him ceased to exist.

Her inner muscles shimmered around his shaft like a million tiny fingers, touching, squeezing, caressing. But he waited. And then he waited some more as she simply braced herself and breathed. It felt like an eternity, but was probably only a few seconds. Finally, he ground out, "You're killing me, woman."

He didn't like the slightly plaintive tone of his voice, but there was nothing he could do about it. The pleasure of being inside her and not moving was torture. Beautiful, exquisite, soul-shaking torture.

"Okay." She nodded. "Okay. I'm ready."

She'd barely gotten the last word out before he was sliding from her body, slowly, closing his eyes against the delicious friction. He continued to retreat, glancing down to see his shaft emerging from her snug grip, shiny with her welcome and her passion. When the flared edge of his head peeked from her pink opening, he gritted his teeth and pressed back home in one hard, unapologetic thrust.

She groaned when his plump tip pressed against the end of her channel and the opening to her womb. It took everything he had to hold himself still and ask, "Y'okay?"

"Oh, yes," she assured him, wiggling slightly, rubbing his head deep inside her. The smell of sex filled the room, the decadent scent of hot skin and needy bodies. And mixing through it all was the sweet aroma of rosewater. It would always, for the rest of his life, remind him of her. "Yes. More, please."

"With pleasure," he assured her, pulling out and setting a rhythm that was meant to slowly drive her to the edge of ecstasy again—and drive *him* to insanity. Over and over he thrust, the friction more delectable with each pass. The desire building with each hot, wet glide.

He could feel her building beneath him. Feel her body sucking at him in greedier and greedier pulls. His orgasm was a living thing now, roaring and growling and begging for release. He held it at bay. Pushed it back and down because he wanted them to come together. He wanted them to jump together. He wanted to see the pleasure on her face at the same time he felt its prurient pull inside his own body.

"Oh God. Dan!" She had one hand braced on the counter as he pumped into her. The other hand was on his hip, egging him on, encouraging him harder, faster. He obliged, reaching around her and sliding his middle finger between her folds. When he found the swollen nub, he rubbed it in circles. Thrusting and rubbing. Thrusting and rubbing. Taking them higher and higher until he could feel her body coiling, her muscles tensing. The sound of flesh slapping against flesh filled the room, competed with their harsh breathing.

"I'm going to c-come," she warned.

"Good," he groaned, feeling his own pleasure building, building, building. It burned deep inside his testicles, raced along his shaft. "Yes, Brooklyn! Let's come together!"

"Oh God!" she cried again, her head falling to hang between her shoulders and little pulses, like the flutter of butterfly wings, started gripping his shaft.

"Lift your head!" he commanded. "I wanna see your face!"

But it was too late. She jumped. Flinging herself from the cliff of physical ecstasy, flying with gleeful abandon into the abyss. She screamed his name, shuddering, her body clamping down on his. Hard. And then she was dragging him with her. The pleasure, the sweet temptation of release too much. He was coming. In hot, heavy spurts that obliterated thought. That squashed all reason. That took him to a place of such ecstasy he wondered if it could possibly be real.

The world turned. Minutes passed. But he was unaware of any of it. Lost. Lost in her. In sensation. Sweet, decadent, glorious sensation that seemed to go on and on. He didn't know how long they stayed there, joined and shaking as their simultaneous orgasms washed over them, through them. But when he finally had the strength to open his eyes, when his mind reasserted itself, making rational thought possible, his first thought was, *Damnit! I wanted to watch her go over!*

He'd been waiting, dreaming, fantasizing for months about seeing her face when he took her to the ultimate heights of pleasure, and he'd *missed* it. With a growl, he pulled from her body, yanked off the used condom—he hissed when the ring raked over his still painfully sensitive skin—and tossed it in the trash can. Grabbing a fresh one from the drawer, he snatched her off her feet, lifted her into his arms, and stalked out of the bathroom.

"Dan? Uh, what are—"

She squeaked when he tossed her on the bed. But before she could scramble away, he grabbed her ankles and dragged her until her ass was at the edge of the mattress. "We're gonna do this again," he said, tossing the empty foil wrapper over his shoulder and sliding the new condom onto his still-erect penis. "And this time"—he positioned her ankles on the edge of the mattress so that her long legs were spread wide, her sex open and ready to receive him—"I'm gonna see your face when you come."

—⁓—

Big. That was the first thought to tumble through Penni's passion-hazy brain when Dan stepped between her legs and angled himself down to enter her. His shaft looked huge, roped with veins and straining the latex of the condom.

Male. That was the second thought she had, her breath catching when he pushed himself partway inside her. With his mile-wide shoulders, heavy pectoral muscles, and that smattering of hair over his chest that arrowed down his corrugated belly until it joined his pubic hair, he was unabashedly male.

And she was small and female. That much was made obvious when he gritted his teeth and slid in further, stretching her, filling her to capacity. She pushed up onto her elbows so she could watch her own impalement. *Sweet Christ.* She wouldn't have thought it was possible to feel needy, to feel achy again so soon. She'd just experienced two of the most earth-shaking orgasms of her life, and one look at him entering her, one peek at his hardened jaw and the glow in his eyes as he watched his heavy shaft part her folds, one glance at the tattoo on his lower belly as his stomach muscles contracted—*No Guts, No Glory*—was enough to have clawing her way toward that peak once again.

Her blood was on fire. Her skin slick with sweat. Her heart thundering and her lungs heaving. "Dan…" She whispered his name because…just because. A verbal connection to go with the physical connection they were making.

"Don't hide from me this time, Brooklyn," he

warned, his eyes boring into hers. "Don't close your eyes or duck your chin." And *why* having him want to watch her, want to see her face while she shattered apart should be the ultimate flattery, the ultimate turn-on was anybody's guess. But it was. Maybe because it was just so…*intimate*.

He waited barely a beat after seating himself to the hilt before he began thrusting. The rhythm he set wasn't slow, but it wasn't fast either. It was simply constant. A cadence guaranteed to build the passion, the pleasure for both of them.

He did come, didn't he?

Yes. She hadn't mistaken the feel of his shaft pulsing deep inside her, or the full look of the condom he tossed in the trash. But you'd never know it by the feel of him now. His erection hadn't subsided one millimeter. If anything, it felt even thicker, even longer.

Can guys be multi-orgasmic?

She'd never heard of such a thing.

That was the last rational thought she had because he leaned forward, coming down on his elbows and sealing their lips in a hot kiss. The rhythmic invasion of his tongue matched the rhythmic invasion of his body. Sure. Steady. Over and over they joined. And the build was slow. Deliberate.

The friction of his coarse chest hairs against the buds of her breasts was delicious. The way his pubic bone ground into her clitoris at the end of every thrust was divine. She hooked her heels above his ass to increase the pressure, to encourage him faster. He obliged her, pumping his hips harder, upping the pace until her body was one big jumble of erotic pleasure. Each nerve ending was alive and screaming for more, more, so much *more!*

The skin of his back was hot and slick with sweat. The muscles beside his spine hard and flexing, creating a deep groove of his backbone. The smell of toothpaste and sex and Dan's clean, electric scent filled her nose, and she was so completely overcome with pleasure, with joy, she thought she may burst with it. Just *boom!* Penni-shaped confetti raining down all around the room. And then she started to. Burst, that is.

Little tendrils of ecstasy wrapped around her womanhood, shimmering through the place where they were connected, twanging against her swollen clitoris, and moving up into her belly, her breasts. She squeezed herself around his plundering shaft, trying to increase the pressure, the pleasure. She was teetering on the brink, unable to topple over. It was delicious. *Maddening.*

"Don't force it," Dan said, breaking the sweet suction of their lips. He framed her face in his hands, his eyes darkened by passion as his hips continued to thrust. Hard and steady. Deep and penetrating. "It'll come. Just ride it out, babe. Just ride it on out."

"Dan…" she said breathlessly, staring up into his handsome, fierce face. Sweat beaded on his brow, dampening the tendrils of blond hair there, turning them brown. *He's gorgeous.* And thick. She would be sore for days to come. But she didn't care. She didn't care if she had to be carted out in a wheelchair. She just wanted it to go on and on, to keep him inside, moving, rubbing, loving her. Forever. The thought was enough to send the pleasure ratcheting higher, tighter. It began to feel as if there was a spring at her core, coiling and coiling. The tension building and building.

"Oh God!" she screamed when, like a flash, another orgasm hit her. This time it was like a locomotive. Hard. Heavy. Unstoppable. She felt it everywhere, clamping her womb like a vise, tightening her nipples until she cried out with the beautiful, painful pleasure of it all. Over and over it hammered her. As if she were standing on railroad tracks, taking blow after blow from each successive train car.

"Look at me!" Dan roared. "Open your eyes!"

She would have thought herself incoherent, but she managed to understand his command and obeyed. His green eyes were full of fire, full of satisfaction, full of triumph as she continued to shatter around him, her body squeezing his, milking his. He thrust deep one last time, churning his hips in a little circle to abrade the screaming bundle of nerves at the top of her sex and draw out her orgasm. Which, let's be honest, already felt never ending. Just *boom! Boom! Boom!* Blast after blast of brilliant, incandescent rapture. Until she was blind with it. Deaf with it. Numb with it.

She had no idea how long she remained that way, riding out the pleasure just as he'd instructed her to do. Letting it crash into her over and over. Again and again. But eventually, the blows turned to ripples, the painful contractions turned to flutters, and her eyesight returned. She saw him smiling down at her with the look of a man who'd just conquered the world. If she'd had a breath left in her, she would have laughed at his blatant expression of victory. Her hearing returned next, and his deep, labored breaths filled her ears along with the sound of a contented growl issuing from the back of his throat. And finally, *finally*, her body came back to her. She could once again feel the rasp of his chest hair against her nipples, feel the full girth of him stretching her walls to—

Wait a minute. What the hey? "You didn't come." She frowned.

"Not this time," he said, still grinning. "Not yet anyway."

"*Can* you come again?" she asked, squeezing her inner muscles around him. His shaft throbbed in response to the caress and a muscle ticked in his beard-stubbled jaw.

"Yes," he admitted, his eyes molten with unquenched desire. "If you think you can handle more."

"You bet your ass," she told him. But when he slowly thrust, one liquid in-and-out, she realized just how sore she really was. Catching her bottom lip between her teeth, she grinned at him and said, "But I think I have a better idea…"

—◊◊◊—

Dan was reminded of a quote from Eminem. *Times are hard and they're getting even harder*. Only in *this* case, *he* was hard and getting even harder. Pulling out of Penni's snug body had been pure agony, but the pain was worth it to see her now, down on her knees beside the bed, lovingly removing the condom and tossing it into the trash can in front of his night table.

A flush had turned her pale skin a delightful pink. *Everywhere*. Her lashes were thick and sooty, hiding her eyes from him as she gripped the base of his shaft. And her nipples stood out in hard points, little punctuation marks advertising her continued excitement. It was enough to make a doubting man believe in God. Who else could have created such a heavenly creature?

"Brooklyn," he husked the nickname he'd given her months ago.

"How do you like to be sucked?" she asked him, her dark eyes lifting to his face. "Tell me."

Sweet Jesus! He'd taught her the game too well. She'd outpaced him, becoming the tease, the temptress. The sorceress. He was completely under her spell. Completely entranced by her. By every tiny thing about her.

"S-softly," he admitted, his voice deep and cracking with need. "Just the tip."

"Like this?" she asked, angling him down and leaning forward. She formed a little ring with her wet, swollen lips, and sucked him softly, slowly inside the hot haven of her mouth.

"Yes," he whispered, his eyes crossing at the pleasure that bordered on pain. His bare toes curled into the boards of the floor. His hips nudged forward of their own accord. It was good. It was too damned good. "Now…" He had to pause and swallow. His throat made a dry, sticky sound. "L-lick my—"

He didn't even need to finish. She plied the slightly rough flat of her tongue over his head, flicking softly at the little slit, coaxing a drop from him. She hummed when she tasted his desire. And the vibration of the sound traveled up his shaft like a bolt of lightning that eventually struck the base of his spine. He cried out, fisting her hair in his hand.

His hips flexed forward again, sliding his shaft deeper, just a little deeper into the wonder of her mouth.

He wanted to thrust unabashedly, over and over. But he was a gentleman first and foremost, so he forced himself to breathe past the urge, to satisfy himself with small strokes that had the flared ring of his head rasping against the pursed ring of her lips. And, little by little, he got himself back under control. Or at least some *semblance* of control.

He softened his hold on her hair, forcing his fingers to release their death grip and said hoarsely, "Now suck on me in long, hard pulls, and fist me in your hand at the same time."

"Mmm," she hummed her pleasure and agreement with his plan. This time he was ready for the vibrations that made his hips arch. She eagerly did as he instructed. And, just like Goldilocks, she did it *just right*. The wet pull of her mouth was perfection. The hard grip of her hand unerring.

"Brooklyn…" Her name was both praise and a curse. "Look at me."

He didn't know why he wanted to see her eyes, but he suspected it had something to do with needing that connection. Needing her to know that it was *him* she was giving pleasure to, taking pleasure from. Needing to remind *himself* that it was her—lovely, sexy Penelope Ann DePaul—who was blowing his mind, his whole fucking world apart.

Her long lashes fanned across her blushing cheeks, creating little crescent shadows in the light streaming in from the leaded-glass window. Then she glanced up at him and he saw that the brown pools of her irises were flashing with desire. She *was* a temptress. A sorceress. An enchantress. And when she sucked, her cheeks hollowing out, her plush, pink lips stretched tight around his thick, veined shaft, he knew without a shadow of a doubt that he never wanted to break free of her magic. Never wanted to escape her sweet, witchy woman's spells. Not for a million and one years.

When her head began to bob, her eyes remaining on his face to gauge his reaction, it hit him... Their connection wasn't just physical. It wasn't just...*this*. It was more. It was everything. And even though it scared him to death to contemplate taking the plunge again—loving meant the possibility of losing, and losing had nearly cost him everything—he just couldn't stop himself.

He cried out her name when she pulled his body over the edge with her talented mouth. But it wasn't just that. It wasn't just a physical release. Because he felt his heart go too. Felt it take the leap out of solitude and loneliness, out of darkness and despair, and straight into that terrifying abyss that was...*love*.

Chapter Twenty

GEORGE HAD A PLAN...

"This had better work," Spider said. "I'm very upset you allowed Winterfield to be captured alive. I don't like the impression it gives that anyone can leave my organization, while away their days selling the information they were supposed to give to *me*, and then face no consequences for their treachery. It doesn't fit my narrative, George. You *know* it doesn't."

"I know, Spider," he admitted, holding his mobile to his ear while nudging the hold-all bag at his feet. He liked the heavy feel of the C4. It grounded him. Gave him a sense of assurance that all could yet be remedied. The aroma wafting up from the plastic explosives was sweet, like almonds, and it mixed with the tangier scents of yeast and fresh-baked bread.

Good old Benton. He was a serious tosser, especially when he called George by that ridiculous nickname, but the kid had come through with flying colors. Not only had there been a car and driver waiting to take George straight to Goose Island, home of Black Knights Inc., when he landed at O'Hare International Airport, but on the backseat had been new papers, two handguns, blueprints for the warehouse that showed the building's structural layout and weaknesses, and a hold-all bag full of enough plastic explosives to take the whole place down.

"But this *will* work," George insisted. "Then everyone will see that you stop at nothing to tie up loose ends. This thing I'm about to do will send an unmistakable message to anyone who might think to double-cross you again."

"Perhaps," Spider allowed. "On the other hand, I would have preferred Winterfield be taken out before he was questioned. There's no telling what that crazy twat is revealing."

"What *can* he reveal?" George asked, soothing Spider's ruffled feathers. "He doesn't know who you really are." None of them did. That was the power of Spider. The man had been able to catch so many people in his web without ever wriggling from the shadows.

"True," Spider agreed.

George blew out a shaky breath. He absolutely *hated* talking to Spider. Like the arachnid he was named after, the man made George's skin crawl. And for good reason. Because *also* like some species of the creature he was named after, Spider could be frightfully deadly.

Taking a quick glance around the little bakery shop located across the street from the massive iron gates of Black Knights Inc., assuring himself the lone customers seated at the high-top table in the far corner had their headphones plugged into their ears while they sipped overpriced coffee and tapped away on their laptops, he got back to the topic at hand: his plan.

"Their cameras only cover the wall and the exterior of the compound," he said. From his seat in the window of the bakery, he had a clear view of the cameras in question. "They don't appear to have any sort of surveillance inside. Probably because they assume no one can breach their perimeter. So once I'm beyond the gate, no one will be the wiser."

"But how will you *get* beyond the gate?" Spider asked. The noise of a rustling newspaper carried over the line. Spider seemed to have only two settings, borderline disinterest or murderous rage. It was terrifying how quickly the man could switch from one to the other.

"Easy," George assured him. "I'll take out the sorry sod in the guardhouse and simply *let* myself in."

For a while there was silence on the other end of the line. It made George nervous. It meant Spider was working through the ins and outs, considering scenarios, contemplating consequences, and staying one step ahead of George and...*everyone*. From what George knew of the man through their various interactions, and from the dealings George had had with others under Spider's purview, it was obvious Spider was too smart by half. Which, if rumor was to be believed, was how Spider had crawled to the top of the heap of so many criminal enterprises.

Finally Spider murmured, almost to himself, "I've had occasion to run into these Black Knights before."

"Have you?" he asked.

"Mmm," Spider hummed. "A few years ago they took my..." He stopped himself. "They took something from me," he finished.

"And they're still alive?" George blurted.

When Spider chuckled, it sounded like dead leaves rustling in the wind. "Some things are better left alone," he admitted.

"Well, today they'll pay for what they stole from

you," he assured Spider. "And Winterfield will pay for his disloyalty. Two birds with one stone."

"Yes, I suppose so," Spider said. "I *can* see how this plan of yours could work." Then he added, his tone taking on a sharp edge, "It had *better* work, George. For *your* sake."

The hard stone of fear that had been perpetually lodged in George's chest since the day he'd begun working for Spider started grinding against his ribs. Despite the cool fall day, sweat beaded on his upper lip. "I won't fail."

"See that you don't," Spider said. "I can't abide another of my employees disappointing me so utterly. I *won't* abide another of my employees being caught."

Spider always referred to the people he kept under his thumb as *employees*. Although *indentured servants* was probably more accurate. They all paid for what Spider had over them by living their lives at his beck and call. And dying at his beck and call too.

As if Spider was reading his mind, he continued, "You know what I'm saying, don't you, George?"

Oh, yes. George knew. And he barely resisted the urge to puke up the sesame seed bagel he'd eaten. A shudder started at his core and worked its way outward, until his arms and legs were shaking. "You're saying that, no matter what, no matter how this goes, I am not to be captured alive."

"Precisely." Spider's tone went back to being bored. And George didn't mistake the sound of a newspaper page being turned.

He blinked away the tears burning in his eyes. "But, Bella... I—"

"Don't worry about her," Spider said. "I will see that she continues her education with the money you socked away for her."

"A-and the evidence against me?" George asked hesitantly, referring to the murder weapon, the gun that could prove his guilt once and for all.

"It will be properly disposed of," Spider assured him. "Your daughter will never know the truth. Your name will remain clear."

Smashing. Brilliant. Except I'll be dead. Although, in truth, ever since joining Spider's ranks he'd very likely been a dead man walking.

"Hopefully it doesn't come to that," George said softly, trying to convince himself more than Spider. He still had so much to live for. He wanted to see Bella pass her A-level exams. Wanted to see which university she got into. Wanted to meet the man she would eventually fall in love with. Wanted to walk her down the aisle…

"We shall see," Spider said offhandedly. Adding, "Good luck, George. Don't let me down."

And with that Spider was gone, cutting the connection without signing off. George blinked down at his mobile, trying to sort out once again how he'd gone so far off the rails on this assignment. But hindsight was 20/20, and there was no use haranguing himself for things he couldn't go back and undo.

At least, no matter what, my Bella is safe. It was well known to everyone who'd ever come into contact with Spider that the man never lied and he *never* broke his word. George could take some comfort in that.

Shoving his mobile into his trouser pocket, he was glancing through the bagel shop's window when the massive gates of Black Knights Inc. swung open. A blond man on crutches escorted a curvy chestnut-haired woman outside the wall. The couple hobbled over to the guardhouse and knocked on the door.

George saw his chance. *Now, now, now!* It would be so much easier *not* to kill the guard at the onset. That way he wouldn't have to take the chance that someone would discover the man's body and sound an alarm.

Quickly shouldering the hold-all, George pushed away from the table and exited the bagel shop. Cool wind whipped off the nearby river and wicked the sweat from his upper lip. Keeping his head down, making sure the brim of his ivy cap obscured his face from any street cameras, he crossed the road. While the wounded man and the pretty woman distracted the guard, he slipped through the quickly closing gates. And then there he was, inside Black Knights Inc. He couldn't quite believe it.

The old saying he and his friends used to chant in the schoolyard came to mind: *Easy peasy, fricaseesey. Wash your bum in lemon squeezy!* He hoped it was a sign that the rest of his mission would go as smoothly.

———

Black Knights Inc., Third Floor
Saturday 3:39 p.m.

"Where else does it hurt?" Penni asked after she'd kissed the bruise beside the crescent-moon scar on Dan's stubbled jaw.

He pushed the covers down to his waist and pointed to the discolored skin on his left pectoral muscle. The Russian's fists had done a number on him. Dan was black and blue. Of course, being black and blue was better than being dead like Kozlov. But no. *No!* She wasn't going to think about that. Not now. Not when she was safe and warm inside the circle of Dan's strong arms.

Coward.

I know! Damnit! I know! she admitted at the same time she pressed her mouth over Dan's heart. She could feel the organ beating steadily, heavily against her lips. Then she caught the little bud of his nipple between her teeth and laved it with her tongue. She just couldn't help herself. It was so flat and brown and tiny. She loved the way it instantly beaded. Loved the low, growly sound of approval at the back of Dan's throat. Okay, so who was she kidding? She just loved...*him.*

And there it was. The truth in all its discombobulating glory. But it's not like it was a grand epiphany or anything. She'd known she loved him since she hopped off the plane in DC three months ago. She'd known she loved him because a hole had opened up in her chest when she watched the jet taxiing toward the runway, ready to take him to Chicago and far, far away from her.

Oh, sure. She'd tried to convince herself that what she felt for him wasn't real. She'd tried to tell herself that it was some sort of hero worship or deep-seated infatuation brought on by the hell they'd been through together, by the way he'd helped her soldier on during one of the most difficult times of her life. But she'd eventually had to admit that it was neither of those things.

Getting to know Dan, seeing his grit and determination and true character shine through in Kuala Lumpur, had been like months of a relationship condensed into just a few days. They'd bypassed all the small talk and bullshit, skipped the part where they each put their best foot forward, and gotten right down to nitty-gritty. Right down to the *core* of each of them. And what she'd found at Dan's core was something good and steady. Something to revere and admire. Something to…yes, *love*. But now the questions were: *Does he see the same things in me? Does he* feel *the same things for me?*

"Does it hurt any place else?" she asked him, determined to shove aside her tumultuous thoughts. She wasn't ready to contemplate them. She wanted just a little more time. A little more happiness. You know, before she dropped her whopping, mega, ginormous bomb on him.

"You're fine just where you are," he assured her.

"Are you sure?" she teased, bouncing her eyebrows. "There's no *other* place on you that hurts? Even a little?"

They'd started this game because they'd fallen into the bed after she finished him off with her mouth—and talk about *h-h-holy shit*; that had been *hot*. And as soon as their heads hit the pillows, they'd both gone out like lights. Just *blink!* Snoozeville.

Multiple, body-shaking orgasms will do that to a person.

At some point though, she'd rolled over, her arm flying wide because she wasn't used to sharing a bed with anyone, and her hand had smacked him on the forehead, directly over his butterfly bandaged wound. He'd yowled and sat up, blinking in confusion. She'd shot out of bed like the mattress had turned into a snarling, toothy beast. But when they realized what had happened, they dissolved into laughter, crumbling back against the pillows.

In contrition, she'd leaned over and kissed his

boo-boo. And one kissed owie had led to another kissed owie. So on and so forth, until they were here now. On their way to another round of getting hot and sweaty. Which you bet your ass was absolutely fine by her.

"Well," he said, his eyes full of warm, sleepy desire, "there is *one* other place."

"Let me guess."

He threw the covers back, revealing his burgeoning erection. It was lengthening before her eyes, filling, thickening, the skin growing dusky with blood.

"Just as I suspected," she said, biting the inside of her cheek. "But if memory serves, I've already kissed that boo-boo."

"True." His expression turned wide-eyed and innocent. "But now it's aching again and—"

"Oh, you're breaking my heart." She pouted playfully.

"And you can see how eager it is for another kiss."

When she glanced down, it was to find him fully aroused—which was always an awe-inspiring sight—and bouncing up and down on his flat stomach above the inky black letters of his tattoo. "All right already, you're making it do that," she accused him.

"Am not."

"Are too."

"Well, maybe," he admitted. He smiled seductively and laced his fingers behind his head so she could fully appreciate the show he was putting on for her, but he inadvertently hit the framed photo on the nightstand, knocking it to the floor.

"Here, let me get it," she said since it had fallen on her side of the bed. She leaned over the mattress and placed it back on the metal and glass table. When she turned back, it was to find Dan's eyes on the picture. The look on his face was soft and peaceful.

"Who is she?" she asked curiously, staring at the red-head, admiring the woman's small, compact frame. People always complimented Penni on her tall, lithe build, but they wouldn't be so appreciative if they were forced to wear her legs for a day while flying coach. Ever since she was a girl, she'd wanted to be short and curvy and—

"My wife," Dan said, his head cocked, his expression all about the *well, duh*.

"Pardon me?" she asked, digging a finger in her ear.

"That's my wife," he repeated.

The bottom fell out of her stomach. Just gone. And her heart dropped down to take up the void. If her life was a movie, this is the part where the sound of a needle scratching across a record would echo in the background. "Y-you're *married?*" She recoiled.

"*No*," he assured her, grabbing her arm and keeping her in bed when she would have tossed back the covers and vaulted off the mattress. "I'm widowed… er…widowered." His frown deepened. "Is that even a word? Whatever." He waved an impatient hand through the air. "You get the point. But I thought you knew."

"N-no," she managed even though her throat was dryer than the Carménère wine her father had liked to drink on Christmas Eve and special occasions.

"Well, I'll be damned." He made a face and shrugged. "Huh."

Huh? *Huh?* That's what he had to say? She didn't… She couldn't… She wasn't…

Shock. Penni was in shock. And she knew her mouth was opening and closing like a fish out of water, but she couldn't stop herself. Questions formed and dissolved one right after the other. A dull *swoosh, swoosh, swoosh* sounded between her ears. And was it just her, or had the room halved in size? The walls were closing in, weren't they?

Finally, one question bloomed to life and retained its shape long enough for her to grab hold of it. "H-how did she die?" she asked, not surprised her voice came out reedy and thin.

Dan's a widower! He had a wife! She couldn't *believe* it! Then again, there was that flash of pain she occasionally saw in his eyes. And she suddenly remembered the conversation they'd had in Kuala Lumpur when he tried to convince her he wasn't worth her time, when he admitted he was dealing with a bunch of personal stuff and was all fucked up about it. But he hadn't expounded beyond that. And she hadn't pressed.

Oh, *why* hadn't she pressed?

Because you didn't want to know, that's why. You just wanted to get naked with him.

True, true. Which just proved, once again, that she was a total ass.

"Violently," he admitted, pulling her from her swirling thoughts. His left eyelid twitched. A muscle in his jaw did the same. *There.* There was that sadness, that flicker of pain. Her heart *ached* for the way it caused his beautiful green eyes to darken. "She was gunned down just inside the gates." He bobbed his chin in the direction of the BKI's entrance. "It's a long story that involves a hired thug, some stolen files that incriminated a U.S.

senator, and a shoot-out. But basically it comes down to her being in the wrong place at the wrong time."

Despite the fact that Penni was reeling, absolutely *reeling* with the knowledge he'd been married before, that he'd *still* be married if life and evil men hadn't interfered and taken his wife—*his wife, Christ almighty!*—from him, Penni was able to whisper, "I-I'm so sorry, Dan." Tears of sympathy gathered and burned behind her eyes. She was feeling a gazillion different emotions, but the ones she could identify were compassion and understanding. So she decided to just go with those. "That's... It's *terrible*. I'm *so* sorry."

"Yeah," he agreed, rolling in his lips, growing quiet. Then, "But it's probably not much different than a nineteen-year-old girl losing her father in the crossfire of two rival gangs."

Her brow furrowed. She blinked. "What the... How do you know about that?"

"I may have done a little research on you when I got back from Kuala Lumpur," he admitted, his expression sheepish.

"Y-you did research on me?"

"Yeah." He nodded, rubbing a hand over his beard stubble. "And I've been wanting to tell you how sorry I am for your loss, but I didn't know how to bring it up. It's not something you just say right out of the blue, you know?" That charming way he smashed his words together made it sound like *right outta th'blue, y'know*.

"Thank you," she told him. The dull ache that knifed into her stomach anytime she thought about the night her father died was so familiar she could ignore it. "It was a really long time ago." And *that* had another one of those flimsy, ephemeral questions swirling around in her head suddenly solidifying. "How long ago did she die?" When she realized how nosy that sounded, and how insensitive, she was quick to add, "Sorry. I'm so sorry. *Geez*. Don't answer that. You probably hate talking about it." After a shake of her head she added, "It has become glaringly apparent to me that I am a blue-ribbon-worthy ass."

"No you're not." He squeezed her shoulder. "You're *wonderful*. And it's okay to ask me anything. I'll always give you the truth."

Yeah, he would. Because he was an honest, upstanding guy. And she was...a blue-ribbon-worthy *ass*. She couldn't help reiterating.

When he squeezed her shoulder again, she instinctively scooted away. All the comfort and ease she usually felt had vanished. It was weird to be in bed with him, naked. You know, what with his *wife* smiling at her from the photograph. She nonchalantly tucked the comforter around herself, trying to play off the move by pretending to pick distractedly at a stray thread.

Dan frowned, cocking his head first at her and then the space she'd put between them. *So much for nonchalant.* "It was over two years ago."

She stilled, her fingers no longer plucking at the string. "Recent then," she said. And what was that she was feeling? She didn't know. It was like a cross between dread and fear and heartbreak. And then a thought struck her like a blindside haymaker from a heavyweight. *Oh, God! Am I a rebound?*

"In some ways it feels recent," he admitted. "In other ways it feels like a lifetime ago. Maybe even *another* lifetime. I guess 'cause going through something like that, losing someone you love so unexpectedly, it… *changes* you. I'm not the same man I was back then. I'm harder in some ways, softer in others. You know what I mean?"

She did. The day her father died was the day her life split in two. There was the Penelope Ann DePaul who'd come *before*. That girl was footloose and carefree. And there was the Penelope Ann DePaul who'd come *after*. That woman was a little bit more circumspect and a lot more serious. But that was beside the point. Because… *just over two years?*

That familiar dull ache in her stomach was joined by a brand-new nauseating pain. "H-have you…" She wasn't sure how to put what she wanted to say without being indelicate. "Um, what I mean is…" *Just spit it out, Penni-pie. No use skating around the truth.* "Have you dated much since?"

"Dated?" The look on his face was incredulous. "No." He shook his head, causing a lock of hair to fall over his forehead, concealing the wound there.

Okay, so was he doing that guy thing where he meant he hadn't "dated" women but he "shagged" a whole truckload of them? "But you've…*been* with other women, right?"

He narrowed his eyes, lacing his hands behind his head and studying her. "Does it matter?" he asked.

"I-I guess not." *You bet your ass it does!* And, shit. That was the first time she'd lied to him. It didn't sit well. But in her defense, it was like she was in the eye of the storm. Her life, and all her dreams and hopes and fears, were swirling around her at 300 mph.

She didn't know how she felt about Dan being a widower—other than knowing she felt terribly sorry for him and the loss he'd suffered. She didn't know what it meant for the future she'd hoped might be possible. She didn't know if it changed—

Aren't you getting ahead of yourself? You haven't even told him what you came to tell him.

True. Too true. And maybe now was the time. You know, what with so many emotional Molotov cocktails having already been thrown. Blowing out a deep breath, scolding her stupid heart for being lily-livered and sinking down to hide somewhere around the vicinity of her knees, she opened her mouth—

"You're the first," he said, preempting what she'd been about to say.

"I'm sorry?"

"Since my wife."

"Come again?" She heard his words but they weren't computing. Or maybe she just didn't *want* them to compute. And *goddamnit!* The room had shrunk again. She would swear the ceiling was slowly falling, getting ready to crush her.

"There haven't been any others," he said.

"Oh-kay." That's what she said. What she *thought* was *Oh, Christ on the cross! I am the rebound!* She felt like crying. Or puking. Or maybe screaming? So she was completely surprised when her next words were "What was her name?"

A brilliant smile spread across his face when he unhooked his hands from behind his head and turned slightly, tapping the traditional heart-and-arrow tattoo on his shoulder.

"What?" She blinked, confused.

"It was Patti," he said at the same time she leaned closer, examining the design. Sure enough. The ink had faded, the tattoo obviously years old, but underneath the heart, inside a waving scrap of ribbon was his wife's name: Patti.

"She spelled it with an *I*," she mused almost to herself. "Just like I spell my name."

"She did." Dan nodded, watching her closely.

"Weird coincidence," she said. Then a thought occurred. A terrible thought. An ugly thought. *She* was the first woman he'd been with after his wife. And his wife's name was Patti spelled with an *I*. And *her* name was Penni spelled with an *I*. "Is that why you gave me that nickname in Malaysia?" she asked, her voice wobbling, her heart pounding. The room spinning and spinning and spinning.

Something flitted across his face. Something that made her breath catch. "Penni," he said, "I—" But then he just stopped, snapping his mouth shut, the muscle in his jaw twitching spasmodically. He wasn't going to lie to her.

"Oh my God!" She slapped a hand over her mouth and jumped from the bed. "You were afraid you'd call me by the wrong name, weren't you?"

"Penni…" He reached for her, his eyes imploring.

She stumbled back, uncaring that she was standing there stark naked and blowing like she'd run a race. A chasm opened inside her. A huge, yawning void that swallowed her heart, her lungs, her ribs. It widened, pushing out until she was totally consumed by it. Lost in it until she was adrift in a gulf of pain and disappointment.

With a sigh, he curled his fingers into a fist and dropped his hand into his lap. "Please don't be hurt. It's not a reflection of you. It was me. I was thinking that I shouldn't... I didn't want... You were just so... *Jesus*, I'm fuckin' this up."

He scrubbed a hand down his face, his eyes searching the footboard like maybe down there he would find the words to make it right. *Forget about it.* There *were* no words to make it right. She thought he called her Brooklyn because of her accent, because it was cute and sweet and special and—

But it was so he didn't mix her up with his dead wife! The horror! The absolute horror!

"Look," he finally said. "You're right. I gave you that nickname 'cause you were the first and 'cause I was scared I'd slip up during the heat of things. And I didn't want to do that, Penni," he implored. "I didn't want to hurt you. You'd been so...*wonderful*. And I—"

Bang! Bang! Bang!

A heavy fist landed on the door, making Penni jump. Her skin felt like she'd run through a clutch of stinging nettles. Her heart felt like it had exploded in that void that had become her chest. She needed to cry, but couldn't. Felt like pulling her hair out, but didn't. She just stood there, staring at the door as every hope she'd had about what she might mean to Dan was crushed into dust.

A rebound. Nothing more. Nothing less.

"You two figure you can stop testing each other's suspension long enough to come down and listen to what Rock has to say about Winterfield?" Boss's booming bass sounded through the door. "We're gathering at the conference table in five…"

When she turned back, Dan searched her eyes, his own pleading for her to understand.

She swallowed the tears burning up her throat, swallowed the cry lodged in the center of her chest, and squared her shoulders. "We'll be there," she called, stumbling into the bathroom to grab her clothes. Hoping beyond hope that she could keep her shit together for just a little while longer.

Chapter Twenty-one

ZOELNER WAS A BALL'S HAIR AWAY FROM DRILLING OZZIE IN the face…

"Are you going to write me up for sexual innuendo?" Ozzie asked Chelsea, who was sitting across the conference table from them. She and Ozzie had been trading banter for what seemed like an eternity—although, in actuality, it had probably only been a minute or two.

"No." Chelsea was grinning coquettishly—there was just no other word for it. "But I will grade you very strictly. I expect nothing but the best when it comes to flirtation."

Zoelner's back teeth set so hard he thought it a wonder he didn't lose a filling.

"Good thing I was always a straight-A student." Ozzie wiggled his eyebrows.

"If you two don't cut it out," Zoelner warned, "I'm liable to revisit those two hot dogs I ate earlier all over this conference table."

"Gross, dude." Ozzie frowned.

"My thoughts exactly." Zoelner leveled him with a look that included Chelsea.

"Aw." Ozzie batted his lashes. "Are you jealous again? I told you there's enough Ozzie to go around.

Come here, you big lug." Ozzie hooked an arm around his neck and dragged his head over. "Let Ozzie give you some more lovin', huh?"

When Ozzie went to kiss his head, Zoelner shoved his hand in Ozzie's face, pushing him away and ducking from under his arm. He was grinning despite himself. Ozzie always had that effect on him. One minute he wanted to kick the bastard in the pork sword, the next minute he was trying not to laugh.

The sound of footsteps pounding down the stairs heralded the arrival of Dan and Penni to the party. "Penni…" Dan's voice echoed around the corner. "Wait a goddamn minute, I—"

Dan was cut off when Penni breezed into the room and asked Ozzie cheekily, "So how was the date with the reporter?"

Zoelner tilted his head, frowning. There was something weird about Penni's face—besides the beard burn that pinkened her cheeks. It was her smile. It looked forced. Brittle. He imagined if someone flicked a sunflower seed at her teeth, every single one of them would shatter. Curious, he glanced behind her to see that Dan was looking… What was that exactly? Distressed? No. Maybe *distraught* came closer to describing it.

Uh-oh. Trouble in paradise. Though what could possibly have happened to pop all those heart-shaped bubbles that appeared over Dan and Penni's heads when they were in the same room together was a mystery. From the sounds he'd heard coming from Dan's bedroom not too long ago, the pair should be moony-eyed and lethargic with postcoital bliss.

"Pssht. I had Samantha Tate eating out of my hand," Ozzie boasted, oblivious to the strained atmosphere accompanying Dan and Penni. "Who wants to bet she'll be phoning me up, asking me to bury my bone by the end of the week?"

"She better not," Boss boomed upon exiting his office. "When it comes to sex with reporters, I'm instating a no-tolerance rule."

"What? Why?" Ozzie ran his hands through his hair like that was the most outrageous thing Boss could have said. When he lowered his arms, his too-long hair was standing out, making him look a little Einstein-esque. "It's the best way to keep her from nosing around here again."

"How do you figure?" Becky asked, skirting Boss's back and grabbing a seat near the head of the conference table.

"One night with the Oz-Man and she'll be too distracted with thoughts of repeating the process to worry about what she thinks we might be hiding here," Ozzie bragged.

Becky snorted. "I swear, just when I think I've seen the outer limits of your ego, there's so much more to be discovered."

"Thank you," Ozzie said, doing his best Elvis imitation. "Thank you very much."

Zoelner realized with a little start that he'd *missed* the Knights in the last three months. He hadn't been with them from the beginning, having only signed on with the outfit a couple of years back. But in that short time they'd become more than teammates and coworkers. They'd become…friends. Family even.

He blinked, a little thrown by the thought.

He'd never really had much of a family before. His

mother had died when he was too young to remember her. His father was a bastard and a half. And his younger brother? Well, Zoelner had spent so much of his life trying to keep the little shit out of trouble—all to no avail—that he'd never really had the chance to develop any sort of familial feelings beyond duty and responsibility.

"I need coffee!" Rock's southern drawl traveled up the stairs before he did. "*Tout de suite!*"

Becky jumped from her seat and rushed over to grab the pot and the stack of Styrofoam cups sitting on a cart by the wall. She filled one cup and handed it to Rock when he appeared at the top of the stairs. After a nod of thanks, Rock grabbed a seat beside Chelsea. Vanessa came out of Rock's office the moment she heard his voice and sat next to him, her expression concerned.

"No worries, *ma chérie*," Rock assured her, squeezing her hand. It was no secret Rock hated doing interrogations. "This one was a piece of cake."

"Good." Vanessa blew out a breath, waving off the cup of coffee Becky offered her. "No thanks. I don't think my stomach lining has recovered since the last time I drank that swill."

"I'll take some," Zoelner told Becky, having grown accustomed to the motor-oil-strength java Boss liked to make.

"Dare I?" Chelsea asked him, eyeing the pot in Becky's hand.

"Depends," he told her. "How strong is your constitution?"

She blanched and shook her head, pushing her glasses up her nose. "I think I'll follow Vanessa's lead and take a pass."

"Probably wise," he agreed, thanking Becky when she handed him a cup. He breathed in the slightly muddy aroma of coffee beans that'd had the shit brewed out of them, but Penni diverted his attention when she sat in the chair next to him, fisting her hands in her lap until her knuckles turned white. He frowned at her, then lifted a brow at Dan, who grabbed the seat at the end of the table. Dan just closed his eyes and shook his head, a classic guy move that said, *I fucked up, so don't ask.*

Zoelner offered him a sympathetic grimace before turning to watch Boss click on the triangular-shaped conference-caller in the center of the table. Boss dialed a number, and after the first ring, an officious-sounding woman answered, saying without preamble, "Please hold for the president."

"The president?" Chelsea squeaked, her eyes wide behind the lenses of her glasses.

She knew the reporting structure for BKI, but as a true blue, wrapped-in-the-flag Intelligence agent, she found it a little awe-inspiring that they had a direct link to the commander in chief. Zoelner knew just how awe-inspiring from experience. The first time President Thompson arrived through the secret tunnel to have a meeting with the Knights, he had sat there blinking at the president, feeling like he'd fallen down a rabbit hole.

"I've got General Fuller with me," Thompson's presidential baritone echoed from the speakers. General Pete Fuller was the head of the Joint Chiefs and the man the Knights reported to. "Who all am I talking with in Chi-Town?" Thompson asked.

Every conference call with Thompson began this way, with a roll call. Boss was the first to make his presence known, followed by Becky. Around the table it went until finally Chelsea said, "Special Agent Chelsea Duvall at your service, Mr. Thompson. I mean, Mr. President. Uh…sir. Shit. Oh, sorry, sir. I mean Mr. President."

President Thomson chuckled and said, "At ease, Agent Duvall."

Chelsea groaned and squeezed her eyes shut. A deep blush stole into her cheeks. *God, she's adorable.* When she blinked her eyes open, Zoelner sent her an encouraging wink.

Ozzie leaned over and surreptitiously whispered, "That woman is a tornado and you, my friend, are a trailer park."

"Meaning what?" Zoelner whispered back, frowning.

"Meaning I see disaster ahead." Ozzie nodded like it was a foregone conclusion.

Zoelner's frown deepened, but even if he'd wanted to argue or make Ozzie explain himself further—which he *didn't*—the conference call was getting underway and he was forced to turn his attention to the topic at hand.

"…able to find out from Winterfield, Rock?" Thompson was asking. "Anything?"

"*Oui*." Rock nodded, taking a fortifying sip of coffee. "Quite a lot, sir."

"Really?" General Fuller's deep base echoed through the speakers. "That surprises me. I would've thought he'd clam up and start making demands before he'd agree to talk."

"Well"—Rock adjusted his green John Deere ball cap and sat forward, resting his elbows on the table—"he *does* want some assurances before he'll give us the details about what all he stole and who all he sold his information to."

"There you go," Fuller said, disgust heavy in his voice.

"What assurances?" the president asked smoothly, ever the professional politician.

"He wants the death penalty taken off the table," Rock drawled.

"Typical," Fuller snorted.

"And he doesn't want to be put in with the general population when he's imprisoned," Rock continued.

"What?" President Thompson asked, curiosity lacing his tone. "Why?"

"Accordin' to him, Spider will be sure to have someone on the inside who'll kill him."

Spider? Zoelner wondered if that was the ubiquitous "him" Winterfield had been screaming about when they were in the van. And now *his* curiosity was piqued.

"Spider?" President Thompson asked. "I'm assuming we're talking about a person and not an eight-legged creature."

"Yes, sir." Rock nodded. "Apparently, this Spider person was the one pullin' Winterfield's strings, the reason the sorry sonofabitch went rogue."

"Explain," Fuller demanded. Just the one word. Patience was not the general's forte.

Rock blew out a breath and settled back in his chair. "First of all, let me state for the record that I'm pretty sure Winterfield's cheese done slipped off his cracker."

"He's nuts?" Boss asked.

Rock nodded, then realized *el Jefe* and the general couldn't see him and said, "As my daddy would say, he's nuttier than squirrel shit."

"So you can't believe anything he says," Fuller grumbled.

"Well, you'd think so," Rock mused. "But Winterfield's crazy leans more toward paranoia and emotional instability, and not so much toward delusions or hallucinations. I think the tale he told me was the truth."

"And what tale was that?"

"It all starts five years ago when Winterfield was runnin' an op in Iraq," Rock began, and by the way the Cajun leaned back and laced his fingers across his stomach, Zoelner knew they were in for a long tale. "He had an asset inside the local al-Qaeda group named Marnia Sultana," Rock continued. "It seems Winterfield developed a little crush on her, and one thing led to another. Durin' pillow talk one night, Winterfield let some sensitive information slip about a shipment of weapons we were handin' over to the Iraqi military. Turns out Sultana was a double agent and she gave that information to her al-Qaeda handlers. An assault on the shipment resulted in the loss of thirty-two American lives, hundreds of weapons, and thousands of rounds."

"I remember that fiasco," Fuller mused. "It happened just outside Mosul. We never could figure out how al-Qaeda knew about the shipment."

"Well, now ya know." Rock scratched his chin. "But this is where it gets weird. Accordin' to Winterfield, two weeks after the disaster he was contacted by a mysterious man who went by the name of Spider. The guy, I'm assumin' it's a guy, had a video confession from Marnia Sultana fingerin' Winterfield with the blame. And Spider used this video to place Winterfield under his thumb, forcin' Winterfield to funnel top secret information to him whenever he came askin' for it."

"And Winterfield never thought to come clean?" Again, Fuller's voice was heavy with disgust. The general didn't suffer turncoats lightly.

"I don't get the impression Winterfield, even when he still had all his marbles, was a man who was fettered by conscience," Rock said. "I suspect even back then his moral compass didn't exactly point true north. He liked bein' a CIA agent. And, if ya ask me, I think he liked the thrill of passin' along information and not gettin' caught."

"So what changed?" President Thompson asked.

Rock tsked. "He got greedy. He figured he was doin' all of that, takin' risks that could get him strung up, stealin' information that was worth millions, all just so this Spider character wouldn't out him for what happened with that weapons shipment. Winterfield took it into his head that he could do a fair bit better on his own and decided to make a break for it. But all the runnin' and gunnin' has since gotten to him. He doesn't strike me as a terribly stable individual to begin with, and I think the stress of it all tipped him over the edge."

"So you think the guy at the airport in Cusco, the one who took out the ground crew and the Russian FSB agent was one of Spider's men?" Fuller asked.

"So says Winterfield," Rock concurred.

"Interesting," the president mused. "I suppose now the question becomes, who the hell is this Spider?"

"Ya got me," Rock said. "And you got Winterfield too. He never met the man, only ever talked to him on the phone. Winterfield doesn't even know Spider's real name, although Winterfield says he has an English accent."

"English, huh?" Thompson mused. "Do we have another Jihadi John on our hands here?"

"He's more than that," Chelsea piped up and Zoelner lifted a brow. "Uh, Mr. President. Sir," she added after a beat.

Adorable. Damnit.

"I'm assuming by the litany of titles being thrown my way that it's Agent Duvall speaking," President Thompson said.

"Yes, sir, Mr. President." Chelsea nodded, her color riding high again.

"Go on then, Agent," Thompson said. "Tell us what you know."

"Nothing, really." Chelsea wrinkled her nose. "Just that a couple of times over the years the name 'Spider' has come up in Intelligence gathering. And not just in connection to al-Qaeda. I ran across a reference to him when I was looking into a human trafficking case. And then another time when I was collecting Intel about an organized crime syndicate that was operating out of Warsaw. But I could never find anything more about him, and since he wasn't pivotal to either situation, I chalked up both references to coincidence. I told myself the third time is the charm and swore that if I heard about him again, *then* I'd get interested in finding out more."

"And *are* you interested in finding out more?" President Thompson asked.

"Uh…yes, sir, Mr. President," she said, her brow furrowed.

"Okay, then," Thompson said. "You're on the case. I'll let Morales know."

"Sir?" she asked, blinking rapidly.

"You were just given an assignment by the president,

Chels," Zoelner informed her. "That's how it's done around here."

"Oh," she said breathlessly. "Oh, yes, sir, Mr. President."

"Sir or Mr. President will do, Agent Duvall," Thompson said. "No need for both."

"Yes, sir, Mr. President," Chelsea said, then made a face like she wanted to die. "Shit. I mean, sorry. Sir." And then she slapped her hands over her face and shook her head.

Thompson and Fuller were both chuckling, Boss was biting his cheek to keep from laughing, and Ozzie slapped a hand over his belly and guffawed. When Chelsea lowered her fingers from her face, Zoelner gave her another wink. The woman obviously needed some support.

"And, Frank," Thompson added. Besides Becky and Michelle, the president was the only person on the planet to call Boss by his first name. "Let's put one of the Knights on the assignment too. I want to scratch some surfaces and see who bleeds."

"Yes, sir," Boss said, looking right at Zoelner. Zoelner shook his head. He'd rather swallow his own foot than be paired with Chelsea on a mission that could last weeks, months, or maybe even *years*. There was no way he'd be able to keep his hands to himself for that long. And if he didn't keep his hands to himself, things could get…awkward. "Anyone in particular you have in mind, sir?" Boss asked.

"How about Dagan Zoelner?" the president said, and it took everything Zoelner had not to groan out loud. "With his training and background as a field agent, he'll be a perfect complement to the work Agent Duvall can do online and through her various sources."

"Done." Boss slapped his hand down on the table like a judge's gavel. Zoelner had learned that when Boss did that, the decision was final.

Fuuuuuck. He forced a false smile on his lips and nodded at Chelsea.

She had a thunderstruck look on her face as if everything was happening too quickly—*yeah, welcome to my world.* Because that's how it worked at BKI. In fact, that's why Thompson and Fuller had *formed* the group. So they wouldn't have to hem and haw around, waiting for congressional permission or for the various Intelligence agencies to fight over jurisdiction, before putting a plan of action into… um…*action.*

"Okay," Fuller said, "anything else you can tell us about Winterfield, Rock?"

"*Non.*" Rock shook his head. "That's it in a nutshell."

"Good," Thompson said. "Then let's find out the who, the what, and the how much of that Intel he stole and sold, and then lock the sonofabitch up and throw away the key."

"I'm assumin' I have permission to agree to his terms then?" Rock asked.

"If he wants to spend the rest of his life all alone in an eight-by-ten," the president said, "who am I to argue with him? And the death penalty's a hard sell these days anyway. So I see no problem meeting his requests. I'll have the paperwork signed and sent over in the next hour."

"Thank you, sir." Rock nodded.

"No, thank *you*," Thompson said. "Thank all of you. Another job well done. And particular thanks to

Dan, Zoelner, and Agent Duvall," he said. Zoelner had
to bite his lip to keep from grinning when Chelsea's
chest puffed out like she'd just had a medal pinned to
it. "On behalf of a grateful nation, I commend you for
bringing that bastard down once and for all. Oh, and
Penni DePaul too," the president added. "I hear you got
caught up in the hubbub, but you performed like the ace
you are. The Secret Service lost a great agent the day
you turned in your badge."

"Thank you, sir." Penni smiled, but it still looked
brittle. Whatever Dan had done, it was bad. Zoelner just
hoped Dan fixed it because, no two ways about it, Dan
and Penni belonged together. It was as obvious as the
noses on their faces.

"You betcha," Thompson said. "Pete? You got
anything to add?"

"Just my thanks for another mission in the bag," was
the general's response.

"All right then. We're done for now." And with that,
the line went dead.

Boss stood and clicked off the conference caller.
"And that's that." He slammed his palm down on the
table again, an audible period to their three-month-long
assignment. That's *also* how it worked at BKI. When the
job was done, it was done. No fanfare. No pomp. Just a
quick pat on the back and on to the next mission.

Everyone pushed up from their seats, and Zoelner
couldn't help but watch the byplay from the corner of
his eye when Dan grabbed Penni's arm and said, "Will
you please—" Dan stopped and ran a hand over the back
of his neck. "Damnit, Penni, we needa talk about this."

"I-I know." She nodded, looking like she was about

to break wide open. Her voice was a little wobbly too. *Shit, Dan Man. What the* hell *did you do?* "But can we do it out in the courtyard? I need some air."

"What's that about?" Ozzie whispered to Zoelner, eyeing Dan and Penni as they headed for the stairs leading down to the shop floor.

"Hell if I know," he admitted.

Of course, he forgot all about Dan and Penni's problems and started cataloging all of his own when Chelsea came over, shoved her hands on her hips like a pint-sized Wonder Woman, and cocked her head. "Hello, *partner*," she said in that low, husky voice that messed with his head.

Chapter Twenty-two

Black Knights Inc., Courtyard
Saturday, 4:19 p.m.

GEORGE HAD DONE IT. HE COULDN'T BELIEVE IT.

In less than forty-five minutes he'd planted his charges around the perimeter of the warehouse and all the various outbuildings. And now all that was left to do was find a way to sneak over the wall or out through the gate, unpack the transmitter that would send a signal to the receiver triggers he'd attached to each load of C4, and press the button. *Boom!* Bye-bye motorcycle shop and hello mission complete!

He was almost giddy with excitement. Giddy with relief. He'd gambled and won. *Daddy did it again, sweet Bella!*

Peeking around the edge of an outbuilding, he saw the coast was clear and headed across the courtyard in a running crouch. He was aiming for the gate that led around the front of the warehouse. He'd nearly made it when the back door burst open and former Secret Service Agent Penelope DePaul came storming out. She nearly bowled him over.

"What?" she squawked when they came nose to nose.

"Bloody h—" That's all George managed before she opened her mouth in what he knew would be a banshee scream. Despite the spike of adrenaline that sliced through his system, or maybe because of it, he had one of the weapons Benton had secured for him out of his waistband and aimed at her face before he finished his curse. "Don't think about it, love," he warned, his heart thundering, the hair on top of his head standing straight.

Shit. Fuck. Bloody, bloody *hell!*

Her mouth clamped shut and she blinked at him. He could almost see her make the decision to turn and run. As soon as she spun, he was ready. Snaking an arm around her neck, he pressed the barrel of the handgun to her temple. "Easy," he hissed, "and you might just live."

They weren't the same words he'd used with that fat airport crewman in Cusco, but it was the same lie. Another thing he'd learned working for Spider was that people became delusional when their lives were hanging in the balance. They would believe *anything* if it meant they could cling to a sliver of hope.

He panted as the fear in him grew. His mind clamored with a million thoughts. But the biggest one was... *what now?*

If he shot her, the bark of the weapon would bring those inside running. And he'd be a dead man. If he let her go, she would scurry inside and alert the others. They'd undoubtedly catch him before he could make his escape. And he'd be a dead man. If he continued to hold her hostage while digging around inside his hold-all for the transmitter, he could push the button and blow the place sky-high. But he was inside the blast radius. So he'd be a dead man.

No matter how he looked at it, he was a dead man.

He nearly cried out in anger, in fury, in hopelessness. *So close. So bloody close.* He was just about to settle for option number three when a thought occurred. And then he nearly cried out in triumph. He didn't just have three options. He had four. He could drag her with him to the front gate and give the guard the choice between opening the gates or watching her die from a fatal dose of lead poisoning. The guard would undoubtedly decide to open the gates. And once George was through, *then* he could grab the transmitter and punch the button.

"Don't say a word," he hissed in the woman's ear. "And come with me."

He'd just started to pull her backward when Daniel Currington pushed through the back door. "Penni, when you asked for bottled water, I didn't know if you wanted still or sparkling so I grabbed both and—" Daniel dropped the bottles when he saw George. The plastic containers bounced against the slate stones making weird *splonking* noises. "You!" Daniel roared.

Then and there, George saw his life flash before his eyes and a terrible certainty filled him. *Sweet Bella, I'm so sorry…*

———

Terror…

That was the only word to describe what Dan was feeling. Straight-up, no-holds-barred, do-not-pass-go terror. It filled him. Ate at him. Consumed him until there was nothing left but the rot. And a fury unlike anything he'd ever known.

Not again. Not fucking again!

He would have roared the words into the sky. Shaken a fist. He couldn't lose another woman he loved to a thug's bullet. Life couldn't be that unfair. The God he wasn't even sure he believed in couldn't be that unfair. *Fuck!*

"I know you," he ground out, trying to force calm into his voice when calm was the dead last thing he was feeling. "I recognize the hat. You were at the bar in the hotel in Cusco. You were watching us."

The man said nothing as his eyes darted quickly right and left, his receding chin twitching side to side. Dan glanced into Penni's wide, dark eyes and wanted to cry for the bone-chilling fear he saw in them, for the terrible flush that blazed in her cheeks, and for the wetness that clung to her lashes. He dipped his head once, trying to convey that everything would be okay. But he wasn't sure he'd succeeded in convincing her. Probably because *he* wasn't totally convinced.

This man, whoever he was, had trailed them all the way from South American to Chicago, and had the audacity to break into the BKI compound. Which meant he was more than willing to go to great lengths to achieve his goal. *Whatever that might be…* Dan didn't dare give himself time to contemplate it.

When one lone tear spilled over Penni's lid, slipping down her cheek and wetting the butterfly bandage there, a lump formed in his throat. And since his heart had already jumped there when he saw Hat Guy with a gun to Penni's pretty head, it was getting quite crowded, making it impossible to breathe.

"Were you the one on the tarmac too?" he asked, taking a step forward.

"Stay bloody well back!" the man shouted, his English accent thickened by fear and adrenaline.

"Are you the one they call Spider?" Dan asked, inching closer still, hoping to distract the guy with questions.

"Ha!" Hat Guy laughed, but it wasn't funny. The sound was filled with hysteria…and a strange sort of sadness. "I am just the bullet. Another man pulls the trigger," he said cryptically.

"Is that man Spider?" Dan asked, shuffling just a little closer. He tried to slow his racing heart using the technique he'd been taught during SEAL training. But it didn't work. The organ refused to cooperate and continued to gallop out of control, sending adrenaline surging through his system until his nerve endings burned, until he could taste its metallic flavor on his tongue. Despite the cool, fall evening, a trickle of sweat slipped down the groove of his spine.

"You have no idea who you're dealing with," Hat Guy hissed. Dan lifted a brow when he saw two fat tears slip from the man's eyes. And now Hat Guy's receding chin was trembling. "You have no idea what he's capable of."

"Who? Spider?"

Hat Guy just swallowed, his face the picture of anguish.

"Please," Dan begged him. Obviously the guy had some sort of conscience, the ability to feel *something*, even if that something was fear. "Let the woman go. We can talk about this. We can figure a way out." He inched closer still, then stopped and raised his hands in the air when Hat Guy pressed his barrel tighter to Penni's temple, making her cry out.

I'll fuckin' kill him! Terror and fury mixed together with the growing panic in Dan's veins to create a deadly cocktail that threatened to melt away his reason, his control. He was about to Hulk out. He could feel it.

"There *is* no way out." Hat Guy shook his head, taking a step back. "You don't *get* out."

"There's always a way," Dan implored him. "Always."

"Please," Penni said, obviously feeling the indecision in the man holding her hostage even if she couldn't see the fear and tears in his eyes like Dan could. "Please, I'm begging you. Don't hurt me." And then she looked at Dan, anguish in her eyes and something...something he couldn't quite put a name to. She finished with a whispered, "I-I'm pregnant."

Dan blinked, thinking he hadn't heard her correctly.

Hat Guy stilled, a flash of horror crossing his panicked face. "Pregnant?" he demanded.

So Dan *had* heard her correctly. Despite the cataclysmic situation, and despite the sudden sensation of having pins and needles prickling every inch of his skin, his mind was ripped back to the bathroom in the basement of the hotel in Malaysia. To Penni having reached her wit's end. To the grief and horror of her colleagues' deaths having finally overcome her. To her asking him to help her forget it all, escape from it all, for just a little while...

"Make love to me," she whispered against his neck between a string of hot, hungry kisses. She lifted a leg, hooking her heel behind his knee and rubbing herself against the raging hard-on that strained the fly of his jeans. He could feel her heat even through her trousers, feel the sultry moistness reaching out to him, surrounding him, tempting him.

"Brooklyn...Jesus," he groaned, flattening his palms against the bathroom door beside her head. And

when she bit his earlobe, his cock throbbed so hard it was a wonder it didn't rip the seams of his jeans.

This is crazy! *he thought. And it was. Crazy hot. Crazy fast. He knew he should stop. A part of him wanted to stop. Now wasn't the time. Not when she was beside herself with grief. And worry and self-reproach. Not when she wasn't thinking straight.*

But then she reached between them to attack the buttons at his fly, ripping them open until the two halves gaped wide. When she shoved her hand inside, past the waistband of his boxer briefs and wrapped her fist around him, squeezing, stroking, he knew stopping her wasn't going to be an option. He didn't have the wherewithal or the willpower. His brain was fried. His synapses firing out one and only one message. Now, now, now!

The skin on her palm was both unbearably soft and slightly callused. He was hugely swollen, so sensitive that her caresses caused both pleasure and pain.

"We shouldn't," he gasped, his head falling back on his shoulders. "Holy shit, that feels good."

"Mmm," she hummed, keeping one hand inside his pants, pulling, petting, stroking, as she used the other to undo the button on her trousers. Her zipper made a soft scriiiitching *sound that was barely audible above their heavy, gasping breaths. Lowering her leg, she toed out of her shoes. She released him to slide her pants and panties down her thighs.*

"Make love to me," she said again, stepping out of the puddle of her clothing and wrapping her arms around his shoulders, going up on tiptoe to realign their bodies. "Make me forget just for a little while."

"Brooklyn, I want to," he groaned, his lungs working like bellows, his heart racing, his cock thrusting unapologetically from the vee of his fly. "But I don't have a condom."

She shook her head. "Forget about it." When she shoved his jeans and boxers down under his ass, his erection sprang forward. She grabbed it, wrapped her leg around his hips, and angled it toward her entrance. "I don't care…"

And then she impaled herself.

Everything after that was a little sketchy. Dan hadn't had many faculties working. But he remembered tight, hot, unbearable wetness closing around his shaft. He remembered their frenzied breaths as they screwed like teenagers up against the door of that bathroom. And he remembered it'd been over very quickly. Because her orgasm had hit her almost immediately, triggering his. And together they'd crashed into ecstasy. Ecstasy that was cut short when a fist pounded on the door, calling them back into action, back into the mission.

And suddenly everything made sense. Penni quitting the Secret Service—no way she could be required to put herself between her protectee and a bullet if she was carrying a child. Penni coming to Chicago to talk to him and then agreeing to fly all the way to Peru when she found out it was possible he could remain on his mission for months to come. Penni's strange expression of fear and indecision when he asked her to help finish the assignment…

She's pregnant. With my child. He knew it as surely

as he knew the stars would all someday fall from the sky, as surely as he knew up from down and east from west, as surely as he knew he loved her. And now he wasn't just terrified to lose her to this madman, he was terrified to lose their child too. Terrified to lose everything that meant anything at all.

"Penni?" Her name was a prayer, a cry, a question all rolled into one. Something hot and wet slipped down his face and dripped from his chin. With a start, he realized it was tears. His heart was aching with love and joy, his soul shaking with fear and dread.

"Yes," she said, her own tears rolling freely. She choked on a sob. And that's when Hat Guy shoved her away from him, straight into Dan's outstretched arms.

He cried out when he felt her skin next to his, felt her arms go around her neck. Squeezing her tight, he reveled in the hot wash of her breath when she tucked her face into his shoulder. But never, not once, did he take his eyes off Hat Guy. He *did,* however, choke on his relief and gratitude when he said, "Th-thank you. Thank you. Now let us help you f—"

"There's no helping me," Hat Guy said, shaking his head, openly sobbing. "There's no hope for me."

Penni turned in Dan's arms, but he refused to release her, determined to keep her close. "There's always hope," she sniffed, her voice full of tears.

Hat Guy shook his head and smiled through the anguish on his face. "Take care of that baby," he said. "Children are life's greatest joy."

And then before Dan or Penni could so much as blink, the man shoved the pistol in his mouth and pulled the trigger…

—~~—

Black Knights Inc., Courtyard
Saturday 5:49 p.m.

"Did you mean it when you said you believed in babies?"
Penni asked Dan, her heart like a boulder in her chest.
She knew the organ continued to pump blood, to fulfill
its function, but it felt heavy, hard, *cold*.

After Mystery Man shot himself, the Knights had
come running out of the shop, locked and loaded and
ready for war. Even pint-sized Becky had been packing. And then for over an hour, the courtyard had been a
scene of chaos. First all the men had run around, retriev-
ing the wired C4—a real nail-biter scenario. The stuff
was stable as long as no one pushed the ignition switch,
but still… And then there had been the president to call
and Morales, the director of the CIA. It'd been decided
by all involved that the local authorities should be left
out of it. You know, given no one wanted to answer any
questions since no one *knew* any answers. Afterward, in
typical woo-woo underworld spec-ops style, the body
had been photographed, fingerprinted, sampled for DNA,
and placed in a body bag—*apparently the Knights just
have those lying around*—and shoved into the Hummer.
Boss, Zoelner, and Chelsea used the underground tunnel
to take it to who knew where. Penni didn't care. She just
wanted to go home and forget any of this ever happened.

But first there was Dan…

It was time, *finally*, to talk about why she'd come.
Why she'd *had* to come. All the fear and excitement
that had forced her to keep her mouth shut was gone.

Probably because her hope for the future, for what they might be starting together, was gone too. Now there was nothing left but to work out the logistics. And it was so sad, so disappointing that it weighed on her, making her limbs feel heavy, numb. Making a dull ache pound behind her eyes. Making each word a challenge.

"Of course I do," Dan said. "I believe in babies, everything else I told you I believed in, and a whole lot more on top of that." He was sitting in the bright red Adirondack chair, his elbows planted on his knees, his big hands dangling between his jean-clad thighs. A whorl of sandy-colored hair fell over his brow and her fingers itched to push it back.

Christ. Even now, even after everything, I still want him.

She figured she always would. The knowledge cut into her, flaying and scraping and making her bleed. She felt like she'd taken a leap of faith and landed in a bed of broken glass.

"Good." She nodded. She was determined to get through this. "Because I'm keeping the baby. I've always wanted to be a mother, and I..." She swallowed. "I think I'd be a good one."

"You'll be a *phenomenal* mother."

"I'm thirty-three years old," she continued as though he hadn't interrupted. "I don't have too many more chances left."

"Penni, I'm *thrilled*," Dan insisted, his smile wobbly, making him look uncertain, boyish. He was choosing his words carefully. "I... It's the best thing that's ever happened to me. A baby. God. I'm gonna be a father! Can you believe it?" He laughed, and there was wonder in the sound.

Yeah. She could believe it. She'd had about two months to get used to the idea. Two months of knowing she was pregnant, relegated to a desk job while she waited to pass the dangerous hurdle of her first trimester. Two months of trying to wrap her mind around the sudden left turn her life had taken.

She swallowed, fisting her hands so tightly she knew her nails were leaving crescent-moon marks on her skin. She shifted on the green lawn chair, trying to get comfortable. It was useless. There was nothing comfortable about any of this. "I don't expect anything from you," she assured him, disgusted to hear her voice was husky and thick, revealing how hard this was for her despite the pragmatic front she was trying to portray. "No child support or anything."

"Penni…" He leaned forward to grab her hand and she flinched away. Not intentionally. Instinctively. If he touched her, she'd forget that he'd called her Brooklyn so he wouldn't mix her up with his dead wife. She'd forget that she was just a rebound. She'd forget that her feelings for him were vastly more complicated, more immense than his feelings for her. *You're the first since my wife…Brooklyn…*

God, she'd been a fool.

"Sorry." She shook her head at the pained look that crossed his face when he quickly dropped his hand. "It's just that…" *Nothing is what I hoped. Nothing is what I wanted.* "I just need a little space," she finally said. Space to breathe. Space to think. Space to let go of her expectations. Space to let go of…him.

The lump that'd been lodged in her throat since the moment she realized her mistake in thinking she meant anything more to him than one small step up through the deep, dark tunnel of mourning grew to disastrous proportions. She was having trouble breathing. And soon, she knew she would have trouble holding back the tears welling in her eyes, the cries clawing in her chest. She needed to leave. She needed to get away.

"You know I care about you," he said, frowning at her. "I—Penni, I think I'm falling in love with you."

Oh, Christ! Just when she thought it couldn't get any worse!

"No." She shook her head, not quite meeting his eyes. She couldn't. She knew if she looked up, she'd see he actually *believed* what he was saying—after all, Dan didn't lie. And if she saw that, she'd want to believe it too. "You just think that because you're beginning to live again, because you're beginning to crawl out from the black fog of grief and despair, and anything that's shiny and new, anything that feels *good* seems more important, *bigger* than it really is."

"That's…" Now his frown turned fierce. "That's what I thought for a while. But it's not true."

"Isn't it?" she asked.

When she saw a brief flicker of hesitation cross his face, she pushed up from the chair. He jumped to his feet beside her. "I know what I'm talking about," she told him. "It's too soon. You're not ready. You said back in Malaysia that you're fucked-up and dealing with shit. Nothing has changed. You still are. You *know* you still are."

A muscle ticked in his jaw. His eyes flared with green fire. "Here's what I know," he said, his voice a low growl of sound. "When I'm with you, there's nowhere else I wanna be. And when I'm not with you, all I can think about is *being* with you."

Please shut up! I can't take it! The last time she'd hurt this bad, felt her heart and soul shredding, was the night she lost her father.

"So please, Penni," he continued, killing her with his face, slaying her with his words. "Don't act like there isn't something between us. Don't act like you don't care about me."

"*Of course* I care about you, Dan." *I love you.* "I think you're…" She shook her head. "I think you're wonderful."

A warm smile spread across his face. Some of the tension in his broad shoulders loosened. "But, please, I don't want to talk about this right now." *I can't think straight when I'm with you. And I need to think straight. Or else I'll let you convince me of something I know can't possibly be true.* "I'm tired. And these last couple of days have been hell. The stress and adrenaline can't have been good for the baby."

When she said the word, his eyes pinged down to her belly and softened. Seeing that look on his face filled her with both joy and sorrow. Joy because she knew, even though he hadn't come right out and said so, that he'd love and welcome the child they'd made together. Sorrow because she also knew that eventually, if she gave him space and time, he would come to realize what she had. That he'd been looking at his feelings for her through the rose-colored glasses of new healing. "I just want to hop in a taxi, catch the first flight back to DC, and sleep for a week," she finished.

"But—"

"After that, we can talk," she said, bending to grab her purse. She could feel it. She was moving closer to the edge. She had to get away. *Now*. But first she needed to make something abundantly clear. "You can be as much a part of this child's life as you want to be," she told him, pressing a hand to her belly, to the tiny, almost infinitesimal pooch that heralded the presence of the beautiful life quickening in her womb.

"I want to be a *father*," Dan said, his nostrils flaring. Were those tears standing in his eyes? *Oh, sweet Lord!* She couldn't stand it. Her own eyes filled. "I want to be in this baby's life in *every* way."

"Good." She nodded, biting the inside of her cheek hard. Her chest ached. She felt like a coward, but she had to leave. She really, *really* had to leave! "I'm so happy to hear that."

"Penni…" He reached for her again.

"No, Dan." She stepped back. "I told you I need some space. And whether you want to admit it to yourself or not, so do you. Space to work out what you're *really* feeling. Space to decide what you *really* want."

He dropped his hand, fisting it. A muscle was ticking in his jaw. "Fine," he finally spat. His temper was flaring. She could see the fire of it in his eyes. Good. Temper was far better than tears. Temper didn't make her want to die. "But know this," he said, his voice low and gravelly. "Whether you wanna believe it or not, I *am* falling in love with you. And I'm not mistaking it for something else because I *want* it to be something else. I've been in love before. I know what it is. I know what it feels like.

"And whether my wonderful wife died two years ago

or twenty years ago wouldn't make a difference. I'd still be mourning her. Forever. I loved her and that's the way it works when you love someone. You never stop mourning them. But, Penni, when I saw your face for the first time in Kuala Lumpur, I knew I'd been missing it my whole life."

Christ! "Please, Dan," she begged him. He had to stop. She couldn't take it.

"So here's how this is gonna work," he went on as if she hadn't spoken, and she could see that the mad was full on him now. She imagined if she squinted she'd see steam puffing out of his ears. "I'm gonna let you go tonight. 'Cause you asked me to, and 'cause I believe you when you say you need space. But I'm gonna call you every Tuesday and Friday night at nine p.m. sharp and I'm gonna remind you of what I've said here this evening, remind you of what I feel for you and remind you that I wanna be with you.

"And for every ultrasound, I'm gonna fly to New York or DC or wherever it is you're living at the time. And I'm gonna be there when this baby comes. And during all that, through all that I'm gonna prove to you that this thing I'm feeling is real. And then I'm gonna make you fall in love with me too."

Chapter Twenty-three

Black Knights Inc., Third Floor
Four weeks later

"So?" Ozzie asked, plopping himself beside Dan on the sofa in the television room. Ozzie had traded his crutches for a rather dapper cane—and kept threatening everyone at BKI that he was going to start wearing a top hat too—but his leg was still encased in a thick brace. After propping his foot up on the coffee table, he pulled a bottle of ginger ale from the pocket of his T-shirt and handed it to Dan. Then he hauled out the bottle of Honker's Ale he'd stowed in his waistband and popped the top. "How did the ultrasound go?" he asked. "Are we talking a tallywhacker or a vajayjay?"

Dan took a sip of ginger ale and frowned. "The technician couldn't get the right angle. The baby had its legs crossed. So we're still in the dark on the sex."

"Mmm." Ozzie tilted the bottle. The smell of barley and hops was delicious and tickled Dan's nose, but he no longer *yearned* for the hooch like he used to. So either his AA meetings were working, or he just had far more important things on his mind. Like the fact that Penelope Ann DePaul was the most stubborn, irritating, *wonderful* woman on the whole goddamned planet. "Well, it's more fun not knowing," Ozzie said. "I like surprises."

"So do I," Dan admitted. "But Penni's a planner."

"Since you brought her up," Ozzie said, not even *attempting* to be subtle, "how *is* Penni?"

Dan took another drink of ginger ale and tried not to squeeze the bottle so hard he broke it. "Beautiful," he admitted. "She's has that glow that expecting women get. And she's starting to show. You can feel the baby move now too. I mean, it's a flutter, but still."

He'd been true to his word. He called her every Tuesday and Friday at 9 p.m. sharp. He asked after her health and the health of the baby. He talked about personal things and mundane things. Then before he signed off, he reminded her that he had fallen in love with her, that he wanted to be with her, and that he wanted a chance to make them a real family. And he'd *thought* he was making progress. Each successive call was less stilted and weird, and the comfort they'd shared with each other from the beginning, the easy way they were together had started to slip back into their conversations—which lasted two, sometimes three hours.

He'd hoped when he flew to DC to be with her for the ultrasound that things would progress even further. But she was still holding back, holding off, not trusting him to know his own mind, his own heart. And for that, he wanted to throttle her. Or kiss her senseless. Sometimes it was hard to tell which he wanted to do first, which he wanted to do *more*. And it'd occurred to him that *this* was why he'd had that portentous sense of doom on the sidewalk in Cusco, that feeling that something awful would happen if he made a wrong move with her.

And, roger that, giving her a nickname so he wouldn't accidentally yell out his dead wife's name while they were doing the deed definitely qualified as a *wrong move*. One she was attaching far too much credence to. One she just would. Not. Let. Go. Even though he'd explained himself a million times, and despite the fact that he sworn on the Bible, the Constitution, and his mother's grave that he would *never* call her Brooklyn again. Although, in actuality, he'd continued to use the nickname after Malaysia *not* because he didn't want to slip up, but because he thought it was sweet and special and something just between them. He'd explained that too. But she was still having none of it.

Fuuuuuuuck! It'd only been a month, but his frustration was reaching disheartening proportions.

"Mazel tov," Ozzie said, clinking the neck of his beer bottle against Dan's ginger ale. "So when are you going back to Washington to see her?"

"Because the baby is healthy, the doc says she won't need another ultrasound before delivery," Dan told him. He'd read *What to Expect When You're Expecting* two times, cover to cover. And given his newfound expertise in pregnancy, he could say that Penni's pregnancy was progressing just as it should. He was so relieved, so goddamned happy about it that sometimes he thought he might break into impromptu song and dance. He was going to be a *father*! How amazing! How wonderful! He was over the moon! "So I told Penni I'd be flying in to check on her every two weeks whether she wants me there or not. It's my kid too, damnit."

"Right on." Ozzie nodded. "I'm with you. Do whatever you have to do to get back where you need to be with her. And in the meantime, you can continue to succor yourself by performing self-love."

Dan felt the tips of his ears heat. He got very still before slowly, deliberately turning to face Ozzie. The asshat was wearing a shit-eating grin. "What the fuck, man?" he demanded.

"Hey." Ozzie lifted his hands. "It's not like I was eavesdropping on purpose. My leg was killing me one night last week, so I got up to come in here and watch some TV. When I passed by your room, I heard heavy breathing."

Shit. Dan was totally busted. Spending hours on the phone with Penni, having her voice swirling around in his ear, always made him painfully hard. He'd taken to…er…*giving himself a hand* the minute they hung up.

Ozzie slapped a hand on his shoulder while taking a deep slug of beer. "No judgment here, dude. Absolutely none."

Dan felt a muscle ticking in his jaw and changed the subject to one he knew would wipe the self-satisfied smirk right off Ozzie's face. "On the subject of women and self-love, how goes it with that reporter?"

Bingo. Ozzie dropped his hand from Dan's shoulder, frowning. "You know Boss said there was a no-tolerance rule," he said.

Uh-huh. "And since when do you ever do what you're told? Becky says Miss Tate keeps calling you and you keep ignoring her. What gives?"

"Becky should mind her own goddamned business," Ozzie grumbled, blatantly ignoring Dan's question.

"Like *that's* ever gonna happen," Dan snorted.

For a couple of minutes they sat in companionable silence, watching the Chicago Blackhawks wipe up the ice with the Minnesota Wild. One of the nice things about living in a major city was that it was chockablock full of professional sports teams. There was always someone to root for, always a game or a match on TV.

After a bit Ozzie ventured, "Zoelner says he and Chelsea might have to make a trip overseas to follow a lead on Spider." When Dan looked over, it was to find Ozzie fighting a grin. "That should be interesting," he added, his tone filled with innuendo.

"Or deadly," Dan said. Ever since being teamed up with Chelsea, Zoelner had been a walking time bomb. All of the Knights had been giving him a wide berth. "They may end up killing each other."

"Or getting down to the business of finally screwing each other," Ozzie speculated. "Which, if you ask me, would make life easier for all of us."

"Mmm," Dan hummed noncommittally, frowning when Ozzie winced and grabbed his thigh. "Still pretty painful, huh?" he asked carefully.

Ozzie's leg was a sore subject, literally and figuratively. And Dan couldn't help but notice that much of Ozzie's jocularity these days seemed disingenuous, *forced*. As if Ozzie was putting on a show for them so they wouldn't know how much he was hurting. So they wouldn't know how *scared* he was. If Ozzie couldn't bounce back from this injury, if he couldn't perform his duty in the field, his career as an operator would be over. None of them wanted to countenance the idea, but it was something they would all be forced to face. Probably sooner rather than later.

"Shooting pains," Ozzie grumbled, waving him off. "I can handle it."

Dan didn't say any more, didn't press. He knew a brick wall when he came up against it. For a while longer, they sat and sipped, watching hockey players battle it out on screen. Then Ozzie said, "You won't get discouraged and give up, will you?"

"What do you mean?"

"On Penni."

"Oh, hell no." Dan shook his head emphatically. "I love her. And if I've learned anything, it's that life's full of uncertainties. But all you need to be able to deal with those uncertainties is one thing, just one thing that's true. One thing you can hang onto and depend on. My love for Penni is that thing for me now. And I'm not giving up on it. Not ever."

"And Patti?" Ozzie asked, his expression curious.

"What about her?" Dan lifted a brow.

"You still love her too, right?"

Of course he did. "I'm gonna love her 'til the day I die," he admitted. "Which sort of reminds me of something a guy said at my last AA meeting."

"What's that?"

"He said love isn't something you find, it's something that finds you."

"It's a nice thought."

"Yeah." Dan nodded. "And how many men get to be found by love twice in one lifetime?"

Something strange passed over Ozzie's face. His lips twisted. "Not many," he allowed. "You're one lucky sonofabitch, you know that?"

"Yeah, I do." And he truly, deeply did.

Now to convince Penni...

———⁓———

Penni's Condominium, Washington, DC
Two months later

Penni pressed the button on her building's intercom system and leaned close to the speaker. "Dan?"

He was early. He wasn't due to arrive until tomorrow and—

"No! It's Becky!" came a reply.

"Becky?" Penni's chin jerked back. The only Becky she knew worked at BKI, but there's no way *that* Becky was here in DC and—

"Becky Knight," the woman said.

Oh-kay. Obviously there is a way.

And then a terrible thought occurred and Penni's heart exploded in her chest. Goose bumps peppered her skin and tears immediately welled in her eyes. Dread and denial made the finger she used to press the buzzer that unlocked the front door of the building shake. Also shaking was the protective hand she placed over her belly.

"C-come up, Becky," she said, her voice hollow and quiet compared to the dull roar sounding between her ears.

She threw open her front door and waited as little stars began to dance in front of her eyes. The hallway was empty but she could hear the elevator begin its climb up to the fourth floor. *Christ, Dan! Oh Christ!* She gripped the doorjamb so hard her knuckles turned white and the wood beneath her fingers creaked a warning. Then with a *ding* the elevator doors opened and Becky emerged. She was quickly followed by Michelle and Vanessa.

Oh Dan! No! Penni had been living with grief most of her adult life, but nothing prepared her for the blow her soul took when three of the women of Black Knights Inc. arrived at her door. It could mean only one thing…

Her legs stopped supporting her and she crumpled to the floor, sitting cross-legged and bawling as her already-broken heart shattered into a million sharp pieces.

"Oh no!" Becky said as the three women raced to her, kneeling beside her where she'd ended up half in and half out of her doorway.

"Dan?" Penni croaked, her throat full of tears, her vocal cords raw from where the shards of her heart had slashed them bloody.

"God, no!" Michelle said. "He's fine." She socked Becky on the arm. "I *told* you we should have called before coming. Look what we've done to the poor woman."

Penni gaped around at them through her blurry tears. "H-he's f-fine?" She sniffed, blinking in confusion, in hope.

"Perfectly," Becky assured her. "He just can't make it this weekend. He's stuck on an assignment that—"

Penni didn't hear the rest because she really started wailing. Only this time it was in relief. In gratitude. When she'd seen all of them, she'd thought for sure Dan was dead. Why else would they be here? And even though she knew now that he wasn't, she couldn't stop the water-works. They kept coming, drenching her face, shaking her chest, making her hiccup on huge, wrenching sobs.

"I *told* you," Michelle said again.

"*Okay*," Becky harrumphed. "You're my sister-in-law and I love you. But you can stop drilling. You struck oil the first time."

"Come on." Vanessa hooked a hand under Penni's

arm. Michelle followed suit on her opposite side. "Up you go. No need to give the neighbors gossip fodder."

Old Mrs. Perkins across the way *did* fancy herself the building's resident reporter, gathering stories about the other tenants and relaying them to anyone who would listen.

Penni pushed herself up, tipping forward slightly because she was unused to her new girth. And, you know, because she was still sobbing. *Why can't I stop crying?* But she knew. Hormones. Hers had been running amok for months. Being pregnant was the emotional equivalent of thirty-seven weeks of PMS.

As if Michelle was reading her mind, she tsked and said, "I know. I know. The hormones are killer. Let's just get you a nice comfy seat, a tissue, and something cool to drink."

Penni realized she was being managed when Vanessa and Michelle turned her into her condo and marched her toward her sofa. Becky followed them inside, quietly closing the door. As Michelle and Vanessa gently pressed her down into her couch, Becky crossed the room and made herself at home in Penni's kitchen. She rooted around in the cupboards until she found a drinking glass.

Penni had just about managed to stop her tears when Becky shoved a glass of water under her nose and Michelle and Vanessa plopped down on either side of her. Like magic, a box of tissues appeared in her lap.

"We're so sorry we scared you," Vanessa said, her dark eyes sympathetic. "We didn't come here for that."

Penni took a sip of water, allowing it to cool the hot

tears gathered in her throat. Then she noisily blew her nose. "Wh-why *did* you come here?" she asked, blinking at the two women on the sofa with her and then over at Becky who'd grabbed a place on the love seat.

"To make you an offer," Becky said.

The determined look on the blond's face had Penni's inner radar beeping. Becky Knight looked like the kind of woman who didn't take no for an answer. Penni darted a glance at Vanessa. *No help there.* The black-haired beauty wore a look very similar to Becky's. *Michelle. She's always the sympathetic one.* Penni looked over only to discover…nope.

She couldn't *begin* to imagine what the BKI women were here to offer. Did they want her to leave Dan alone? Did they think she was trying to trap him? Did they come here to make sure she didn't try to wriggle into their tight-knit group?

"Wh-what offer is that?" she ventured hesitantly, pulling a fresh Kleenex from the box and dabbing her eyes. The tears had *finally* stopped. But Christ knew they'd start again at the drop of the hat. Yesterday, she'd broken down for ten minutes after watching a commercial for Android phones. The son and father scene had just been so touching. And she'd imagined that someday Dan and their child would—

"The offer of a home in Chicago," Vanessa said.

"I'm sorry?" Penni felt her brow furrow. She tucked a stray strand of hair behind her ear.

The move drew Michelle's eyes. She smiled and sighed. "Man, your hair looks great. All shiny and thick. These middle months are a dream, aren't they? When you no longer have morning sickness? When you're feeling all vibrant and healthy and *I am woman, hear me roar*?"

"I—" Penni shook her head, confused. "I'm sorry. What's happening here?" She turned to Vanessa. "Did you just offer me a home in Chicago?"

"Yepper," Becky said. When Penni glanced at her, it was to find her expression was even *more* tenacious. Becky reached into her hip pocket to extract a Dum Dum lollipop. After unwrapping it, she continued, "See, the three of us have been talking."

"A lot," Vanessa added.

"And scheming," Becky stressed.

"A lot," Vanessa said again.

"And to the everlasting exasperation of the men in our lives," was Michelle's addition to the conversation.

"And we think you should come to Chicago," Becky finished.

Penni opened her mouth, but before she could say a word, Becky pointed her sucker between Penni's eyes. "No. Just hear us out. See, we think it's unfair to make Dan fly to DC every other weekend to check up on you."

"That was *his* decision," Penni said in her own defense, feeling her cheeks heat. Somehow, with these women sitting in her living room, she felt like she'd done something wrong. Which she *hadn't*, but—

"I know," Becky allowed. "Still, he's got an important job to do."

"They all do," Michelle added.

"And it'd be easier on him…" Becky said.

"On all of us, really…" Michelle contributed. Penni was getting dizzy from the tag-team conversation.

"If you just moved to Chicago," Becky finished.

For a moment Penni could do nothing but sit there blinking. Of all the presumptuous—

"Not forever," Becky was quick to point out. Like somehow that concession made her preposterous idea easier to swallow. "But at least for the remainder of your pregnancy. And maybe for a few months afterward as well. When the baby is new and you need help."

"And you *will* need some help," Michelle insisted, nodding knowingly. "Take it from a woman who's had two. The first three months are the hardest."

"I—" Penni started, but Becky spoke right over her.

"And I don't mean you'd have to move into the warehouse. That's asking too much." Oh, *that* was asking too much? Not the thousand-mile move? "But we have a friend, well…" Becky made a face, shoving the lollipop in her cheek. "She's more of a sister-in-arms, really. Her name is Delilah and her uncle rehabs houses. Last year he redid a three-flat in the Gold Coast."

"Which is a *great* neighborhood," Vanessa insisted. "And only a couple of blocks from Northwestern Memorial Hospital, so *super* convenient for a woman in your condition."

"And speaking of your condition," Michelle said, "there's a wonderful OB-GYN who works there. You'd love her. She's this old hippie who has five kids of her own and is totally pragmatic about childbirth. The woman's a friggin' *rock* in the delivery room. Which is exactly what you want."

"Ladies," Becky harrumphed. "I'm trying to paint a word picture of Delilah's uncle's place here. Stop interrupting me."

"Oh." Michelle nodded, rolling her hand. "Proceed."

"Thank you." Becky nodded and sniffed like she was auditioning for the role of Queen of England. "See, the three-flat is an old greystone. The top two floors have been rented, but the bottom is free. It's fully furnished, has these gorgeous dark wood floors, marble counter-tops, two bedrooms, and a lovely view out the big bay window onto Astor Street."

"Which is this quiet, tree-lined street right off the Magnificent Mile," Vanessa added.

"And Delilah's uncle says you can live there for as long as you need at the family rate," Becky continued. "Which is free except for utilities."

Michelle glanced around the condo. "You could easily put all your stuff in storage for a few months. And once you've cleared this place out and slapped a new coat of paint on the walls, I bet it'd sell like a hotcake at a hotcake convention. Then, after the baby is born, and when you're ready to go to work for your uncle—"

"*If* that's what you decide you still want to do..." Becky interjected.

"Then all you'll have to do is pack your bags and call the movers," Michelle finished.

Penni's head was spinning. "You guys really *have* been talking and scheming," she said, lifting a hand to her throbbing forehead. "But...*why* would you be willing to do this? Why volunteer to help with—"

"Because we love Dan," Becky cut her off, her expression plastered with *duh*. "And Dan loves you and that baby you're carrying." When Penni opened her mouth to argue about the first part of that sentence, Becky once again pointed her Dum Dum right between Penni's eyes. "He's family, which makes your baby family, and *you* family by extension. We take care of our family."

And here Penni had been so scared of what Dan's friends and coworkers would think of her once they knew. Here she'd thought they'd close ranks around him and push her out. But instead they were opening their arms and offering her a place within the fold. A *new* family to replace the one she'd lost when—

Oh Christ! Emotions filled her like suffocating smoke, making it impossible to breathe. Her face exploded. Once again it was all tears and snot and deep, racking sobs.

"Hormones," she heard Michelle say knowingly.

———

303 North Astor Street, Chicago, Illinois
Three months later

Penni was as big as a house, overdue, and on a mission…

Oh, and cranky. She was really, *really* cranky. In her own defense, carrying around a nearly eight-and-a-half-pound baby—according to her obstetrician's estimates—who seemed determined to stay inside to practice backflips atop her bladder would put any woman in a bad mood. And have any woman willing to try *anything* to speed the birthing process along. Hence, the mission.

If Dan will just hurry the hell up!

She waited impatiently by the front door of her greystone, straining her ears for the sound of his monster Harley. *There.* From up the street came the rumble of rolling thunder. She stepped onto the stoop and craned her head, her eyes searching. A flash of shiny red caught her attention. Heartbreaker. That was the name of his bike. And it looked the part. From its intricate cherry bomb–colored paint job, chrome battery box in the shape of a cracked heart, and twisty, turny exhaust pipes that grumbled and coughed and shook the air around them, it was enough to make every female—and male, for that matter—stare and wonder and ache and *wish*.

But right now, the only thing *she* wished was that Dan would get his fine ass moving. Because now that she'd made her decision, now that she had her mission set before her, she was ready to get going on it. *Beyond* ready. Like, she wanted to kick her own butt for not thinking of this yesterday.

Just keep calm and carry on.

Stuff it! she told the annoying voice.

Dan roared up to the curb, looking frustratingly handsome in biker boots, jeans, and leather jacket. Oh, and thin. He looked thin and comfortable and *not* nearly thirty-nine weeks pregnant. The bastard.

"I had to wait thirty minutes in line," he told her after shutting down Heartbreaker's engine and pulling off his helmet. He shook out his shaggy hair. The blonder streaks caught in the afternoon sunlight, glowing like a halo. But she knew for a fact the man was far from a saint. And to that end, she planned to insist he join her on a sinning spree very, very soon. "And then when I ordered the hot dogs with extra, *extra* peppers, they had to go in the back and open a new tub."

"Forget the damned hot dogs," she called, waddling— yes *waddling*, there was just no other way to describe it—down the steps and toward the curb.

He stopped making his way up the walk, his chin jerking back. "Forget the hot dogs? Did you miss the part where I just said I had to stand in line for thirty minutes to—"

She closed the distance between them, grabbed the lapels of his biker jacket, and silenced him with a kiss. *Oh my…* For a second she forgot everything—her plan, her reason, her surroundings. Because his lips were smooth and firm, just as she remembered them. His tongue wet and bold, stealing into her mouth to conquer and claim. His arms strong and sure as they wrapped around her waist. No, not waist. She hadn't seen her waist in months.

But that was neither here nor there, because *Christ*, she'd missed his kisses. Dreamed about them…every flippin' night. And had been so tempted by the thought of them, the memory of them, that she'd almost said *screw it* to all her reasons for not pursuing the physical side of their relationship during these past—

"Mmm," he hummed into her mouth. His breath was fresh and minty. Then, to her everlasting annoyance, he was breaking the suction of their lips and staring down at her, his eyes narrowed. "What…?"

He didn't say anything more. Didn't need to. Because her MO ever since those crazy two days surrounding the events of Cusco and Chicago had been to keep him at arm's length. It had been difficult enough to harden her heart against his declarations of love and support, and she'd known it would have been hopeless to try to maintain her position once he took her to bed, once she allowed herself to revel in his arms, in his knowledge-able, soul-shaking lovemaking. So she'd implemented a no-nooky policy after she moved to Chicago and a no-dirty-talk policy during their daily—yeah, they'd eventually become daily—phone calls.

And talk about torture. It'd been nearly impossible to keep her hands and her mouth to herself. Why pregnancy should have evolved to make a woman horny out of her mind was something she did not understand. *I mean, the deed is already done! Why saddle a woman with an increased urge to mate?* And then, while Dan had been out hunting for hot dogs with extra peppers and she'd been lying on the sofa trying to find a comfortable position—and cursing Dan's name for doing this to her—she'd had a grand epiphany.

"I want you to make love to me," she told him now, dragging him with her up the walk and the stoop. Pulling him inside the bottom-floor apartment.

"Excuse me?" he asked after he booted the door closed. "I thought you said you—"

"Shit, I *know* what I said," she groused. "But forget about it. I don't care about any of that right now. The tacos from last night didn't work. The Thai food for lunch didn't work. These extra peppers on the hot dogs aren't going work. That old saying about spicy food must be a myth. And I'm tired of not being able to get comfortable. I'm tired of being fat—"

"You're not fat." He smiled, his eyes roaming over her as if he'd never seen anything so beautiful. She wanted to punch him in the face. "You're gorgeous and glowing and—"

"And I'm tired of waiting for this kid of yours to decide that he or she is ready to make an appearance." She grabbed his lapels and yanked him down until they were nose to nose. "Sex can induce labor. So let's have some sex."

"Penni"—he curled his hands around hers, forcing her clawed hands to release the leather of his jacket—"you're not thinking straight. You're exhausted and—"

"Damnit, Dan!" she hissed. If she could have shot fire from her eyes, she would have set his hair ablaze. "You put this thing inside me. Now you help me get it out!"

He stood to his full height, hooking his thumbs in his belt buckle so that his fingers made a frame of his man bits. The man bits she was *trying* to make use of. Glancing at his face, she saw his lips quirking.

She pointed a finger at him. "Don't do it. Don't you laugh at me."

He rolled in his lips, his big chest quaking.

"You really don't want to test me right now," she warned. "I'm this close"—she held her thumb and forefinger an inch apart—"from taking out my frustration on various and sundry parts of your body. Starting with your smiling mouth."

"Ahem." He studiously wiped away his smirk, trying his best to compose himself. "Come here," he said, herding her toward the couch. Yes, herding. Because she was as big as a cow. Thanks to him. The bastard! "Let's sit down and let's talk about this."

"I don't want to *talk* about it," she growled. "I just want to *do* it." Still, she sat on the sofa, jamming a pillow behind her aching back and putting her swollen feet and ankles up on the coffee table. Cankles. She never thought she'd see the day she had cankles.

"Believe me," Dan said, sitting beside her and putting

his big, warm hand on her belly. He always did that when he came to visit her. Sat with his hand on her stomach as if he wanted to touch her and the baby at the same time. "I wanna do it too. Jesus, Penni, I've been *dreaming* of doing it for the last six goddamn months."

"So what's the problem?" she demanded.

"The problem is I promised myself that if we made love, *when* we made love"—she narrowed her eyes because the way he said it made it sound like it was a foregone conclusion. Now she added the word "arrogant" in front of the word "bastard" when she silently cursed him—"that it would be because you've accepted that I love you. And you've admitted to loving me too."

"Dan," she said, sighing, "I've already told you—"

"I know what you've told me, damnit!" Dan cut Penni off. He'd tried to play nice. Play it cool. Tried not to broach any of their issues because every time he did, her face twisted up like someone had shoved a porcupine up her tuckus, and he worried what her stress could do to the baby. But he was done being patient. They were having their heart-to-heart right goddamned *now!*

"But you're wrong," he said. "You think you're a rebound, but you're not. It wouldn't have mattered if I'd dated and slept with fifty women between Patti and you, or zero women between Patti and you, because the moment I met you, the moment I saw you, I knew. I knew *you*, Penelope Ann DePaul. And I knew I wanted to be with you."

"Dan, I—"

"Shut up and let me finish," he growled, pinning her with a fierce look.

"Continue," she allowed with a sniff. And she was so damned beautiful, she made him ache. Pregnancy looked *good* on Penni. It made her round and soft. All dewy and pink. It'd been torture these past few months keeping his dick in his pants, but that's what he'd done. Because that's one of the rules she'd imposed when she agreed to move to Chicago.

Dan would thank the BKI ladies until his dying day for convincing Penni to do that. He'd *loved* seeing her blossom. *Loved* watching his child grow within her. *Loved* going to Lamaze classes. *Loved*…her.

"You think the only reason I've stuck around as long as I have is because you're pregnant, but that's not true," he insisted. "Baby or no baby, I would have pursued you exactly the same," he continued. And the look on her face said she *desperately* wanted his words to be true. "Because I believe with my whole being and everything that I am that we belong together. You and me. Forever."

"Dan—"

"And you think because I loved my wife with my whole heart that there's no way I could love you the same." He cut off whatever protest she'd been about to make. Now that he was talking, he was determined to get it all out, lay every single one of his cards on the table. "But again, you're wrong."

"But—"

"See, my love for her doesn't lessen my love for you," he said, his eyes boring into hers, insisting she hear and understand and *believe*. "'Cause love is endless, boundless. Just when you think there couldn't possibly be any more in you, you look and see a well of it just waiting to be tapped." And it was a miracle. He was awed by it. Humbled by it.

"I loved Patti. And I love you. And I'm so…lucky…" His voice hitched. Oh, and great, now *he* was the one with tears welling in his eyes. "So fucking *lucky* to have had the opportunity to love two brilliant, beautiful woman in my life. So fucking *lucky* to have found a soul mate twice."

"Soul mate," she whispered.

"That's what we are," he insisted, wiping a hand under his nose. "When I think back on it, I've known since the beginning. It's that strange connection we share. That odd sense of peace and comfort we get whenever we're near each other."

"That bizarre feeling of knowing and being known." She sighed.

His heart leaped. Did she…*finally*…believe him?

"Exactly." He nodded. "So I'll make love to you, Penni." Oh, how he'd make love to her. Over and over. Twice for every time he'd wanted to in the past six months. "Just as soon as you tell me you believe me. Just as soon as you tell me you love me too."

He held his breath, searching her face. And then he saw it in her eyes. She believed him. *She believed him!*

"Dan…" She whispered his name and he hoped to hear it on her lips for a hundred more years. He didn't dare move. Didn't dare blink. His heart was a fist, huge and hammering against his sternum. "I believe you," she said, wrapping her arms around his neck and hugging him tight. "And I love you," she confessed in his ear.

He sucked in a breath of triumph, tightening his

arms around her, *knowing* they would stay around her. Forever. Tears rolled down his face, soaking into her hair. He didn't care.

"I told you back in Malaysia I was looking for something more in my life," she whispered. "For *someone* more. But I think the truth was I was aching for love, aching to *be* loved. And I'm so humbled, Dan." She was openly sobbing. The sound made his own tears flow faster. "I'm so humbled and fortunate and *happy* that my questing heart found you…"

"Penni." He framed her face, his heart bursting with love and happiness, his shoulders shaking. It caused the new ink he'd gotten yesterday, the fresh ribbon with Penni's name in the center that he'd had tattooed just below Patti's—when their baby was born, his or her name would go on a ribbon too—to rub against the material of his T-shirt and burn. "You've just made me the happiest man alive."

"Good." She nodded, her smile a little wobbly through her tears. "Now would you *please* make love to me and help me make this kid to hurry the hell up?"

"It would be my pleasure," he growled. And it was…

Read on for an excerpt from

Hell or High Water

The first in The Deep Six, a pulse-pounding new
series from Julie Ann Walker!

Present day
10:52 p.m....

"AND THE *SANTA CRISTINA* AND HER BRAVE CREW AND CAP-
tain were sucked down into Davy Jones's locker, lost to
the world. That is...until now..."

Leo "the Lion" Anderson, known to his friends
as LT—a nod to his former Naval rank—let his last
words hang in the air before glancing around at the four
faces illuminated by the flickering beach bonfire. Rapt
expressions stared back at him. He fought the grin curv-
ing his lips.

Bingo, bango, bongo. His listeners had fallen under
a spell as deep and fathomless as the great oceans
themselves. It happened anytime he recounted the
legend of the *Santa Cristina*. Not that he could blame
his audience. The story of the ghost galleon, the holy
grail of sunken Spanish shipwrecks, had fascinated
him ever since he'd been old enough to understand
the tale while bouncing on his father's knee. And that
lifelong fascination might account for why he was
now determined to do what so many before him—his
dearly departed father included—had been unable to

do. Namely, locate and excavate the mother lode of the grand ol' ship.

Of course, he reckoned the romance and mystery of discovering her waterlogged remains were only *part* of the reason he'd spent the last two months and a huge portion of his savings—as well as huge portions of the savings of the others—refurbishing his father's decrepit, leaking salvage boat. The rest of the story as to why he was here now? Why they were *all* here now? Well, that didn't bear dwelling on.

At least not on a night like tonight. When a million glittering stars and a big half-moon reflected off the dark, rippling waters of the lagoon on the southeast side of the private speck of jungle, mangrove forest, and sand in the Florida Keys. When the sea air was soft and warm, caressing his skin and hair with gentle, salt-tinged fingers. When there was so much...*life* to enjoy.

That had been his vow—*their* vow—had it not? To grab life by the balls and really *live* it? To suck the marrow from its proverbial bones?

His eyes were automatically drawn to the skin on the inside of his left forearm where scrolling, tattooed lettering read *For RL*. He ran a thumb over the pitch-black ink.

This one's for you, you stubborn sonofagun, he pledged, flipping open the lid on the cooler sunk deep into the sand beside his lawn chair. Grabbing a bottle of Budweiser and twisting off the cap, he let his gaze run down the long dock to where his uncle's catamaran was moored. The clips on the sailboat's rigging lines clinked rhythmically against its metal mast, adding to the harmony of softly shushing waves, quietly crackling fire, and the high-pitched *peesy, peesy, peesy* call of a nearby black-and-white warbler.

Then he turned his eyes to the open ocean past the underwater reef surrounding the side of Wayfarer Island, where his father's old salvage ship bobbed lazily with the tide. Up and down. Side to side. Her newly painted hull and refurbished anchor chain gleamed dully in the moonlight. Her name, *Wayfarer-I*, was clearly visible thanks to the new, bright-white lettering.

He dragged in a deep breath, the smell of burning driftwood and suntan lotion tunneled up his nose, and he did his best to appreciate the calmness of the evening and the comforting thought that the vessel looked, if not necessarily sexy, then at least seaworthy. *Which is a hell of an improvement*.

Hot damn, he was proud of all the work he and his men had done on her, and—

His men…

He reminded himself for the one hundred zillionth time that he wasn't supposed to think of them that way. Not anymore. Not since those five crazy-assed SEALs waved their farewells to the Navy in order to join him on his quest for high-seas adventure and the discovery of untold riches. Not since they were now, officially, *civilians*.

"But why you guys?" The blond who was parked beneath Spiro "Romeo" Delgado's arm yanked Leo from his thoughts. "What makes you different from all those who've already tried and failed to find her?"

"Besides the obvious you mean, *mamacita*?" Romeo winked, leaning back in his lawn chair to spread his arms wide. His grin caused his teeth to flash white against his neatly trimmed goatee, and Leo watched the blond sit forward in her plastic deck chair to take in the wonder that was Romeo Delgado. After a good, long gander, she giggled and snuggled back against Romeo's side.

Leo rolled his eyes. Romeo's swarthy, Hispanic looks and his six-percent-body-fat physique made even the most prim-and-proper lady's panties drop fast enough to bust the floorboards. And this gal? Well, this gal might be prim and proper in her everyday life—hell, for all Leo knew she could be the leading expert on high etiquette at an all-girls school—but today, ever since Romeo picked her and her cute friend up in Schooner Wharf Bar on Key West with the eye-rolling line of *"Wanna come see my private island?"* she'd been playing the part of a good-time girl out having a little fun-in-the-sun fling. And it was the *fling* part that might—scratch that, rewind—*did* account for the lazy, self-satisfied smile spread across Romeo's face.

"I'm serious, though." Tracy or Stacy or Lacy, or whatever her name was—Leo had sort of tuned out on the introductions—wrinkled her sunburned nose. "How do you even know where to look?"

"Because of this." Leo lifted the silver piece of eight, a seventeenth-century Spanish dollar, from where it hung around his neck on a long, platinum chain. "My father discovered it ten years ago off the coast of the Marquesas Keys."

Tracy/Stacy/Lacy's furrowed brow telegraphed her skepticism. "One coin? I thought the Gulf and the Caribbean were littered with old doubloons."

"It wasn't just one piece of eight my father found."

Leo winked. "It was a big, black conglomerate of ten pieces of eight, as well as—"

"Conglomerate?" asked the brunette with the Cupid's-bow lips. Tracy/Stacy/Lacy's friend had given Leo all the right signals the minute Romeo pulled the catamaran up to Wayfarer Island's creaky old dock and unloaded their guests. It'd been instant sloe-eyed looks and shy, encouraging smiles.

Okay, and confession time. Because for a fleeting moment when she—Sophie or Sophia? Holy Christ, Leo was seriously sucking with names tonight—sidled up next to him, he'd been tempted to take her up on all the things her nonverbal communications offered. Then an image of black hair, sapphire eyes, and a subtly crooked front tooth blazed through his brain. And just like that, the brunette lost her appeal.

Which is a good thing, he reminded himself. *You're gettin' too old to bang the Betties Romeo drags home from the bar*.

Enter Dalton "Doc" Simmons and his nearly six and a half feet of homespun, Midwestern charm. He'd been quick to insert himself between Leo and Sophie/Sophia. And now her gaze lingered on Doc's face when he said in that low, scratchy Kiefer Sutherland voice of his, "Unlike gold, which retains its luster after years on the bottom of the ocean, silver coins are affected by the seawater. They get fused together by corrosion or other maritime accretions. When that happens, it's called a conglomerate. They have to be electronically cleaned to remove the surface debris and come out looking like this." Grabbing the silver chain around his neck, Doc pulled a piece of eight from inside his T-shirt. It was identical to the one Leo wore.

"And like this," Romeo parroted, twirling the coin on the chain around *his* neck like a Two-Buck Chuck stripper whirling a boa.

Their first day on the island, Leo had gifted each of his men—*damnit!*…his *friends*—with one of the coins, telling them their matching tattoos were symbols of their shared past and their matching pieces of eight were symbols of their shared future.

Leo tipped the neck of his beer toward Doc. "Maritime accretions, huh? You sound like an honest-to-God salvor, my friend."

Doc smirked, which was as close to a smile as the dude ever really got. If Leo hadn't seen Doc rip into a steak on occasion, he wouldn't have been all that convinced the guy had teeth.

"But even a conglomerate of coins wouldn't be enough to guarantee the ship's location," Leo added, turning back to the blond. "My father *also* found a handful of bronze deck cannons. All of which were on the *Santa Cristina*'s manifest. So she's down there… *somewhere*." He just had to find her. All his friends were counting on that windfall for various reasons, and if he didn't—

"But, like you said, your dad tried to find this Christy boat for"—Leo winced. Okay, so the woman seemed sweet. But the only thing worse than mangling the name of the legendary vessel was referring to it as a *boat*— "like twenty-some-odd years, right?"

"And Mel Fisher searched for the *Atocha* for sixteen years before finally findin' her." He referred to the most famous treasure hunter and treasure galleon of all time. Well, most famous of all time until he and the guys made the history books, right? *Right.* "In shallow water, like that around the Florida Keys, the shiftin' sands are moved by wind and tide. They change the seabed daily, not to mention after nearly four centuries. But with a little hard work and perseverance, you better believe the impossible becomes possible. We're hot on her trail." Her convoluted, invisible, nonexistent trail. *Shit.*

Doc slow-winked at the woman by way of agreement, twirling the toothpick that perpetually stuck out of his mouth in a circle with his tongue. It must have dazzled poor Sophie/Sophia, because she sucked in a breath before batting her pretty lashes and sidling her lawn chair closer to him. Throwing an arm around her shoulders, Doc turned to wiggle his eyebrows at Leo. Just like the others, Doc was never one to pass up an opportunity to feed Leo a heaping helping of shit. Par for the course considering Leo was...*fuck a duck*...used to be their commanding officer, a prime target for all their ass-hattery.

Yeah, yeah, Leo thought, quietly chuckling. *So, I pulled the Roger Murtaugh, I'm-gettin'-too-old-for-this-shit bit. And you think I screwed up royally when I turned down what she was offerin'? So, go ahead. Rub it in, you big corn-fed douche-canoe.*

"Why do you need to find that old treasure anyway?" the blond asked. "You have a private island." She motioned with her beer toward the rippling waters of the lagoon, tipsily splashing suds into the fire and making it hiss. "Aren't you r—" She hiccuped, then covered her mouth with her fingers, giggling. "Rich?" she finished.

"Ha! Hardly." Leo rested his sweating beer bottle against the fabric of his swim trunks. Here in the Keys, shorts and swim trunks were interchangeable—unlike his possible bed partners, apparently.

Come on, now! Why can't you get Olivia Mortier out of your head?

And that was the question of the hour, wasn't it? Or more like the question of the last frickin' *eighteen months*. Ever since that assignment in Syria…

"But if you're not rich," the blond insisted, "then how can you"—*hiccup*—"afford to own this place?"

No joke, Romeo had better double-time her up to the house and into his bed. One or two more brewskies and she'd be too many sheets to the wind for what the self-styled lothario had in mind for her. Romeo may be a horndog extraordinaire, with more notches on his bedpost than Leo had sorties on his SEAL résumé, but like all the guys, Romeo was nothing if not honorable. If Tracy/Stacy/Lacy was too incapacitated, Romeo would do no more than tuck her under the covers with a chaste kiss on the forehead. And as their SEAL Team motto stated: *Where's the fun in that?*

On cue, Romeo turned to Leo, snapping his fingers, a worried frown pulling his black eyebrows into a V. Leo hid a smile as he reopened the cooler and dug around inside until he found a bottle of water. He tossed it over the fire, and Romeo caught it one-handed. Then Mr. Slam-dunk-ovich made quick work of exchanging the blond's beer with the H_2O. "Try this, *m'ija*," he crooned, really laying his accent on thick before leaning over to whisper something no doubt highly suggestive into her ear.

The blond giggled, obediently twisting the cap off the water bottle to take a deep slug.

"We don't own the island, darlin'," a deep voice called from up the beach. Leo turned to see his uncle coming toward them. The man was dressed in his usual uniform of baggy cargo shorts and an eye-bleeding hula shirt. His thick mop of Hemingway hair and matching beard glowed in the light of the moon, contrasting sharply with skin that had been tanned to leather by the endless subtropical sun.

Bran Pallidino, Leo's best friend and BUD/S—Basic Underwater Demolition/SEAL training—swim partner, had once described Leo's uncle as "one part crusty sea dog and two parts slack-ass hippie." Leo figured that pretty much summed up the ol' coot in one succinct sentence. "My great-great-I've-forgotten-how-many-greats-grandfather leased the island for one hundred and fifty years from Ulysses S. Grant."

"*President* Grant?" the brunette squeaked, coughing on beer.

"The one and only," Uncle John said, plunking himself into an empty plastic deck chair, stretching his bare feet toward the fire, and lifting a tumbler—filled with Salty Dog, John's standard grapefruit, vodka, and salted-rim cocktail—to his lips. Ice clinked against the side of the glass when he took a healthy swig. "You may not know this, Tracy," he said—*Tracy*. Leo snapped imaginary fingers and endeavored to commit the name to memory—"but ol' Ulysses smoked 'bout ten cigars a day. And my great-great"—Uncle John made a rolling motion with his hand—"however-many-greats-grandpappy happened to be the premier cigar-maker of the time. In exchange for a lifetime supply of high-quality Cubans, Great-Grandpappy secured the rights to make a vacation home for himself and his descendants on this here little bit of paradise for a century and a half." Uncle John's familiar Louisiana drawl—the same one Leo shared, though to a lesser extent—drifted lazily on the warm breeze.

The Anderson brothers, Uncle John and Leo's father, James, originally hailed from the Crescent City. Like their father before them, they'd trained to be shrimp-boat captains in the Gulf. But a chance discovery during a simple afternoon dive off the coast of Geiger Key had changed everything. They'd found a small Spanish gun-boat equipped with all manner of archeological riches, from muskets to daggers to swords, and the treasure-hunting bug had bitten them *hard*. The following year, when Leo was just five years old, the brothers moved to the Keys to use their vast knowledge of the sea to search for sunken riches instead of plump, pink shrimp.

Unfortunately, they never found another haul that could compete with that of the gunboat. Uncle John gave up the endeavor after a decade, settling in to run one of Key West's many bars until his retirement six months ago. But Leo's father had continued with the salvage business, splitting his time between jobs and hunting for the *Santa Cristina* until he suffered a heart attack during a dive. Leo took solace in knowing his old man had died as he'd lived, wrapped in the arms of the sea.

"Ulysses S. Grant? So that had to have been, what? Sometime in the eighteen seventies?" the brunette asked.

"You know your presidents, Sophie." Uncle John winked, taking another draw on his cocktail.

Sophie, Sophie, Sophie. Leo really should have paid more attention to the introductions. I mean, seriously? What was his problem? If a woman's name wasn't Olivia Mortier, it just went in one ear and out the other? *For shit's sake!*

"I teach history at the Girls' Academy of the Holy Saints High School in Tuscaloosa." She hooked a thumb toward her friend. "Tracy teaches home ec."

Leo nearly spewed his beer. It wasn't high etiquette, but it was damn close.

"Ah." Uncle John nodded sagely. "Well, that explains it. And you're right. It was in the eighteen seventies."

"So then"—Sophie's lips pulled down into a frown—"you're kicked out in, what? Five? Ten years?"

"Eh." Uncle John shrugged. "We can't really get kicked out because it was never really ours to begin with. Besides, this crew will have found the *Santa Cristina* by then." John had moved out to Wayfarer Island under the auspices of "helping" Leo search for the ship. But really Leo suspected the old codger was just bored with retirement and looking to take part in one last hoorah. "And," he continued, "they'll have enough money to buy whatever house or island they want. Am I right, or am I right?"

"Hooyah!" Doc and Romeo whooped in unison, lifting their beers in salute.

Leo didn't join in. He wasn't a superstitious man by nature, but the ghost galleon brought out the avoid-the-black-cat, throw-salt-over-my-shoulder in him, and he didn't want to jinx their chances of finding the wreck by treating it like it was a foregone conclusion. He also didn't like to think that in a few short years he and his

uncle would lose the lease on the island that had seen
generations of Andersons for spring breaks and summer
vacations, for Fourth of July weekends and the occasional Christmas getaway. It wasn't until Leo arrived
with his merry band of Navy SEALs that anyone had
attempted to live on the island permanently; it was just
too isolated.

"And speaking of the crew…" Uncle John said. *Crew*.
Leo rolled the term around in his head and figured *right.*
I reckon that's a label I can work with. "The other half
of 'em just called on the satellite phone."

Because when Leo said isolated, he meant *isolated*.
The nearest cell tower was almost fifty nautical miles
away. Which begged the question: What the ever-lovin'
hell had Tracy and Sophie been thinking to let Romeo
sail them out here? They were damned lucky Romeo
was a stand-up guy and not some ax murderer. Had
Leo felt more obliging, he'd have given the women a
well-deserved lecture about the ill-advisedness of hopping onto a catamaran for a four-hour sail with a dusky-
skinned gentleman sporting a too-precisely trimmed
goatee. But right now, he had more important things
to discuss.

"What'd they say?" he asked his uncle, referring to
his three friends who'd spent a week across the pond in
Seville, Spain.

"They said they finished photocopyin' and digitizin'
the images of the documents in the Spanish Archives
yesterday afternoon and sent all the data to What's-his-
name, that historian you've been talkin' to online."

Online via the Internet connection Leo had estab-
lished using the satellite he mounted to the top of the

house. Because while he and the guys might've been fine to forgo cellular signals, there would have been serious mental and emotional fallout had Mason "Monet" McCarthy not been able to watch his beloved Red Sox play on their lone laptop or Ray "Wolf" Roanhorse not been able to Skype with his bazillion loving relatives back in Oklahoma. And the satellite was one *more* reason Leo's savings account and the savings accounts of the others were barely in the black.

God, we need a salvage gig. A big one. Because they only had enough funds left to fuel the search for the *Santa Cristina* for two, maybe three more weeks. And that wasn't going to be enough.

Of course, before they could start advertising their services, they needed to actually incorporate their fledgling business. Which meant paperwork and opening accounts and coming up with a *name* for their company. Leo was not happy with Romeo's suggestion that they should call themselves Seas the Day Salvage. I mean, he enjoyed a play on words as much as the next guy, but, come on now, that was just *bad*.

Pushing his cash problems and the long list of things he still needed to accomplish aside, Leo got back to the point at hand. The historian he'd been emailing.

"Like I've told you twenty times before, the guy's name is Alex Merriweather," he scolded his uncle, not pointing out that John had no trouble remembering the names of Sophie and Tracy, two women he'd just met— *the lecherous old fart*. "And he assures me that if there's anything new to discover in those documents, he's the man who'll find it."

Treasure hunters die old and broke. It was a saying

Leo sure as shit didn't want to see come true for him and the guys, which meant he was exploring every possible avenue he could. Including hiring an overpriced historian to go through all the old documents that pertained to the hurricane of 1624 and the fate of the Spanish fleet.

"Hmmph." His uncle made a face. "I doubt some library nerd is goin' to be able to tell you anything more than—"

"So what else did they say?" Leo interrupted, not willing to engage in that argument. *Again*. "After receivin' the digitized copies, did Alex gave 'em any indication that—"

"Hold on there, Leo, my boy." Uncle John raised the hand not wrapped around his cocktail glass. "Don't let your mind go runnin' around like a gnat in a hurricane. First of all, they didn't go into any detail with me. Second of all, I don't think they've *got* any details. The sorry sonsofbitches have been stuck on a transatlantic flight all day long. They just landed in Key West a little while ago. They're goin' to rack out there for the night and head here first thing tomorrow mornin'. You'll have to hold your questions until then."

Leo sat back in his chair, frustrated by the delay but comforting himself with another long pull on his beer.

"I need to run to the little girls' room," Tracy suddenly announced. "Want to"—*hiccup*—"come with me, Sophie?"

After a quick look at Doc, Sophie pushed up from her lawn chair. "Of course," she said, giving the back legs of her Daisy-Duke-style jean shorts a quick tug. It didn't do a damn thing to cover the lower curve of her ass cheeks peeking from beneath the frayed denim.

"I'll show you the way." Romeo bolted up from his chair. The guy knew an opportunity to move things along when he saw one. "You coming, *vato*?" he asked Doc, one black brow raised meaningfully.

"Be there in a sec," Doc said. The three of them still seated around the fire watched, heads tilted, as Romeo herded the women across the sand toward the house. *What?* They were all healthy, red-blooded, heterosexual males, and the sight of long, tan legs and sweet, heart-shaped derrieres was not something to be missed.

"Hey, LT," Doc said, taking the toothpick from his mouth, "if you've changed your mind about Sophie, I'll gladly hara-kiri myself."

"You'll what?" Leo turned away from the view.

"You know," Doc snickered. "I'll fall on my sword so *she* can, uh, fall on *yours*."

Maybe he really *was* getting too old, or maybe he just had other things on his mind—*not Olivia, not Olivia… okay, probably Olivia*—but Leo just couldn't force himself to feel any enthusiasm about the prospect of another meaningless one-night stand. "Thanks for the offer, even as distasteful as you just made it sound." He grimaced. "But believe me when I say she's all yours if you can get her."

"Don't you worry." Doc winked, pushing up from his seat, throwing the toothpick into the fire, and turning toward the rambling old house. "I'll get her."

Yes, sir, Leo figured Doc probably would. After all, a woman had once told him that Doc was the spitting image of some big French actor. And though Leo hadn't the first clue who she was talking about, he figured from her dreamy expression that the comparison was meant to be a compliment. "Me and Uncle John will hang out here. Give you all some time to do your wooin'."

"If that's the case, you may be here all night," Doc boasted. "My wooing has been known to last—"

"Yeah, yeah." Leo waved him off. "Get lost, will you? I'm tired of lookin' at your smug face." And sure enough, Doc's expression became even more…well… *smug*. Leo grinned because he knew just what to say to get rid of it. "Besides, you stay here too much longer and you may give Romeo time to convince dear, sweet Sophie that a little two-for-the-price-of-one action could be lots of fun."

Doc's grin melted away as he called Romeo a foul name beneath his breath. But to Leo's surprise, Doc didn't hightail it up to house. Instead he angled his head, his eyes searching Leo's face over the glow of the fire.

"Well?" Leo asked. "What are you waitin' for?"

"It, uh…" Doc lifted a hand to scratch his head.

"What's up, bro?" And, yes. More than his *men*, or his *friends*, or even his *crew*, the five guys who'd hitched their wagons to his mule were his *brothers*. In every way that counted.

"You know, the, uh, the way I see it," Doc said haltingly, "part of our pledge included no more pussyfooting around when it comes to going after the things we really want." Leo watched Doc unconsciously rub the tattoo on the inside of his left forearm. "And it's been obvious since day one that you want Olivia Mortier."

Damn. Just hearing her name spoken aloud made the hairs along the back of Leo's neck stand up.

"So, why don't you send her an email, huh? See if she'll take some time off from The Company to come down here for a little visit." And now that smug smirk was back on Doc's face. "Maybe after she's wobbled your knob a time or two, you'll stop mooning around like a lovesick teenager."

Sonofa—Sometimes it sucked ass living in such close quarters with a group of men trained and tested in the fine art of observation. "Wobble my knob? What are you? Thirteen?"

"Avoiding the question?"

Damnit. "For the record," Leo growled. "I don't *want* her to wobble my knob, as you so eloquently put it." A voice inside his head warned him his nose would be growing Pinocchio-style any minute now.

All right. So, if he was totally honest, he *would* have liked to see where things with Olivia were headed. He would have liked to know if all those not-so-subtle flirty looks and that one ball-tightening kiss could have turned into something more—knob wobbling included. Unfortunately, Fate had intervened in the form of the goatfuck of all goatfucks, which had precipitated his exit from the Navy and negated all chances that he'd ever again work in the same arena as one oh-so-tempting Olivia Mortier.

He was a civilian now. And civilians and CIA field agents weren't exactly known to find themselves in a position to mix it up. So even if he *could* convince her to take a vacation from missiles and mayhem, it's not like there was any real chance at a future for them. After all, the woman was all about the adrenaline high, and he was…well…*retired*.

Acknowledgments

It should come as no surprise to fans of my books that my first round of thanks goes to my husband. Sweetheart, you're my sounding board when I need advice, my inspiration when I've run out of ideas or funny bro-isms, and my biggest cheerleader when I start to doubt myself. I couldn't do any of this without you. I love you!

My second round of high fives goes to my editor, Deb Werksman. Deb, your ability and willingness to brainstorm with me, not just about my books but about the path of my career, is invaluable. Thank you so much for going above and beyond, for not only caring about the stories but about me. I couldn't ask for a better advocate. You da bomb, lady!

A big round of applause and giant thanks to all the folks at Sourcebooks. I cherish the day I signed the contract that made Sourcebooks my publishing home and all of you my publishing family. I couldn't ask for a better team. Huzzah!

About the Author

Julie Ann Walker is the *New York Times* and *USA Today* bestselling author of award-winning romantic suspense. A winner of the Book Buyers Best Award, Julie has been nominated for the National Readers Choice Award, the Australian Romance Reader Awards, and the Romance Writers of America's prestigious RITA award. Her latest release was named a Top Ten Romance of 2014 by *Booklist*. Her books have been described as "alpha, edgy, and downright hot." Most days you can find Julie on her bicycle along the lakeshore in Chicago or blasting away at her keyboard, trying to wrangle her capricious imagination into submission. Be sure to sign up for Julie's occasional newsletter at: www.julieannwalker.com.

And to learn more about Julie, follow her on Facebook: www.facebook.com/jawalkerauthor and/or Twitter: @JAWalkerAuthor.

I Own the Dawn

The Night Stalkers

by M. L. Buchman

NAME: Archibald Jeffrey Stevenson III

RANK: First Lieutenant, DAP Hawk copilot

MISSION: Strategy and execution of special ops maneuvers

NAME: Kee Smith

RANK: Sergeant, Night Stalker gunner and sharpshooter

MISSION: Whatever it takes to get the job done

You wouldn't think it could get worse, until it does...
When a special mission slowly unravels, it is up to Kee and Archie to get their team out of an impossible situation with international implications. With her weaponry knowledge and his strategic thinking, plus the explosive attraction that puts them into exact synchrony, together they might just have a fighting chance...

"The first novel in Buchman's new military suspense series is an action-packed adventure. With a super-stud hero, a strong heroine, and a backdrop of 1600 Pennsylvania Avenue and the world of the Washington elite, it will grab readers from the first page." — *RT Book Reviews*, 4 stars

For more Night Stalkers, visit:

www.sourcebooks.com

Take Over at Midnight

The Night Stalkers
by M.L. Buchman

NAME: Lola LaRue

RANK: Chief Warrant Officer 3

MISSION: Copilot deadly choppers on the world's most dangerous missions

NAME: Tim Maloney

RANK: Sergeant

MISSION: Man the guns and charm the ladies

The past doesn't matter, when their future is doomed

Nothing sticks to "Crazy" Tim Maloney, until he falls hard for a tall Creole beauty with a haunted past and a penchant for reckless flying. Lola LaRue never thought she'd be susceptible to a man's desire, but even with Tim igniting her deepest passions, it may be too late now…With the nation under an imminent threat of biological warfare, Tim and Lola are the only ones who can stop the madness—and to do that, they're going to have to trust each other way beyond their limits…

"Quite simply a great read. Once again
Buchman takes the military romance to a
new standard of excellence."—*Booklist*

"Buchman continues to serve up nonstop
action that will keep readers on the edge of
their seats."—*Library Journal Xpress*

For more M.L. Buchman, visit:

www.sourcebooks.com

Light Up the Night

The Night Stalkers
by M.L. Buchman

—᠁—

NAME: Trisha O'Malley

RANK: Second Lieutenant and AH-6M "Little Bird" Pilot

MISSION: Take down Somali pirates, and deny her past

NAME: William Bruce

RANK: Navy SEAL Lieutenant

MISSION: Rescue hostages, and protect his past—against all comers

They both have something to hide

When hotshot SOAR helicopter pilot Trisha O'Malley rescues Navy SEAL Bill Bruce from his undercover mission in Somalia, it ignites his fury. Everything about Trisha triggers his mistrust: her elusive past, her wild energy, and her habit of flying past safety's edge. Even as the heat between them turns into passion's fire, Bill and Trisha must team up to confront their pasts and survive Somalia's pirate lords.

—᠁—

"The perfect blend of riveting, high-octane military action interspersed with tender, heartfelt moments. With a sigh-worthy scarred hero and a strong Irish redhead heroine, Buchman might just be at the top of the game in terms of relationship development." —*RT Book Reviews*

For more M.L. Buchman, visit:

www.sourcebooks.com

Pure Heat

The Firehawks

by M.L. Buchman

These daredevil smokejumpers fight more than fires

The elite fire experts of Mount Hood Aviation fly into places even the CIA can't penetrate.

She lives to fight fires

Carly Thomas could read burn patterns before she knew the alphabet. A third-generation forest fire specialist who lost both her father and her fiancé to the flames, she's learned to live life like she fights fires: with emotions shut down.

But he's lit an inferno she can't quench

Former smokejumper Steve "Merks" Mercer can no longer fight fires up close and personal, but he can still use his intimate knowledge of wildland burns as a spotter and drone specialist. Assigned to copilot a Firehawk with Carly, they take to the skies to battle the worst wildfire in decades and discover a terrorist threat hidden deep in the Oregon wilderness—but it's the heat between them that really sizzles.

"A wonderful love story…seamlessly woven in among technical details. Poignant and touching."
—*RT Book Reviews* Top Pick, 4.5 Stars

For more M.L. Buchman, visit:

www.sourcebooks.com

Full Blaze

The Firehawks

by M.L. Buchman

—∿∿—

These wilderness firefighters battle more than flames

The elite fire experts of Mount Hood Aviation fly into places even the CIA can't penetrate.

She's just jumped square into the heart of the blaze

When Australian helicopter pilot Jeannie Clark rescues wildfire photographer Cal Jackson from a raging burnover, she doesn't know she's bringing aboard a firebrand. Cal is quickly recruited for MHA's covert operations that reach far beyond the flames. Together Jeannie and Cal are assigned to an overseas operation with a lot more at risk than burning trees. And they'll need all the skill, love, and trust they can muster if they're going to survive the heat of this jungle battle.

—∿∿—

"A richly detailed and pulse-pounding read that balances fast-paced drama and romance. Buchman again pens an excellent read!" —*RT Book Reviews*, 4.5 Stars

For more M.L. Buchman, visit:

www.sourcebooks.com